SHADOWS OF WAR

FADED EMBERS

ANNE WHEELER

ISBN: 978-1-951910-01-3

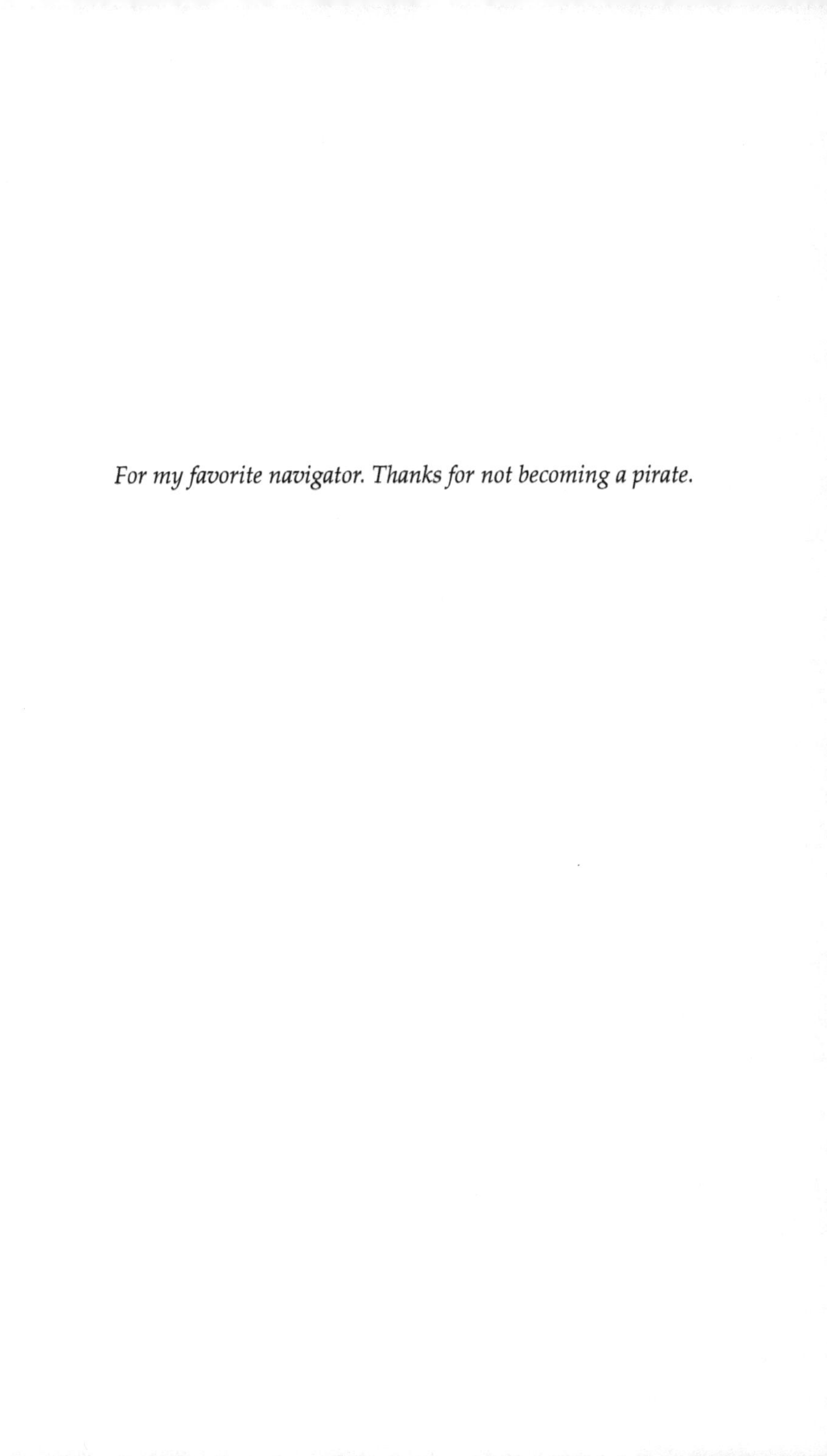

For my favorite navigator. Thanks for not becoming a pirate.

Blessed are the merciful, for they shall receive mercy.

MATTHEW 5:7

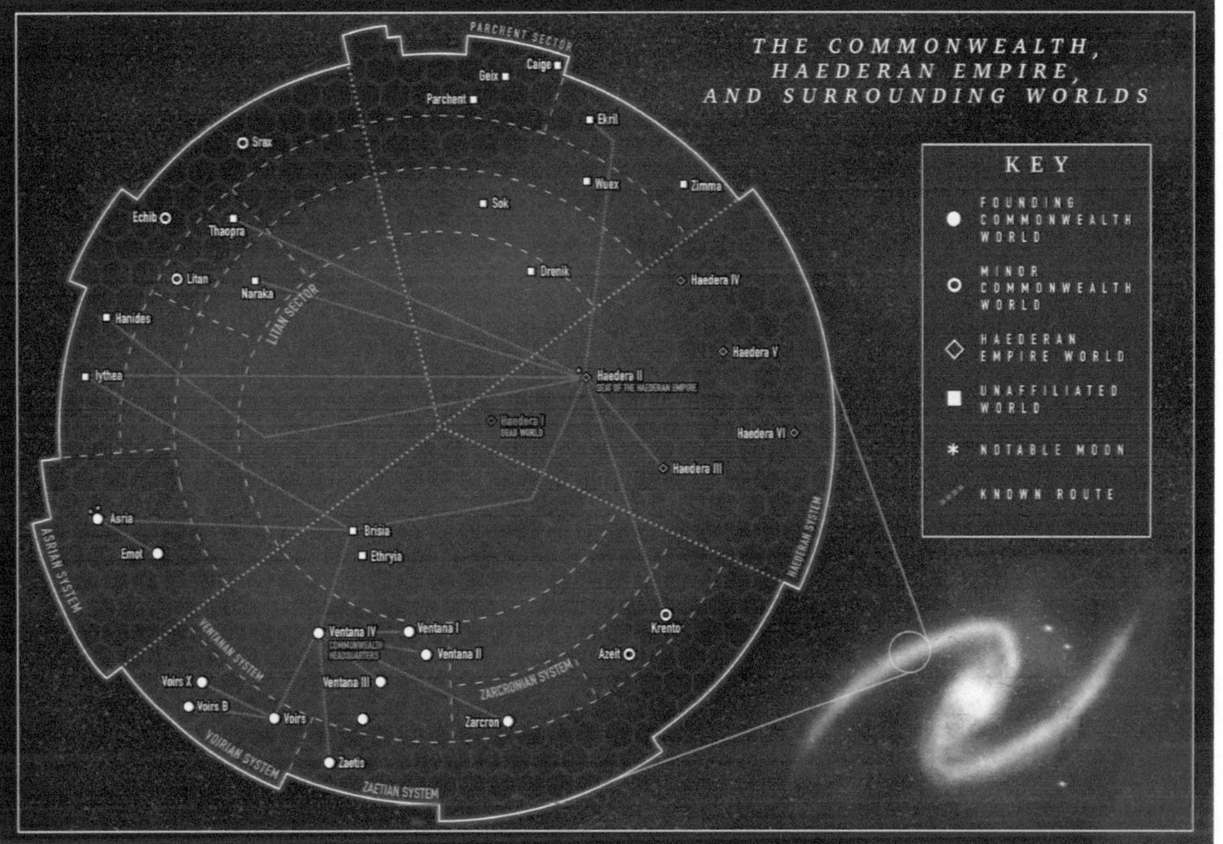

THE COMMONWEALTH, HAEDERAN EMPIRE, AND SURROUNDING WORLDS
PARCHENT SECTOR
Caige
Geix
Parchent
Ekril
Srax
Wuex
Zimma
Sok
Echib
Thaopra
Drenik
Haedera IV
Litan
Naraka
LITAN SECTOR
Haedera V
Hanides
Haedera II
SEAT OF THE HAEDERAN EMPIRE
Iythea
Haedera I
DEAD WORLD
Haedera VI
Haedera III
HAEDERAN SYSTEM
Asria
Brisia
Emot
Ethryia
ASRIAN SYSTEM
Ventana IV
COMMONWEALTH HEADQUARTERS
Ventana I
Ventana II
Krento
Azeit
VENTANAN SYSTEM
Ventana III
ZARCRONIAN SYSTEM
Voirs X
Voirs B
Voirs
Zarcron
VOIRIAN SYSTEM
Zaetis
ZAETIAN SYSTEM
KEY
FOUNDING COMMONWEALTH WORLD
MINOR COMMONWEALTH WORLD
HAEDERAN EMPIRE WORLD
UNAFFILIATED WORLD
NOTABLE MOON
KNOWN ROUTE

CHAPTER ONE

The Valko swerved in the harsh winds, knocking Avery against her harness. She kicked it left again, but it wasn't far enough to right the spacecraft entirely. Not only because of the training ship's incessant desire to disobey her commands—the winds at Alcaris were bad that day—but because the calm she normally felt in space turned to anxiety the closer they got to the ground. Her heart was pounding, but that was no surprise. What was surprising was how much her hands were shaking.

Because this wasn't how it was supposed to go. Not her first suborbital flight in a Royal Asrian Defense Forces trainer after months of technically flawless atmospheric flight. Not after she'd begged and pleaded with Merritt, who'd claimed the idea of her flying again was horrifying. Not after she'd submitted dozens of pages of paperwork proving that she was, in fact, fit to fly again— at least with a copilot.

Fox Espelt shot her a look from the right seat as she struggled with the controls. The captain might be five years younger, but right now he seemed just as unflappable in the Valko as he'd been for the past three months. He appeared to have no fear or anxiety about flying with his queen—his combat experience in the Haederan invasion several years before probably had a lot to do with that. Avery tried to ignore his surreptitious glances and gently brought the Valko back to center.

There.

With a light finger, she made constant corrections as they hovered over the center of the landing pad, and the anxiety turned to pride. Espelt was smart enough to ignore her whispers, the continual instructions to herself and the Valko. She'd told Merritt she could do this, and as soon as they landed, she'd call him and—

The gust, stronger than any they'd encountered so far, caught her by surprise.

"I've got it," Fox called, his calm tone unchanged. Pain shot through her wrist and the ship banked to the right—violently, that time.

Without argument, she pulled her hands back. Fox brought the ship to the middle of the landing pad and set the Valko down so gently she wouldn't have been able to tell they'd hit the ground if she hadn't been watching the altimeter. Within seconds, the landing crew surrounded them, and he popped the hatch on his side and took a breath of fresh air, silent.

"I knew we should have tried it in the simulator first." She stared straight ahead, unable to look at him. The early confidence slipped away like she had dreamed it—even though her dreams these days were nightmares.

"The Valko can be flaky in winds like this. Bad wing design. It's meant for space." In the corner of her vision, he shrugged at his obvious excuse and pulled off his helmet. "We'll try it again next time. You'll get it. There's no rush." His tone was easy, but he had to have known how much this flight meant to her.

No rush.

"Yeah. Thanks, Fox."

Avery unlatched her harness and poured herself out of the starship on legs that barely held her up. New plane, new flight, new muscles, new weaknesses. The space part had been easy, the atmospheric flight slightly less so, but the landing? She'd forgotten the physical demands of that segment of flight.

Kusir, she wished she could forget the entire thing. No matter. She let the pending demands of the day rush over her, pushing the tightness in her chest down. With her rushed schedule, there would be no debriefing with Fox today, not even an informal one, which meant Wynne would be waiting for her. She would vent to her head of security on the way back to the palace, then throw herself into her official work. And then, once things settled down and she felt up to it, she would contact Fox and ask for another flight. It was the only thing to do, really. She wouldn't squander this opportunity to fly with the Defense Forces when her calendar allowed—it was one of the few things from her past life she was still allowed to cling to.

She crossed through the hangar, stepping aside to let the crew pull in the Valko for inspection and refueling. The door opposite opened right outside an adjacent fence, and on the other side of that fence was a small park. It was in the center of the base and secure but empty now, and that peaceful area was where she needed to be that very second. Her authorization token let her through the fence gate, and she breathed a sigh of relief.

Freedom.

Wynne would be waiting for her—she'd doubtless been watching the sky for hours—but she had a few minutes, and the park was a shortcut to the aeroflyer pad where Wynne was waiting, anyway. And she needed the time alone. Needed the wind, the sun, and the birds singing in the tree above her, for Wynne was going to take her back to be locked inside the senate building for a few more hours—or the palace, which was pretty much the same thing. It was rare she and Enric even let their royal charge escape to the palace gardens to contemplate life without following along, which Avery couldn't understand. It wasn't like the Imperial Haederan Army troops who remained on Asria were allowed anywhere near the place. There was no danger.

Grass crunched across the park as she let her eyes drift closed.

Heart pounding, she jumped to her feet and squinted into the sun at the figure walking across the small lawn. Wynne must have become impatient. But this didn't look like Wynne, wasn't walking like Wynne.

Chase.

Avery stood without a word—or even an acknowledgment—and headed back the way she'd come. It would take longer, but if she walked fast enough, she could double back through one of the restricted hangars and lose him. Who had he coerced into giving him access this time? Maybe no one. Maybe he'd simply walked on. It was absurd that a Haederan was allowed on a Defense Forces base to begin with, and Chase especially had a habit of talking himself into places where he wasn't otherwise welcome. But that was part of the agreement she'd been forced into with the Haederan Empire, even if she'd been trying to find a way out ever since.

Faster, faster.

It didn't matter. With her legs still weak from the flight, Chase easily caught up to her before she reached the fence. He stepped in front of her and threw his arm across the gate as she reached for the keypad.

Her teeth ground together of their own accord.

"We had an agreement," she said, focusing on his boots.

"About me visiting Alcaris?" His lilt was so foreign on a Defense Forces base that she looked up.

"That uniform." Avery met his eyes, skipping over the crossed swords on his collar as she lifted her head. A flashback now would be humiliating. "You were not to wear it in my presence."

Not that she'd ever seen him in anything else, cultural attaché game or not—it was just the first chance she'd had to admonish him for it.

Chase glanced down at his green Imperial Security fatigues, the ones she still saw in her nightmares, and frowned.

"Our agreement was that I wouldn't wear it at the palace.

This"—he looked around toward the fueled Valko on the ramp—"is not the palace."

She would have blamed Haederan culture for his obstinance, but this intentional literal-mindedness was pure Chase. There was no winning with him.

"Never mind," she snapped. "I don't care what you wear. Get out of my way."

Chase took a step to the side. "Your Majesty, your secretary told me you were here. You know I wouldn't have come unless it was urgent."

"When I'm here, it's Captain Rendon. And stop bothering my secretary. Who let this man in here?" she yelled over the fence at a group of Valko mechanics leaning against the hangar on a break. One of the women raised her eyebrows at Chase and ducked around a corner—to find security, she hoped.

"Really. A promotion?" His grin faded as his eyes fell to her collar, like he'd just now noticed what she was wearing. "You deserve it, Your Majesty," he said quietly.

"It's old." The Defense Forces had matched the Commonwealth rank she'd earned during the war. And Chase knew everything that went on around Asria, especially when it had to do with her. She hated him for it. But a deal was a deal, even if she'd made a bad one with him. "And don't pretend you didn't know about it before now."

"Of course I did. But seeing it in person is something else."

At least he wasn't denying he knew her every move. "Move, Colonel. Or I'll—"

"Or you'll what?" His arm stiffened across the gate at her furious expression. "Look, five minutes. Please. You'll want to hear this."

"No."

She turned on her heel and darted through the park, though his footsteps were close behind. Her personal aeroflyer was parked right where it was supposed to be, and her sudden pace kept Chase far enough behind her until she caught sight of Wynne and Enric in the aeroflyer's rear seat. Wynne tossed her tablet to the side and hopped out to confront him as Avery skirted around her.

"Leave her alone, Colonel," she said with more patience than Avery knew she possessed.

Chase narrowed his eyes. "I need to talk to her."

"Then get on her schedule or get Ambassador Neave to do it for you." Wynne tossed her dark hair over her shoulder, the very picture of a Cadena socialite—albeit one carrying a pistol under her fitted jacket. "You don't need to be following her around town. I know you have more sense than that."

"I was in the area."

Wynne snorted. "Try again."

Chase glanced at Avery, then back to Wynne. Good. He'd decided he wasn't going to be able to get closer. She sank back against the seat and re-knotted her hair, brushing off Enric's questioning look and banal pleasantry. Didn't he know he was impeding her eavesdropping?

"Major, it's urgent."

Wynne looked back into the aeroflyer and rolled her eyes. Avery could only hear snippets of her quiet reply—but whatever she said, it worked. Chase glanced inside, halfway apologetic that time, and gave her a quick wave before heading back in the direction he'd come.

Wynne sighed and climbed inside, across from her and Enric. "Sorry about that," she said. "But he's gone now."

"I need to know your secrets for making him give up," Avery said. It wasn't like Chase to surrender so easily. Or at all. Wynne must have threatened him with bodily harm. "What did you tell him?"

"Just that you'd had a bad day, and that he was making it worse, which I knew he didn't want to do." She squinted at Avery. "You did, didn't you?"

"How did you know?" How was it that everyone was better at reading people than her?

"If you hadn't, you'd have argued with him rather than running away."

"Hmm." Avery tapped a finger on the window as the flyer lifted off and banked toward the palace. Wynne wasn't wrong. "Flight didn't go well."

"And you're not looking forward to your coronation tomorrow."

That was an understatement. She'd taken her oath upon her father's death and her election, another lifetime ago. What was the point of a huge celebration? But she'd delayed the ceremony for months now, and she was out of excuses, though caring for a newborn and recovering from an enemy occupation made good ones.

"Hardly. Some of our traditions are antiquated, and you know it, Wynne."

"Well, you already know my opinion." Wynne's eyes darkened, and it wasn't due to the evening shadows. "There's too much unrest to go through with this ceremony now."

But no one listens to my opinion was her unspoken complaint. Avery smiled as Enric choked down a laugh. Wynne never changed. Threats were everywhere to her.

"The unrest is directed at the Haederans, not me," she pointed out.

And that was the truth. Only a small minority had remained on Asria after their failed invasion—Chase included—but they weren't popular with Asrians. And their permanency didn't make sense. What were they running from? Emperor Owin had promised her a kinder, gentler Haedera, and going back to their home planet had to be better than living on a planet where they were hated.

Then again, even Owin couldn't change centuries of Haederan culture. Nor did he truly want to, she suspected. Haederans were Haederans, no matter what, even the ones living on Asria, and Chase was proof of that. Their insistence on maintaining their navy's orbital base was even more proof.

"And there haven't been any specific threats, have there?" she asked.

Enric hedged as Wynne glared out the window.

"The usual. Nothing specific." He leaned back in his seat and crossed his arms. "I'm afraid you're not getting out of it this time, my lady."

"Avery. Please." She'd trained Wynne in her preferred informality—while they were alone, at least—but Enric was another matter. "You don't think he really had something important to tell me, do you?"

"Colonel Chase? Maybe, but I doubt it." Wynne looked down at Alcaris, where Chase was an ant-sized dot on the ground. "But even if he does, it can wait. Right?"

Avery forced a smile. Her unease was a result of nothing more than the mediocre flight and impending coronation. Yes, that was all. Chase wasn't worth concerning herself over, not with her coronation looming.

"Right."

CHAPTER TWO

Hundreds of Asrians—or maybe thousands—milled about the plaza below her. Avery couldn't hear them through the thick glass, but she could see them, and that was worse. If only a sudden rainstorm would flash through the capital, flooding the streets and postponing the festivities, but there was no chance of that today, the meteorologists had assured her. She pressed her nose against the window, grateful she was a dozen stories up and that the crowd couldn't see her through the dark tint.

Not yet, anyway.

"It's really too late now, isn't it?" she asked the window.

Merritt appeared behind her, and his hands coiled around her waist. "It was too late a few years ago, love." His lips touched her bare neck, and she shivered. Never again would she take his touch for granted. "But this is a good thing."

Easy for him to say. Today he would blend into the crowd. He'd go unnoticed, as he usually did, because all eyes would be on her. She turned around to face him, the grin on his face infinitely more pleasant than the crowd outside.

It faded when he saw her look. "You can smile, you know," he said. "It's not a betrayal of him if you do."

How had he read her mind? The heavy velvet coronation robe

draped across the chair in the corner said otherwise. Worn by fifteen generations of Rendons, it still looked new, the trim elaborate and exquisite. The indigo matched the lace of her dress—not that anyone would see how fashionably and uncomfortably she was dressed under all the fabric.

"This is supposed to be a celebration." With a freshly manicured finger, she traced the embroidered asters and stars that edged the bottom of the robe. Twinkling stars against the dark velvet night. Like she'd seen yesterday, flying the Valko. "But how am I supposed to celebrate when he never got to wear it? When no other Rendon is here to see me?"

Her uncle had been the last Rendon to wear this coronation gown, long ago, before she was old enough to remember the ceremony. Not her father. It should have been her father. Her father who had taken his oath after his brother had abdicated, but who'd been killed by the Haederans before Asria had been able to celebrate his ascension. The elder Lucas Rendon deserved to wear it now. Maybe even Quen, but her brother had been gone for years.

It was too heavy a burden to bear.

"Lucas is here. And your father would be proud of you." Merritt sighed and adjusted the high collar of his formal uniform. "He would be thrilled to see you wear it."

Avery pressed herself against the window. "I think he'd rather be alive."

He flinched, then nodded slightly, conceding that point.

"Baylen's outside," Wynne said, ducking her head around the corner. "Everyone's ready."

Except you was left unspoken. But she wouldn't tell Wynne—again—how terrified she was. It was time to do what needed to be done, even if most Asrian traditions were silly and ancient and too much of a spectacle. She plastered a fake smile across her lips as the prime minster stuck his head inside.

"It's time, Your Majesty."

Avery blinked, but Grant Baylen didn't disappear like she'd hoped. No, he stood there in the hallway looking as well dressed as ever, and she caught her hand before it could smooth her skirt of its own volition. It wasn't Baylen's fault that he was a sharp dresser. It wasn't even his fault that she was about to walk out in front of a crowd of thousands, and that was the real reason she was annoyed by his appearance.

For how could she feel self-conscious today? She looked fine—beautiful, Merritt had said earlier that morning. Her brown curls were caught up at the nape of her neck, except for the few unruly ones around her temples, and the aster earrings and sparkling gold eye makeup, gaudy on any other day, certainly helped. It all made it easier to accept that she wasn't just Avery today, but Her Majesty the Queen of Asria.

She gave Baylen a quick smile, the only way she could hide her distress, and reached for the robe as Merritt held it out. It was heavy on her shoulders as he fastened the clasp on her throat, and she closed her eyes against the weight. It was too appropriate, perhaps. Had every other Rendon monarch felt the same?

Before she knew it, the small group was downstairs and the cool breeze was washing across her face as the doors were pulled open. And was that—was that cheering? Such a strange reaction to her appearance. Such an unwelcome one. She didn't deserve this. She hadn't been born for this. It wasn't her place.

Down the lift, out the back door, through the plaza, and into the temple.

It would be easy. She just had to force her feet to do it.

Light flashed like a million vidcams just a pace away. Or maybe it was the lightning she'd prayed for hitting the temple. But that was a foolish idea. It wasn't storming, and the Holy One didn't answer prayers like that. It had been a beautiful day when she'd stood up there staring out the window, with no clouds in sight, and—

An unseen force threw her to the pavement, scraping her cheek open. Heat, fire, cold, ringing, deafness—she reeled under the rapid-fire assault on her senses. She tried to stagger to her feet, into the fire. Wynne pushed her back down, her lips moving in some sort of command, though Avery couldn't hear anything through the unnatural silence in her own head. Ash drifted downward, falling on her head and that worthless blue cloak. Someone else yanked her up by the arm, and before she could argue, she was pulled, not carefully, along the no-longer-white but red and gray stone path. Her shoes slipped on the ash, her ears rang, and where—where were Merritt and Lucas?

She threw the strange arm off and spun around, desperate.

"Not the flyer," Wynne's face was pale as she hollered at Baylen's security team, her smooth cheeks smudged with black soot. Enric was nowhere in sight. "Senate building. Basement. The entire building's been cleared. Now!" She pushed on Avery's back, almost as forceful as the explosion had been.

"But Lucas and Merritt." Avery slid on the ash, and Wynne pulled her up once more.

"They're fine. Go!"

Wynne was lying. She was lying because she'd seen them herself and she knew they weren't alive. They were dead, they had fallen back there somewhere on the hard ground, and Wynne wasn't saying anything because they weren't her first priority.

But no. There was Lucas, at least, a little brown-haired sack thrown over Enric's shoulder as they darted inside. His gray eyes focused on her, wide with fear.

Avery scrambled forward as he reached for her, his cries propelling her onward and through the glass doors at the back of the senate building. Someone else grabbed her arm as soon as she stepped foot in the small lobby, then pulled her down a flight of stairs before she reached him. Maybe several. It was impossible to tell, especially through the crowd of security that had suddenly surrounded her.

She tried to push by them. Freedom. She needed freedom. Nothing mattered but Lucas and Merritt. Didn't they understand? Nothing mattered now but getting to them.

Wynne appeared on her right arm as she gasped for air.

"I need to check you out," she said. "Let me make sure

you're all right, let them make sure Lucas and Colonel Rendon are all right, and then I'll track them down for you. Can you do that?"

Avery nodded, heart pounding. Wynne would get her way. There was no use arguing with her.

"As long as they're fast," she whispered.

"They will be." Wynne jerked her head at the medic who'd pushed his way through the crowd, a uniformed security guard behind him. "Second office on the left."

He nodded, and she and Wynne followed him into the dark room. Wynne flipped on the lights and shot her an apologetic look. Avery shook her head as she sank into the upholstered chair just inside the doorway and closed her eyes. Wynne couldn't help the bright lights, and if Avery couldn't see the guards outside, couldn't see the light that bathed everything in that peculiar radiance, couldn't see the walls that were threatening to cave in on her, everything would be just fine.

"Your Majesty?" The medic sounded nervous. "Could you look at me? I need to check your pupils."

Reluctantly, she opened them to stare at his concerned face. "I don't have a concussion," she said, tilting her head up. "I didn't hit my head. Just my shoulder. And it's not bad."

"Shrapnel?" Wynne's voice was sharp. Neither she nor the medic pointed out that Avery had, in fact, hit her face.

The medic gave Avery a questioning look.

Through all this fabric?

"It's just my ears. And my cheek." With tentative fingers, she brushed her face, coming away with blood. No one looked too concerned about that, though. The scrape couldn't be that bad.

"No headache?" he asked.

She shook her head.

Please don't touch me.

"Then I'll just clean up the scrape and be out of here, my lady. The hearing should resolve itself soon. If it doesn't, we'll worry about it later."

He pulled a small wrapped package from his bag, and she flinched as his hand moved toward her cheek.

Ice.

It was odd how something so small, so insignificant, so innocuous could be a horrible reminder of what had happened to her during the war.

Her fear must have been written on her face, because his lip twitched and he held the package out to Wynne instead.

"This doesn't require my attention. If anything changes, come find me. Loss of consciousness, headache, slurred speech . . . you know the drill." He ducked out with a curt and rather confused nod at both of them.

Avery ran her hands over her face. "Just stick it on and let's be done with it, Wynne. There's nothing wrong with me, but I suppose a scar might frighten Lucas."

Lucas. She was going to have to fight her way past Wynne to find him.

Wynne pushed herself off the desk. "You start feeling ill, you tell me." At Avery's silence, her voice grew harder. "Promise me."

"Yes. Fine. I promise."

Wynne, while only four years older, could still make her feel like a child, even on the day of her coronation.

"Good."

Wynne opened the pack, and Avery looked away as she smoothed the clear plastic ice on her cheek. It was cold, yes, but Wynne's fingers were warm, unlike the chilled hands of the Haederan medic who'd treated her injuries deep in that prison under Cadena. She wasn't living the past—but was the future any better?

"Your Majesty?"

It was another medic, but this one—her heart almost stopped—this one had Lucas clinging to her shirt. With a cry the whole basement probably heard, she grabbed him and sank down against the wall, the dark velvet cloak pooling around her like blood. He laid his head on her shoulder, soundless.

"Is he all right?" She tried to push his head off her to assess him, but he tightened his grip on the shoulder of her dress, still silent. "Why isn't he saying anything?"

"He's just scared." The medic tried to smile. "Wanted his mother and lovey."

At that, Lucas looked up with wide eyes. "Lovey?"

Avery blew out a choked laugh. "We'll find that later. When we get home." She glanced up at the guards outside the door. "Can we get home?"

"They're clearing the palace now. Once we make sure it's secured and find a safe route, we'll get you back."

Avery nodded and squeezed Lucas so tight he began to cry. "Sorry, boo." She kissed the top of his head, the softness of his hair at odds with the rest of her emotions. Baylen slipped into the office past the guards, and she jerked her head off Lucas's. "What happened?" she asked him.

"Three bombs," he said with a glance at Wynne. "Two inside the temple itself and one in the smaller shrine outside. Someone really wanted this to work."

"Do we know how bad yet?"

Wynne shifted.

"Seventeen dead so far, Your Majesty. Countless injuries."

Seventeen. Seventeen futures gone and families ruined. More of Asria destroyed. They were supposed to be celebrating, reveling in something that hadn't happened in so long, and instead . . .

Their deaths were on her. They'd been here to see her, and she was responsible. Lucas squirmed and whined in her grip, but she couldn't take her gaze off Baylen.

"Senator Perera and Senator Comelles and her husband are among the dead. It'll take a while to identify most . . ." He must have mistaken her silence for interest.

"I understand." Her voice broke. She knew why he'd trailed off. She'd never seen that horrified look on his face, not even on the night they'd both been arrested by the Haederans. She hadn't known it was possible to feel worse, but this—this was ghastly. It would take weeks, if not months, to identify the remains. "And the target?"

A stupid question, perhaps, but she needed to hear someone say it. Maybe this wasn't her fault. Maybe someone had a personal issue with one of the other guests.

Three bombs, Avery. Two in the temple, precisely where you'd have been standing five minutes later. Who else would they be after?

The prime minister narrowed his eyes at her. Yes, Baylen had always thought her naïve, but the question had probably surprised even him. She looked away, at Wynne. Her head of security pressed her lips together. Sympathy? Sadness? Anger? It was impossible to tell.

"Your Majesty?" a new voice interrupted.

Why wouldn't they leave her alone? Why did they insist on calling her that? She didn't deserve the title. People were dead because of it.

"What now?" Wynne snapped.

A plainclothes guard stepped around Baylen into the increasingly crowded office. He nodded at Baylen and shot Wynne a sharp look, but he'd never cross one of the queen's personal bodyguards further. Not now.

"There's a Haederan upstairs, Your Majesty," he said apologetically, one hand reaching to scratch his neck. "He wants to see you. Says he has information. He wouldn't leave us alone until I agreed to come down here and ask you in person."

Chase. Who else could it possibly be? It was just like him to show up in the middle of everything. The guard held out a thin slip of metal to her, and Chase stared back from the Asrian residency permit she'd personally authorized, that familiar blank look with a hint of disdain across his face.

"Let him down here." She shifted Lucas in her lap so she could rub her eyes with the inside of her wrist, holding the permit between her fingers like it was toxic.

"Your Majesty, it's likely this was the act of Haederan extremists. It's not wise—"

"No. Let him through." The more people around her who didn't want her dead right now, the better, and paradoxically, Chase was one of the few she trusted to not kill her, Asrian or Haederan—even though his sudden appearance all but verified that his position as cultural attaché at the Haederan embassy was a sham. He had to be rattled to let on so clearly that he was just as much Imperial Security Command as before. "Just search him first. If he tries anything, you can be the one to shoot him, I promise."

The guard's lip twisted, but he turned on his heel, returning five minutes later with Chase. Even before Avery caught sight of him, his footsteps down the hall, quick and urgent, sounded ominous. As did the fact he was wearing civilian clothes, more casually dressed than everyone else milling about.

"I'm sorry," he said, his eyes widening. Apparently deciding the small amount of blood on her cheek was of no real concern, he relaxed his shoulders. "I never thought—" He ran a hand through his hair, then glanced around and the small crowd. Just the idea of Chase being on edge put her even more on edge. "Can we talk in private?"

"With Wynne." How desirable Wynne's normally unwelcome protection was now.

He nodded easy agreement, and that was disquieting, too. Avery pushed herself off the floor and handed Lucas to one of Baylen's personal guards. The ceremonial cloak came off too, and she threw it unceremoniously onto the desk. A silly, useless thing that so many had died for. Wynne followed her and Chase around the corner. It probably wasn't as private as Chase wanted, but she wasn't about to go into one of the empty conference rooms with him, even with Wynne trailing them.

"It was just speculation," he said as they stopped in the hallway, far away from the crowds. Only muted voices, plus the occasional cry from Lucas, followed them this far down. "Not this. Not so soon. I don't even know how he got to Asria so fast. Or that he wanted you dead so badly."

He was rambling. Chase in civilian clothes, rambling at her, his usual calm demeanor gone . . . this was a terrifying thing.

"Who? What are you talking about?"

Chase took a breath and his voice grew lower.

"Five weeks ago, Owin attended a memorial ceremony on Iythea. You know the deal, give a speech, lay some flowers. He cried when he arrived, when he saw the things . . ." He swallowed, then licked his lips. "The things we had done there. He's trying to smooth things over with the Commonwealth, Your Majesty, and he wanted to do this publicly so the entire quadrant knew where he stood. But there was an explosion. He's safe and on his way back to Haedera as we speak, but ten others weren't so lucky. The habitats are damaged beyond repair. He's agreed to personally compensate the Iythean Research Association for the loss of their structures."

For the structures, perhaps, but the loss of life? From what little she'd heard of the Haederans' occupation of Iythea, the devastation was probably a blessing in disguise. Slave labor, executions . . . the entire planet needed to be washed away and built anew. Or perhaps left as a reminder of the things that could happen when power became more important than life. But Iythea was Iythea. Asria was Asria. Things like that didn't happen here.

Or maybe they did. The peaceful planet where she'd grown up was gone now.

"I don't understand," she said. "What does that have to do with me?"

Chase sighed. "Because it was Quen Rendon who set them off."

CHAPTER THREE

SHE MUST HAVE MISHEARD HIM. HER EARS WERE STILL RINGING, NOT as loudly as before, true, but certainly . . . no, she'd misheard him. Avery cast a glance at Wynne, but it did nothing to lessen her confusion.

"Quen?" she asked. "My brother Quen?"

How long had it been since she'd said his name? A year, at least. Her parents hadn't talked about him much after he disappeared. Drex had, but he'd stopped a few years before the war. Merritt had never even met Quen. People just didn't talk much about Quen these days. She'd told Chase about him, though, hadn't she? It was one of the holes in her memory.

Chase pressed his lips together. "We've been tracking him for a while now—"

"We?" Avery snorted at his admission.

Chase gave a sullen smile at being outed as Imperial Security. "After the explosion on Iythea, he disappeared, but for just a week. He popped back up almost right away, begging passage to Emot on a freighter out of Brisia." He narrowed his eyes at Wynne. "He wasn't difficult to find. Aren't your people still looking for him?"

"Colonel, leave her alone." Wynne didn't need her defense, but Chase was irritating at the best of times, and this was certainly not the best of times. "No, they haven't been looking for him in a long while. I don't believe the senate had any reason to keep searching for him since my election. Not during the occupation and certainly not since the armistice. I've always been curious about where he disappeared to, what he's been up to, but Quen doesn't want to be found. He's given up on Asria and his position."

If they take me back to Asria, it won't be alive.

It'd been Quen's last message, sent to her in a private comm while she'd been a cadet on Ventana IV. She'd turned it over to the senate's investigators but hadn't heard anything since, and with the war, she had never expected to. Perhaps Quen had been killed —it was certainly a fate she'd considered.

Until now.

"How do you know he was responsible for what happened on Iythea?" she asked. "Was this what you wanted to tell me yesterday?" Chase might be reaching with this claim. Quen had been rebellious, yes, and he'd certainly frightened her on a few occasions, but he couldn't have murdered almost a dozen people.

Chase looked at his feet. "He didn't claim responsibility for it, if that's what you're asking. But—but yes. Imperial Security believes he was behind it. I can't tell you more, not here." He glanced down the hallway and sighed. "I don't suppose I can get you to the embassy, can I?"

Wynne shook her head. "Once they've cleared the palace, you can have the ambassador set up a meeting in Her Majesty's office there."

It was clear Wynne's use of her title was intentional, a reminder to Chase that former prisoner or not, Avery was the queen of Asria and he was a guest of her planet for however long that welcome persisted. If the senate had anything to do about it after this attack, that wouldn't be for long.

His shoulders sagged. "It'll have to do, I suppose. But please, let's not wait very long. I'm concerned—"

"Avery?" The familiar voice called her name again down the corridor. "Avery!"

Merritt.

He was covered in soot and dust, his arms and face scratched, but he was alive. He embraced her before she could ask if he was uninjured, before she could make sure she wouldn't harm him further by touching him. He squeezed her so tightly she could barely breathe, but she didn't care. It didn't matter that she was gasping for breath or that he smelled like explosives or that he was covered in someone else's blood. She just clung to him. How many more second chances could they possibly deserve?

"I'm sorry. I'm so sorry," he murmured in her ear. "They needed help up there. If I'd known you were panicking—I told them to tell you—Grant said he would, as soon as he saw you."

"I think he was distracted. It's all right," Avery managed to tell his shoulder. "I'm just glad you're here."

She cringed. How could she say she was glad he was uninjured when so many others were wounded? Her family was uninjured, but how many others weren't? How many families had been torn apart today for nothing?

Seventeen dead so far, Your Majesty . . .

"I know." Merritt ran a finger across her cheek, dislodging the thin plastic. She pulled it the rest of the way off. Pointless thing. "How bad is this?" he asked.

"It's not." She nestled her head into his shoulder. They'd have to pry her away. "Not at all. Not anymore."

* * *

It was ten more hours before they were allowed home. Ten hours to make certain the palace was secure and to triple the amount of guards on patrol—most borrowed from the local Cadena police, some from the Defense Forces directly. Avery had coordinated the protection of the rest of the senators herself, and, like the security officials had pointed out earlier, some in the senate believed the attack was the work of Haederan extremists.

She sat cross-legged on Lucas's floor in the dark as he slept, her eyes closed. If she breathed slowly enough, if she concentrated on the feel of the soft wool under her, if she told herself over and over again that the lights were off only because *she* had waved them off, then the panic retreated into the shadows for a time. It wouldn't be long until it came for her again, but there was enough time to ask the question.

How could You let this happen?

The death toll had hit thirty-five by sunset. And if Chase's intelligence was correct, it was by her own brother's hand, no less. Hadn't Asria suffered enough? An invasion, an occupation, and a terror attack—it was too much.

And now this. Why couldn't she change the past? Why wouldn't the Holy One change the future? All questions she would never have an answer to.

The shadowy panic began its expected march toward her as she continued to beg. Stiff, she pushed herself off the lush rug and nodded to the guard sitting in the corner of Lucas's room. The young woman from Wynne's former Defense Forces security operations unit seemed competent enough, but she shouldn't be in here at all. The royal family's privacy was just one more intangible thing Quen had taken from her.

He'd stolen their security, too. Merritt would never admit how much he needed the feeling of safety, but she knew. She knew it in the nightmares he still had, in the way his hands turned clammy whenever an Imperial Haederan Army soldier crossed his path in public, in the way he never talked about his experiences after his capture. He would deal with this newest situation with his usual unemotional facade, but it wasn't fair to him. Hadn't he suffered enough?

She passed another six guards on her way to their rooms, not counting the ones stationed just outside Lucas's door. With a sigh, she crept downstairs instead of going inside, through the gallery and toward the Blue Room. Merritt loved the peacefulness of the small parlor, and on his worst nights, spent hours there. It was where he'd first met Victor, after all, who'd blessed their relationship. Where his world had changed for good so many years ago—even though he couldn't have known the extent at the time. She couldn't blame him for wanting to focus on the good memories in a futile attempt to drive out the bad.

She didn't make it that far. Light filtered out under the door to Merritt's private office—the room he hated to use. *This is all so formal*, he'd once said. *I don't need an office in our home.*

Clearly, though, tonight he needed that mostly unused office more than he needed the tranquility of the Blue Room. The lights were on inside, and—and were those voices? Avery tiptoed closer, and the lilting Haederan accent coming from inside couldn't have been more familiar or unwelcome.

Chase was in Merritt's office?

She froze just before reaching the door. Merritt would have had to authorize Chase's access to the palace personally, especially tonight, but he hadn't mentioned anything to her. And Chase hadn't yet made his urgent appointment with her, so if he and Merritt felt the need to hide a conversation, it was something worth listening to.

At least they were *attempting* to hide it—neither was being very quiet about their clandestine summit beyond closing the door. One of the regular palace guards down the hall caught her eye as she pressed her ear against the door, and she put a finger to her lips, knowing how ridiculous the order was.

"I told you a long time ago that you didn't need to worry about her safety when she was with me," Chase was saying. "Did you think I didn't mean it?"

Merritt snorted, and despite Chase's already refuted claim, Avery bit back a smile.

"You told me that," he replied, "but then you tortured her. So yes, I'd say you didn't mean it. And I'd say you're mad for even suggesting this."

"Don't exaggerate, Colonel. I'd think you of all people would know the difference between torture and humane interrogation." A chair squeaked, like Chase had just flopped into it.

"You call what you did to her humane?" Merritt's voice became low, dangerous. Did Chase know how explosive he was about to become? "She sleeps with the lights on every night. She has panic attacks. You nearly destroyed her!"

"She'll get over it."

Avery didn't need to see Chase's face to imagine the indifferent look on it, undoubtedly accompanied by an infuriatingly dismissive shrug. She held her breath and waited for whatever came next, but Merritt's voice grew quieter until she couldn't make out any words between them. After an almost-silent twenty minutes, a chair creaked as one of them stood.

"Well, think about it," came Chase's voice. "And try to convince her."

More footsteps. Avery whirled around for a hiding spot, but there was none. She flattened herself against the silk-paneled wall as Chase swung the door open. Maybe he wouldn't see her, even in this empty hallway. It was dim, after all.

Chase screwed his face up in disgust at her sudden appearance.

"Still eavesdropping in hallways, I see. That worked out so well for you last time." Without another word, he stalked off down the corridor, a previously hidden sentry behind him.

She wasn't sure whether to laugh or snarl back. "I live here," she called after him. Laughter won out. Who did he think he was?

Merritt ducked his head outside and rolled his eyes. "Sorry about that. How much did you hear?"

Avery shrugged as she perched on the chair next to the door. Nothing more than Chase trying to justify his interrogation methods, which was not something she wanted to think about or discuss.

"Well, then you're going to love this." Merritt leaned against the doorframe, out of striking distance.

"Let me guess. He suggested some bad things were going to happen without giving you detail or explaining how serious he was."

"No. He's sorry he didn't push you further the other day at Alcaris, and that he didn't make you listen to him about the current threat. I do believe he feels quite guilty about that, maybe even partially responsible. After Wynne made him leave, he sent official word through his, ah, secondary office, but it didn't reach our security teams in time. But the intel about Quen really was vague—he showed me part of it."

"Intel?" she asked. "He showed you? Why not me?"

"Because you wouldn't give him an appointment for another day, and he didn't think it could wait that long. And"—Merritt chuckled—"I do believe he's a little frightened of you."

"Frightened of me? That's absurd."

With a nervous laugh, she glanced down the corridor. Merritt was reaching. Chase couldn't be frightened of her, because she was terrified of him.

"You have quite a bit of power over him now, love. I'm not sure you realize how much." Merritt grinned. "You also have a rather poor reputation for how you take certain news. Honestly, I can't blame him much for—"

"Fine, Mer," she snapped. "What else?"

"Well, he wants to help."

That wasn't surprising. For over a year, Chase had been trying to absolve himself of the things he'd done to her. As much as she didn't need his help, he probably believed saving her from Quen would be his utmost accomplishment.

"Help how?" she asked.

He ground his palm into his forehead, clearly irritated at having to tell her the news himself.

"Promise you'll hear me out, love?" he asked. "Don't shoot the messenger, remember? I had nothing to do with this, and that look on your face right now is exactly why he pawned this off on me."

Avery gritted her teeth. "How, Merritt?"

Merritt sighed and closed his eyes. "He wants to take you to Haedera."

CHAPTER FOUR

Avery stared at him. "I'm not going to Haedera with Gareth Chase."

Merritt shrugged, like Chase had suggested something as simple as having a second glass of wine at dinner.

"That's what I told him. He was rather insistent that I try to change your mind."

No wonder they'd been in Merritt's office for so long. Merritt would have said there was no chance of that, and then Chase would have told him to talk her into it anyway, and Merritt would have said, *There's no talking Avery into anything, and you know it.*

"Yeah. I'm sure he was insistent," she said. "Because he knows better than to ask me himself. I'm not going."

She sprang to her feet and headed back to their rooms, trying to ignore the two unfamiliar security personnel who had suddenly appeared behind them. How were strangers in the palace supposed to make her feel better? They'd of course been thoroughly vetted by Wynne and her team, but what if . . .

"I just think—" Merritt darted after her down the dimly lit gallery and up the wide marble staircase. "I think you should consider it," he said when he finally caught up. "It's not such a bad idea."

Not such a bad idea?

She didn't reply, just ignored him and went through her evening routine, checking the lights in the bedroom, parlor, bathroom, and dressing room. All half lit. The palace staff were learning. Maybe one day she wouldn't have to do this any longer, but the advantage of not being able to see the dark circles under her eyes and the stretch marks on her waist couldn't be denied. Still, she tore off her dress and threw on a jade silk negligee as fast as she could. Merritt didn't get to see her like that tonight.

He frowned at her from the bathroom, then waved off the light. She ignored his disapproving look as she collapsed on the bed and ran her fingers through her curls. The room was silent except for the quiet tones of the guards outside.

"You think I'm being ungrateful, don't you?" she finally asked.

Of course he did. It was obvious in his tone, in the way he was siding with Chase, in the way he was watching her—cautiously now instead of disapprovingly, like she would bite his head off if he got too close.

He sat down next to her, still out of striking distance. "Ungrateful? No. I completely understand why you don't want to take him up on his offer. I'll admit I'd have a hard time doing it if I was in your position. But Haedera is the last place Quen will ever look for you. Haedera is the last place anyone who knows your history would ever think to look for you."

"Could that possibly be because Haedera is the least appealing option possible? That it's also the least safe place?" Avery glared at him, but he waited in patient silence. "Then you think I should do this."

Merritt flopped on his back and looked over at her. "I think there are ten guards outside that door right there, another five down the hall with Lucas, and none of them are going to be enough if Quen wants to kill you. And I know you're just used to Wynne and Enric, but . . ."

"But Haedera, Merritt. I can't. I just can't. He threatened to send me there, and you don't know what that was like." She blinked back tears. The last interrogation session with Chase was never far from her memories.

The night it'd all become too much.

The night nothing had mattered except living one more day.

The night she'd broken.

"He said they would take me there. That he didn't want to do it, but there was nothing he could do about it any longer, all because I wasn't telling him what he wanted to know. I knew they would execute me once I got there. He told me they would. That they'd kill me in front of the emperor himself. After, they did even worse things to me." Her voice cracked. "I was so afraid of stepping foot on Haedera, so afraid of dying, so afraid of more pain, that I—"

Said too much.

Betrayed Hadley and Feye.

Committed treason, even though Hadley forgave me.

"—I told him things I shouldn't have. And now the two of you are asking me to go, and it brings me right back. It feels like I have no choice."

She took a shuddering breath and rubbed her eyes against the sight of Chase leaning against the table in that bright room. That was the past. It was Merritt next to her now, and they were in the palace, and the Haederans had—mostly—been ousted, and she was free, and Merritt and Chase were asking her to go of her own free will . . .

"Completely different circumstances this time, love."

Merritt rolled toward her, and she buried her face in his chest, not caring that she couldn't breathe through her hair and his shirt. He brushed the curls away, and she pressed closer. The hair had been hiding the tears.

"I know it is," she said. She did, didn't she? Then why did it feel like she had no choice? Why did it feel like they were forcing her to go?

"It's your decision, of course, but this is a good thing this time."

"Then you think I should go?"

"I do."

"And you can't." It wasn't a question.

Merritt sighed. "Doubtfully. Not without arousing more suspicion. Certainly not without violating my orders. But I'm not worried about myself. It's you and Lucas who need to be scarce for a while."

Avery closed her eyes. Merritt had been able to hang on to his position in the Defense Forces after marrying her, if only half time, but he was right—his job meant he couldn't leave Asria now, especially for Haedera. He certainly couldn't do it without telling General Teruel and probably a lot of other people who didn't need to know. Well, nothing could be done about that.

"I assume you see the irony in me going to Haedera for my own safety," she said.

"More than anyone except you and Chase, probably." Merritt chuckled. "And you know he's secretly enjoying that irony right now."

She made an unflattering noise. "I'm sure he is. He's probably whistling his way back to the embassy with that repulsive grin of his right now."

"So tell me you'll consider it?" He ran a finger down her jaw, signaling the end of the discussion.

She leaned into him and closed her eyes. For the first time, hope overwhelmed the fear.

"I'll consider it."

* * *

The next evening was oddly warm for early spring in Cadena. Brooks Neave stood next to her on the boarding ramp at the shuttleport outside of town, concern written on his face. It wasn't like the calm and composed Haederan ambassador to show anxiety, and that meant he'd seen the intel Chase had shown her four hours earlier.

And that Quen was trying to kill her.

"I needed a vacation anyway," Neave said, giving her a forced smile. "And I hear northern Emot is nice this time of year."

"I'm so sorry for the deception." Avery shifted from foot to foot as Wynne and Enric loaded the rest of her belongings themselves. Ramp crew talked, an unnecessary risk. "I know you have work to do on Asria."

"Nothing as important as this, my lady, and I can do everything I need to do from Emot. I'm happy to help out, as long as you give my regards to His Majesty."

That pleasantry was forced, too. Even the emperor of Haedera didn't know about this trip. Owin would never know of Chase's plot—even being former brothers-in-law—or the queen of Asria's departure, or of her stay at Chase's estate on Haedera, or that his ambassador to Asria was hiding out on Emot to cover the Rendon family's use of his personal starship. Even Owin might talk to the wrong person.

"I'll be sure to do that," she lied.

Neave nodded. "And please make sure—"

Wynne pushed between them as a shadowy figure moved on the opposite side of the ramp. She needn't have bothered. Even at this distance, the uneven gait gave him away.

"Merritt?" Avery called quietly.

Merritt crossed the ramp, silent as the stars, and dropped one last small bag on the boarding ramp at her feet.

"Teruel gave his approval for a 'very long leave to wherever I deem appropriate,'" he said with a laugh. "As long as I don't leave the quadrant. He didn't ask many questions, either. I rather suspect he's given up when it comes to you."

"I'm sure he has." Giddiness welled up in her stomach. She clenched her hands into fists to keep from running her hands over him in front of Neave. "But that means more people know where I'm going."

"Still not many. Baylen. Teruel. Wynne and Enric. His Excellency. And Colonel Chase, wherever he is."

Avery wanted to sigh. "He's already inside with his daughter, so I suppose it's time we go, too." She turned to Neave. "Your Excellency?"

The ambassador gave her a quick bow. "Have a pleasant trip, my lady. Stay safe." His footsteps clicked across the ramp as he left.

Avery turned to Merritt. "That's it, then. Ready?"

"Ready as I'll ever be. Enric?"

Enric tossed Merritt's bag inside and nodded. "All set. I'll see you when I see you, Your Majesty. Good luck."

"Good," Chase cut in from behind them. "Because they're ready up front. Shall we?"

No backing out now. With Wynne behind her, Avery climbed the boarding ramp into the main corridor. It felt like stepping foot onto Haedera itself. Instead of the ivory carpet and leather preferred on the royal Asrian couriers, Neave's ship was dark yet strangely open. Real wood, probably local to the ambassador's part of Haedera, covered the wall, and the sconces were something one could find in a temple instead of a starship. All she wanted to do was run her fingers over the intricate whorls that danced down the hallway.

Chase led her forward to an unmarked stateroom while Merritt took Lucas for a look at the flight deck.

"The three of you get the big suite this trip," he said. "Major Ferran will be right across the hall."

He slid the door open, revealing a large suite with a bed square in the center. An impractical headboard stood behind it instead of the usual storage, so necessary in a cramped courier ship. And plants? Three of them sat by the large viewing window, a large artificial light above them. An overstuffed pine-green velvet chair sat nearby with its own light attached—a personal solar room, something even Asrian courier ships didn't bother with. Neave's apparent wealth put even the Rendon family money to shame.

But it was the young girl kneeling in front of their trunks who captured and held Avery's attention.

"Oh, good," Chase said, turning to Avery. "This is Fiona."

The girl spun around at his voice. Young. Perhaps ten years younger than herself. No frown lines, no lines around her eyes, no dark circles, and probably no stretch marks. It wasn't hard to make her feel old these days.

"Your, ah . . ." Avery raised her eyebrows in question. *Older daughter he'd never mentioned? Mistress?*

Chase frowned at her, perhaps reading her thoughts, then gestured her back into the corridor. "Sophie's maid."

"You brought your maid?" Avery asked. After rushing her and Lucas and Wynne out of the palace with practically nothing but the clothes on their backs?

"I couldn't exactly leave her on Asria," he said. "She's my entire household here, and I'm responsible for her. Anyway, Sophie doesn't need a full-time servant, though she'd tell you otherwise, of course. So for the trip, and while you're on Haedera, she's yours."

"No. Absolutely not." It was a blunt answer, but one had to be blunt to have a chance of outwitting Chase.

"No, what?" Merritt appeared through the doorway to the flight deck, Lucas squirming in his arms, and she breathed a sigh of relief. Merritt would stop this. She reached out for Lucas, and he happily threw himself at her.

"He wants to loan me his servant, Mer." Only the fear of Lucas picking up less-than-royal habits kept her from rolling her eyes.

Merritt narrowed his in amusement. "Well, why not?"

It sounded like Chase's favorite phrase. Why not indeed?

"Because I don't need one," she said petulantly, avoiding Chase's mocking stare. "I never have."

She was more than capable of unpacking, and she could certainly dress herself. The Rendons had scarcely used servants in Sabino; even her uncle had made his own breakfast most days. And in slightly more formal Cadena? The palace servants were trained to be unobtrusive, but that wouldn't be possible on a small starship. Fiona—a Haederan, no less—would be in the way. Did Merritt and Chase think she'd had people doing her hair during her short stint as a military cadet?

"A twelve-year-old girl doesn't need a full-time servant either," Chase said. "You'd be doing me a favor, Your Majesty."

Who says I want to do you a favor? "It's not a favor. I know it's not. You don't need to have people spying on my every move. And I'm not going to allow it, no matter what reasonable-sounding explanation you come up with."

There. It was said. No one related to Chase in even the most tangential way could be allowed in her and Merritt's quarters.

Chase burst into laughter. "If I had someone spying on you, you would never know it." He cut himself off at her furious expression and Merritt's chuckle. "Look, if you can't stand having her around after a few days, I'll send her back to Sophie. But please, give her a chance. It's one of the few things I can do to help right now."

Her shoulders sank as she nodded her agreement. The Commonwealth psychologists had reassured her that caving to Chase's minor requests was normal—he'd threatened her life back then if she hadn't immediately acquiesced to his demands, after all—but that justification had never made her feel better about her compliance. Her mind should be long past the fear, and yet it wasn't. Chase had won this one.

Again.

* * *

She crawled into bed that night wanting nothing more than to be left alone. Lucas had clung to her for hours, distraught by the loss of his lovey blanket they'd forgotten to bring in their rushed departure. Merritt had sided with Chase, about a servant of all things, something she still couldn't believe. And although Fiona had escaped to her quarters next to Wynne's after the blowup with Chase in the hall, she was back. Too tired to argue over something so trivial, especially since the maid hadn't had a say in the situation, Avery let her turn down the bed and brew a pot of tea.

Turning a bed down on a courier ship. Chase had to know how ridiculous that kind of luxury was.

She rubbed her head and tried to focus on the words that swirled over the tablet. Baylen had loaded it up with inconsequential issues to address, documents to sign, things to keep her occupied—minor paperwork that wouldn't matter if it fell into Haederan hands. Which it would, if Chase had any say in the matter. *Kusir*, he'd probably downloaded the entire contents of the tablet already. She blew out a deep breath at the thought.

"They mistreated you. Didn't they?"

"Excuse me?" Avery looked up from a list of Defense Forces retirement certificates.

"Before. During the war." Fiona pulled another blanket from a drawer under the bed to replace it with clothing, her cheeks red at the audacious question.

Avery met her eyes. "Yes. They did."

It might have been too frank an answer, but she wasn't going to pretend what had happened hadn't. And it wasn't as brusque as what she'd wanted to say. *Yes, Colonel Chase did* was the whole truth.

Fiona swallowed, then looked away. "I can tell by the way you look at me, my lady. By the way you look at him. And I'm sorry about whatever happened to you, more than you'll ever understand." She went back to unpacking the trunk. "But he's a good man, you know."

"Then you don't know what he does for a living." Avery set the tablet to the side. It was hard to believe, but who knew how Chase ran his household? He had a good reason for hiding most of his professional life from his servants. If it was even possible to hide something like that. He had to be wearing his uniform when he left his home in Cadena every morning.

Fiona froze for a moment, then smoothly folded another of Merritt's shirts and put it away.

"I know what he does."

"And you aren't afraid of him?"

There was an even longer pause. "Why should I be? I am a loyal Haederan subject."

And people called her naïve. How many loyal Haederan subjects had been caught up in one purge or another over some illusory betrayal? Avery gave Fiona a slight nod and went back to signing retirement certificates. Destroying Haederan delusions was something best saved for another time.

CHAPTER FIVE

How long had she slept? Not nearly long enough, for she was exhausted, so tired she couldn't move any part of her body, not even her little toe. The only thing she could do was stare at the familiar figure leaning against the table across the small room. He was shrouded in shadows, but she knew who he was. She knew what was coming. It would be impossible to forget. All she wanted to do was close her eyes against the future, but even that was a staggering effort, one she couldn't manage. All she could do was stare.

Chase set a tablet aside and crossed his arms, watching her with something that looked like compassion.

"Just before you came in," he began, "I received another order for your transfer to Haedera. I'd hoped to hear otherwise, but they've denied my request to keep you on Asria."

She wanted to dash out the door to certain freedom, but she was frozen, cold and stiff. Invisible bonds held her to the chair. She opened her mouth to speak, but her lips moved without a sound.

"You didn't think they'd give me forever to do this, did you?" Chase shook his head as he pulled her to her leaden feet. "I'd hoped this would have ended differently for you, Your Highness."

Why couldn't she move? Or speak? Why was Chase calling her *Your Highness*?

He merely looked frustrated at her silence as he led her through the shadowy halls to her cell. Was the ten minutes without the guards a reward for the treason she would surely commit before her execution on an enemy planet? Or a strange kind of goodbye? She couldn't calm her racing thoughts enough to decide what his intentions were nor form any words until he had deposited her on the cot inside. Her brain argued for ignorance, the obliviousness protection from her fate, but her mouth, finally semi-functional, demanded answers.

"Colonel?" She hated the uncertainty in her voice.

He turned in the doorway, his eyebrows raised in silent permission, the rest of his face impassive.

She almost faltered, but there wouldn't be another chance. She wouldn't go into her future blind, like some mute animal led unknowingly to slaughter.

"What's going to happen to me?"

"On Haedera?" Chase tilted his head and regarded her for a moment. No, he looked through her. Like to him, she had ceased to exist. "You don't want to know." He slammed the door shut, plunging her into icy darkness.

Avery's eyes snapped open.

It was dark and cold in the suite aboard the courier ship, but Merritt was snoring softly beside her, and no wonder—he'd had his nose stuck in a tablet for the past fifteen hours. She pulled the blanket she'd kicked off during the night back over her and nestled against him, reveling in how tangible and solid he was. As she listened to him breathe against her, her own breath became regular again, and the chills, as real as they'd been in her dream, died away in the warmth of his body. He shifted at the feel of her cold feet against his, but she clung to him until he relaxed back into his deep sleep.

His touch allowed her to move just enough to wave on the light. It shouldn't have been off. Merritt knew better. Wynne knew better. Fiona, it seemed, did not, and that lack of knowledge would need to be remedied first thing in the morning.

With the light calming her, she rolled over on her back and stared unblinkingly at the ceiling. She'd thought the nightmares were over. At least the vivid ones, the ones that were far more realistic than her dwindling memories. For the past few months, her dreams had merely been images and feelings. Not—not whatever that had been.

Sleep wouldn't come again, though, and if she was honest with herself, she didn't want it to. Why risk another dream? She crept out of bed and slipped on a pair of soft leggings and a thick tunic, then glanced back at Merritt. He was still asleep, for once untroubled by his own dreams of war, and as much as she wanted his company and touch, she wouldn't disturb him now.

Quietly, she stuck her head out into the corridor. Laughter filtered down it. Lucas's laugh. Struck with guilt that Wynne or Fiona had been roped into supervising him in the middle of the night, Avery made her way to the passenger lounge. Lucas had pulled himself up from his hands and knees and was working his way across the large viewing window, falling and laughing every so often while Wynne coached him from a chair in the corner. His mouth split into a smile when he saw her, and he went crashing to the floor again. Avery darted for him, but his cry must have been embarrassment, for it turned to an ecstatic babble as soon as she picked him up.

"You look terrible," Wynne said in greeting.

"Just a bad dream." Avery stuck her nose in Lucas's hair. There was no need to relive details in front of Wynne. In the morning, Merritt would ask why she'd disappeared in the middle of the night, and it was something she couldn't even tell him. Details weren't needed, though. Wynne and Merritt could guess. "How long has he been up?"

"Two hours. I wish I could borrow some of his energy. That Haederan woman fell asleep an hour ago. I sent her to her cabin."

"I'm sorry your workload has doubled," Avery said, slipping into the lounge chair next to Wynne. Would she ever stop feeling guilty about the pressure her very existence placed on everyone else? Leaving Asria had made things worse.

"I don't have anything else to do," Wynne replied. "Work keeps me busy."

"Still, I feel bad you've had to leave Asria." Wynne had never mentioned a family, and she was at the palace most of the time, but there had to be someone she cared about back home.

"It's a much-needed break, my lady."

That didn't sound like Wynne. But yes, there it was—a slight sadness in her eyes.

"From what? I hope you're not staying with me if you don't want to. Do you want your Defense Forces job back?"

It was possible. Maybe it hadn't been Wynne's decision to work for the Rendons once her father had become king. She was supposed to have been on a temporary loan from the military, after all, but these things had a way of becoming permanent.

Wynne smiled. "No. I'm perfectly happy here. It's just that—" Her smile faltered. "There was someone. Carles. He was killed in a car accident a few months before the Commonwealth arrived. Some nights I deal with it better than others."

"Oh, Wynne." She squeezed Lucas tighter. "Why didn't you tell me?"

"I don't like sympathy. And I couldn't stand the looks people gave me, so I finally stopped talking about it. No one at the palace knows." Her eyes became haunted, distant. "We were so close to the end. I suppose, more than anything, I never got over him dying when Asria was still under Haederan control. I keep picturing how we would have celebrated the liberation together, and that's harder than anything else."

"I'm so sorry." If only time didn't march forward in one direction. "I wish there was something I could do."

"You have nothing to be sorry for. Nothing," Wynne repeated as Avery licked her lips to speak again. "I know what you're thinking, and I am so happy that everything worked out for you and Colonel Rendon."

Before Avery could reply, there was a quiet knock at the door. Chase stood outside in civilian clothes, wide awake.

"I heard voices," he said apologetically. "And I was wondering if we could talk, Your Majesty." Chase glanced around the lounge, his eyes landing on Wynne. "In private."

She must have flinched at his question because Wynne, ever the observant one, shook her head disapprovingly. Chase narrowed his eyes in similar displeasure and opened his mouth.

"It's fine, Wynne," Avery interrupted before he could speak. Anything to dispel the impending argument between the two of them. There was no avoiding their interacting, not in these close quarters, so she had to do what she could to keep the peace for everyone's safety and her sanity. She lifted Lucas and kissed his cheeks. They were warm, like Merritt had been. This child was her reality, not that dream—and he didn't need to witness any of this unrest, even if he couldn't possibly know the meaning behind it. "You keep Miss Wynne company for a while, all right?"

He babbled happily in reply. Wynne stalked out with Lucas's hands wound through her hair, but not before dimming the lights halfway. *Bless her.* Avery blew out a breath and motioned Chase to Wynne's chair. Any talk with him could only happen in this room, with space on the other side of the windows, a fact he had to know. A fact which probably, despite his claim of being curious about voices, explained his appearance now.

Chase sat and leaned toward where the stars would be if the ship wasn't streaking so fast through space, elbows on his knees, avoiding eye contact. For almost five minutes, the lounge was silent except for one loud shriek from Lucas, cut short by the closing of a door. Avery stared at him, waiting to be included in the conversation, but he might have been in his own world for all the talking he was doing.

Finally, he sighed and turned toward her.

"I need to ask your forgiveness."

"For what?" It wasn't like Chase to apologize for something minor. Or anything at all, really. Anxiety washed over her. What had he done now?

A bit of familiar mockery appeared on his face at her question, though it seemed to be directed at himself this time.

"If I'd known you'd have forgotten so easily," he said, "I wouldn't have bothered." He cocked his head at her, more than polite interest on his face. "I'm sorry for what I put you through. All of it. I'm even more sorry that you're still paying for it now."

Oh. That.

Avery tucked a foot under herself and stared at him. In the middle of the night, on a civilian ship, in civilian clothing, with the earnest look he was giving her, he seemed harmless. But then, he'd seemed harmless for a Haederan long ago on the street in Cadena, dressed as an Imperial Haederan Army captain. Before he'd revealed his true identity. Before he'd destroyed her life. And how many before her?

No, Chase was the furthest thing from harmless. Regardless of whatever diplomatic job he'd been playing at since the armistice, he was still Imperial Security, and still dangerous, even now.

"Who says I'm still paying for it?" she asked.

Calm. Stay calm. Maybe it was a foolish hope to project such a confident front, but it was humiliating for Chase to know just how badly he'd affected her.

"Colonel Rendon." His lip quirked up.

"Oh."

Right. The quiet conversation in Merritt's office she hadn't heard all of.

"He promised he'd kill me if I hurt you again. I'm fairly certain he meant it."

"Merritt wouldn't—"

She broke off her protest. Maybe he would. And it wasn't as though she was obligated to ease Chase's guilt about torturing her. She blinked away the memory of him appearing in her cell in Cadena, the moment that he'd shattered everything, and stared out the window.

"You don't need to apologize," she told the void. How easily those words slipped out. She didn't mean them. "It was war."

"It was wrong," Chase said quietly. "I knew that going in, and I still did it." He leaned forward and rubbed his forehead with the heels of his hands. "I think you can figure out most of the whys at this point. But they're no excuse."

Avery pressed her lips together and shook her head. It would have been impossible for Chase to escape the life he'd been born into, even if he'd wanted to. Sophie, sleeping alone in his cabin down the hall, never to see her twin again, was proof of that. Still, her compassion toward him could only go so far.

"You still don't need to apologize to me," she said. "It's not my forgiveness you need."

"I have His. I—I would like yours."

She closed her eyes. Chase was asking too much.

"If it's too soon or not something you can do at all, I understand. I know there's nothing I can do to change the past or heal the things I've done."

"I would like to forgive you. I know I need to."

Tears welled up behind her eyelids, and she wanted to scream at him. How dare he make her *feel*? How dare he bring this up tonight? Didn't he know how much progress she'd made in the past year, progress he'd just smashed to bits?

"I'm not trying to guilt you over this, Your Majesty. Please believe me."

"I know you aren't." She pressed her fingers against her eyes and drew in a shuddering breath.

"Quite the opposite, in fact. Do you remember the night we met?"

She nodded, even though reliving the past with Chase was the last thing she wanted. She experienced that almost every night, even without his prompting.

"You called me a hypocrite."

"I did." She laughed and wiped the tears away. With youth came foolishness, it seemed. Maybe it was just the benefit of hindsight. "And you were. Though I didn't know just how much of one at the time. I wouldn't have been brave enough to say a word to you had I known."

"No one was brave enough—or cared enough about me to risk it, perhaps. No one had ever challenged me before. Not one person had ever confronted me, made me stop and consider the lie I was living. And you of all people should have been terrified of me, but you sat there with that arrogant look on your face and insinuated I couldn't truly worship the Holy One and serve an empire that cheapens life at the same time." His smile became lopsided. "I owe you for that. More than you know."

"But you still—"

"If we're fortunate, it takes less than an eternity to turn things around." His gaze flickered out toward space. "And if it makes you feel any better, when I wasn't with you or sleeping, I was in your temple praying for guidance. For protection for my family. For forgiveness for the things I'd done and the things I was going to do. For peace in the quadrant, though I had absolutely no right to pray for that. It's no wonder He ignored me."

"I remember the incense." The scent of him, fresh from the temple, haunted her dreams. Maybe more than the memories of the threats, the exhaustion, the beatings. "I hated you for it."

"You have every right to hate me. For a lot of things." He tilted his head to the side, his unwitting tell for more questions. "How bad is it?"

She blew out a breath. It was none of his business, but something made her want to answer, desperately.

"The flashbacks are going away," she said, "but I'm sure you know about the nightmares. They're impossible to hide, especially since I always look like I've been up all night. Sometimes I wonder why the Asrian media hasn't reported on them." The dark circles weren't just from Lucas like she always claimed.

"I have nerve damage in my wrists. My left thumb is numb most of the time. At first they thought it was from the pregnancy, but once I told them how long it had been going on, they wrote it down as 'induced neuropathy due to overzealous use of restraints.' It didn't respond much to treatment, and I finally told them no more. I can fly the Valko like this most days. But my eye —my eye is the worst."

She blinked away tears as the bad eye went blurry. Chase knew what had happened there. He hadn't seen the soldiers slam that stun pistol across her face, hadn't heard her cry out in pain, but he'd seen the aftermath, even blamed her for the injury. There was no need to relive it in front of him now.

"But you're flying," he said.

"Badly. I'll never fly alone again. I'll never fly in combat, even with a secondary, no matter how desperate Asria gets. They're only—" What was the word? Her memory was mush. It happened most of the time she was anywhere near Chase. "They're humoring me. It keeps me happy, and it's a good public relations trick. Because I'm worse now than I was a year ago. I don't know how to explain it. As soon as I knew I was safe, everything slammed into me. I remember things I couldn't before."

So many things.

How the soldiers would stick her arm with a needle, pretending to inject who knew what.

The speculation of her execution and the vile things they wanted to do to her body afterward, discussed loud enough for her to hear.

How their hands felt each time they'd searched her. She'd retreated into herself every time, a broken and empty shell lit with pinpricks of rage. Where did they think she could have found a weapon?

The Imperial Security medic. He'd healed some of her injuries, yes, but he'd also subjected her to unimaginable cruelty.

How the wounds on her back had bled through her thin prison

clothing. She'd cried at the sight of the stains, something she hadn't even done during the lashing that had caused them.

Being chained to the wet and frozen floor, hooded, for two days while they tossed buckets of ice on her from time to time. She hadn't thought the cell could get any darker or colder, but she'd been wrong.

Her back began to ache where they'd struck her, a stinging pain long forgotten, and she looked back at Chase before the memories took an even stronger hold. Even so, she shivered, and by the way he pulled at his collar, he noticed.

"The physical pain," she said, "that's easy to forget when I let myself. It fades, or at least moves around so often that I can't focus on one memory. That helps. But you—" Confessing anything to Chase was so difficult. For weeks back then, she'd convinced herself that showing vulnerability in front of him was the worst thing in the world. "You may not have done those things yourself, but you broke me. So thoroughly that I don't know I'll ever be whole again. And I can't forget that, as much as I've tried."

"I'm sorry," he said. "I know how trite that sounds, but I've never told you like this before, and you deserve to hear it out loud."

"You don't need to keep saying it. I know."

"I wish I could change things. I wish I could change so much. Believe me." At her silence, he sighed and stood. "I'm going to go check on things up front. I hope you can get some sleep tonight."

"Wait." Something stirred inside her, and she twisted around and spoke over the back of her chair. "I don't mind if you stay. I can make us some tea. Or coffee, if you'd rather," she added hastily. Anything to keep him from walking away when they were right on the verge of—something. "Merritt probably didn't tell you, but being alone bothers me sometimes."

Right now, just the idea of walking back to her quarters alone bothered her.

"I can get Major Ferran for you." Chase gestured toward the

door and took another step in the same direction. "Because you did once say you'd rather waste away in a prison cell than have my company."

"Did I?" She must have blocked it out, because she couldn't remember ever saying that. What else was she unable to remember? She'd experience everything again in her dreams at some point, that was for sure. "I'm sure I must have meant it at the time. But if we're to have a chance at a new start, Colonel . . ."

Chase laughed, though it sounded tense. "If a new start is what you'd like, then please, call me Gareth, Your Majesty."

Her smile faltered a little at that. Words were easy, but the promise he'd just made was not. She stood and stuck her hand out to conceal her uneasiness at both his touch and what she was about to say. He already knew everything about her—what more could a name possibly mean?

Everything.

"Then it's Avery."

She held her breath as he stared at her hand and frowned. The frown disappeared as he grasped it, and her heartbeat slowed. What must he be thinking? Did he understand the trust she'd just extended to him? He squeezed her fingers and smiled, so perhaps he did.

"Tea, then?" she asked as he dropped his hand.

"If you'd like. But allow me." Chase turned toward the small water dispenser.

"Haederan style, if you don't mind, please."

He chuckled and reached for two of the delicate porcelain mugs that sat on a polished wood shelf above the sink. Neave's love for luxury, even in deep space, extended to the little things as well.

"I don't mind," he said. "Though I'm a little surprised you—"

Blue porcelain shattered on the steel floor as the courier ship reeled violently to port. Avery grabbed the arm of her chair as the deck tilted beneath her. Her fingers slipped, and pain shot through her knees as they hit the floor.

Chase was next to her in an instant. "Are you hurt?"

"I'm fine." She tried to slide away from him, but the ship was listing at such an angle that her body wouldn't respond to her commands. "But I don't think I want to be in this room with those windows right now."

"No argument from me there." He pushed himself up, steadier than she could ever be, then reached out for her.

Avery jerked her arm away. "Don't touch me."

Her voice shook more than it should. She pulled herself up on the chair instead, then made her way to the door, a hand on the wall, him trailing behind her. Only the thought of falling backward into him kept her upright.

The ship lurched as she reached for the keypad, to starboard that time. Her forehead slammed against the wall, and it was only Chase's presence that kept the curses unspoken.

"Stay here."

Chase smashed his hand against the emergency button and pushed her out the door, then down to the floor in the hallway.

"Don't tell me what to do." Avery crawled to her feet as the ship shuddered, an unworldly noise echoing through it.

"Then don't try to get yourself killed."

He stepped toward her, probably planning to shove her to the deck again, but Wynne appeared at her side before he could. She didn't glance at Chase, just shouldered Avery toward her cabin.

"Do me a favor and listen for once." Wynne looked rattled as she pushed Avery down the corridor, and Wynne never panicked. "Pirates. Just light-years off our nose. Time to hide."

CHAPTER SIX

A‌VERY TUCKED HER LEGS UNDER HER AND SQUEEZED L‌UCAS TIGHTER. His eyes were round, but he was silent for now. Sophie pressed against her, hair disheveled from her midnight wake-up, her eyes red from crying.

"They'll go away," Wynne whispered to her. "We don't have anything they want."

"As long as they don't destroy the ship in the process."

Wynne sounded too optimistic. It was a miracle that their shots hadn't yet breached the hull or that the ship hadn't been torn apart by the barrage modules that had dropped them from hyperspace. Whatever she thought of the Haederans, even they didn't mess with that technology. The magnetic fields strung between the modules had slowed Neave's ship to sublight speed like they'd smashed into an asteroid—which meant they'd been lucky. The technology had the unfortunate side effect of destroying ships, killing the crew and passengers in the process. Whether the Haederans were afraid of Commonwealth retaliation or simply had a bit of humanity left in them didn't matter. Barrage modules were solely within the purview of pirates.

And rarely used by even them, thank the stars.

"Let's hope they don't," Wynne replied. "It's held together so far, so we may be lucky. They just launched a pod, and their ship is waiting for them to return. Could be a quick boarding." She put her finger to her mouth and shook Sophie by the shoulder. "Silent, remember? Until Lady Avery says otherwise."

Sophie nodded and pressed harder into Avery's side. The closet in her and Merritt's cabin wasn't so tiny that she needed to, but Avery didn't mind. The two small ones clinging to her diluted some of her own fear, and having something to focus on besides the people who were about to board the courier might be lifesaving. The diminutive stun pistol in her pocket didn't hurt either—not that it would be much use against a gang of pirates armed with who knew what.

"All right. See you in a bit." Wynne patted Lucas on the head and swung the door shut.

The closet went dark. Avery's heartbeat thrashed in her ears, but she could hear Wynne moving about the cabin, arranging the linens in an attempt to make the room look unoccupied. If Wynne wasn't successful, Merritt would have to convince the pirates that he was the cabin's sole occupant. She took a deep breath, her nose in Lucas's hair. He squirmed, and she released a bit of the pressure.

"Listen up, you two." She grappled for Sophie's hand in the dark. "We're going to play a game. Whoever is quiet the longest gets a surprise."

"What kind of surprise?" Sophie sounded doubtful.

You get to live?

"I don't know yet. We'll figure out when we reach Haedera, yes?"

Sophie squeezed her hand in return.

"Good. Now no more talking until Wynne or your father comes back." If only she could order the same of Lucas. His breathing was slowing, and he was growing heavy, like he was on the verge of falling asleep, but that could change in an instant.

The cabin grew deathly quiet after Wynne exited. No light filtered through the almost-sealed closet door. It was impossible to tell what was going on in the cargo bay or if their attackers had retreated to their own ship. Perhaps they would. Perhaps they'd recognized the ship and had decided not to bother a Haederan vessel. Perhaps—

Shouts.

She couldn't understand the words through the cabin door, but they didn't sound friendly. She clung to Lucas, asleep over her shoulder. Asleep and silent. Next to her, Sophie gave a quiet whimper, and the child's fear seemed to seep through her hands. Avery tried to yawn, tried to push the panic down, but it was too late, her breath already short. Oh, of all the inopportune times for a panic attack . . .

The cabin door slid open with a high-pitched hissing sound that was audible even in the closet. Voices, not Asrian or Haederan, filled the small space. Avery flinched as containers hit the door, the one thin piece of metal shielding her and Lucas and Sophie.

"Search those storage compartments."

The accent wasn't familiar, but the order left nothing to the imagination. Someone yanked open each wardrobe in turn, starting on the opposite side of the cabin. The handle on the door next to them jiggled—it had been sticky the entire voyage. Avery clutched Lucas even closer and searched for Sophie, but she'd pushed herself into the far corner, just close enough for Avery to brush her fingers.

Lucas shifted.

Sophie whimpered again.

Avery tightened her grip on the stun pistol.

The door flew open.

She blinked in the bright light. A group of them stood in the cabin. For a long second, time stood still, as if she and Lucas and Sophie had surprised the pirates as much as the pirates had surprised them out in deep space. The one who'd flung the door open grabbed for Sophie, but Avery's first shot hit him square in the chest.

With a cry, Sophie darted out of the closet and tripped over the unconscious body lying in front of her. The sandy-haired man standing by the bed grabbed her by the wrist and yanked her up, his decidedly non–stun pistol at her head. Was he wearing thin armor under those black fatigues? His colleague certainly wasn't, so perhaps not, but—

"Drop it."

And he had a Brisian accent. *Fantastic.* Brisian loyalty was only to money, which meant someone had hired him, and there would be no talking them out of this attack unless she could offer more. What else was there to do? Avery shifted Lucas to a more secure position and tossed her pistol out into the room, right to the man's feet.

He ignored it and jerked his head at her. "Out."

Pain shot through her calves and knees as she stood, clutching Lucas.

"Hand him over."

Somehow, she found her voice. "No. I'll pay you. Just tell me how much, and I'll pay you more."

"Now." He pushed the gun harder against Sophie's head. "Or you can scrub her brains out of the rug."

Her gaze shot to Sophie. The girl's eyes were red and wet, but she wasn't making a sound. She didn't move either, didn't shake, didn't fight, didn't do anything except stare back.

And before the emperor pulled that knife, even before he ordered that child to kneel in front of him, I knew what we had done.

Brennin Kern's voice burst into her mind like a lightning bolt. Losing Sophie after what had happened to Marc would kill Chase. Lucas struggled and whined against her hold, but Avery wound her arms tighter around him. She pressed her lips against his head, inhaling his scent. She couldn't let them harm Sophie, but she couldn't hand over Lucas, either.

"You don't want to do that," she said, her voice shaking. "You don't want to harm her."

"No," he agreed. "I don't. But I will if you don't hand him over in the next five seconds."

She swallowed. This was a nightmare. It wasn't happening. Any second now, she'd wake up next to Merritt, or perhaps Chase would saunter in wearing that dreadful Imperial Security Command uniform, full of threats and mocking intimidation. That was how all her nightmares went.

"Then step out into the center of the room."

Oh, more orders—but they hadn't shot Sophie or made a move toward her. They were going to pry Lucas from her hands, then.

Fine. She'd fight them. They didn't know how much she'd fought in the past, didn't know what she was capable of. Handing over Lucas directly was out of the question, but she could move out of the closet. Yes, she could walk just a few paces. On shaking legs that had to belong to someone else, she took three steps, then stopped. Lucas began to wail. Even a toddler could sense the tension in the cabin.

One of the men circled behind her, and Avery fought back her own whimper. Was there any point in pretending she wasn't afraid of them? Her terror had to be written all over her face. Hadn't she learned anything from her dealings with Imperial Security?

Hide your fear. Always hide it.

But bravery was just talk when it came down to it.

A hand curled around her upper arm and yanked backward, nearly pulling it from her shoulder. She didn't have a chance to turn toward her attacker before her wrist went weak—hadn't she just told Chase how brittle they were?—and her hand slipped from Lucas's chest. He fell toward her waist with a cry, and before she could breathe, before she could grab him, he'd hit the floor.

Lucas screamed, actually screamed, and the shorter pirate scooped him up and tossed him over his shoulder. Avery stepped toward them, but the searing pain in her shoulder became torturous as the man behind her yanked harder. There was no way she could move now, but she would kill him. All of them. As soon as she got the chance, they'd be dead.

"That wasn't so hard, was it?" the Brisian asked. He shoved Sophie toward the door, into the arms of one of the others. Lucas's captor followed, an arm around his flailing legs. "Now be good, and they'll be safe."

The door opened to release the two pirates, then hissed shut. The man holding her relaxed his grip on her arm, and Avery jabbed him hard in the stomach with her elbow and darted toward the door. He stumbled after her, but the inconsequential injury she'd inflicted didn't matter. There were two of them left in the cabin with her—conscious, at least—and both now had stun pistols pointed right at her chest. She stumbled to a halt, hands out at her sides.

"I wouldn't call that good," the Brisian said. At least he'd swapped his gun for a stun pistol while she hadn't been looking. Some rational part of her brain told her that meant something. They were here for her, and they wanted her alive. "On the deck. Facedown. Now."

The luxurious rug didn't hide the cold of the steel deck underneath it. The chill ate into her cheek, her palms, her shoulders, her knees, even though the rest of her body was burning up. But Lucas was safe. He had to be safe. They'd only grabbed him to ensure her cooperation, hadn't they?

"Hands behind your back."

Her terror wouldn't let her fight that order, either. Handcuffs dug into her sore wrists, and she fought back a scream as he wrenched her shoulder further.

Calm. Stay calm.

"Just the shocker?" he asked, with a quick glance at his unconscious colleague.

"Yes." Her voice was a breathless whisper. This one. This one had to be in charge, and she could reason with him. With a careful and, she hoped, unobtrusive shift in position, the pain in her shoulder subsided. "But this is a diplomatic courier. We don't have any cargo that would interest you."

"This isn't a diplomatic ship." His hands swept down her sides and around her waist, brisk and efficient, like he was making a superficial check of an animal for fleas, then he sat back on his heels and examined her. "It's the personal courier of Brooks Neave, the Haederan ambassador to Asria—which means whoever he loaned it to must be very important, no?"

Fear, raw fear, settled in her. He laughed as tears spilled onto her cheeks.

"That's what I thought." The door hissed open, and he jumped to his feet. "Yeah?" he asked someone behind her. "You got them all?"

The newcomer grunted.

Merritt. Wynne. Chase. Fiona. The pilots. They had to be all right. Had to be.

"Good. Get him out of here." He gestured at the unconscious pirate, then knelt next to her. "I'm going to let you see them, but the first wrong move you make, I pick them off one by one. Understand?"

He seemed to take her silence for acceptance and yanked her off the floor and into the corridor. Red emergency lights provided the only illumination. Avery shifted her weight toward the bridge and Lucas, but the man pulled her in the opposite direction toward the cargo bay and four figures approaching them in the dim light. Three were moving in an unfamiliar manner, but one, yes, the one in the middle she recognized.

Her stomach fell all the way to her feet. Not Merritt. Of course, if they knew who she was, they wouldn't allow her to see Merritt. They wouldn't give her that kind of hope.

They'd brought Chase instead.

Chase squinted at her as the two groups closed the distance, then sighed when the pirate holding her jerked her to a stop a few paces away.

"This is a diplomatic ship," he said slowly. "But if you leave now, maybe we'll forget this happened."

The pressure on her arm disappeared as the Brisian walked slowly toward him, head tilted, eyes focused on nothing but Chase. Avery tried to back away toward the flight deck, only to stumble into two more men.

"Funny, that's the same thing your Asrian friend just said. You never were very creative in your threats, Colonel."

That strange voice, that Brisian accent that she'd only heard once or twice in her life, had transformed into something much more familiar. Familiar and sinister. And he . . . and he knew Chase?

Their hijacker was Haederan.

Avery blinked. That didn't make any sense. None at all. She tried to catch Chase's attention with her eyes, but he ignored her.

"And you were never very good at following rules, Burrier. But this . . ." Chase eyed each of the pirates under the flashing emergency lights in a long, languid sequence, skipping over her anguished expression. "Well, I have to say, I'm a little surprised."

"Then this will surprise you even more."

The punch caught Chase right across the mouth. His head flew sideways, but he didn't make a sound as he ran his tongue across the blood from his split lip.

"You're right," he said. "I'd have thought you'd put a little more behind it."

Was he trying to get himself killed?

Burrier shook out his hand and grinned. "I was warming up. Want to try again?"

Chase opened his mouth. Probably he did.

"Stop!" Her shriek surprised everyone, including Chase, who jerked straight up like he'd just realized she was there. "Stop. Don't hit him."

"Well, look at that." Burrier turned toward her. "Who'd have thought the Asrian queen would have a soft spot for you, sir?"

"She has her moments."

Burrier chuckled. "I'm sure she does." He jerked his chin at Chase. "Tell her what you're supposed to tell her."

Chase sighed again, the suffering sound of a man who wasn't used to being ordered around.

"The others are alive and unharmed and will remain so as long as no one tries anything reckless." He glanced back at Burrier. "Close enough? Can I go back and deliver my news to them now? You did promise, after all." His tone made it clear just what he thought of Burrier's promises.

Burrier looked Avery up and down. "No. I think we'll let them worry about her—and you—a little while longer." He pointed toward her cabin. "Both of them in there."

"Sir." The pirate behind her didn't seem pleased with the instruction. "You're stretching us too thin."

Burrier chuckled. "You're worried about a middle-aged paper pusher and an academy dropout, Groves? Throw them in there, then meet me back in the cargo bay. Now."

* * *

Without any formality, they shoved Chase facedown on the deck. He grimaced as he hit the ground but lay completely still. It wouldn't be any surprise to Avery if he'd trained himself to hold his breath for minutes at a time, no matter how much pain he was in. Burrier pointed to her, then to the empty spot between Chase and the bed.

"Down."

He had to be kidding. Lie next to Chase? Avery opened her mouth to argue, and he put his hands on her shoulders.

"Now. I won't ask again. You wouldn't want to break that lovely nose if it were to hit the floor, would you?"

Avery jerked away from him and knelt, then collapsed to the floor as gracefully as she could manage with her hands behind her back—which wasn't very. She couldn't look at Chase. The silk hanging over the edge of the bed provided a much more pleasant visual than anything else in the room. And the pattern—Haedera did have lovely textiles. If only she could run her fingers across it, use it to soothe herself like Lucas would.

"That was easy enough, wasn't it?" Burrier kicked her left ankle across her right, and she bit her lip in fury. "See you both in a bit."

Footsteps, dampened by the thick rug, paraded out of the cabin, followed by the hiss and click of the door.

"They're all gone." Chase's voice was barely a whisper. "Look at me."

Avery shook her head. The sheets were the lightest blue silk, almost white, edged with a flowing, repeating leaf that she hadn't noticed until now. So organic. So beautiful. Had the seamstress who made them ever imagined they'd be splattered with blood?

"My lady, look at me. I need to make sure you're all right."

With great effort, she switched cheeks. No matter what had happened, it wasn't worth ignoring him like a petulant child. Chase smiled at her as their eyes met, blood still oozing from his lip.

"You're bleeding all over my rug." Her laugh was breathless and high-pitched, but at least it was a laugh.

"The ambassador's rug," he corrected, smearing most of the remaining blood onto the luxurious wool. "I do hope you'll do the honorable thing and buy him a proper replacement. Did they hurt you?"

Avery shook her head. "But they're on the bridge. Sophie and Lucas." Her voice cracked. She'd trained herself early not to show distress in front of Chase—though she'd never been successful—but this was different, wasn't it? It wouldn't be a show of weakness if she cried now. "I couldn't stop them. They just took them."

"That's not your fault. Get that out of your head right now. No one expected you to take on a group of pirates with nothing but a stun pistol. And Burrier's a bastard, but I don't think he likes killing children."

Did he have to be so blunt?

"And Merritt? Wynne?"

"Cargo bay with the pilots and Fiona, like he said. And fine, also like he said. I don't suppose I have to point out that they're after you. Wholesale murder would bring too much notice down on them."

"That man. Burrier. The rest must be Brisian, I suppose, but he's Haederan. He knows you. How?"

Chase shifted. "I have enemies."

She choked down another feverish laugh. "Why am I not surprised? And this particular one?"

"A former Imperial Haederan Navy navigator with a book-making habit and an even worse insubordination problem."

Ah.

"One who's been subjected to your talents, I assume?" A lame attempt at humor was the only thing keeping her from sobbing.

He narrowed his eyes. "It was brief and efficient. He knew he was caught and had no reason to fight. But yes, he hates Imperial Security for ignoring his commander's request for leniency and despises me especially. As though his release from the navy and imprisonment was my personal vendetta against him and not less than a standard sentence. Seven years. He deserved a hundred times that, but when your father has the ear of the emperor, things tend to . . . well, he got the leniency he wanted by imperial decree. He's lucky his entire family wasn't executed."

Avery wrinkled her nose.

"Anyway, he disappeared from Haedera shortly after his release. We knew what he was up to out here, of course"—Chase managed a laugh—"but it didn't seem important enough to do anything about. He wasn't bothering Haederan subjects, after all. Until now."

"That you knew of."

He tried to shrug. "That we knew of."

"And then Quen hired him."

"It would appear so."

"And he hates you."

"Indeed. Even more than you do, I'd imagine. You, at least, never called me a—"

"I get it." She flushed. "So we're in a lot more trouble than you implied before."

Chase closed his eyes. "Oh yes."

CHAPTER SEVEN

"Oh yes?" she repeated. "Well, that's comforting. So what now?"

Chase sighed, then rolled his shoulders back, still on the floor facing her. From this close, the cut on his lip didn't look quite as bad, but she was relieved it wasn't her.

"You're going to lie right there and not do anything," he said.

"And you?"

"I'm going to do the same thing."

"Colonel—"

Chase didn't answer, just closed his eyes and took a deep breath. He wasn't sleeping though, there was no doubt about that. The look of concentration on his face deepened, and his spine curved slightly.

"Colonel, picking those handcuffs isn't quite what I'd call lying there and doing nothing."

"Maybe if the Commonwealth had taught you things like this before they set you loose in the middle of a war zone," he said, opening his eyes and pulling his right wrist free, "you wouldn't have come so close to getting yourself killed." His chin jerked in that familiar arrogant manner as he sat up, tossed the cuffs behind him, and smoothed out the wrinkles in his sleeves. "Though I don't know why I'm complaining. It certainly made my job easier."

"How dare—"

"Shh." Apparently oblivious to her discomfort, he clamped his hand over her mouth. "Do you want them to hear you?"

No. She wanted his hand off her body. Had he forgotten she'd done the exact same thing? Untrained, no less, then she'd followed that feat by stealing one of his navy's fighters. She tried to kick him, but he sat up before her foot met its mark. All she could manage through his palm was a grumbling noise.

"I'll take that as a no—and your promise to be quiet." Chase removed his hand. "Now stay down and play along," he said as he stood.

"Play al—"

"Hey!" His voice echoed through the cabin. Avery stared at him, horrified, unable to order her muscles to move enough to roll over. "Can we get some water in here?" Chase ignored her shocked look and pressed himself against the wall beside the door.

"What are you doing?" She shook her head frantically. "No. I don't want them back in here. I don't want—"

The door clicked, then slid open. In one fluid movement, Chase had the man who entered flat on the deck, his own pistol pressed under his ear. The door closed again. Avery squashed her face back into the rug.

Too much death.

"You can shut up and stay alive," Chase whispered to him, "or you can shout for them and die before help arrives."

Silence.

"Good choice."

There was a crash and a soft grunt, and Chase reappeared by her side. "I'm going to check things out. Stay right there and be quiet."

"Stay here?" she asked under her breath. "Like this? With him right there?" Deep pain shot through her wrists and shoulders as she struggled against the handcuffs, trying to wiggle them loose. "But what if they come back? What if they come looking for him? What if he wakes up? What if they come back and you're not here? Or what if they see you skulking around out there? It's a courier ship, not a cruiser. You don't have much space to work with." She couldn't hide the fear in her voice, though whether it was about their situation or the fact Chase might have killed someone in front of her was debatable.

Chase blew out a deep breath. "You need to learn to trust, my lady. Believe me, he's not waking up anytime soon. Or at all, if I hit him hard enough."

Avery stilled and looked closer at the man on the floor. Shallow breaths shifted his torso. Her frustration with Chase, with her imprisonment, with this invasion bubbled out in a low growl. *Trust?* Did he even realize what he was saying? Trusting the wrong person could get one killed. She didn't trust. She couldn't trust him, not as a person, not as a whatever he was pretending to be now. He might know a few little tricks, might know how to pick handcuffs, but taking back a ship from belligerents was completely different. If he made the slightest error, it was Lucas's life at stake. What was Chase going to do, talk their captors to death?

"Let me go," she snapped. "Let me go, and I'll stay right here, I promise. At least untie me!"

"And if I do, you'll stay right here and not try anything I'll regret?"

"Yes!" She'd do anything, even hide back in that dark closet, as long as he released her.

Chase leaned over, and she froze. Her heart thrummed at his closeness, closeness that had only meant one thing during her imprisonment—more pain. This time, though, there was no slap, no threat, no strong fingers forcing her to make eye contact, just a long silence as he knelt there and observed her from a breath away.

"Well?" she finally demanded.

He moved closer, his lips almost meeting her ear. "I don't believe you, Your Majesty."

"I'm going to kill you." Oh, how she'd wanted to say those exact words for so very long.

Chase shifted out of her path before she could strike at him.

"No, you're not. You're going to stay right here until I find out what's going on out there." His face grew serious. "Listen to me—if by some chance they come back, I don't want their wrath directed at you. Quen might want you alive, but if you anger them, there's no way to know what they'll do."

Her heart hammered in her chest, panic rising at the thought of continued captivity. Her worst memories washed over her, but she fought back to the present. Chase was tormenting her on purpose, surely, but his justification made sense. She found herself nodding through the panic.

"Lucas is up there."

As if he could forget Sophie was, too.

"I know he is, but I won't let any harm come to him. Or you. You need to believe that. Can you do that for me?"

All she could do was stare at him. Yes, she believed what he'd said about Lucas, but . . . he wouldn't let any harm come to her? The man had the shortest memory in the quadrant.

But maybe that didn't matter any longer. Keeping Lucas safe was all that mattered, and that meant she had to trust Chase, had to take him at his word. It meant spite for the sake of spite was a useless emotion, a wasted effort when they could be working together.

"I'll—I'll try," she said.

"Good. I won't be long." He gave her a quick pat on the back of her shoulder, a gesture she supposed was meant to be comforting, and disappeared out the door.

* * *

Chase had lied. It had been fifteen minutes since he'd left her lying there, or so the chronometer by the bed told her when she wrenched her neck around to see it. Fifteen minutes was a long time, long enough for the chill of the metal floor to seep through the rug.

Avery took a deep breath and flipped herself to a sitting position. It would infuriate Chase, it would infuriate their captors, but her shoulders couldn't take the tension anymore. She rolled them in small circles as she leaned against the bed, wishing she could reach a drink. Or turn the sink in the bathroom on. Anything to quell the raging thirst that had popped up. Maybe she could turn the faucet on with her teeth.

The door clicked again before she could rise and try. Hot fear rose from her toes as she slid back to the floor and pushed her face into the rug.

Too late. It was too late.

"That's what I thought. You couldn't do what I ask if your life depended on it—which it does, by the way. Turn yourself loose. You've done it before."

Chase's sarcasm was followed by a pin hitting the rug next to her head. Avery suppressed a sigh as she struggled back to a sitting position. He'd finally remembered that she'd escaped Linden. Well, there wouldn't be a repeat of that feat, not now.

"Do you think we have time for your petty retaliation?" she snapped at him. "Let me go. What's going on out there?"

"Don't think I won't remember your asking me for help." Chase reached behind her, and with a few deft flicks of his hand, the cuffs fell to the floor. She refrained from rubbing her wrists in front of him, but just barely. "They're not patrolling the ship. Six of them in the cargo bay with the pilots, Major Ferran, and Colonel Rendon. I don't know how many on the bridge."

"So now what?"

"They've got to be planning on transporting us on *Mayfair* herself—there's no sign of their ship any longer. Someone will be along to help us soon. We're just drifting—it'll be obvious something's wrong with us."

She rubbed her sore shoulder. "Not that obvious unless someone's paying attention. And if they get things under control and set us underway again, we'll be in a bad spot. I don't suppose you know if the pilots were able to get a distress signal out before we were boarded?"

Chase shook his head. "Maybe. Doubtful. There's no way to know, and it's not as though I can ask them now."

"Then we need to do that first, and we can't do it from here."

He sat back on the bed, looking cautious. "If we try to take the flight deck . . ."

Sophie and Lucas will be in danger.

"I know." Why wouldn't her voice stop cracking? "But listen to me. It needs to be done. If we can get up there and send a distress signal, we can also . . ."

The jumble of random thoughts that had raced around her brain while she was lying on the floor suddenly coalesced into a clear plan. This would work, wouldn't it? It had worked, albeit unintentionally, on the fighter she'd stolen off *Aurora*. It had almost killed her.

The words spilled out.

"Lower the pressurization. We can depressurize it slowly enough that they won't realize what's happening."

"The engineering panel in the cargo bay will clue them in."

"If they're paying attention. They're guarding five people, most of whom have at least a little hand-to-hand training." She stifled a laugh. Wynne was the one they needed to worry about, but she wouldn't insult the pilots like that. Old loyalties died hard. "They've got their hands full back there, and if they discover we're on the flight deck, you know they'll send reinforcements. They'll be too busy to check pressurization. I think we can do it."

He stood and began to pace. "It's risky."

She pushed herself up. "You're worrying about risk after you just spent twenty minutes skulking around the ship?"

Chase grinned and held out a stun pistol he'd pulled from his pocket. "Stay behind me, all right? Colonel Rendon won't be happy if I get you shot."

Her hand closed over the pistol's grip. "It's a deal."

* * *

Chase beat on the reinforced door of the flight deck so loudly the entire ship must have heard him. Behind him, Avery pressed her back against the wall—they only had a few seconds before someone from the cargo bay came to investigate. The door slid open, but the woman who'd opened it wasn't looking at them, her gaze over her shoulder toward the flight deck seats instead.

Wrong move.

Chase pressed his pistol against her forehead before she realized the visitors standing in the corridor weren't colleagues.

"Hands up," he said. "Two steps back onto the flight deck, then on your knees. Now."

The pirate's lip curled as she raised her arms to her sides, but she did what Chase ordered. Avery stepped through the door behind him and slammed her hand against the close button. The flight deck was lit with a dozen panels to either side of the main controls a dozen paces away through a smaller arched opening. Lucas and Sophie were nowhere to be seen, but a short, stocky man with dark blond hair was rising from a curved chair in front of the viewscreen.

Her shot hit him before he could draw a weapon. The pirate collapsed where he stood, half on his chair, half on the deck, hand nowhere near a weapon. With a grin, Chase gestured her around him. She darted by him as Sophie's dark head poked around the corner by the viewscreen. The girl was holding something to her chest, and Avery's knees nearly gave out as she approached.

Lucas.

His cheek was on Sophie's shoulder, but she could feel it on hers. She didn't even need to touch him to realize he was stirring from a deep slumber.

"More of them?" She nudged the unconscious pilot with her foot before grabbing the pistol from his pocket. All she wanted to do—desperately—was to touch Lucas, to bury her face against him, but he was safer in that corner with Sophie for now.

Sophie shook her head as she stood. "Just the two of them," she whispered, ducking her head around the pillar that didn't quite conceal Chase. He'd presumably relieved the woman of her weapons, for she was kneeling on the deck against the dark consoles, hands on her head. "Is he going to kill her?"

Did the girl honestly believe he'd never done such a thing? Or maybe she believed Chase had done it all too often. With as much gentleness as she could, Avery pushed her back against the wall. If he did shoot the woman right there as she knelt, Sophie didn't need to see it.

"Colonel?" she asked.

"I'm not going to kill her." Chase sounded exasperated at the question as he dug through the nearest cabinet with one hand, presumably looking for something to tie the pirate up with. "But I'm not leaving her to attack us, either." His gaze landed on the stun pistol in her hand. "Toss that over."

Avery stepped slowly toward him instead, set the pistol in his outstretched hand, then turned away toward Sophie to prevent her from seeing the shot. If only she didn't have to hear it. She reached out for Lucas as he began to cry in Sophie's arms and brushed her fingers against his downy hair, his velvety cheeks.

"Shhh. You're all right." Her brain recognized the absurdity of standing there on the flight deck of a hostage courier ship in the middle of space holding a crying baby, but she couldn't take her hands off him.

"I hate to interrupt," came Chase's voice, "but we need to get moving on this. Sophie, hold him, will you? We're going to try something."

"Yes, sir," Sophie said quietly. She held her hands back out to Avery. "My lady?"

Yes, sir? Was their relationship that strained? It wouldn't be surprising, but sadness washed over her. That was no kind of bond for a child and father. Avery gave each of Lucas's cheeks one last kiss before relinquishing him for the second time in two hours. He giggled at Sophie, the tears forgotten, as she spun him over her head. Maybe the girl was the right person to watch over him after all.

"All right," Chase said, sliding into the control seat next to her. "Do you have any idea what you're looking at? Because I don't."

She smothered a nervous chuckle as she swiped a finger through the environmental pages of the multifunction display. It refused to display on the heads-up viewer, so Chase leaned in toward her. All she wanted to do was smack him away.

"This"—she pointed at a set of numbers in the top corner—"is the readout for pressurization in each zone. It looks like there are almost a dozen of them, one for each cabin, plus the main corridor. The flight deck and cargo bay are separate, thankfully."

"So this should be easy."

"Easy but slow." She touched the flight deck number, and it flashed red under her finger. "If they find out we're in here before we can get them to sleep, it won't be good."

"Then how about a distress signal first?"

At least one of them was thinking clearly. She certainly wasn't, not with him looming over her shoulder. Whenever she blinked, she was in that bright room of her nightmares again.

"Good idea. But could you back away a bit?"

"Sorry." Chase shifted back in his chair as something strange crossed his face. He hadn't taken offense to her words, certainly—Chase didn't take offense to anything, it seemed—so could it be shame?

"Thank you." She took a deep breath and reached for the comm panel.

"Wait." His hand clamped over hers and she yanked it back

from the glass, her heart racing. "They could be monitoring communications back there. Is there any way to do this covertly?"

On a civilian transport? Chase was reaching. It wasn't as though she could jam anything.

"Well, if they're monitoring us, they're monitoring us," she said. And if they were, it was already too late to avoid their retribution. A vision of Merritt sprawled on the deck, covered in blood, a bullet hole in his head, passed through her mind. She tried to blink the image away, but it didn't dissipate. "I don't think they'll be able to see this, though."

Chase nodded.

"All right." She reached for the comm panel again. "Do you know if there's an auto-distress button?"

He looked blankly at her.

"For hijackings."

The blank look didn't change, and she sighed, then licked her lips. "Verbal distress signal it is, then." She flicked the push-to-talk with her nail. "Mayday, Mayday, Mayday. This is the Haederan courier ship *Mayfair*. Last known coordinates . . ."

She rattled off the coordinates from the slip of paper Chase held out. Distance and relative bearing off Haedera II, of course, not from the center of the quadrant like the Commonwealth and Defense Forces used. It was hard not to roll her eyes at the ethnocentrism, but if the Commonwealth received their message before the Imperial Haederan Navy did, they could translate the nonsense, even if she couldn't do it in her head.

"Ship has been taken by hostiles, request immediate assistance. Repeat, ship has been taken by hostiles, request immediate assistance." She leaned back and examined the controls. "Happy?"

He grinned. "Ecstatic. Now how about that pressurization?"

Why was her head pounding? They weren't messing with the environmental system on the flight deck. "Sixteen will be enough to knock everyone out but not do any permanent damage. We're at twenty-one now, so we'll go down one every twenty minutes. It'll take some time, but hopefully they'll never know what hit them." She brought up the environmental system page again and rubbed her head as she glanced at Chase. "There must be a way to automatically step it down, but we don't have time for me to flip through every screen and find it. So time me? Starting now?"

He nodded and checked his chronometer. "Mark."

"To twenty, then." She flicked the number with her finger and focused on the panel, suddenly conscious of how long she'd been staring at his face. "And now we wait."

"Isobel hated them." Chase smiled, either oblivious to or enjoying her self-conscious flush.

"Hated what?" *Kusir*, he'd noticed her gaze, and in pure Chase fashion, had called her out on it.

"You're staring at my freckles." He shrugged. "Isobel hated them, and I've never minded. She used to complain about it whenever I stopped lightening them for a few weeks. I can't believe the arguments we used to have over it."

"Do you miss her?" Of all the things to ask. Of course he did. The pain he carried along with him was evident.

"Every day, and more during the night. She was the other half of my soul." He glanced in the corner at Sophie, asleep with Lucas curled in her lap. "Sophie looks just like her. So did—so did Marc. He was a little version of her with blond hair."

"I'd love to see a picture of him."

"Maybe once we get to Haedera. Isobel carried one around, but I never did. I was always too afraid that would make him a target."

His voice cracked on the last word, and she changed the subject. "You never told me she was the emperor's daughter. It explains so much." And it was such a strange detail to leave out. Did Chase think he could hide it forever?

He waved an awkward hand and chuckled, just a little bit.

"Oh. Well, it was a delicate situation. I told you on *Imperieuse* that I needed you to trust me, and what would you have thought of me if you'd known he was my father-in-law? You'd have wondered where I was hiding my horns."

"Horns?"

"Horns." He wriggled his fingers on top of his head. "Like the *kaldrens*, mythical Haederan demons that are said to haunt the forests in the mountains near Windhaven."

Avery couldn't hide her own laugh that time. Oblivious, indeed.

"That's not when I would have started wondering if you were a demon, Colonel," she replied. "Perhaps the first time I saw you in that uniform."

Chase flushed that time. "Yes, I suppose that would have been it." He leaned back in his chair and studied her as she checked the readouts again. "So this is what you'd have been doing if things had gone differently."

"Knocking out pirates in the cargo bay of a Haederan ambassador's private starship?" she asked. "Hardly."

"Flying, I mean." His voice grew quieter; his stare grew more intense. "I saw a photo of you a long time ago. From when you were at the academy before everything. I made sure I knew everything there was to know about you before I caught you on that street."

Silent, she fiddled with the flight deck temperature control. Where was he going with this? Was he trying to make her feel worse?

"You looked so confident in that uniform. So arrogant. Like you planned on taking on the entire Imperial Haederan Navy by yourself and were daring us to do something about it. I hated that look. You had no right to be arrogant when I knew, and you didn't, that Asria would be ours before the season turned. I decided right then and there that I would knock that arrogance out of you, even though I hadn't even met you yet."

Her face grew hot. He'd beat more than arrogance out of her.

"Why are you telling me this?" she asked.

Chase cocked his head in a manner she was all too familiar with.

"Because every so often, I catch a glimpse of it, and I wish I could see that arrogance from you again. I hope one day I will." He checked the time. "That's twenty minutes."

She turned the pressurization in the courier down another notch. "That was another person, Colonel. Another time."

"I don't know," he said wistfully. "You may not believe it, but I think there's a lot of that person left still."

* * *

She and Chase had been wrong about how long depressurizing the rest of the ship would take. They decided to halve the rate, and it was another two hours of awkward conversation with Chase, hugs from Lucas, and sullen stares from Sophie before Avery leaned back from the console. There had been no communication from the cargo bay—apparently their captors hadn't checked on their prisoners in the large suite.

"Sixteen," she said. "I've leveled it off."

"Goodnight, everyone," Chase said. "Sweet dreams."

"We should probably bring the friendlies back up here as soon as we can. I don't like the idea of keeping them at near vacuum that long. And it would be nice if you could find me a pilot. Preferably one of yours, but Merritt can fly if it comes down to it."

His lip curled. "It's a little late for that now. You've been doing just fine—you can't fly it?"

"It's not a fighter, Colonel." Chase couldn't be allowed to see how badly her palms were sweating. "It's a decidedly unstealthy, sluggish starship with no armament, designed for two pilots. In the navy, we liked to call those targets. If those pirates out in space overheard our distress call, they're not going to be happy, and if we need to run, having help familiar with all the systems would be wonderful. Find a spare mask or something. At least one of them should wake up quickly once they get oxygen."

"Of course, my lady." He rummaged through a rack next to the main control and came out with two masks. "See you in a bit." His words became muffled as he strapped one over his face.

The flight deck door slid closed behind him, and Avery took a deep breath. He'd slipped out too fast for the low pressure in the main corridor to affect the flight deck beyond a sudden and soft whoosh of air, so her shortness of breath had to be in her mind. She checked the pressurization on the flight deck anyway—normal. Was it just the panic of being alone? *Alone and responsible for two children?*

For the first time, she was glad for Sophie's help. The girl sat in the corner on the floor, playing peekaboo with Lucas like absolutely nothing had happened. Like they were in a garden in the palace in Cadena on a sunny day with nothing to worry about but a bit of sunburn.

"Haederan courier ship *Mayfair*. Haederan courier ship *Mayfair*. This is the Commonwealth Navy cruiser *Terigon*. If you hear this, please respond."

The call crackled at first, then stabilized. Avery darted for the comm panel and slammed her hand against the visual button. The Commonwealth Navy commander who appeared on the viewscreen squinted at her, then made a slight motion off to his side.

"We're responding to a distress call, ma'am—do you still require assistance?"

For the longest second, she couldn't do anything but nod.

"At least seven belligerents, hopefully unconscious in our aft cargo bay. Possibly more elsewhere on the ship." The bricks that had descended on her shoulders when Chase had headed back that way lifted a little. "Along with five friendlies and an additional conscious Haederan officer. You'll need suits."

He nodded, then snapped his fingers off to the side, and shadows moved. "Medical assistance?"

"Thank you." Her voice had become breathless again. "Not on the flight deck. We're locked in. In the cargo bay—no, I don't think so. I hope not. Just some oxygen for them, I hope. But I don't have good information."

"We'll take care of it." He nodded at her, and the viewscreen went black.

"Now what happens?" Sophie looked pale.

"Now we wait. They'll let us know when it's safe to leave here." The girl's lip quivered, so Avery dropped to the floor next to her and reached out. "Come here."

Sophie flopped down next to her and smiled at Lucas, then closed her eyes and leaned against Avery's shoulder. She sat there, one arm around Sophie and Lucas curled up in her lap, for what must have been an hour before Sophie spoke.

"My lady?"

Avery pried her eyes open. "Hmm?"

"Do you know what my father does?"

A hot flash shot through her heart.

Better than anyone else on this ship but him.

"He works for Ambassador Neave, of course." She kept her voice steady. "Cultural things. He's working on relations between our planets."

"Yes," Sophie said. "But before that, he did something else. You know that, don't you? And sometimes I worry that he may do it again." She glanced up at Avery with something like shame.

"Oh." How was she supposed to respond to this? "Well, I—"

Could there possibly be a more uncomfortable conversation? Naturally Sophie knew her father was Imperial Security—Chase still wore the uniform, and she was Haederan, after all—but she couldn't possibly know everything that meant. Not the interrogations, the torture, the executions. Not as young as she was. But then, if she knew about Marc's death, maybe she did.

The flight panel began to beep before she could figure out what to say, and Avery jumped to her feet. Someone—the Commonwealth, if everything had gone according to plan—was raising the pressure in the rest of the ship. The cameras were still cut, and a sudden pounding on the door echoed through the flight deck as she poked around the menus to find a work-around.

"Get in the corner." She pushed Sophie and Lucas back behind the pillar and grabbed the pistol Chase had left. "Don't move until I tell you it's safe."

With the gun raised in front of her, she tiptoed toward the door. Out of habit, she glanced up at the monitor connected to the camera outside. Still black. Part of her wanted to run back and ask *Terigon* if these were friendlies, but something told her they were —and that they were bearing bad news. Hand shaking, she reached for the opener.

When the door slid open, a Commonwealth marine in full battle armor stood in the doorway. He—or she, it was impossible to tell—lowered their rifle upon seeing the small group. Wynne stepped out from behind the hulking figure, a mask hanging from her neck and blood covering her hands.

Her legs wouldn't support her any longer. The pistol fell from her hand and crashed to the deck, but even that sound wasn't as loud as the rushing blood in her ears. The vision of a body lying on the floor of the cargo bay flashed through her mind again, and even as she tried to blink it away, it refused to disappear.

"Merritt," she whispered.

"Is fine," Wynne said. "But they're transporting Colonel Chase to *Terigon* now. He was . . ." She swallowed. "Shot."

CHAPTER EIGHT

The Commonwealth officer who met them at the hatch stuck out her hand. "Jaxi Bretel, Your Majesty." Her accent confirmed she was a Ventana IV native, and a deep pang of unexpected homesickness shot through Avery. Would Ventana ever stop feeling like home? "Protocol department. Welcome to *Terigon*. Anything you need, let me or the security team know, and we'll make sure you get it."

"I need to see the Haederan officer you brought on board earlier, Commander. The one with the gunshot wound." She'd already waited too long to ask. Even with her constant reassurance that, yes, they were completely unharmed, it had taken forever for the Commonwealth medics to make sure she and Sophie and Lucas weren't injured.

"I'm not entirely sure what the situation is with him," Bretel replied, flashing a brilliant smile. "But I can certainly find out his status once you are all settled in your quarters."

Why did she feel like she was being manipulated? This woman wasn't even good at it. She was too friendly, too slick, too something. On the other hand . . .

Protocol.

That explained everything. She was supposed to be charming

and slippery. Some people appreciated that, perhaps. Probably male people.

"I'd like to see him now, please." Avery firmed her voice. *You'll provide me with anything except intel on the Haederan I just asked about, isn't that right, Commander?*

"Colonel Rendon and the children—including the young Haederan lady—are already settled, my lady. I'm sure the princes are anxious to see you."

Avery shook her head. "Sick bay first. Please."

Bretel sighed at her refusal to back down and gestured down the hallway. "This way."

* * *

It was an uncomfortable walk through the cruiser, more so for Avery than anyone else in the small group. Personnel in gray and blue Commonwealth uniforms scurried around her, some casting curious glances at her and Wynne in their civilian clothing—bloodstained, in Wynne's case—but most were too busy to realize that the queen of a Commonwealth planet was standing in their midst.

Avery ignored the stares as Bretel led them through one more hangar bay. A shortcut, it had to be, which meant the woman knew the ship well. Knew the fastest route to her quarters after a long shift, knew the best ways to avoid the smell of old food that drifted out of the mess halls, knew just the right place to watch the stars when *Terigon* was traveling at sublight speed.

This would have been her life had things gone according to plan. Half her brain wanted to ask for a tour of the barracks and the Comet hangars, but the other half—the sane part—told her that visions of her past life would be more painful than she could handle. And she did need to find out about Chase first.

Perhaps a tour could come later.

"Your Majesty." The doctor who greeted her in the doorway of the main sick bay on level fourteen sounded surprised to see her, then confused as he glanced at Wynne and Bretel. "Is everything all right? We were told—"

"It's not me." She'd probably just given the man a near stroke with her appearance. "I'm looking for Gareth Chase. The Haederan who was brought in earlier. He may have been in some dark gray pants and a checkered blue sweater." Thank whatever luck remained in the quadrant that Chase hadn't been in uniform when the pirates boarded. It might have intimidated their attackers, but it would have had exactly the wrong effect on the Commonwealth. "How is he?"

The doctor's face went blank, and she bit back a gasp.

Chase was dead.

It was the only explanation for the doctor's reaction. She'd been too late. Too late to say thank you for saving *Mayfair*, too late to say goodbye. There was nowhere to sit, but she only wanted to collapse in a chair.

"He's . . ." The doctor frowned at her, then Wynne, then Bretel, as if he wasn't quite certain who to give his news to. "He's out of surgery and doing fine last I heard, but he's not here."

"Where is he?" Bretel sounded as curious as Avery was anxious.

The doctor blinked in confusion. "In the infirmary in the brig."

She didn't think, didn't wait for Wynne or Bretel, just turned on her heel back through the maze of corridors. Left, right, and left again, and then—and then she was totally and completely lost in the labyrinth of steel. She stopped and leaned against one of the smooth gray walls, out of breath, face red with anger. She'd never find the brig on her own, and it wasn't surprising there were no signs directing meddling guests like her.

"Hold on, ma'am." Bretel jumped in front of her as Avery tucked a stray piece of hair behind her ear. "You don't know where you're going, and you certainly can't barge into the brig and demand to see him."

"She's right," Wynne added, not short of breath at all, though her disapproval of the entire situation was clear. "We'll figure something out." *You can't barge into the brig without having a panic attack, and you know it* was left unsaid.

"He doesn't belong there, Wynne. Something's wrong."

"Come on." Wynne tilted her head toward one of the corridors like she knew where she was going. Probably she did. Likely she'd been counting turns and memorizing corridors since they'd arrived. "Let's get everything settled in your quarters, and we'll figure out what's going on."

Avery ignored her—something she'd have to grovel for forgiveness for later—and turned to Bretel. "I need to know he's all right, Commander. Now, not in six hours."

Bretel blew out a deep breath and looked from her to Wynne's stony face.

"Let's go. Maybe they'll allow a short visit if he's well enough. But don't get your hopes up. I don't have any control over what happens in the brig."

* * *

Wynne placed her pistol and comm on the metal table in the brig's processing area and turned her pockets inside out for the warrant officer sitting on the other side. He'd taken Avery's word that she wasn't carrying a weapon or anything else illicit. Finally, the benefits of her status were beginning to outweigh the drawbacks.

"Are you going to be all right?" Wynne asked her quietly.

Avery nodded. It was a lie—her legs had already weakened at the sight of the thick metal door that led into the secure section of the brig. But she owed Chase, didn't she? She closed her eyes as the warrant officer walked them through the entrance. That small motion didn't do much to dispel the memories of her own captivity. This was different though, wasn't it?

"You've got ten minutes," he said as he deposited the group in front of a closed door inside the small infirmary and pressed his fingers to the keypad. "If you need anything or want out sooner, just knock. We'll be right outside."

The door opened, revealing a room larger than she had expected. Wynne and Bretel stepped to either side, clearing the way for her to enter. The sour bite of antiseptic combined with a citrus cleaner assaulted her, so different from the stagnant, grease-filled air on the rest of the ship. To the side, a few machines she couldn't identify beeped ceaselessly.

And there was Chase.

He was pale, which wasn't surprising for someone who'd lost so much blood. There was a large bruise on one side of his head, clearly visible under his light hair. In fact, he didn't look good at all, no matter what the doctor in the central sick bay had told her. The rest of his injuries were hidden under a thin sheet, and she was grateful for that. But he was awake—*alive*—and smiled as she stepped inside.

"I have to say, Your Majesty"—his eyes flitted from her toward the slowly closing door—"I'm honored that you were worried enough about me to step foot inside the brig."

"Stop it." The plea came out as an order, something she'd never have been courageous enough to do before. But how could he make jokes now? The warrant officer finished sliding the door shut behind her, and she took a deep breath, forcing her body to remain facing Chase. "I was terrified you hadn't made it. And when they told me you were here, I didn't know what to think."

"A misunderstanding." Chase cocked his head to the side as if to emphasize the error. His easy tone should have been accompanied by an offhand wave, but his wrists were chained to the sides of the bed.

"This is some misunderstanding." There weren't any chairs in the stark room, and her knees weren't going to hold her up much longer. Leaning against any of the equipment was out of the question. What if it was keeping him alive? Avery rested on the side of the bed by his feet instead. "What happened?"

Chase closed his eyes and took a labored breath.

"Apparently the Commonwealth has been searching for me for quite a while. War crimes, they tell me."

"War crimes?" She cut herself off as his eyes flicked up at the camera in the ceiling. "What are you supposed to have done?"

He sighed. "Oh, the usual. What they'd presume of any Imperial Security Command officer. Rape. Torture. Experimentation. You know."

"That's ridiculous."

The words were out of her mouth before she could stop them. Of course he'd done horrifying things to her, but rape? No. Experimentation? What was that supposed to mean? And torture?

Well.

Torture had such a nebulous definition, didn't it? And it didn't matter, because they couldn't prove anything. They didn't know what he'd done to her.

"The charges get more specific, of course." Chase waved his hand in a limited and vain attempt at indifference, and his eyes landed on hers. "Refusing to acknowledge the military status of a Commonwealth Navy prisoner of war captured on Asria. Compelling a Royal Asrian Defense Forces prisoner of war to serve in the Imperial Haederan Navy."

Oh.

Her chest constricted like all the air had just been sucked from the room. The Commonwealth—beyond Special Operations Forces, many of whom knew her story but were closed-mouthed as a rule—had found out about her. They'd found out about Lieutenant Colonel Stev Kanmar.

She brushed a hand across her hot cheeks, but it didn't do much to dispel the anxiety. No, not only anxiety—the certain understanding that whatever trouble Chase had escaped in the past, he would never find a way out of this. Not if the Commonwealth had found out the truth, the truth from so long ago. She'd forgiven Chase for his part, hadn't she? Of course she had. It shouldn't matter any longer what he'd done to her. And spinning Stev Kanmar's sacrifice for his planet and queen into a war crimes charge for the person who'd helped saved both was all a misunderstanding, like Chase had said.

A misunderstanding the Commonwealth had jumped on. A year ago, she wouldn't have blamed them.

"It's all very ridiculous, yes. But we don't need to talk about it now," he added casually, his stare anything but. "Once they inform Ambassador Neave of my situation, I'm certain everything will work out. The princes are unharmed?"

The princes. Not Lucas and Colonel Rendon. His underlying meaning was anything but casual.

They do not know the Commonwealth prisoner of war was you, he was saying. *Do not tell them it was you. Not yet.*

"Everyone is fine. Lucas is a little traumatized, but he'll be fine with time. Merritt has some scratches." She watched Chase breathe, trying to transmit what she wanted to say.

Please tell me you have a way out of this.

"I'm glad to hear that," he replied.

"And you? What happened on *Mayfair*?"

Chase tried to shift in the bed but flinched instead. "I got to the cargo bay, and they were all unconscious. We'd done it. But the mask I'd taken for myself started running low, so before I woke one of the pilots up, I had to search for another one. If I had to do it over again . . . Anyway, your Commonwealth friends showed up before I had the chance to restrain the rest of the belligerents. Burrier, when I rolled him over to check his pulse, had a pistol and just enough cognizance . . ."

Avery couldn't pull her hands away from her mouth. She'd sent Chase into that situation. This, what had happened to him, was her fault.

He smiled at her. "Don't look at me like that. A three-hour surgery and I'm as good as new. No broken bones, no implants required, and I didn't need that spleen, anyway." A flash of that familiar amusement flickered across his face. "Though I don't think I'll be doing any mountain climbing for a while. Better than Burrier, though. He won't be doing any breathing."

"Are you in much pain?" He had to be, of course, and if the

medical personnel weren't helping with that out of pure anti-Haederan vengeance—

The door slid back open, and she jumped to her feet. "It's not been ten minutes!" she protested.

"Sorry, ma'am." The gray-clad guard gestured her out. "Commander Bretel wants to talk to you."

How restrictive her life had become. She gave Chase a quick goodbye smile, though she was certain the attempt just made her look ill, and followed the guard back outside.

"You seem to know the prisoner fairly well, Your Majesty. I'm surprised," Bretel said from her spot against the wall.

"You were watching me?" Her voice became high pitched. How much had Bretel heard? How much had she been able to piece together?

"Not closely." Bretel frowned, and Avery silently kicked herself for giving a hint that something was wrong. Bretel would pull the recording now and give it to her security people to watch it over and over and over, reading into her and Chase's conversation. They'd both said too much already. "But you were on a ship in deep space together, and no one's explained exactly why. And you were so very insistent on visiting him."

Next to Avery, Wynne shifted to her other foot.

"He works directly for Ambassador Brooks Neave at the Haederan embassy on Asria," Avery said. "We've met in the course of official business, of course. I know the ambassador will be looking for an update on his condition as soon as he learns of the situation and thought it best the news come directly from me."

"And you had no idea that he is Imperial Security Command?"

All she wanted to do was look at Wynne for guidance. For reassurance. Or at her feet, for whatever wisdom they could give her. Or the wall. Or anywhere but Bretel's eyes. It took everything she had to stare at Bretel without blinking.

"I suspected."

"And you didn't bother to tell anyone your suspicions?"

Who did this woman think she was? She wasn't under obligation to tell the Commonwealth a thing about Chase.

"He's a middle-aged man working as a cultural attaché at an embassy on a planet vaguely hostile to his own, Commander," Avery said. "Of course I suspected he was intel. I'm sure everyone who met him did. There's nothing I could have done about it even if I knew for sure."

"Intel is a rather innocuous term for what he is, don't you think?"

She jerked her chin in the expected affirmation. Why was this beginning to feel like an interrogation?

"Maybe. I wouldn't know."

"Having lived on a Haederan-occupied planet, you must have some idea of the kinds of affairs Imperial Security is involved in. Maybe you even have some personal experience that you'd rather forget." Bretel glanced at Wynne. "Perhaps you do, ma'am?"

Wynne took a step in between them. "Commander Bretel, this is rather inappropriate, don't you think? Her Majesty has no influence on Haederan embassy personnel on Asria, official or otherwise. Any speculation about his true identity before now would have been just that—tactless speculation."

Bretel looked at her boots. Guiltily, if such a thing were possible.

"Perhaps you're right."

"Good." Wynne nodded toward the door. "Then you'll excuse the queen while she gets some rest. It's been a rather traumatic day for all of us."

Bretel nodded in return, though her eyes were still sharp. Wynne guided them the whole way back to their quarters, pointedly not asking for navigational assistance this time.

* * *

Merritt poured his second glass of wine in ten minutes and leaned against the table to stare at her and Wynne.

"I'm glad he's alive. But while you two were gallivanting around the ship and spending time in the brig, I had three visitors questioning me about my relationship with him." He glared at Avery as she settled on the leather sofa across from him. "A nonexistent relationship that I don't care to explain, regardless."

"What kind of visitors?" she asked.

"Hell if I know. Commonwealth Special Security, I think. Some kind of intelligence types, anyway. They never think they're as obvious as they are."

He downed the rest of his glass in two swallows. "What I do know is," he said, pointing a finger at her, "it won't take more than a day until they figure out *your* association with him. 'Refusing to acknowledge the military status of a Commonwealth Navy prisoner of war.' Dammit, Avery. You told him you were a military officer, and in true Imperial Security Command style—no, in true Gareth Chase style—he ignored it. I don't care who he's related to. There's no way out of this for him now."

"There has to be. What he did to me may as well have been a million years ago." *If you don't count the nightmares and flashbacks.* "I don't know how they found out, anyway. And I won't speak against him. I won't. I'll refuse. You know how much I owe him. How much you and Lucas owe him. And think about what he did for Asria. He's practically the reason for the armistice!"

"Oh, of course you won't speak against him." Merritt's sarcasm made her flinch, but Wynne covered a smile. "And you know what they'll say to that, don't you? That you're brainwashed. That he coerced you—or worse."

Kusir. She didn't even want to imagine what *worse* meant to the Commonwealth.

"I'm not brainwashed," she insisted. "And he didn't coerce me. Not into standing up for him, anyway."

Merritt stared at her as if he couldn't believe what she'd just said out loud.

"I know that, you know that, he knows that. But think of how this looks to the Commonwealth. Think of how it looks to any sane person who knows what he is."

"And now everyone does." Avery sank onto the sofa and let her head fall into her hands as the doorbell buzzed. "Bretel's not really from the protocol office, is she?" she asked.

Merritt huffed. "You think?"

Bretel's voice all but echoed through the cabin as she stepped inside, around Wynne. "I know you know Colonel Chase, Your Majesty. And I know how."

Avery stood and drew herself up to her full height. It still wasn't enough to put her past Bretel's shoulders.

"Fine," she said. "I know him. I've known him a long time. And I know what he does."

And just what are you going to do about it, Commander?

"Avery," Merritt said under his breath.

Bretel glanced at him, then back to Avery, the brilliant smile from earlier back on her face.

"They can compel you to testify against him about what happened on Asria during the war, Captain Rendon," she said easily. "All I have to do is tell them you're here."

"You wouldn't dare do that." Why hadn't she filed that paperwork to sever herself from the Commonwealth military once and for all?

Right. Because she thought her commission hadn't mattered any longer. They'd released their claws for the time being, and she'd thought the freedom permanent. What a foolish lack of foresight.

Or was complacency truly the reason? If she was honest with herself, didn't giving up her commission mean so much more? Like giving up the dreams she had when she was young?

"I don't want to have to," Bretel said, drawing her thoughts away from the past.

"Then don't! If you're the only one who knows, then don't. Not right now, at least. You don't understand." A flash of inspiration ran through her. Perhaps . . . perhaps if Bretel knew the entire story, things would be different. "Is there somewhere we can talk in private, Commander?"

Bretel glanced around the cabin, eyebrows raised in feigned innocence. "This is private, ma'am."

"I think you know what I mean," Avery ground out between her teeth.

Bretel looked from Merritt to Wynne, more cautiously that time, like she didn't trust any of them. "You don't have a comm device on you, do you?"

Avery pulled it out of her pocket and handed it to Wynne. "Not anymore."

Merritt threw his hands in the air.

Bretel eyed her for a long time while she held her breath. "Then let's find somewhere more private."

Somewhere more private turned out to be just where Avery had expected—an unmarked set of offices through an unmarked hatch a level up from her luxurious temporary quarters. Bretel waved on the lights inside the first one, a small, sparse room containing nothing more than a comm desk and two chairs.

"Interesting place for a protocol officer to be holed up." Avery ran her finger along the edge of the empty desk. "No signed photos of the last royalty to visit *Terigon*? What a shame."

Bretel sighed and pushed a small button on the panel above the desk. *General Torin said you were a pain in the ass,* she was probably thinking.

"You have your somewhere private, Your Majesty," she said instead. "No cameras, no microphones, no anything. It's as clean as it gets on this ship, and if you need me to clear out the recordings from your suite, I can do that as well. What do you want?"

"First, I want to know your real name."

Bretel sat, directing her glare somewhere between Avery's hairline and her ears, her mouth pressed shut.

"I'm going to be completely honest with you," Avery added. "I'd rather you be just as honest with me."

"It's Jaxi Bretel." Her stare was directly challenging now.

Avery sat and crossed her arms.

"Fine." Bretel plucked at something on the sleeve of her gray-and-blue Commonwealth Navy uniform. If that wasn't a dead giveaway, nothing was. "It's Jaxi Bretel. Lieutenant Colonel Jaxi Bretel, Special Operations Forces. But it seems like that doesn't surprise you, Your Majesty."

"Ah. A colleague then. Wynne and I figured as much." She'd ceased to be surprised by Commonwealth games, at least from Special Operations Forces. Hadley would approve of this one's deception.

"A—a colleague, ma'am?" Bretel stuttered.

"I'm sorry. Are we only Special Operations Forces colleagues when you're using my history with the Commonwealth to threaten me—ma'am?"

You called me Captain Rendon not twenty minutes ago. Don't play games.

Bretel blew out a deep breath, and Avery couldn't help feeling a little sorry for her. She probably had no idea how etiquette demanded she approach the situation. Queen of a Commonwealth planet, Commonwealth officer, no matter how far removed from the fleet, apparent Haederan sympathizer . . .

"My only interest here is your safety," Bretel said. "That's my assignment. There was some concern when we identified the occupants of the courier, and the higher-ups felt it was wise to have someone to handle you personally." She shrugged and gazed at the door. "It's an overreaction, clearly, and you're here as the queen of Asria, so if you'd prefer, I'll contact the protocol office to take care of you. I couldn't care less what happens to Colonel Chase."

"Well, I care."

"Why?" Bretel's eyebrows scrunched together in confusion. "The man tortured you."

The man tortured you.

The words made her stomach churn and her mind spin. How much did Bretel know? Had she read the reports from her debriefings with General Torin? Those were supposed to be sealed—or mostly sealed—because of the verium information. The idea of dozens of people knowing what she'd gone through made her sick.

"Do you want the short version or the long one?" she asked.

"Whichever one you feel like telling," Bretel replied.

Neither of them.

Avery took a deep breath. "All right. Yes. Colonel Chase—" She couldn't say the word. "He did. If you know who he is and how we know each other, then you know I was working for General Torin during the war. You know I was arrested by the Imperial Haederan Army because of my status as the princess-elect, and you also know that during that time, the Imperial Security Command ascertained that I was a Commonwealth agent."

As long as she stayed detached, that was all easy to say. None of it was much of a secret, anyway. Practically all of Asria knew it.

"And yes, I was interrogated by Colonel Chase." Her voice broke, even though she'd been fighting to control her emotions since she'd walked in. "Extensively. If you'd like to call what happened to me torture, I would be the last to disagree."

Bretel leaned forward and folded her hands on her desk. It was clear she'd heard all that. Perhaps she knew Hadley personally. It wouldn't be a surprise if she'd known Elex Feye. The community was small, indeed.

"But what you don't know," Avery went on, "and what very few know is that he was instrumental in my return to Asria when my ship was captured en route to Ventana IV, in the rescue of the prince consort from Haederan custody, in the protection of my unborn son, and, eventually, in the cessation of hostilities between Asria and Haedera. All at great risk to himself from his own people in both Imperial Security and the Imperial Haederan Army, I might add. So yes. I care about what happens to him."

"And you were what? Escorting him back to Haedera?" Bretel's face softened. "To avoid prosecution, perhaps."

"No. I didn't know the Commonwealth was searching for him." Avery looked at her hands. *I'd never have let him leave Asria if I'd known.* "You may have heard about the bombing on Asria during my coronation. The person responsible for that was my own brother."

Unlike recounting her experience with the Haederans and Chase, that accusation hadn't become any easier to say over the past weeks, no matter how detached she kept herself. Bretel's manner said she knew that information, anyway. How had the Commonwealth found out so quickly?

"Intelligence has been limited on my brother's current location and intention," she went on, "so Colonel Chase offered me his estate on Haedera as temporary protection. After an attempted assassination on the Haederan emperor on Iythea a few months ago, Colonel Chase believes—we believe—that Quen Rendon hates Haedera enough that he'll never set foot on the planet."

She pressed her lips together and waited for Bretel's reaction to that confession. There wasn't much of one, not that the woman's flat expression surprised her.

"I can't get him out of the brig," Bretel finally said. "If his appearance had been kept secret, then perhaps . . . yes, I might have done something about it then. But too many people have seen him now. Too many people know he's here. This was the regular security folks' doing, not Special Operations Forces."

"I understand." Her heart sank anyway. "But there has to be something you can do."

Bretel sat back and examined her. "If you'd like to continue to Haedera without anyone knowing where you disappeared to, I can certainly help you there."

It was the safe decision. The one she should make, and the one Chase would expect her to make. Then why was it so hard to agree to her offer?

"We will discuss it with Wynne. But I need to see Colonel

Chase before we decide on anything." Her voice cracked again. "Please."

* * *

Merritt came this time. Avery had insisted on it. She clutched his hand as Bretel, now in that familiar indigo Special Operations Forces uniform, spoke under her breath to the guard, then ushered them inside the infirmary room. It seemed Bretel had also lied about her ability to influence the brig personnel, and Merritt's distrust was tangible. It was surprising that she could read his body language so easily now, as if they'd become one person.

Chase looked better. Not wonderful, but better. He wasn't nearly as pale as he had been earlier that morning, and his smile was a little less forced, though he shot Bretel's new uniform a sharp look.

"A group," he said. "Come to break me out this time?"

Avery tried to smile back. "Lieutenant Colonel Bretel has found a way to get us out of here and on our way." Why wouldn't her voice stay even?

"Why would you trust her like that?" Chase didn't sound angry. Just perplexed. "That doesn't sound like you."

She gripped Merritt's hand until he flinched.

"I was able to get in contact with Major Hadley, sir," Bretel cut in. "He confirmed the queen's account of what happened last year on Asria—of your assistance in his mission there. I can't promise it'll change any minds that matter, but"—she cleared her throat, hands on her hips—"it changed mine."

"She's going to get us off the ship," Avery added. "If—if—" *You give me your blessing.* Her mouth had gone dry all of a sudden. They couldn't leave Chase. She couldn't leave Chase.

"Then go." He flicked his hand as far as the chains would allow. "As soon as you can. Don't wait around here to see what happens to me. You'll take Sophie, I assume?"

"Yes." Those hated tears welled up. "Yes, of course."

"I don't want you here." Chase shifted under the thin sheet. "Do you understand that?"

"Yes." Reduced to one-word answers. That's what the situation had done to her. "I understand."

"If everything goes well, we'll be out of here in the next few hours," Merritt said. His lip twitched, the only indication of his distress. "Sophie—I'm sorry, but they absolutely refused to allow her in here. But we'll take good care of her until we reach Haedera, I promise. She has family there?"

Punishment. Not letting him say goodbye to his daughter was nothing but punishment. As soon as they got back to their quarters, she was going to grab Lucas and never let go.

"Servants." Chase's jaw was tight, though whether it was from fear or sadness or pain was impossible to tell. "She's more than capable of running Windhaven with their help."

An eleven-year-old girl, motherless and alone, running some large estate . . . it was too much.

"Lieutenant Colonel Bretel will keep an eye on you as much as she can." Avery brushed away the unrelenting tears. "At least until you're well enough to be transferred to Ventana."

Holy One, comfort him.

Merritt tugged gently on her hand. "I think it's time, love."

"Fine. Yes." She let him pull her toward the door behind Bretel but turned back to Chase at the last second. He frowned at her, looking more like someone who needed a nap and some pain medication instead of a goodbye, and the tears fell harder. "I'm sorry. I'm so sorry."

And then Merritt pulled her through the door, his arm around her, and Chase was gone.

CHAPTER NINE

HER EYES FLUTTERED OPEN AT THE SOUND OUTSIDE, BUT AVERY pressed her body into the soft bed and closed them again. There was no mistaking the visceral strangeness of a foreign land, and that was something she couldn't face, not yet. A smile crossed her face as she reached for Merritt, but her hands came up empty.

Of course. Merritt always had been an early riser, and since they'd left Asria, he'd been working too much. She might as well stay in bed if that's how things were going to be. Still, she could only take the stiffness of a night's rest for so long, and reluctantly, she sat up, blinking away the sunlight that streamed over the bed. It was surprising she'd been able to sleep so long.

In the dark of the night before, the guest house at Windhaven had seemed luxurious enough, but her current surroundings were more than she could have ever imagined. Floor-to-ceiling windows rose from two sides of the bedroom, broken only by a large wooden support beam that ran around the entire room. She could practically see herself in the polished shine of the wood as she pushed the silken sheets to the side.

Windhaven was perched on top of a large hill—or small mountain—surrounded on all sides by rocky outcroppings covered in giant cactuses. In fact, the entire estate clung to the side of the cliff, separated from a steep drop by only a row of large, decorative boulders. And outside her window—she'd heard of the famed giant Haederan cactuses, had seen pictures, but nothing had done them justice. Three of them, at least ten times her height, soared into the sky just outside, large white flowers obscuring their tops. Smaller cacti surrounded them in varying shades of amethyst, no less majestic in their youth.

She couldn't tear her eyes away from them. How had she ever believed Haedera was a desert wasteland? Carefully, on legs still shaky from long-range spaceflight, she made her way to the window and pressed a hand against it.

"We can go for a ramble after breakfast, if you'd like." Merritt grinned at her from the doorway.

She jumped at his appearance, then nodded, unable to verbalize her reaction to the wild beauty outside.

"So, breakfast? You can eat in the great room and stare outside while you do it." Merritt pulled her close and ran a palm under the silk that barely covered her thighs, then grinned at the goosebumps on her arms. "But as much as I love looking at you like this, you'll want to dress first. You have a visitor outside." His smile grew sheepish as he drew his hand back. "Though I suppose I'm not helping."

"A visitor?" she asked, sliding her hand under his shirt. "I think whoever it is can wait a bit."

Merritt raised his brows and backed away, and she sighed her surrender. Fiona had been efficient in unpacking their belongings, and she stepped out into the sunlit great room less than five minutes later, wearing the least wrinkled dress she'd been able to find. The man sitting in a chair by the window stood when she entered, and to her surprise, she couldn't contain her delight at his familiar face.

"Captain Kern!"

"Major Kern, my lady." He raised his shoulders in acknowledgment. "Welcome to Haedera—and Windhaven."

She tilted her head at his clothing: slim gray pants and a loose, long-sleeved azure shirt. It wasn't the feared Imperial Security uniform she would have expected on him, but the bulge at his left side gave her pause.

"Then you're still—"

"Colonel said no uniforms." Kern gave a proper imitation of a gracious smile. "He said they might upset you."

"I see." The confusion turned to a frown at the mention of Chase. "That was kind of him."

He let the smile disappear. "Yes. It was."

There was no point in mentioning Chase's fate had been out of her control.

"And you're here to . . . ?"

"To show you around after breakfast, of course, my lady."

"Just to show me around?" She sank onto the sofa diagonal from where he'd been sitting, eyeing the trays of fresh fruit that she couldn't identify. One had been cut into brilliant pink squares, then nestled back into its dark green rind.

And keep an eye on you was what he wasn't saying. Well, maybe that wasn't such a bad thing. There were an infinite number of more pleasant people to be around, but probably not many who were as competent as Kern. Or as feared—especially on Haedera. She picked at a piece of the pink fruit and stared him down.

"I think I did a damn good job keeping you alive before, despite your best attempts to circumvent my effort, no?" Kern sat and clutched his coffee, not breaking the mutual glare.

One more person who questioned her intelligence and decision-making. What had Kern expected her to do? Sit around and let his people do whatever they wanted to her planet? Even Chase knew better than that. How could he have honestly expected her not to fight the occupation?

Only Merritt's appearance saved her from a regrettable argument. He settled onto the opposite end of her couch and grinned at the piece of fruit hovering in her hand.

"Try it," he said.

She shot him a mistrustful look and stuck it in her mouth. "It's spicy!"

Merritt laughed. "It's dusted with chile-infused sugar. It wakes you up, at least."

Her mouth burned. "I think a walk might accomplish that, too."

With less pain.

Kern took a long sip of his coffee. "Then if you're ready . . ." He gestured toward the main door of the guest house.

Or maybe not. Anything was preferable to a walk with Kern.

"Merritt?" she asked.

"I'm going to stay here." Merritt leaned over and gave her a long kiss on the cheek. "Lucas and I are going to wait until it cools off a little. I've got some reports to go over in the meantime."

Her lip quirked up. Was this just another excuse to bury himself in work? He was only supposed to be working part time for Teruel now, and surely the general would understand if he took a break while they were on Haedera. Most everything was too sensitive to work on here.

"Lunch together later, then?" she asked. "I won't care how spicy it is once I've been awake for more than half an hour."

"It's a deal."

She squeezed his hand goodbye, brushing her fingers over his to suggest what lunch would really consist of, then wandered down the hallway that led to the main foyer. The little gold-and-wood dragons on the side table there stared at her as she waited for Kern to follow. They were identical to the one on the Haederan flag and looked ancient. Unsettled by the horns on their heads, like the ones on the demons Chase had mentioned, she shifted her gaze to the door, to the square blocks of glass set in between some exotic Haederan wood she couldn't identify.

"It's not glass."

"Hmm?"

"You're worried about the glass in the door." Kern ran his fingers across it as he pushed the door open. "Don't be. It's bullet-proof, laser proof, and every other kind of proof you can think to worry about. The emperor used to stay here when he visited."

Her distaste must have shown, because he laughed—the first real laugh she'd ever heard from him. "The servants changed the linens, I'm sure."

Avery bit her lip to keep from laughing out loud. "You do have a sense of humor. I was beginning to wonder."

"Every so often."

"And that means you've visited Windhaven frequently."

"No. I came here for the first time a few days ago to look around and secure the place. His message didn't come until then." Kern pinched the bridge of his nose in frustration. "It's not easy to secure an estate this large, even if it's hanging off the side of a mountain—which you should be thankful for, by the way. Just don't wander too far off into the desert. There's only so much terrain they can patrol."

"So there are more of you around." An unpleasant slithering sensation crept down her back. It was one thing to know Imperial Security was all over Chase's estate, but she wouldn't be able to hold herself together if she *knew* knew. Or saw them.

"You won't see them. And if you do—sorry."

He gestured her through the door into the expansive court-yard. It'd been dark when they'd entered the night before, and the beauty would have warmed her heart if it'd been anywhere else. The far wall was tiled in a dark teal mosaic in stark contrast to the brown of the guest house. A flame flickered from a niche in the center, and the same giant cactuses she'd seen from her own window stood silent guard on each side.

He wasn't sorry, she realized as they stepped outside, and there was an underlying coldness in his voice that went along with the strange way he'd trailed off. She wanted to shake it off, but there was no point in letting resentment fester.

"You're angry with me about what happened to Colonel Chase," she said.

"How—"

"I've known you long enough." To her eternal regret. "It's pretty obvious. But it's his own fault, you know."

Her cheeks grew red at her accusation. How easy it had been to be merciful toward Chase on *Terigon* and how easy it was to hate him again now that she was finally on Haedera without him.

"His own fault?" Kern looked around, probably for bystanders to their impending and vocal disagreement. "Do we have to discuss this now? Here? Can we at least pretend we've never met? I think that would be easiest for everyone involved."

"It's a little late for that now," she grumbled, brushing the sweat away from her forehead.

"Too hot, Your Majesty?" Kern asked with feigned deference. "We can skip the tour if you'd prefer to sit inside and protect your complexion."

She clenched her hands at her side. It was becoming harder and harder not to roll her eyes. *Not on your life, Kern.*

"It's not so bad, Major. Ventana was—" *Hot and humid, and I survived three years there,* she'd been about to say. Still, saying anything to him about Commonwealth headquarters seemed inappropriate. They might not be enemies, but they certainly weren't friends. "It was . . . hot," she finished lamely.

He tilted his head in a Chase-like manner, and she flinched at the sudden memories.

"Then let's be on our way, shall we?"

"Lead on."

There. If they could only hold on to this passive-aggressive sociability, all would be well. They walked along the stone path that connected the guest house to the main building while Kern pointed out the various plants and identified a few small lizards that darted away from their footsteps. To her surprise, the tour became enjoyable. It wasn't as terribly hot as it had seemed when they'd first stepped outside, and Kern didn't make a bad tour guide, just an especially Haederan one.

And the views. The landscape was stunning. How far could they see from this vantage point? Kilometers, no doubt, though there was no other civilization in sight. It was surprising Chase ever managed to leave this place—a haven, it certainly was.

"The sunsets here must be spectacular," she said.

"Mm-hmm," Kern said. "And the sunrises, if you're into that sort of thing."

She laughed. "You've met Lucas. I've seen more sunrises in the past year than in the rest of my life combined."

He gave her a polite smile that faded as fast as it'd come. That was odd. Intimidating, professional Kern was jealous of a child? Well, Chase had mentioned there'd been a woman—and that Kern had been afraid she wouldn't be around when he returned home from Asria. It wasn't hard to figure out what had happened. This empathy for Haederans was a new thing.

She mulled over the uncomfortable emotion as Kern led her through a long hallway, not as grand as the front gallery at the palace in Cadena, true, but filled with similar paintings of someone's ancestors. Likely the imperial relatives of Chase's wife, since he didn't resemble any of them. Avery was staring at one that contained a woman wearing fashions that would have been at least three hundred years out of date on Asria when a dark purple flash turned the corner just in front of them, then disappeared.

"Sophie?" she called quietly down the corridor.

There was a pause, then Sophie's dark head poked back around the corner. The girl was as immaculately dressed as she'd been on the courier, but her eyes were red this time, her cheeks swollen. She glanced from Avery to Kern, then dropped into a brief curtsey.

"That's—that's really not necessary." Avery ignored Kern's quiet snort. All she wanted to do was take Sophie in her arms and wipe the tears away.

"I'm sorry, my lady." Sophie's voice was raspy. "I didn't mean to spy on you. I just heard voices, and I was afraid . . ."

Afraid of what? That Kern was here to make her disappear too? By the furtive and terrified looks Sophie was giving him under her eyelashes, that fear wasn't too far off. After all, it'd been

Imperial Security who'd taken Marc away from Windhaven to his death.

"Major Kern was just giving me a tour of the estate. Maybe you'd like to come with us?" Anything to not be alone with Kern. Anything to prove to Sophie she was safe. Sophie probably made a much better tour guide of Windhaven than Kern did, anyway, and it didn't look like the girl needed to be alone.

Sophie shook her head and dashed down the hall, then disappeared through a large set of doors. Avery looked at Kern, who shrugged like nothing had happened, then motioned down the gallery.

"We'll cut through here for now. I'll show you around the main house next," he said, focusing out the floor-to-ceiling windows as they passed through a vaulted three-story room. "If you like the view, you won't want to miss this."

"Hold on." She pointed out the window. "What's that?"

The small white building outside was surrounded on all four sides by a wrought-iron fence, arched along the top. A gate led into the courtyard, the entirety of which was covered in various cactuses of every shade of green and purple. Flame flickered through the open door, and she took a deep breath as she stared. Could a building call to you? This one certainly seemed to.

Kern shrugged. "Private family chapel."

"Can we go in?"

"If the gate's unlocked, I don't see why not."

They made their way down the steep hill to the stone structure that was half-built into the side of a small cliff. She stumbled a few times on the loose rock, but Kern was smart enough to do nothing more than offer his arm—a gesture she took him up on. He pushed on the gate, which wasn't as ancient as it'd appeared from the main house, and it swung right open. She tiptoed into the courtyard after him, the sanctity of the place flowing about her.

Sanctity? Here? With someone like Kern next to her?

Her cheeks grew warm at her own arrogance as she stepped

carefully down the stone walk that led to the chapel. Even Drex would be disappointed in her, for the Holy One didn't limit Himself to Asria, especially since the Haederan faith, according to Commonwealth intelligence, predated even Asria's. Yes, the priests had spread the truth to Haedera long before they'd ever reached her own planet. This building was proof enough, wasn't it?

Ethereal shadows sparkled on the white rock inside. It was smaller than she'd expected, just a few paces in each direction. And it wasn't just a few candles, either. The entire interior was lit by dozens of them, some on wrought iron tables, some set into niches in the white walls. The warmth of the desert outside felt like an ice storm compared to the heat that radiated from each tier of small white votives.

She chose an unlit one and ran her finger around the smooth bottom, her gaze drawn to the framed photo that sat on one of the higher tiers, surrounded by fresh flowers yet unwilted in the heat. It seemed someone else at Windhaven cared for the place as much as Chase must have when he was here.

"Marc?" she asked. An unnecessary question, since the boy looked just like Chase but with Sophie's brown eyes, dark hair, and delicate chin.

Kern dipped his head, his lips pressed together in a thin line.

Avery reached for a match and held it and the candle up toward him.

"Do you mind?"

He shrugged, his jaw tight. "Not my place to say no."

Any friendly progress they'd made earlier had been lost, it seemed. Clearly, she'd stumbled upon something else uncomfortable for him. She wanted to do nothing except bolt back to the guest house, but she pushed her curls over her shoulder and lit the candle in front of her.

"What happened to him?" she asked the candle.

"Colonel Chase told you what happened." Kern dusted off the frame—everything outside at Windhaven was dusty—and replaced it. "I told you what happened. Do we really need to relive those details again?"

"I'm not talking about Marc." *And you know it, Major.*

Kern turned away from her and pushed three unlit candles together.

"Emperor Devan II was murdered in his sleep." He pressed his fingers to his forehead and lit one of the candles. "One shot to the head—they say he never knew what hit him. We never found the assailant, their method of entrance, how they were able to sneak a pistol into the palace, nor how they were able to escape. It was like a wraith slipped in and did it. That's what everyone likes to believe now, at least, especially in Rebet."

"I'm surprised you weren't able to figure out who the assassin was," she said. A shiver ran through her despite the heat that blazed through the chapel. "It seems like a strange failure for *Imperial* Security."

Kern lit the other two candles and turned back to her, his eyes like ice.

"Who says it was a failure?"

CHAPTER TEN

FOUR WEEKS.

For four weeks she'd been wasting away at Windhaven, pretending whatever she was doing on Haedera was the right thing. She was alive, yes, and safe, and so were Lucas and Merritt, but there was no proof they wouldn't have been fine back home in Cadena. Or anywhere else on Asria. Even Emot could have been an option. She was a coward, just like she'd once accused Victor of being.

She was different from her uncle, though, wasn't she? It was a different situation. She had a family to protect now. A child. Yes, it was Lucas who'd brought her to Haedera. She'd do anything for him.

But herself? She should call it what it was, and that was cowardice—and it had gotten Chase arrested. That guilt plagued her hourly. Memories of him were all over Windhaven, from the sadness in Sophie's eyes and the hostility in Kern's to the way the servants all seemed to be afraid of her, as if she might eventually be responsible for their arrests, too.

Afraid of her. An Asrian woman who was terrified of them. How absurd.

Merritt's cough broke into her thoughts, and she shifted

toward him, thankful for the distraction. Guilt or not, there were worse things than curling up next to one's husband on a warm afternoon as he worked—and few things more extravagant since she'd become queen.

He adjusted the blanket back over her and smiled. "I'm about ready for a break. Want to go for a walk?" he asked.

Avery snuggled down next to him. "I'm pretty content right here—but yes, if you'd like. You probably need the fresh air." She wouldn't be selfish this time. It'd been days since Merritt had left the guest house. "A walk sounds wonderful, too."

Merritt laughed. "You have to crawl out of bed first."

Reluctantly, she tossed the blanket to the foot of the bed. "We should bring Lucas."

Merritt kissed her ear, then jumped out of bed before she could put her hands on him in return. "How about just the two of us this time?"

He sounded too serious to argue, so she let him pull her out of bed and toward the door, though he didn't drop the tablet until they'd reached the foyer. *Always with the work.* He set it on the table with the Haederan dragons by the main door, and she frowned at it.

"Should you leave that there?" she asked.

Merritt gave it the briefest of glances. "It's nothing important. But I need the reminder when we come back."

Being irresponsible with important information didn't sound like the overly conscientious man she knew, so it had to be true. She managed to kick on a pair of shoes before he had her out the front door and into the blazing sun. In the early evening, the heat wasn't as oppressive as usual.

"Close your eyes," he said.

She narrowed her eyes at the order, then squeezed them shut.

"Now pick a direction." Merritt spun her around a few times, then stopped her against him.

She pointed, her eyes still closed. "That way."

"East. Good choice."

"Why?" She stared east, over the walls and out into the desert. Nothing was out there but the same giant cactuses and a few hawks, circling over what little water they could find.

"Why not?"

"Good enough answer for me." She took his hand again as they climbed down the steep rock stairs that led to the iron gate at the edge of the estate. "It's funny how I always thought Haedera would be brown. What else am I going to be so wrong about?"

The desert was anything but brown today—perhaps this was usual for this part of Haedera. In front of them ran a rocky wash surrounded on both sides by short trees, their slim green leaves blowing in the breeze. The sky was as blue as the desert was green, without a single cloud to cut through the azure heavens. So much color for what she'd thought would be such a dreary place.

Merritt raised his eyebrows.

"Don't answer that," she added.

"I wouldn't dare." He laughed. "Not with you looking at me like that. And although I know you won't believe me—love, you're doing fine. I wish you'd believe that."

She blew out a breath. "I ran away."

"And what would Asria do if something happened to you? We're muddling through everything right now, but who else is there? Until Lucas is old enough, unless the senate starts talking about electing someone outside of your family, you're it. We don't want or need a repeat of . . ." He looked uncomfortable for the first time, then swallowed. "Of the situation in which your uncle left us."

And that was the truth, wasn't it? Asria didn't need a monarch —most planets didn't have one, had never had one—but tradition was tradition, and Asrian tradition was precise and narrow-minded indeed. The aftermath of an invasion was exactly the wrong time to be talking about major cultural changes.

"You know I'll do my duty." She kicked at the small pebbles that lined the ephemeral creek, now dry. Speaking of change on Asria was a waste of breath. Speaking of duty made her ill. "They have washes like this in the Ritan Mountains on Ventana, out where I used to hike," she said. "For some reason, the locals still spoke about them in Old Ventanan—*sapas*."

"Brennin had some old-style Haederan name for it that even he couldn't pronounce." Merritt laughed. "We'll just call it a wash."

Brennin?

"You've been talking to Major Kern? Socially?" Merritt wouldn't betray her like that, would he?

"Just a bit here and there about the local area." He glanced at the hawk that had landed in the top of the tree in front of them. "He's rather open once you get to know him. And friendly."

"He's not friendly," she said. "He's Imperial Security."

"So?"

"What do you mean, 'so?'" She yanked her hand away. "So he's horrible. Repulsive. A murderer, for all you know. The things he's done here on Haedera—he's evil, Merritt."

Yet *evil* seemed a stretch. Was looking the other way after his emperor was murdered really so bad? If one wanted to talk about evil, that man had been the personification of it. And Kern had been more broken up about witnessing the murder of Chase's son than she ever would have expected. Was it possible he had a conscience just like the one Chase had shoved somewhere deep inside himself?

Anything was possible, of course. Admitting it . . . well, that was totally different.

"He helped save your life," Merritt said, waving at the hawk, about as blasé as she'd ever heard him. It flew away at his movement. "He ended up detained on Asria for months after the prisoner swaps began because of it."

"Months? That wasn't supposed to have happened." And she'd only visited him once, just before leaving Villiers after the armistice. No wonder he hated her.

"Well, for whatever reason, it did. They probably lost his paperwork. You know how that goes. And you can't avoid him—

or Imperial Security—forever. Not for now, at least. Probably not even once we get back to Asria. You know they're all over the planet, as much as we try to keep them out."

Was he trying to start an argument? Merritt knew how terrified she was of Chase's organization, knew how the senate had been deporting each one who popped up on Asria. It was never-ending work—the snakes. Well, she'd finish this fight before it began, right here, right now.

"Just like *you* can't avoid every single Imperial Haederan Army soldier in Cadena for the rest of your life," she snapped at him.

"That's completely different." Merritt's voice went cold. "You think you know what happened, but you can't possibly know what I went through, what they did to me after—"

He quickened his pace, leaving her behind, kicking rocks as he went.

She had to jog to catch up, a difficult movement in the loose sand and gravel. She yanked him to a stop by his sleeve, and he skidded on the slick surface of the wash.

Merritt jerked his shirt away and narrowed his eyes.

"You do know, don't you? How?" His shoulders sank. "Never mind. I should have known. That man couldn't mind his own business if his life depended on it. How long have you known?"

It was such a hazy memory—but not hazy enough to forget what Chase had implied.

"He told me on *Imperieuse*," she said quietly. It seemed like forever ago. "I'm sorry."

"Of course he did." Merritt sighed as his gaze shifted downward. "Let's walk a bit first. Let me get my thoughts together." He held his hand back out. "And hold my hand. Please don't be angry with me about earlier. I didn't know Kern was such a sore subject with you. You treat him so politely. But I should have known. There's terror in your eyes whenever he's around, Avery, and I want to kill him for it."

Avery brushed his fingers with hers. They were cold. Such a strange feeling in this hot place.

"I treat him politely because there's nothing else I can do. I'm afraid of him. Of the things he's done and the things he may still do. Not to me," she added hastily as Merritt's expression grew icy. "Never to me. He frightened me, but not in any way that truly mattered. He was always more standoffish than anything else, like he somehow respected me underneath that cold exterior, and now I understand why. I was never as afraid of him as I probably should have been."

"You don't need to explain. I shouldn't have pushed you about it." He squeezed her hand and looked up. "The birds around here are amazing. There must be a pond or lake or something near here for this place to be so alive."

"There's supposed to be a lake just over that mountain to the south." She pointed with her free hand, swinging Merritt's hand with her other. "Maybe one day we can take a hike out that way?"

"A lake in the middle of the desert?" Merritt laughed. "We'll have to make a plan, then. I can't miss that. Can you imagine what kind of strange Haederan fauna must frequent it?"

What kind of fauna must frequent it? This wasn't Merritt talking. It didn't sound like him and it didn't look like him. They'd headed down a one-way canyon, and the only thing left to do was smash into the wall on the other end.

"Next week sometime?" How she wanted to be headed back to Asria in a week, but that seemed to be a futile hope. Enric hadn't sent any messages yet, and until he said it was safe, they weren't going anywhere.

"Sure. Next week sounds great."

Wordlessly, they walked along the dry riverbed away from Windhaven, their footsteps stirring up dust and disturbing the odd lizard. Avery wanted to laugh at how easily the reptiles scurried to a new perch to stare unblinking at the interlopers who'd disturbed their peaceful morning, but the unease that permeated the air was unshakable. She focused on the clean smell of rain in the distance, but it didn't do any good. Silence between Merritt and her had never been awkward before.

"Merritt—"

Let's go back. Let's ignore what I asked. Let's ignore what happened. It was so long ago—

"They raped me," he interrupted. "They broke my legs"—he tapped his thigh with the hand that wasn't clinging to hers, at the metallic implants that allowed him to walk—"so I couldn't even think of escape, so I couldn't fight back, and then they raped me."

The constant desert breeze blew harder between them.

"I'm sorry." What a silly, shallow response. She dug through her mind for something better and came up empty. "I wish I knew what else to say. I love you so much, Merritt, and I—"

Merritt's grip tightened. "There's nothing you need to say. You aren't responsible. No one is except them. After I tried to escape . . . Well, it hadn't been pleasant before, but it got a whole lot worse after that. I didn't think I'd live through it. I didn't want to live through it."

"I wish I could change the past," she replied. "I wish I could have prevented it somehow. I wish those responsible—that there was some way they could be held accountable."

"I know you do. But good luck getting the Haederan Army to release any of the names. I wish you could, but think of how Owin would laugh in your face if you asked." Merritt looked out over the mountains in the distance. When he spoke again, his voice shook. "And may the Holy One forgive me, but I'm glad Perrin's dead. If he was still on Asria, still in Cadena, I don't know if I could stand it."

She'd barely given Taln Perrin's suicide a second thought lately. But the former military governor of Asria had so many crimes to answer for: summary executions of civilians, the six hundred dead at Tarragona, the roundups of Defense Forces personnel and their families. Ordering Merritt's torture was just one of many. She'd never spoken to Owin about what'd happened to Merritt, but maybe it was time. At the very least, if anyone responsible was still on Asria, they could be deported. Let their own people deal with them. The armistice with the Haederan Empire hadn't included sheltering war criminals.

"I can't say I don't sleep easier knowing Perrin's gone, either," she said.

"You don't sleep easily at all, love." Merritt gave a strangled laugh. "Especially last night."

Why did his laughter make her cry? He was right, though—the nightmares last night had been worse than they'd been in a while.

"Neither do you."

He pulled her against him and nestled her head under his chin. "I can't imagine what being here must be doing to you. I guess we'll just be screwed up and exhausted together then, yes?"

"There's no one else I'd rather be exhausted with."

Merritt made a sound quieter than a sigh but louder than his usual breathing. "We screwed up," he said slowly. "I should have known . . ."

"Mer, you don't need to talk about this." He'd never spoken about the failed mission to take back the Defense Forces head-quarters at Alcaris in the early days of the war, and she'd never asked. Hadn't read the reports, either. She had access to them, but they were too personal. It had to be Merritt's decision.

"No." He pushed her away so she could see him. "I need to. Debriefings are one thing, but this . . . this is different."

Avery nodded and sank to the ground, right there in the middle of the wash. He followed, seemingly grateful for the excuse to sit.

"Teruel didn't know, not at first," he said. "It was the Minister of Defense's idea—you know how that woman's never met a gutsy plan she didn't like."

Especially when it wasn't her own gut on the line. But however much Avery wanted to believe otherwise, what happened hadn't been Lidia Grec's fault.

"Politicians," she said, shaking her head.

"That's you too now, love." Merritt brushed her hair away from her cheek. "Somehow she'd gotten word that the Haederans hadn't destroyed the Nightflares. We figured it was a suicide mission, but Teruel asked me if I wanted to take part. He didn't order it. He knew how much I'd been chafing under Haederan control, that it had affected every single part of my life." *My relationship with you*, his eyes said.

Her heart began to race. She'd told Hadley about the Nightflares—a trivial bit of information she'd learned while eavesdropping in the palace. Had she been responsible for Merritt's capture? He'd never forgive her if she had, would he? She blinked, trying to work through the foggy maze of thoughts and memories.

No. The Commonwealth intelligence community, or at least Hadley, wouldn't have been keyed in to the Defense Forces like that, not then. Somehow, Grec had found out the same thing from one of her own sources. Her conscience was clear.

"Avery. I should have stayed. I should have been there for you."

Were those tears? Merritt didn't cry. *Hadn't cried.* The war had changed things.

"You needed me more than Asria did. I don't know if I'll ever forgive myself for leaving you there alone. I know," he said, holding his hands out. "I know you can handle yourself and that you don't need a savior. But what that bastard did to you—"

Avery took his hands between hers. "That doesn't matter now. They would have arrested me with or without you around. If you'd tried to stop them, the same thing would have happened to you. You did what you thought needed to be done with the information and options you had at the time." She smiled. "Some really smart guy told me that once."

"Hmm." He wound his fingers between hers. "Just a smart guy?"

"Well . . ." Heat rose in her cheeks, and this time, it wasn't from the warmth of the desert wind. "He's pretty good-looking, too."

Merritt smiled in return at the expected answer, but it was a false one. "So the night before I said goodbye to you, I made some visits. Handpicked a team of people I trusted. I couldn't give them more notice than that, even though I wanted to, in case the Haederans got wind of it.

"There were fifty-three of us. Pilots, Avery. A bunch of pilots. We didn't know anything about infiltrating an enemy base. What chance did we have? We tried our damn best, though. Two of the teams were supposed to create a diversion on the other side of the base—and they did. Stev Kanmar was in charge of one of them, and I'll never forget the sound of those explosions. They meant freedom. They were going to get us into space, and I could die there. I would have been happy dying there. I think everyone would have been happy dying after taking out a few of those ships. I found out later that the Haederans had set off the charges so we'd make our way to the hangar without being suspicious."

He pulled his hands away from hers and gripped the top of his head. "We got to that hangar, just dreaming of those stars up there, and it was empty. Just—empty. I knew right away . . ."

His voice cracked, and she knew he was seeing that empty hangar again in his mind.

"There wasn't anything we could do except retreat and hope we could take a few of them out on the way and that the reprisals for our actions would be minor. But they'd rigged the fire suppression system in the hangar with some chemical, and the next thing I knew, I was waking up flat on my stomach with a rifle against my skull. They brought everyone in except for the few casualties we'd incurred on the way in earlier. We all just stared at each other. We knew we'd been had—but why? It didn't seem to have any purpose. You could tell no one had any idea what was going on. And then Perrin arrived."

"Mer." She reached out a hand, and he took it, squeezing so hard she thought her fingers might break.

He didn't look at her. "They separated us. No pattern that I could tell. Thirty-some on one side, the rest of us on the other.

They marched most of my group out, everyone except Kanmar and me. And then . . ."

"It's all right," she said. "You don't need to say it. I know."

. . . and then the Haederans had executed them.

His shoulders sagged. "One by one. It took forever. And when it was all over, I screamed at them. Yelled at them to get up and move, but they didn't. Perrin—the man just laughed. And then right before he walked out, he kicked me in the face and ripped the rank pins right off my collar." Merritt stared into her eyes, though Avery wasn't sure he was seeing her. "Those were for you, weren't they?"

"Yes," she whispered. "They were."

She could still see those silver stars in Perrin's open palm the night Merritt had been captured. Mocking her, mocking her grief. They sat in a box now, hidden away in her rooms at the palace . . . proof that hope was something to cling to, no matter what happened.

"And then they must have hit me again, because when I woke up, I was in that cell. I was ready for interrogation. I could have handled that. They'd done that before, right after the annexation. Instead, they laughed at me. Said you were dead, but I wouldn't get off that easily. Then after the first beating, they told me you were alive, but I'd never see you again, and that you were going through worse. The things they said they were doing to you—I wanted to kill them, Avery. And I tried. So help me, I tried to get out of there."

The pain in his voice brought tears to her eyes. "Mer, they were lying. I won't pretend they didn't break me, but those soldiers didn't know where I was or what was happening to me. I doubt they knew if I was alive or dead." Some days she doubted Lient had known what was going on.

"I believed it all. Every word they said." Not only pain now, but guilt. "And once I figured out their schedule, I decided I'd make a run for it. They'd cracked a few ribs that morning, and when they sent in some private with food they knew I couldn't eat, they weren't cautious about it, and I grabbed him. Only he wasn't armed like he usually was, and it didn't take long until they caught me. And after they were done beating me, they marched me to the infirmary on two broken ankles. I thought they'd finally realized how much trouble they were in, that they were going to let the medic fix me, but instead—"

His ring ground into the delicate skin on the side of her finger, and she fought to control her breathing, fought to keep from gasping.

"There was this—this infantryman. Crimson Regiment. And the entire time he was—" Merritt drew a ragged breath and closed his eyes. "He called me Your Highness. Told me you were next. That he couldn't wait to go see you after he was done with me." He looked up, haunted now. "And that if by some miracle we both survived, you would never want me again, because I was his."

Heat like she'd never felt before settled into her middle.

Holy One, why?

"No." Her firm voice surprised her, but Merritt needed that certainty. She forced the tears away, forced her stomach to settle. "That's a lie. I don't care. I don't care about that, or the implants, or the nightmares. Or any of it." She jerked at his hand, more violently than she'd intended. "You are mine, Merritt Rendon, every part of you. No one else's. And I'm yours until the last breath I take. That's how much I love you, and anyone who says anything else is a liar. Do you understand me?"

Merritt released a little of the pressure on her fingers and exhaled.

"You are my heart. I love that you waited for me. I love that you made it through what you did. And I love you for being you."

"Me too." She drew the back of his hand to her mouth and kissed it, then pressed his palm against her cheek. "And we're going to be just fine. Right?"

Because even if Owin laughs at me, I'm going to find out who did this. And if they're still on Asria—

They both jumped at the footsteps behind Merritt.

"I hope I'm not interrupting anything." Wynne came around the corner of the wash, kicking up pebbles behind her. She frowned at them both but didn't say anything. "But there's a little problem up at the main house."

"Just a walk." Merritt swore under his breath and pulled Avery to her feet. "It's past time to head back in. What's wrong?"

Wynne's face was unreadable. "You'll never believe who just showed up."

CHAPTER ELEVEN

Chase leaned against the mosaic fireplace in the small dining area off the kitchen, eyeing each one of them in turn. His hair was longer than usual, his freckles darker, but he didn't look nearly as injured as he had when Avery had said goodbye on *Terigon*. The defiant look that hardened his eyes, though—yes, that was familiar enough.

"So this is what this feels like." He shifted against the tile and rolled the sleeves of his silk shirt to his elbows, looking uncomfortable despite his flawless attire. "I'm not sure why you're all looking at me like this. Can't a man return to his own home without a bunch of suspicious stares and questions?"

Avery stirred scratched at the linen of her chair with a fingernail as she looked from Merritt to Wynne to Kern. It was the wrong move—at the sound, all three transferred their stares from Chase to her. Why did this fall to her? Why did all the unpleasant matters fall to her? What business was it of hers if Chase was here or not? Did they think she had any control over him?

Oh, fine.

"You know exactly why we're all looking at you like this," she said. "The last time we saw you, you were lying in the brig's sick bay on *Terigon* with a few bullet holes in you, accused of war crimes. Don't pretend it's not at least a little suspicious that you've suddenly shown up at Windhaven—on Haedera!—without telling anyone you were coming."

"And I told you back then." Chase's gaze wavered to the crystal light above the table in front of her, then to Kern, then to the open foyer doors, out toward the mountains in the distance. "It was a mistake."

"Accusations of war crimes aren't a mistake. The Commonwealth—"

She leaned back in her chair and frowned at her hands. The Commonwealth what? Had every reason to hold him? Wouldn't have let him go? Wouldn't have made a mistake of this magnitude? There was no polite way to finish her statement.

"Sir . . ." Kern began, then shuffled from foot to foot.

Good. Someone else was just as confused as she. Chase might lie to her, but he'd never lie to Kern. Would he?

"Look," Chase said, rubbing his eyes. "The ambassador's request finally reached the Commonwealth, as did His Majesty's. There's no issue anymore. The mistake was sorted out. You know how these kinds of things go."

Silence. Merritt raised his eyebrows at her and edged toward the open patio doors and freedom. "If we're done here, I have work to do."

Don't leave me here, Merritt. Don't leave me with him. Don't leave me—

"Same. It's about time for another patrol." Kern shot Merritt a look, and they disappeared out the double doors onto the terrace together.

"My lady?" Wynne asked. "I'd like to shadow him this time—make sure everything's covered."

Not you too, Wynne.

"Fine." Avery waved a hand toward the mountains outside, and Wynne darted out behind Kern. She leaned back in her chair and glared at Chase. "So?"

"So what?" He pushed himself off the fireplace with his foot and eased down in the chair across from her. Gingerly, like he was still in some pain this many weeks later. "I just told you what happened."

"You said the mistake was sorted out. What kind of mistake was it? Did they confuse you for someone else?"

"No. It was just a mistake."

She raised her eyebrows.

"I have diplomatic immunity on Asria," he said slowly, like the excuse had just occurred to him for the first time. "They realized they shouldn't have been holding me in the first place—that they couldn't without causing an interstellar incident."

Was this what interrogating an uncooperative subject felt like? Besides the warm desert breeze filtering in through the open doors and the luxury surrounding them, it certainly felt like it. How had Chase kept himself from wrapping his hands around her throat when she'd given him nonsensical answers like this?

"You weren't on Asria when the Commonwealth arrested you, Colonel. Your diplomatic immunity granted by the Asrian High Senate does not extend into Commonwealth-controlled space. Nice try, though."

Chase sighed dramatically and tapped his fingers on the table. A rare sign of anxiety from him.

"Have you forgotten who I am to Owin?"

Oh.

Yes, he'd mentioned that Owin was responsible for his release, but in her surprise at seeing him reappear, she'd forgotten Chase had been married to the man's sister. The Haederan ambassador to Asria and the emperor of Haedera himself would have made a formidable team, even against the Commonwealth.

"I—I suppose I did." She recrossed her ankles. "I'm happy to hear that Owin and Ambassador Neave were able to smooth things over."

Still . . .

Refusing to acknowledge the military status of a Commonwealth Special Operations Forces prisoner of war captured on Asria.

Compelling a Royal Asrian Defense Forces prisoner of war to serve in the Imperial Haederan Navy.

Something odd fluttered in her chest. Owin and Neave would have had to work a miracle to clear him of those charges. Yet there was no way Chase could have lied. If Owin hadn't managed to free him, he'd be on his way to Ventana IV right now.

"Good. Then you can drop this unfounded suspicion. You know how it gets you into trouble. Would you care for tea?"

"Tea?"

Kusir, she sounded like a robot, only able to repeat his words back to him. Between her conversation with Merritt and Chase's reappearance, she felt like someone had struck her in the head with a log.

"Yes, tea. It's been a long trip, and I'd like some Haederan tea. Preferably not on my own—I spent enough time alone in the brig. I'm sure you know what that's like. Or do you have somewhere else you need to be?"

Against her will, her heart melted. Those days alone in the brig on *Imperieuse* might have been his fault, but Chase was right—she knew what that kind of isolation felt like, and she wouldn't wish it on anyone. Even if she didn't relive it in her nightmares, she felt it each time she entered a small room. She'd spent weeks with the walls closing in around her, screaming until her voice was gone. When they'd finally released her into Chase's custody, her fingernails were broken off from clawing at the door and her eyes were unable to focus on anything past arm's length. The navy guards hadn't been harsh like the soldiers in Cadena, but perhaps having nothing to focus on but her bleak future was worse than torture— for on her darkest days, she'd known she would never leave whatever desolate prison on Haedera she was destined for except as a small container of ashes.

And hadn't Chase visited her then? Hadn't he brought tea and conversation and worked for hours to calm her, even if she hadn't approved of his methods in the moment? He'd waited until she'd pleaded to see him, true, but after she'd escaped with that fighter, not even Chase was cruel enough to force his presence on her when it was unwanted. Not when she'd been as broken as she'd been. Not until he was invited. If nothing else, she owed him for that consideration.

"No," she said, batting away the pain that never seemed to end. She tried for a smile, more to forget the memories than to console him, and the guilt of her selfishness ate at her, too. "I don't have anywhere else to be. Tea would be nice."

"Good, because it's already on the way."

"Gareth!" A freckled, elderly woman stuck her head around the corner from the kitchen and hurried over to him, her eyes alight. "They said you were home, but I didn't want to believe it until I saw you with my own eyes. I've been so worried about you," she said, holding out her arms. "And Lady Sophie has been distraught."

"I came from her rooms before they all cornered me in here." Chase stood with a grin and pulled the woman in for a hug. He towered over her slight frame, and her head only came halfway up his chest. Once he released her, she patted him on the cheek, looking for all the world like a worried mother whose child had returned from . . . well, Chase had certainly returned from something.

Avery couldn't help gaping.

Chase turned his grin to her. "By the way you're staring, it looks like no one's introduced you to Lara."

She shook her head, unable to form words at the sight of someone who—cared for Chase like this? Someone who wasn't afraid of him? Fiona certainly gave him a respectful distance, and the rest of the servants tiptoed around Windhaven like they were terrified of him. It was impossible to believe this slip of a woman didn't fear him, yet there wasn't any other explanation for her actions. Could she be his mother?

"Lara is Windhaven's head housekeeper," he explained. "She keeps us—keeps me—together. I can't believe you haven't met her yet."

"Don't bother her like that, Gareth. The queen needs rest—in private, not by being dragged all over the estate. And unlike you, I know my place."

Avery's hand met her mouth to hide her smile. Had his housekeeper just scolded him? Right to his face?

His grin faded. "You're right, of course. Your Majesty, allow me to introduce Lara. If there's anything you need that they haven't provided, you can let her know. Lara, I—I think it's time for that tea now. Perhaps something special for Sophie in case she decides to show. And please let Zavis know I have a small bag of things on the aeroflyer."

"Certainly, my lord." She backed away with a slight bow.

"How did they treat you on *Terigon*?" she asked as Lara disappeared from sight. Half of her didn't want to know—didn't want to remind him of what he'd been through—but half of her was desperate to make sure he hadn't been abused. What a strange impulse that was.

His eyes sparkled as they met hers. "Feeling a little guilty about your former employer's actions toward me, are you?"

Current employer, occasional as they might be. And maybe.

"Of course not," she said. "It's just that you looked like you were in so much pain when we left, and I haven't been able to get it out of my mind." How easy it was to confess all sorts of things to him now, even fear. "Yes, I suppose I'm bothered by what they might have done to you."

Chase laughed, though it seemed forced. "I'd just had a few bullets removed from my abdomen. When I wasn't in pain, my mind was numb from the meds. But yes, I'll ease your worry— which is very flattering, by the way. They treated me well. I got a cell to myself, decent food, and even a long chat with a Voirian security officer whose great-great-grandfather defected from Haedera." He waved his hand in that familiar, dismissive way. "It may as well have been a holiday, albeit one with limited sightseeing opportunities and an indefinite conclusion. Is that good enough for you?"

"Thank you," she breathed. "I just needed to know."

Chase nodded, then leaned back in his chair and tilted his head slightly. "How are you liking Windhaven?"

"It's beautiful, both the house and the grounds. I had no idea the desert could be so lovely. Is it your family's estate?" He'd seemed too proud of it to have inherited it from his wife's side.

"For seven generations, though the main house isn't that old, of course. My father was an Imperial Haederan Navy admiral, fifth generation, and my mother . . ." He smiled, though it was tinged with sadness. "I'm sure you saw the paintings in the gallery. She was a remarkable artist."

"They're beautiful." Her forehead wrinkled. "Owin once mentioned your mother was a relation."

He laughed. "All the nobility is related on Haedera II, some more closely than others. Her great-great-grandfather was Emperor Owin I, so yes, that means I have the unfortunate consequence of carrying both my parents' family titles and Isobel's decidedly longer one." He paused to smile at Lara as she dropped off an iron teapot with a Haederan-style dragon as a handle. "Don't ask Brennin about his, by the way, not unless you want a three-hour lecture on equality, the class system, and why he decided Imperial Security was a better use of his time than gallivanting around his hometown spending his father's money."

"Don't worry, there's no chance of that." Learning Kern's motivation for subjugating his own people instead of enjoying his family's wealth and privilege in a more innocuous fashion was the last thing she wanted to do. "But you know I have to ask."

Chase poured her tea, then focused on his own. "You really don't, my lady."

"I do. Three separate hereditary titles, and you're just now mentioning them—this must be good."

"Good is not the word I would use." His cheeks grew red as he exhaled a wary surrender. "His Imperial Highness Prince Gareth Merion of the Sacred Empire of Haedera, the Most Righteous Margrave of Rebet and Fifth Earl of Windhaven."

Her hand flew to her mouth; her teeth sank into her lower lip to stop the laughter. Why hadn't it ever occurred to her that Chase was a prince of Haedera?

"You can see why I prefer my father's name. It was my sole act of rebellion." The flush deepened and his eyes danced, even though he was clearly trying to steel them. "I'm not offended if you laugh. It's truly ridiculous."

"I would never." She knew her expression told a different story. "Family is—can be—"

"Difficult," he finished.

"To say the least."

"And you don't have anything so absurd on Asria."

"It used to be close." Chase had to know that. If any Haederan had done their research before arriving on their conquered planet, it would have been him. "Before the Civil War, the aristocracy consisted of a full tenth of the planet. They wiped all of them out after the surrender and revoked all titles except for Mauris Rendon's immediate family and descendants. Even then, there were close to a hundred of them." She shrugged. "Now it's the opposite—the royal family has shrunk to nothing. It's not supposed to matter, since the senate can elect anyone they want, but they're worried. I get messages about it almost weekly."

Messages that offended Merritt in particular.

I'm not going to breed you, then let them take you to the slaughterhouse, he'd said after the last one. *How are you not furious about this invasion of privacy?*

She'd laughed at his stony expression, but he hadn't relented. Yes, Merritt had a long way to go until he accepted his new life.

"Somehow I think you're not going to cave unless you want to." He took a sip of tea. "How much of Haedera have you seen?"

"Only Windhaven." Chase should have known that. "I'm not here to sightsee. Or make an official visit. I can't even visit the palace without your media being all over it."

And what would the imperial palace in Rebet be like? Not like her own home on Asria, that much she knew. Haedera was different. It was exotic. No one she knew had even considered visiting. She stretched her toes, ready to run all the way there that very second.

"So we don't tell Owin. If he hasn't already heard from Kern's men, he's not going to. And I know Brennin has had you cooped up here—I can see it in your eyes. Not that I'm surprised. He's dependable, but he doesn't trust you."

"I can't imagine why not." A laugh broke through. For some reason, just the fact that Chase could laugh at Kern's dislike for her made it a little better. Maybe he wasn't as angry with her as Merritt had implied. Maybe he was . . . just Kern. "It's definitely a tempting offer. But I don't want to cause any trouble."

"You, cause trouble? I don't believe it." His eyes crinkled. "I can keep up. And Brennin can try. If you could go anywhere on Haedera—and keep in mind there are a lot of places you don't need to be going, places that wouldn't be safe if you were recognized—where would it be?"

Freedom. She could taste it. A thousand ideas rolled about in her mind—no. Not rolled. They jumped gleefully. How many other Asrians had the opportunity to explore Haedera with someone as well-acquainted and safe as Chase? It was a chance not to be squandered. Mountains, deserts, holy sites, ruins of the first Haederan people to make planetfall . . .

"For the next two weeks, I'm your personal tour guide." Chase poured her another small cup and pushed it across the table. "If you want to think about it or ask Colonel Rendon, just let me know in a few days."

She swirled the thimble-sized porcelain. Visions of thousand-year-old imperial artwork dissolved in a heartbeat as another less exotic but infinitely more divine thought took its place.

"No. That won't be necessary. I know exactly where I want to go."

CHAPTER TWELVE

THE AEROFLYER SANK LOWER IN THE CLOUDLESS SKY, BUT THE SANDY ground outside barely changed. Maybe there were a few more plants than she'd been able to see at altitude, but the desert looked the same. Avery leaned against the window and tried to figure out exactly what she was doing in this remote part of Haedera as Kern's voice broke the silence that had filled the aeroflyer for the past hour.

"I'm surprised you wanted to join us, Colonel Rendon. You must have enough to do back at Windhaven."

Merritt gave him a sharp look, the one that said, *Back off or else.* Even she'd been the recipient of that look a few times. Queen or not, marginal senator or not, there were some things Merritt kept close—or at least had kept close until they'd arrived on Haedera. One had to respect him for that.

"Official work can always wait. It was important to her, so we're here. Though I have to admit, I don't quite understand the lure of flying halfway across the planet."

He was exaggerating about the distance but not about his confusion over their excursion. She'd tried to explain the night before, but the words and pleas had sounded vague and irrele-vant to him—she could tell. Not that she blamed him. How was she supposed to describe a nagging feeling in her heart that never quite went away?

"I just—" She stopped. Maybe simpler was better in this case. "It's just somewhere I need to be."

No, Merritt couldn't understand the reason for this trip. Just like she still couldn't believe she'd prevented Feye and his rifle from shooting Chase from that cliff so long ago, and just like she hadn't been able to explain that strange compulsion to Hadley, she couldn't explain the pull that had led her to this small town over three hundred kilometers from Rebet.

And it was small. If they'd had enough time before landing, she'd have been able to count the houses that lined the main road. Dunes surrounded the village, but no roads ran out of it. It was as cut off as some cities in the mountains on Asria, but for such a different reason—even on the beaches she'd frequented on Ventana IV, she'd never seen so much sand. If there ever was a good reason for aeroflyers, Esro was it.

As she stared at the enclosed town, Chase smiled at her like he'd read her mind. "The dunes kept covering the road. They finally gave up and let it happen instead of digging out every few months."

"But why the desert?" she asked. "You have this whole planet —why all these settlements out here? So far from the forests? The water?"

She must have looked as baffled as she felt, because Kern laughed.

"It's mostly cultural," Chase said. "There've always been myths about monsters that roam the rainforests north and south of here. And those are just a thin strip at best. It was more productive to make a way of life in the hotter and drier parts of the planet. Which we did," he finished, sounding pleased with himself and a thousand years of Haederans. "We terraformed Haedera I first, and after that disaster, this was easy. Not needing to terraform always is."

Yes, it'd taken them six hundred years to terraform a planet before the first atmospheric holes had appeared—followed shortly by the loss of carbon dioxide, and, eventually, the catastrophic terraforming failure. The Haederan Empire had lost thousands of colonists before evacuating. It'd always been a vague story, something she'd read about in history class, but being here now . . .

Her chest tightened. Why hadn't they settled Haedera II first? Yes, the desert had overtaken most of the planet before humans had arrived, but they'd been here thousands of years now, managing and thriving—enough so that they'd been able to attempt to expand their empire several times over. So much death could have been avoided.

So much death.

"And the monsters?" she asked. The small animals' influence was all over Haedera, from the flag to the teapot she and Chase had used at Windhaven days before, and even monsters were a better topic of conversation than Haederan imperialism and war. "Are they some sort of *kaldren*?"

"*Aligs.*" Kern drew out the *i* in what had to be an extinct Haederan dialect and laughed. "A native Haederan lizard. They prefer to avoid humans, but they're slightly venomous and don't have any problem defending themselves if provoked. Now we know they're just easily spooked, but it gave the early colonists the wrong idea. Just imagine coming across one of them in the desert, then finding your missing companion grasping at his throat, bloody saliva running from his lips as the venom paralyzes his diaphragm."

Merritt raised his eyebrows.

Wynne's lip curled. "Is that kind of detail really necessary?"

"Has your stomach turned weak, Major?" Chase favored her with an all-too-familiar mocking tone.

Avery wanted to sigh. Chase was usually polite enough to Wynne, but since his return to Windhaven, he'd been curt with almost everyone. Even her a few times, like the day before when he'd threatened to cancel the trip over some vaguely cited security concerns. When she'd pressed for details, he'd snapped at her—

then relented, apologetic beyond reason after she'd flinched in fear. He claimed he wasn't in pain any longer, but who knew? Maybe he was healing slowly, but that couldn't be the only reason for his moods lately. It had only been the pull of this place that allowed her to tolerate him for an inescapable five-hour aeroflyer ride.

A short second later, the aeroflyer came to a blessedly gentle bump in the sand outside a group of large sand dunes. The pilot could have half crashed the ship for all Avery cared, as long as she was free from the hostile atmosphere inside. She pushed against Merritt, but he was too absorbed in the view to notice she was trying to escape.

Wynne, ever the lucky one, hopped out first and scanned the distance to the dune field, frowning.

"Is it always this empty here?" she asked.

"Only a few hundred people still live in town." It was Kern who answered that time as he jumped out behind her. A familiar sneer was on his face, the one that meant he hated being this far from an actual city.

"Small enough we should see any trouble coming," Wynne said.

"That's the idea."

Chase ignored them all, his eyes swiveling about.

"You said it would be safe here." Avery shot a glance at Wynne. Chase's concern was making her heart beat faster.

"Safe enough," Chase replied, gesturing them toward the single transport that sat outside the perimeter fencing. "But it never hurts to be cautious. You should have allowed us to come and check things out before, my lady. I'm not liking the fact we don't have a presence here beyond an informant, and that we weren't able to clear the place beforehand. When I told you I'd take you anywhere—"

"You don't like the fact you're in civilian clothes," Avery interrupted as Merritt helped her out. Chase and Kern both wore similarly loose shirts and had the same uneasy look about them, even armed to the teeth, so it was probably the truth. "Which was your own decision, so you will not blame it on me." *Kusir*, that felt good to say, even though Merritt snickered out loud at her challenge. "No one knows we're here, anyway. No one even knows I'm on Haedera."

"No." Chase tried to smile but didn't quite succeed. "No, they don't. Well . . ." He blew out a deep breath and smoothed his shirt over his pistol. "Shall we, Your Majesty?"

* * *

The graveyard was as large as the town was small.

Avery tried to ignore Wynne and Kern circling the perimeter as she and Merritt followed Chase around the haphazard grave markers. The young man who'd driven them out to the edge of town leaned against the transport outside the electrified fence—presumably the single Imperial Security Command informant around. He hadn't said a word to any of his strange visitors.

"I'm surprised Captain Linden is buried here," she said to the surrounding dunes as much as to Chase.

He turned, his face grim. "His family's lucky I was able to work this out. The emperor wanted—well, he wanted to make an example of him. I managed to convince His Majesty"—there was derision in the title—"that handling his burial in that manner would lead to too many questions about the verium and your escape. The official story was treason, of course, which is why he's buried here and not with honor in Rebet, but the details of his alleged crimes were classified. It was the best I could do at the time. Perhaps one day Owin might . . ."

His voice trailed off, but the longing was obvious.

"It was a poor decision on his part," she said, "not treason. It's not as though he intentionally allowed me to escape. He didn't deserve to be treated like this."

And it's my fault.

Because if she hadn't escaped, if she hadn't stolen that fighter,

Linden—and Chase's son—would still be alive. Months of pondering had brought her right back to the same answer, and she hated herself for it.

"No," Chase said. "He didn't deserve this. But now, at least, his family has a place to go."

"And they're expecting us?"

Merritt squeezed her hand. He'd been so silent, but hopefully the place was acting on him as well.

"In a few hours, yes." Chase pointed toward a smooth rock set apart from the rest of the stone markers. "Right here."

Unlike the rest in the desolate cemetery, Linden's marker was flat and unmarked. Just a rock, and not even an attractive one, brown and dingy and blending into the sand. Even to an off-worlder, the meaning was clear.

This was a traitor's grave.

She knelt beside it, Merritt next to her, and brushed the sand away. Insignificant, perhaps, since the desert would reclaim the marker within hours, but the small action felt holy in a way.

"Can you tell me about him?" she asked. There had to be so much more to Rhys Linden than what she'd learned of him in a short hour or so—which was very little.

Imperial Security Command captain.

Quite trusted, since Chase had left her alone in his custody.

Educated, by his voice.

Father of a child he'd never met.

And—she had to admit it—he'd been civilized. At least, he'd ordered the soldiers not to harm her, and they'd feared him enough to obey.

Those five facts were the sum of everything she knew about an entire life, one she'd played a part in ending. It didn't seem nearly enough.

Chase sighed and crouched next to them. "Rhys Linden was . . . he was fun."

She settled the rest of the way into the sand. It filled her shoes, but that didn't matter. "Fun? I didn't think you knew the meaning of the word."

He smiled in return, though it looked weary.

"I met him almost ten years ago when he was a recruit assigned to System Intel. He was young, brilliant, and determined. And, though you'll think this odd for Imperial Security, he loved people. It was refreshing, even to someone as cynical as me. I stole him as soon as I could, and it turned out to be one of the best—and worst—decisions I've ever made."

Speaking of bad decisions . . .

"And Elex Feye's sister?" Oh, she'd been wondering about that for so long.

"Another mistake." Chase made an unflattering noise. "Maybe one day I'll tell you the entire story, but suffice it to say, it's a relationship that should have never happened. But that was Rhys. He'd plow headlong into whatever he wanted, no matter the cost, and it seemed he wanted her. Some good came out of it, though. It always does when the Holy One can put His hand on it. That baby—she's beautiful. I know she'll do just fine in life. Maybe one day she'll even visit her father's planet."

"Did he ever say anything about me?"

"Avery . . ." Merritt's voice was low, warning. He of all people knew she didn't need to relive those days, especially in front of Chase. But she was fine. With him next to her, she would always be more than fine.

Chase gave him an apologetic shrug. *I can't refuse to answer the queen*, it seemed to say. *You know what she'll do to me.*

"Oh, he had lots and lots to say about you," he said. "Mostly that he should have stunned you or drugged you or bashed you over the head with his boot when he had the chance. And that I did a piss-poor job of turning you, of course. Over and over and over with the second-guessing the entire way back here."

He rubbed his eyes as the wind picked up, scattering sand. "That's partially my fault. There were so many things we could have done differently, so many poor decisions made on a second's notice—he blamed himself, I blamed myself, he blamed me, and I blamed him. But in the end, it didn't matter. You were gone, along with that fighter, and someone had to answer for that."

"I would do the same thing again." She stiffened, even with Merritt's hand protectively on her back. "I've prayed for so long to be able to say otherwise, but I can't make myself believe it. Which means this is my fault."

She wouldn't cry. She wouldn't. Even though she felt the chill of that shuttle, felt the handcuffs cutting into her wrists, felt Linden's and Chase's eyes on her as the ship lifted off, transporting her to a fate worse than death. She'd felt the same guilt before, yes, of course, but not like this. It hadn't mattered on Asria. There, Linden's death had been a vague event that might as well have never happened. But here, in his hometown in the region of Saer, sitting in front of his grave . . .

"I would always expect you to make the same decision, my lady. You did the honorable thing in a shameful situation, and what happened afterward is no one's fault but the man who pulled that trigger."

"I wish things were different," she replied.

She leaned into Merritt. Repeating the same thing over and over didn't change the past. It didn't make the future easier. And having Chase forgive her actions—it was just too much.

"I know. But all we can do is move on without forgetting." Chase pulled a small object from his pocket and held it out to her. "I hope this doesn't offend you. I've wanted to leave it here for a long time, but when I had the opportunity, it wasn't safe, and once it became safe, I was so far away . . ."

It was a pin. Just a small one, crossed silver swords identical to the ones on the Imperial Security uniform. Had the emperor taken that honor away from him as well? Likely.

She brushed her fingers against the polished metal, even though the memories made her shake.

"I don't mind," she said. It was a lie. She did mind. She

minded a lot, and that wasn't going to change any time soon. "Do you think—do you think he would mind if I prayed?"

Chase smiled. "He might. But the Holy One won't."

He placed the pin on the rock and began a prayer under his breath, and somehow, whatever Linden thought of her and what she thought of the pin didn't matter. She could mind and still forgive—and maybe already had.

CHAPTER THIRTEEN

THE HOUSE BELONGING TO LINDEN'S OLDER SISTER WAS OLD BUT WELL kept. Surrounded by a low wall that looked to be made of mud and sand, a small room off to the left suggested it might have been nothing more than a shack at some point, but even in this part of Haedera, time marched on, for the main house was at least ten times the size.

The sisters might have lost their titles and standing in the nobility when they'd married commoners, but they hadn't lost every bit of their wealth, and it was clear what money remained had been spent outdoors. A garden, riotous with color even in this wasteland, surrounded the main building. Avery couldn't take her eyes off the large clay containers filled with jade and lavender succulents, the fountain that burbled and spit more water than she'd seen since they'd left Windhaven, and the canopied trees with some kind of yellow fruit.

She inhaled their spice on the breeze as Chase pounded on the teal front door, trying to squeeze the image from her mind of him and a group of Imperial Security officers doing the same—only in the middle of the night. It helped. A bit. At least enough for her to chance another look around at the garden. She could have stood right here in this paradise for hours, but the door immediately swung open.

The woman who stood in the doorway was at least fifteen years older than Avery with the same light-brown hair so common on Haedera and eyes as dark as any one would see on Asria. A smattering of freckles covered her cheeks and nose, and a thin layer of makeup had been pressed on top, but it was clearly perfunctory. Viessa Rowe didn't look like she cared what anyone, including the Imperial Security Command, thought of her. She glanced from Avery to Chase to Kern, then motioned them inside, wordless.

If only Merritt and Wynne were here—but as Merritt had rightly pointed out, too many visitors would be counterproductive and overwhelming for the sisters. Wynne had agreed with him after a few sharp words to Kern behind their backs. Threats of what she'd do to him if Avery wasn't returned unharmed, no doubt. It was only Chase's outstretched hand that forced her forward. Anything to avoid him taking her arm to escort her anywhere.

She found herself in a small sitting area with whitewashed walls and large windows covered by gauzy white drapes. A multibranched cactus in a copper pot sat in one corner by what must have been the original fireplace, a circle of aqua cushions across from it. They were almost the cerulean blue she was so accustomed to, and as she sat between Chase and Kern and tucked her feet underneath her, the familiarity reassured her. Haederan, yes, but they were still people. Still mourning—and she and Asria knew mourning.

"Thank you for seeing us." Chase's voice echoed through the silent room. "Especially on such short notice."

"I didn't have a choice." Viessa's hands—and voice—shook as she sat the *alig*-embellished teapot on the polished piece of wood in front of them. "One does not turn down an order from Imperial Security."

Not if one wants to live.

"You always have a choice with me, Viessa," he said, a little softer. "It was a request, not an order, and it was personal. I'm here as Rhys's friend. No one else, not even his commander."

She started a bit at that, then nodded and began to pour the tea.

"Where's Gweyr?" he asked.

"Right here, Colonel," came a cheerful voice.

The younger woman who came out of the kitchen couldn't have been more different from her sister. Where Viessa was understandably terrified of two-thirds of her visitors, Gweyr didn't look like she could be afraid of anyone, even Imperial Security. A slight grin was plastered on her face, and her sandy hair was untamed, like she'd just spent the past few hours letting the desert style it. She looked just like Linden, and Avery stared at the floor as Gweyr sat next to her sister.

"Good." Chase exhaled. "I'm sorry for another visit, but there are some things that need to be said."

Her cue. Avery grabbed one of the small teacups and wrapped her hands around it. One day she would learn to control her fidgeting. Victor had been so adept at it.

"My name is—"

"I know who you are, Lady Avery." The wrinkles around Viessa's eyes grew deeper. "Do you think we're too backward here to know about anything outside of Haedera? I knew who you were as soon as I saw the three of you coming down the walk. But what I haven't been able to figure out is what you're doing here with two Imperial Security officers." She raised graying eyebrows. "So? What is it?"

"Viessa, really." Her words were a rebuke, but Gweyr's eyes focused on Avery, her earlier friendliness gone.

"I knew your brother." Avery brushed a curl from her forehead. The house was cool, but her skin was burning. "Briefly. Not well. But I wanted to tell you in person how sorry I was to hear about his death."

"His murder." Viessa gave Kern a sideways look, apparently

suspicious of the entire group. Not suspicious enough to avoid criticizing the empire, though.

"Yes." Avery licked her lips. They were about to crack again. How did people manage in this climate? "His murder."

"My brother did not commit treason," Viessa said. "He loved Haedera."

The low whir of an aeroflyer in the distance cut through the hostile silence. Avery tried not to flinch, though visions of an invasion flitted through her brain. *Just a resident coming home from wherever. Not an attack.* Windhaven suddenly seemed more of a haven than usual.

"We've been through this," Chase said, the only one not looking out the window. "The people who matter know the truth."

Viessa whirled on him, her earlier fear gone.

"And if she's here to apologize for whatever role she had in his death, then she needs to hear it from the people who are hurting more than you!"

The tips of his ears turned red, but he nodded at her as the aeroflyer noise grew louder, then disappeared completely. Had it landed nearby?

"He loved Haedera," Viessa repeated as she turned back to Avery. "He would have done anything for his empire. And now— you can't imagine how people talk around here. I'm happy our parents are dead, because if they weren't already, this would have killed them. He was their baby, the one they prayed to come along for years but thought would never appear. They thought the family line and title had died out. And then, when he was selected for Imperial Security Command, they were so proud of him . . ."

"I'm sorry."

Why did the words mean so little? What else could she do but apologize over and over and over? Did Viessa know that if she had the chance, she would have escaped from Linden again? Did it matter? This had been a terrible idea, coming all this way to apologize to people who hated her without even knowing why.

A commotion at the door drew her attention. Kern jumped to his feet and headed for the door, but he didn't look anxious about whoever was there. Expectant, perhaps?

"I wish I had other words," she said. "But I still wanted to come here and tell you—"

"Sir," Kern interrupted, the door cracked open, his fingers on the handle.

Chase sighed and stood. "Gweyr, Viessa, I'm sorry I didn't tell you about this part"—his gaze moved to Avery—"and certainly sorry I didn't tell you, my lady, but I wasn't entirely sure on the schedule, and there were some security issues that precluded informing you before."

"What now?" Viessa snarled.

Kern pulled open the door to reveal four uniformed Imperial Security Command men. They swarmed inside with sensors, through the sitting area, the bright yellow kitchen, and what had to be bedrooms toward the back. Viessa and Gweyr stumbled to their feet as they entered. It was all too obvious who would follow once the house was cleared, and as soon as the officers nodded at Chase and headed back out the front door, Owin II, Emperor of Haedera, stood there on the doorstep, a single plainclothes guard behind him.

Viessa was finally mute.

"Gareth," Owin said as Kern shut and latched the door behind him and his guard, "stop grinning at the back of Lady Avery's head like a fool and introduce me."

Avery's head snapped around just as Chase managed to wipe the smirk off his face.

"I am terribly sorry, sire." He followed the apology with a bow. Gweyr and Viessa matched him, Viessa a little slower. "Your Majesty, Gweyr Wells and Viessa Rowe. You know Lady Avery, of course."

Gweyr and Viessa looked at each other with the same question Avery had.

What is he doing here?

Owin waved them all to sit, though he remained standing in front of the door. Had he planned a short visit, or was he nervous about something?

"I won't take too much of your time," he said. "But I have a proposal for the two of you."

Gweyr fidgeted with the hem of her shirt. Viessa just glowered at him.

"I'll just come right to it. I would like to have Captain Linden's remains transferred to Rebet, if you're willing. To Imperial Security headquarters where they belong, along with the ceremony to which his service has entitled him."

Viessa's glower faded a bit. Likely it was the first time anyone had referred to Linden by his rank since well before his death.

"That doesn't change the past, sire," Gweyr mumbled to her feet.

"I can't change the past. I wish Captain Linden was standing right here, and I wish I had a better explanation for what happened, but he's not and I don't. I can only right part of what has been wronged."

Silence fell, broken only by sniffling. Which sister it was, Avery was too afraid to move her head to find out.

"By all means, take a few minutes to decide." Owin's smile landed on Avery. "My lady, if I could have the pleasure of your company for a short walk?"

"No." Viessa's refusal was abrupt; she didn't look at Gweyr. "I don't need time. We would like that very much."

Chase's shoulders relaxed.

"Good," Owin said. "The details have already been worked out, and I'd like you to be my guests in Rebet for the ceremony. Major Kern will fill you in on everything. But I'd still like to explore your lovely gardens with Lady Avery." He grinned at her. "I'm not certain my curiosity can handle one more moment of wondering what the queen of Asria is doing in Esro."

* * *

Owin's guard, plus Chase and Kern, stayed inside, and Avery tried not to be offended at their lack of concern. She and Owin meandered down the stone walk of the courtyard in silence, just like they had outside Cadena so long ago.

"So?" he asked, stopping under one of the spicy yellow trees. "To what do I owe the honor of this unexpected visit?"

"Colonel Chase didn't tell you?"

Of course he hadn't. Her visit to Haedera was supposed to be secret, after all. Owin shook his head, so she gave him the brief version of Quen's threats and Chase's plan to hide the royal family on Haedera—Chase himself would have to fill in the gaps later. It was a fitting punishment for this kind of surprise.

"And Brooks Neave sends his regards. I didn't ask for this kind of favor, though," she said, gesturing around the courtyard. "Only to visit his grave and his family. I didn't know Captain Linden. I only met him once. But a long time ago, Colonel Chase told me what had happened after he returned to Haedera, and I . . ."

Owin inclined his head. Naturally he knew Linden's story if he was offering this kind of imperial favor. "Understood. And Gareth is proving to be a suitable host?"

"He—"

How to reply to that? *He hasn't tortured me in a secret dungeon at Windhaven, but he's been in a foul mood ever since the Commonwealth released him and is making all our lives miserable?* That was probably not an appropriate answer for Chase's imperial master and brother-in-law.

"Windhaven is beautiful," she said instead. "And even though I miss Cadena, we're very comfortable there."

"That's a dance around the truth if I've ever heard one." Owin laughed. "If he becomes a problem, you let me know immediately." His voice sobered enough that it was clear he knew just how she'd become acquainted with Chase. "Major Kern can get you in touch with me."

"I appreciate that." Owin was probably one of the few on

Haedera who could control Chase. "But since you're here, there is one thing I'd like to discuss with you." Her heart began to pound, right there in the middle of the garden paradise. "Owin, I need a favor. A personal one."

He smiled. "Repatriating Captain Linden's remains to Rebet isn't indulgence enough?"

"That was a favor for Colonel Chase. Not that I disagree with your decision, and if I'd known it was a possibility, I might have beat him to the request. But no—this is about Merritt. What happened to him after his capture at Alcaris."

The smile turned to a frown. "What was that?"

She dipped her fingertips into the fountain, avoiding the striped insects that hovered just above the water.

"Careful," Owin said, a questioning expression on his face. "They sting."

She jerked her hand away. "He was tortured on Taln Perrin's order. I realize Haedera isn't a party to the Voirian Accord, but what Perrin's men did to him is far beyond what anyone would consider acceptable treatment, prisoner of war or not. I want names. And if those men are still on Asria, I want them gone. I would prefer they answer for their crimes on Haedera"—*or on Asria, though we all know that's not going to happen*—"but I'll settle for their deportation from my planet."

There. That hadn't been so bad.

"You realize the magnitude of what you're asking."

It was a warning, but she pushed on.

"I'm not asking for anyone's death. I may be asking for absolutely nothing—in fact, the soldiers in question could very well be back on Haedera already. If that's the case, you have nothing to lose by verifying their locations and status for me. And if by chance these names include other high-ranking officers, then I would leave their futures to your discretion."

Owin sank onto one of the low stone walls surrounding the fountain and considered the sand under his polished shoes. "I don't have as much sway over the Imperial Haederan Army as you probably imagine I do." He looked back up. "That's all you're asking?"

"That's it."

"Then I'll consider it."

It didn't sound like a yes. It didn't even sound like a maybe. Still, it wasn't a no, even from a Haederan. The wildest, most inappropriate idea sprung into her head. Dare she ask? Avery glanced around, but the courtyard was empty and silent except for the breeze scattering pebbles and the dunes singing in the distance.

Say it. Say it before you lose your nerve.

"Although—I hope you'll also consider the withdrawal of all Haederan troops from the Asrian surface."

Owin leaned back and crossed his arms, then burst into laughter.

"Gareth never told me you had such a sense of humor, my lady."

Avery steadied her feet—and her gaze. "I wasn't joking. We've done everything you've asked. You have a commercial group mining your verium outside Tarragona. I fought for months with the Commonwealth to have diplomatic relations approved. You've built your orbital surveillance station, and we've made no effort to fight its staffing."

Her voice wavered a bit at that. The surveillance station in question had been a sore point in Asrian-Haederan relations— such as they were—for months now, and she was in the middle of it. The Defense Forces hated having what amounted to an enemy base in orbit. The Imperial Haederan Navy had made it clear that the armistice allowed for "whatever surveillance they deemed necessary to protect Haederan troops and citizens planetside."

Worse, just two weeks before her interrupted coronation, Senator Roviro had blamed her publicly in an interstellar security committee meeting for the grip the Haederan Empire still had on Asria. It was only a long tea break with Baylen that had convinced her to stay in the senate building at all. She still hadn't attended the next committee meeting. Didn't Asria understand? Would they prefer all-out war? Some would, probably.

Get rid of the troops, and you'll get rid of that orbital base.

"Yes, you have done everything we've asked," Owin said. "And if you'd like peace to continue, you'll continue to oblige our demands and cease with absurd requests like the one you just proposed. The terms of the armistice can always be unilaterally renewed in a way you may not like—or annulled altogether."

The words were a jumble at first, then her face grew hot as their meaning coalesced; her knees began to shake.

Owin was just like the rest of them.

How easy it was to forget that, armistice or not, Asria was still controlled by the Haederan Empire. The new surveillance station she'd never rid her system of was proof of that. The two men waiting for her inside the small house might as well still be her jailers. Her position was a sham, a pretense at normalcy and sovereignty, her title just a few meaningless words strewn together in front of a name that held her hostage.

But that didn't matter. She would free Asria—for good—or die trying.

She opened her mouth, but before she could form any words, the yellow tree above her and Owin exploded into shards of clove-scented wood.

CHAPTER FOURTEEN

Avery flattened herself next to the wall on the cool stone patio. The bullet had missed Owin's shoulder by a hair, and her head by less than that. Another bullet whizzed by, embedding itself lower in the tree's trunk. Spice mixed with the unmistakable scent of a high-energy projectile weapon filled the courtyard. She suppressed a hysterical laugh as she crawled toward the front door, her clothing catching on the rock with each pace. Did the shooter know they'd almost taken out the leaders of two planetary systems?

Of course they knew.

Another shot flew past, but this one didn't hit anything nearby. She looked up as much as she was able. Yes, the front window was open. That last shot had come from inside. Before Avery had a chance to debate which of the three armed men in the house were shooting out toward the desert, the front door cracked open. It was Owin's plainclothes guard, his pistol raised. He pointed at her with his free hand and gestured toward the door.

He didn't have to tell her twice. With a deep breath and a prayer, she pushed herself to her feet and ran at him, still half crouched. He shoved her inside as soon as she came within grabbing distance, straight into Kern's arms. Where he and Owin disappeared to after that, she didn't see. Their own flyer, likely, where the rest of his guards waited.

"Get down," Kern hissed, pushing her to the floor. "Are you hurt?" She shook her head, but he ran his hands over her anyway. Apparently finding no blood mixed with the dirt on her clothing, he caught her by the elbow. "This way."

"Hold on." She dug her heels in as he tried to pull her up and toward the back of the house. "Where are we going?" Not back outside, that was for sure.

"Ferran is headed this way in the flyer." Kern pushed her into a small washroom, just far enough from the back door to escape again if the assailant came through it. "We're going to draw the shooter's attention from the side. You're going to hide back here until they get the emperor away in his aeroflyer, then we duck into ours once it gets here."

It sounded like as good of a plan as any.

"What about them?" She nodded toward wherever Viessa and Gweyr had hidden. The kitchen? A cellar? Surely not. Kern would have thrown her down the stairs if one existed.

"Once the two of you are out of here, they're safe. In addition, it seems Captain Linden's sister doesn't care one bit that she's not supposed to have that rifle she just pulled out. They'll fight to the end."

That didn't sound like as good of a plan, but there was no point in arguing with him. Not while shots still echoed outside. She wanted to cover her ears, but that was impossible in front of Kern. He wasn't even flinching—how was that possible?

"Don't they need you out there?" she asked.

Kern shot her a glare from his crouched position on the floor near the door. "Colonel Chase is handling it. I'm handling you."

How lucky.

Another crack echoed, closer that time. It had to be Chase now. Had to be. The initial shot hadn't come from anywhere close to the house, but the gunfire and unmistakable sounds of plasma weapons were getting louder by the second. If it wasn't Imperial

Security firing from Owin's flyers . . . well, the alternative wasn't good. How long could they hold off the attackers?

"It doesn't sound like they're handling it."

"That's the emperor's full security team circling back around from the air. But you're right—it sounds like more than one shooter, and they're going to be leaving in the next few seconds. Can't risk him, especially with snipers out there. Takes balls to hide with no cover."

Kern was right. The aeroflyer had dropped the three of them off in an empty field in front of Viessa's house, but outside of the lush courtyard, there wasn't anywhere to hide this far from a small village. Just empty desert for miles. Not even the dunes on the far side of Esro provided any protection.

"How do you know it's Owin's team firing?" *Kusir*, why had her voice just cracked?

Kern flinched at bit at her casual use of his sovereign's name, then recovered. "I know what Imperial Security weapons sound like." She hadn't heard arrogance like that in his voice since the night they'd carted an unconscious Victor out of the palace, though it was tempered with concern this time. "They train for this. Don't worry."

"I'm not—"

Four rhythmic knocks on the door cut her off. Kern stood, pistol raised at shoulder-level, but it was Chase who slid it open. He gave her scarcely a glance before nodding at Kern.

"Two of the team down outside. He's away. Our aeroflyer's three minutes out. Sit tight."

He darted off, leaving Kern to close them in again. He resumed his protective position in front of the door, and Avery wrapped her arms around her chest and stared at him.

Three minutes. How could three minutes seem so long?

"I'm sorry," she said to his back. The apology was out before she realized what she was saying. But Chase had done it, hadn't he? And his sins were greater than hers. If he could say the words and mean them, then so could she.

Kern turned away from the door for just a second. "For what?"

"For leaving you at Villiers." She blew out a deep breath. "For not checking on your paperwork and working to have you released sooner. I didn't realize how long the prisoner swaps would take, but that's no excuse. I owed you more than that, and I'm sorry that I didn't follow up. I knew how badly you wanted to get home, and I failed you."

"Politics takes a long time." He looked back at the door and shrugged. Was it her imagination, or had his breathing become irregular?

"It does. But I—I am politics on Asria, and I should have visited at the very least."

"Yes. You should have." The hum of Chase's personal aeroflyer in the distance interrupted him. "They're close."

He hadn't forgiven her. She'd wasted an apology on a man who would hold a grudge until his dying day. And how could she blame him? She stood as the engines spooled down for landing, desperate to escape the hostile atmosphere inside the small room. Kern motioned her next to him, then cracked open the door. Chase was down the hall by the exterior door, his pistol drawn.

"Twenty paces," he said to Kern, then turned to her. "Unfortunately, it's open desert out the back. No landscaped patio to hide in out there, but the front is pretty well covered by the shooters. They'll open the flyer door for you once you're out, but you've got to be fast. I'll cover you the best I can. Ready?"

"Yes. And you'll be behind me?" How welcome the formerly unwanted Imperial Security Command presence was now. In a million years, she'd never have imagined needing Chase close by.

"As close as we can."

Avery took a deep breath at his promise and stepped around him into the hallway.

"Hey." Kern cracked a smile as she passed. A real one, like she'd seen her first morning at Windhaven. "Apology accepted. But don't let it happen again."

She gave him a breathless laugh. "I promise I will never let you wither away in Defense Forces custody for almost a year ever again."

"I'm holding you to that." He gave her a gentle push toward Chase as she stood frozen next to him in the doorway. "Run fast."

Run fast. Right.

She stopped next to Chase as another shot sounded in the front of the house. That one sounded like whatever illegal weapon Viessa had been using.

"I'm not so sure about this," she told him.

By the look on his face, Chase wasn't, either.

"They didn't back off much when the emperor left. Either they're after you or they aren't taking any chances that a decoy boarded his flyer. We don't have a lot of time before they make their way closer to the house. We need to be gone, and soon."

"What about them?" She jerked her head toward the front of the house at Viessa and Gweyr.

"They won't leave. Viessa said the neighbors couldn't run her off when Rhys was declared a traitor and neither would a—well, I won't repeat what she called whoever's shooting at us."

"Colonel, you have to make them leave!" He and Kern couldn't possibly be thinking of leaving two women here alone. A hot flush spread across her face. Anger or fear, she couldn't tell. Was he mad?

"That's not my decision to make. I promised Viessa after Rhys died that her fate was her own. Dragging them out of here at gunpoint for any reason is exactly what they don't want." Chase cracked the door open, just enough to see his aeroflyer parked outside. Wynne's face was pressed up against the glass, shimmering in the heat. "Ready?"

She wanted to search the house and drag Viessa and Gweyr out with her, but she nodded and slipped out the door. The desert heat hit her face like the afterburners of a Dragonfly. But there didn't seem to be any shots from behind the house—not that she could hear anything through the rush of blood in her ears. The flyer glistened as she ran toward it, then Wynne opened the hatch.

Five paces.

Three paces.

Almost there.

A blast of cold air hit her face, tripping her. *Just the flyer. It's just air from the flyer.* Wynne reached down and grabbed her hands, and the next breath she took was from the cool steel floor.

"Stay down."

It was Wynne's voice and Merritt's hand on the back of her head as he crouched next to her, keeping her safe like he'd said he should have done from the very moment the Haederans had arrived on Asria. She stayed flat, even though all she wanted to do to was spring up and wrap her arms around him. Kern and Chase would be inside the flyer at any moment, and then they'd be off to Wind—

Another shot.

Merritt's hand pushed her cheek harder against the metal floor, and she flinched. There was only one reason he'd be that rough with her. That shot had hit the flyer. He swore out loud and released her, and her stomach dropped when she looked toward where he'd disappeared.

Kern had collapsed halfway between the flyer and the back door of Viessa's house; Merritt and Chase were darting toward him from opposite directions. Freed from Merritt's hold, she pushed herself up and crawled toward the flyer door, but Wynne grabbed her by the arm.

"Are you trying to get yourself killed?"

"Wynne, he's—"

The man on the roof stole her attention. How had he—oh, he'd climbed one of those beautiful spicy trees of Viessa's, the ones that were just the height of the flat-roofed building. He probably hadn't even broken a sweat scaling them to get up there. One of the Imperial Security Command men? No. Not dressed in those desert-colored fatigues like he was. He aimed his rifle at Kern again just as Merritt crashed to the ground next to him.

She didn't think, couldn't tear herself away from Wynne's

grip, just screamed Merritt's name and pointed. He whirled around toward the house, pistol in hand, still on the ground next to Kern. She knew that look. Determination. Resolve. Even the light armor the gunman wore over those chilling fatigues couldn't protect him. He dropped off the roof from Merritt's single shot like he'd been hit by lightning.

Wynne pulled her back toward the interior of the flyer as the desert became silent again. Avery collapsed on the rear seat, unable to tear her eyes away from Kern. Chase looked like he'd dived to the ground to protect him from the second shot, but Kern wasn't moving. He'd just been speaking with her, had just been joking with her, had just forgiven her for treating him so poorly . . .

Merritt pulled himself to his feet, apparently uninjured, and said something to Chase. Then—then something to Kern?

Tears sprang to her eyes for the first time since the ordeal had begun. Why was Merritt bothering? Kern was dead. She ignored Wynne's disapproving stare and leaned forward toward the open hatch, ready to yell for Merritt to pick up his body and run. They could mourn later.

But no. Kern had rolled over on his side and was nodding at Merritt.

"They need to hurry," Wynne said under her breath.

As if he'd heard her, Merritt yanked Kern up and toward the flyer. With Chase behind them, running backward, his eyes swiveling from roof to desert, it was less than five seconds until he threw Kern's limp body in and climbed inside.

Chase slammed the door shut behind them. "Go!"

The pilot didn't hesitate at his order. They lifted off and tilted immediately into a bank away from the house. Merritt reached to help her strap in, and Avery shook her head.

"How is he?"

"I'm hurt." Kern opened his eyes and tried to laugh. "It's only a scrape. Just one that surprised me more than it should have."

"More than a scrape." Wynne cut his sleeve away with a pair

of scissors from the med kit, then pulled away the burned fabric and grimaced, her face pale. "That's almost all the way to the bone."

"Better my arm than my head."

"So?" Merritt asked as Wynne cleaned Kern's wound. The scent of burned flesh slowly turned to something more medicinal as she worked. "Who were the unwelcome guests? And how did they know she would be there?"

"Wish I knew." Chase shrugged. "I suppose we'll find out in a few hours. I'm going to have to call in some reinforcements, though."

Reinforcements? More Imperial Security troops at Windhaven? Would she see them this time? Of all the horrors, Chase might even decide to station some inside the guest house now. Avery clutched Merritt's hand, certain the blood had drained from her face. The uniforms, the nightmares . . .

Chase's lips thinned as she began to shake. He'd always been able to read her too well. There was no hiding her fear from him, even as she shifted against Merritt to control the trembling. His body felt safe, yes, but the imagined visions of Chase's men yanking her from a cell didn't disappear, even as she tried to blink them away.

"You won't see them. I swear to you, my lady, you will not see them, even if I have to put them on the roof," he added, unlike Kern's not-promise when she'd first arrived. "But I'm sorry. I know this will dredge up more disagreeable memories, and I hate to do it, but the most important reinforcement . . . well, this evening may be a little unpleasant for you."

Just this evening? Had he already forgotten what'd just happened to them? She glanced from Merritt to Wynne to Kern, but Merritt and Wynne only looked confused. Kern looked confused as well, and then, after a few exchanged glances with Chase, sheepish. Something was up. Her stomach twisted, and that time it had nothing to do with the aeroflyer's turns.

"Unpleasant how?"

CHAPTER FIFTEEN

AVERY DECLINED A GLASS SIX TIMES BEFORE ACCEPTING, BUT whatever ancient wine Chase had pulled from the cellar at Windhaven had worked its magic, and after four sips, she stopped shaking. Not even the long ride back to the estate, nor a hot bath, nor Merritt's attentions had accomplished the same. Near death was becoming harder and harder to recover from.

But at least she wasn't in Kern's position. He sat in a chair in the corner of the vaulted library, the color back in his face but thick bandages showing through his loose, open-necked shirt. That meant energy weapons, for if dermtape hadn't healed him in the past few hours, things were bad indeed. She flinched at the idea of the open burn wound as Chase poured a second drink and set it on the table next to her.

"When you're ready for another," he said.

She waved him and his liquor off. The last thing she needed was to succumb to whatever was in that bottle. Not with Callum Lient on the way. No, she needed to be wide awake and fully functional when the head of the Imperial Security Command arrived with whatever new intelligence he had.

Lient.

The name filled her head. On second thought, maybe her

shaking wasn't only from the recent assassination attempt. Because even she knew him. Or of him, to be accurate. Not only was Lient the head of Imperial Security, but he was the right hand of the emperor himself. Devan, Owin, whoever came next—it didn't matter. Emperors came and went, their names barely known.

But Lient was different. Imperial Security was different, and even though some of her early fear had faded out of proximal necessity, it rushed right back as a servant escorted him into the library. She tried to stand, but Merritt gracefully pushed her back to her seat.

Right. You don't stand. In Cadena, in her office, she greeted diplomats and maintenance personnel alike with a handshake, but Merritt was right—here, on Haedera, the Haederan Empire needed every reminder that they were to respect her and her role as queen of Asria.

Lient gave her a formal bow as he entered, completely out of place with the events earlier in the day and her own tenuous status on Haedera.

"I'm so happy to meet you, Your Majesty," he said with a tight smile. "I wish it was under better circumstances, but it seems Gareth has his secrets."

Avery smiled at him and his Owin-like comment. It was the best greeting she could manage to give this slight man, even though he was nothing like she'd expected. Like Chase and Kern, he wore no uniform. He stood only as tall as Merritt's chin, perhaps, with soft brown eyes and the even skin tone of the Haederan lower classes. How then had he risen to such a position? It seemed uncouth to ask Chase, but maybe after another glass of wine and Lient's departure she'd be curious enough to risk it.

"It's no exaggeration," Chase broke in. "He really is happy about it. He's been talking about meeting you ever since I did." He took a sip of his own drink, though unlike hers, it wasn't his first and it was something decidedly stronger than wine. "And he's even happier that he's meeting you at Windhaven—where he can borrow from my library—and not in a prison cell, which is where he wanted to send you three years ago. Even before that stunt Major Hadley pulled with you in Cadena. He'd planned on a good long stay for you, I might add. You'd probably still be there."

Her mouth dropped open.

"Really, my lord." Lient sighed as he accepted a glass of wine from Kern. No Windhaven servants attended the meeting, though whether that was because of the secrecy or their understandable fear of Lient was hard to say. "The past is the past, and you don't need to keep dredging it up, especially in front of her. Isn't that so, my lady?"

She stifled the urge to reach a hand toward Merritt. The past was never the past, especially here at Windhaven.

"I—then I'm happy for the same. And happy to meet you as well, General."

Chase had the decency to look penitent about his comment as he waved them to the cluster of chairs in front of the empty fireplace. She could hear Wynne pacing in front of the main door— the only anxiety she'd ever show in front of strangers. Merritt slid his hand over hers as he sat, and she wound her fingers through his, her breathing slowing. She'd survived introductions, the worst part. It would be easy from here on out.

"Owin is unharmed?" she asked.

Chase hadn't sounded certain when she'd asked him the same thing hours earlier. And Owin's guards had seemed competent, but—on the other hand, if anything serious had happened, Lient would still be in Rebet.

"He is," Lient said. "Though I think he's beginning to realize just how serious this business is." He kicked back in the deep leather chair Avery hadn't chosen for fear of falling into it and turned toward Chase again. "You and Major Kern racked up quite the body count this afternoon, my lord. Three already dead when reinforcements arrived. Two more died before we could transfer them out of there."

She didn't ask if they'd been helped along toward death. But, no, dead men couldn't talk, and the Imperial Security Command would want them talking. It was the survivors who were the unlucky ones today.

Chase's contrite look drained from his face, only to be replaced by his usual arrogance.

"Did you or did you not want His Imperial Majesty walking out of that house alive, sir?"

"Cut it, Gareth. He shouldn't have been out there in the first place."

"His decision." Chase waved his hand as if Owin had decided to visit Esro all on his own.

"Yes." Lient stared him down. "I'm certain that no one in my organization would have put the idea in his head."

"He's an adult, sir." Chase took another sip of liquor.

"An adult whose safety you—and I, I might add—are responsible for. Sometimes I think you forget your oaths, Colonel. Do you think I want to lose two of them in a year? I don't know about you, but I'd like to keep my head."

"If His Majesty is dead, your head is safe by definition, sir."

Avery's mouth dropped open for the second time in five minutes. Was nothing sacred to him? Merritt raised his eyebrows at her, and she shook her head. There was no chance of explaining Chase to someone who hadn't figured it out on their own. He was simply Chase, and one just had to accept his impertinence. Or not.

Lient curled his lip and turned his stare toward Kern, apparently having given up on Chase.

"And you? What do you have to say for yourself?"

"Nothing, sir." Kern shifted uncomfortably, and it didn't look like it was because of his arm. His gaze darted toward the door and freedom, but he swallowed and added, "It was a mistake. It won't happen again, sir."

"Hmm. Make sure that it doesn't, Major." Lient shot Chase one last glare, then focused on Avery and rattled off a few Haederan names. "They've been on the radar ever since His Majesty's ascension and the withdrawal from the Commonwealth planets. They're not too happy with you either, my lady. The overly lenient, inexperienced emperor and—I'm sorry, my lady—the despised queen of Asria in one small, unguarded building? Perfect opportunity."

"They knew I was here?" A chill ran down her spine. "How?"

Lient spread his hands. "We suspect they simply recognized you once they trailed the emperor to Esro. But now your presence here won't be a secret for long. Whoever has the money will know you're on Haedera. Including"—he shot Chase another look—"Quen Rendon."

"How long do we have?" Merritt asked.

"A few days, perhaps, though I would expect Windhaven is safe enough for now," Lient said. "But if there are no objections, my lady, we should consider moving you somewhere else."

"Like where?"

"The imperial palace is out of the question after this attack. There are some garrisons, or perhaps we can find a suitable safe house."

"I don't want Lucas seeing the inside of an Imperial Security Command garrison." Merritt's hand grew heavy over hers. They didn't know it was really her that couldn't see the inside of one, would they?

"It may be your only choice," Chase said. "You've survived it before."

He was wrong. At Tarragona, yes, she'd survived, but just barely. It wasn't an experience she cared to relive, and that garrison had been an Imperial Haederan Army one—the only uniforms there that had struck her with dread had been Chase's and Kern's. Still, Avery favored him with a small nod. She would figure it out if it came down to it. Protecting Lucas came first, even if she had to curl up and cry for a week straight.

"Then Gareth will find a few suitable places for you to pick from. Now, if you'll excuse me—my lady, Colonel Rendon—there are some things I need to discuss with him in private."

"Nothing's private around the queen, sir." Chase tossed back the rest of his glass. "She eavesdrops."

Lient sighed.

Chase didn't blink, didn't argue again, simply motioned him toward a door on the far side of the fireplace. His private office, it appeared. The two disappeared through the door, and Kern blew out a deep breath.

"I'll see you both in the morning," he said. "It appears I have some research to do for Colonel Chase."

Avery leaned back in her chair as he shut the library door behind him.

"So? What do you think?"

Merritt shrugged. "I think Windhaven is pretty remote. And I don't like his idea of hiding you in an Imperial Security garrison. Physical safety doesn't mean much if . . ."

"If what?"

"You know." *If you have a nervous breakdown* was what he meant. He plucked her second glass of untouched wine from the table between them, took a sip, and frowned. "This is terrible."

"He's got gin on the bar, I think."

"That sounds much better." Merritt pushed himself up and began to dig through the bottles on the lower shelf, then froze.

"What's wrong?" she asked.

Two ice cubes clinked into a glass.

"You can hear them, can't you?"

"Not a thing, actually." He popped the lid off a crystal bottle and focused, too intently, on pouring the straw-colored liquor. "Thick door."

"Mer!" She darted at him, but he stepped in front of her. "You're a terrible liar."

"And you're a terrible eavesdropper." He pushed her a few paces away. "He all but told Lient you were going to do it."

"And Lient didn't believe him," she whispered, hand on his chest. "Let me at the door."

"Avery!"

"Admit you're just as curious as I am."

Merritt rolled his eyes.

"Admit it."

"Fine. I'm just as curious as you are—only I know better."

"Well, I know better, too, only I don't care."

He heaved a sighed and stepped to the side. "I hope you don't regret this."

Avery favored him with a look. "Silence."

Merritt stalked back to his chair and flopped into it with his drink, only to stare at her with raised eyebrows. She took a breath and pressed her ear to the door.

"—know I'm not interested in that anymore, sir. You know I've never been interested in it. I don't care what he says. We're going to rue the day we ever came into contact with the stuff, and you know it." Chase sounded unreasonably irritated.

"You've had plenty of time to come to your senses. What's gotten into you, Gareth? What really happened on *Terigon*?"

A familiar chuckle. "Are you afraid the Commonwealth tortured me, sir? That I talked?"

"I'm afraid something happened that made you lose your nerve, even if it was only coming that close to landing in prison. We need your skills. We need your knowledge. Without you . . ."

"I'm no scientist. Or doctor. Or pharmacist or anything else. Someone else can take my place—they've been doing it for the past few years while I've been on Asria, haven't they?"

"That's another thing." Lient's voice grew dark. "How did you talk the ambassador into that position?"

"He requested me. Knew I knew Asria better than most."

Silence. Lient was probably sighing. "Look, I'm not going to order you to do this," he said after a moment.

"Unless I force you into it, isn't that right, sir?"

"You have an obligation to the empire."

"Not if I retire."

Lient uttered a few soft curse words. "Your service ends with your death, in case you've forgotten. Not when you decide it's no longer worth your while."

Her heart skipped.

"Is there something I can help you with?"

Kusir. She jerked away from the door at Kern's voice. He was leaning against the library door, his forgotten tablet hanging from his hand, arms crossed, an amused look on his face. The amusement had to be feigned.

"I was just—"

"—listening?" he asked. He glanced at Merritt, who was sprawled in his chair, shaking his head, his empty glass dangling from his hand.

"I was looking for more ice."

"You could have asked, my lady." In a few steps, he reached the bar and dumped a few cubes into a clean glass. "I wouldn't want you sitting here without a drink. Someone might wonder what you were doing so close to the door. Someone not as accommodating as I."

She stumbled back to the chair next to Merritt with her glass of ice, her legs shaking. *Kern had come to her rescue?* Before she could ask why, the office door swung open and Chase stormed out. He didn't give her or Kern a second look before slamming the library door shut behind him. Lient followed, eyes on his feet, though he shot her a quick nod as he passed. Kern darted to open the door for him, then resumed his cross-armed position against it.

"So? Did you hear anything interesting?" he asked.

She swiped a finger around the cut crystal. "If I did, I wouldn't tell you."

Kern recoiled a bit. "You really don't like accepting help, do you?"

Was it possible he had no idea what was going on in there? Wouldn't Kern know everything that was happening at Windhaven? Maybe—but maybe not when Lient was involved.

"I don't like people hiding things from me," she said. "Especially when my child's safety is at stake."

"Those two have nothing to do with your security. They only like to pretend they do." He cocked his head. "What did you hear in there?"

Her chest tightened again.

He's curious. He's just curious, like he's always been.

"She didn't hear anything." Merritt lifted the hand that wasn't clinging to the now-sweating glass, and somehow, her body followed. "Let's go, Avery."

She opened her mouth to argue, then shut it. What would be the point? Merritt could feel her terror, knew when a flashback was coming on. If she hurried, if she swallowed her pride and let him lead her back to the guest house, they might be fast enough that she could fall apart in private. The tears would hold off for that long, wouldn't they? As long as they ran, as long as she clutched Merritt's arm—

Merritt jerked her to a stop, and she looked up to see Kern's arm across the door.

"I wouldn't eavesdrop like that again if I were you, my lady," he said. "Especially on Haedera."

Merritt shoved him aside.

"And I wouldn't threaten her like that again if I were you, Major. Especially in front of me. Excuse us."

CHAPTER SIXTEEN

KERN HAD BEEN RIGHT ABOUT ONE THING—THE SUNSETS AT Windhaven were one of the most stunning things she'd ever seen. Magical, even. Clouds were building in the distance, clouds that spoke only of a small break from the heat instead of rain, and they shattered the normally solid orange into brilliant streaks of red and gold. It was unlike anything she'd seen on a dozen planets. This foreign, terrifying place was lovely—a realization almost impossible to wrap her mind around.

"It's beautiful, isn't it?" Chase hopped down the last small drop behind her and sank to the ground a respectful distance away.

Avery took a long sip of water and smiled at him. It was just like Chase to ignore the prior evening's events like nothing had happened. If he was here, speaking to her like he was, that meant Kern hadn't said a word to him about her activities—she was safe. And if she could smile at him like she had, that meant she'd survive an entire conversation without panicking. Yes, life was looking up.

"It's like fire," she said. "I wish Merritt could see it."

He laughed. "Before you leave, I hope he's able to pry himself away from work and explore like you've been able to."

"One of us needs to be productive while you've got us stashed here." She looked away. Her concern about Merritt's strange actions with the tablet was probably written across her face, and Chase could read everything about her. He'd never let up until he found out a truth she didn't know. "What about you? Have they not allowed you back to work?"

"We all need time off once in a while. I told them I was technically on a leave of absence from the embassy." He licked his lips, his eyes dark in the shade of the mountain. "I'll tell you . . . I need the break. The same problems will be waiting when I return. They always are."

With the sun as high as it was, the night air hadn't chilled at all, but she shivered anyway. No matter how kind he was to her, thinking of Chase's professional problems would always have that effect. There wasn't any way around it.

"Speaking of that, Brennin found a place for you. It's a garrison outside of Laegih, and it'll be safe. There's no family housing there, but I didn't want to take you somewhere that had it—it would be the first place Quen will look for you. The crew quarters there aren't comfortable, but it's temporary," he added hastily. "Don't forget it's temporary."

"I know. And you know I don't need comfort." Temporary or not, her hands shook at the thought. Chase knew all too well what kind of austerity she could survive. *Had survived.* "I appreciate everything you've done for us."

"You're welcome. I'm happy to do it." His attention turned to the darkness of the desert. "I'm afraid," he said abruptly. "I don't think I've ever said those words before."

Chase, afraid?

"Of what?"

"That Owin won't be able to hold on to power. There are already mutterings within Imperial Security about his lack of ambition as far as the rest of the quadrant goes. In the army, the doubts are even more open, no matter how we try to quash them. Maybe we weren't ready for this new era." He looked back at her and swallowed. "I'm afraid this peace won't last. Just like his rule began, everything could change in a heartbeat—or the end of one. I pray every day that I'm wrong, but sometimes I feel we're all living on borrowed time. What happened in Esro is a symptom of a larger problem."

His predictions were chilling. She'd hoped the attack on the Linden house had been an isolated incident.

"Is there any reason Owin can't hang on?" she asked. He'd expressed that same fear to her a million years ago, though, in a muddy field outside Cadena. *That kind of leniency would be too much of a risk to my life.*

"He's too kind—you know that. Benevolence isn't looked fondly upon here. You know the story of how humanity came to Haedera?"

Avery shook her head.

He leaned back against a rock and studied her. "How much do you like mythology?" He laughed at her expression. "Some say the Holy One blinked us into being right on the planet as a sign that we were His chosen people—though why a deity who had the entire universe and then some to choose from would have chosen Haedera is beyond me."

He shot her a grin, a real one with a touch of self-deprecation.

"But you didn't hear me say that out loud. The real story is much simpler. You know of the old interstellar arks, of course. A group of colonists meant to try for Clellau, but there was a revolt aboard one of the ships. The records aren't clear—something about work schedules and food rationing. It was quashed as they approached what we now call Haedera V, but the damage had been done. Weapons fire had almost destroyed the engineering section, and there was no way they'd make it to Clellau any longer. Instead of leaving them to perish in space, the captain of the colonial fleet decided to cut the trip short and settle in this system instead. I like to think it was a small act of mercy that gave us our only hope of salvation."

She shifted on the hard ground. To think of the promise of Cleplaum . . . A paradise compared to Haedera.

"But, it seems, mercy is the last thing we're taught now, the last thing we value, the last thing we'll ever care about. They tolerate Owin for the time being, but he's too merciful. Haederans, in general, want justice. They don't care how it happens. Perhaps we're still bitter that it was mercy that led us to this system."

"Mercy is never wrong." Owin was the last person she'd call merciful after their earlier conversation, but the tiniest voice suggested Chase wasn't talking about his emperor any longer. She brushed her hair out of her eyes. The wind was picking up, and it scattered a small vortex of sand in front of her. "Nor is . . . nor is forgiveness."

Even in the glowing shadows, she could see his eyes light up.

"You didn't need to say it," he said. "You don't even need to think it if you're not there yet. I certainly don't deserve it."

"You may not, but I'm hardly innocent. What right do I have to withhold forgiveness from you? The Holy One forgave my doubts over His very existence. Surely I can forgive you for things you've tried to make amends for. You've suffered enough without me holding onto this hate." Her voice broke. "It's time for me to move on. It's time for our people to move on. And I'm trying the best I can."

"I know you are. And you're doing an amazing job of it—not that I'm surprised. I only wish you'd believe in your own strength."

In the dark on the hill above them, there was a quiet cough. Chase blew out a breath and pushed himself to his feet. "That would be Brennin. I'm going to walk the perimeter with him. You should get inside. *Okaucros*, you know."

"I will. Just a few more minutes." She looked around for the doglike animals and laughed. "And I'm not worried about the *okaucros*. There're plenty of rocks to throw at them if they decide to get brave."

Chase stared at her for a moment like he couldn't decide if she was joking or not, then returned a chuckle. "I'd say you're adapting to Haedera much faster than I ever thought you would."

He waved over his shoulder as he left, and she closed her eyes as the sound of sand crunching under his shoes became quieter and finally disappeared. She needed to get back up to the guest house, to Merritt and Lucas, to a long bath to wash the dust off herself, but this—maybe this was what real peace was. A quiet evening, a diamond sky turned vermilion, and the feeling of tranquility and stillness that could only come when one had just done something right. Chase would sleep well tonight, probably for the first time in years, certainly since he'd met her, and perhaps she would, too. Why rush the feeling away?

Footsteps and the sound of loose rocks echoed on the hill below her and she traced an idle design in the sand. The noise was in the opposite direction from the main house, but maybe Merritt had finally pried himself away from his reports and gone for a walk. She sighed inwardly. The sun was behind the mountains now, leaving only a blank sky studded with high-altitude clouds. He'd missed the best part. They were always missing the best parts.

She craned her neck for a better look. "Merritt? Is that you?"

There was no answer from the dark figure that crested the hill a dozen paces away.

"Colonel?" It had to be Chase, circling back around on whatever search he was doing with Kern. "Gareth?" she tried. That would elicit a laugh, at least. Anything to dispel the shiver that had started at her toes and was working its way upward. "Who's here?"

There was no answer. No answer except the wind whistling through the desert and across the mountains, a small animal scampering somewhere in the underbrush, a larger animal howling off in the distance, quiet voices drifting down from the estate, and—

"Hi, Avery."

She scrambled to her feet at the unfamiliar voice, pebbles scattering under her shoes as the dim figure came closer. Her pulse began to race, and she took a deep breath. It was nothing. She was safe.

"Who is it?" she called.

An Imperial Security Command guard, it had to be. One Kern had promised she'd never see. But *Avery*? An unfamiliar Haederan wouldn't call her Avery. Not even Chase had ever called her Avery after her initial invitation. No one on this planet except Merritt called her Avery, and this was not Merritt.

Why hadn't she gone up to the house with Chase?

"You don't recognize your own brother? I'm hurt." There was a pause, then the sound of rocks shifting as the figure walked toward her. "Hurt but not surprised, I suppose."

"Quen," she breathed, a sickening feeling wrapping around her heart.

"Quen," he agreed, stepping onto the little ledge where just minutes ago she'd been as safe as she ever thought possible. Her estranged brother, standing right there in front of her.

His skin had tanned—but then, it had been years since she'd last seen him. Who knew what he'd experienced since then? His hair, dark like hers when he'd been a teenager, was streaked with gray, and his eyes were lined, like he'd spent the years away from Asria squinting and frowning. He wiped sweat from the back of his neck and grinned at her, though it wasn't friendly. Just cold— the coldest thing in the desert next to the pistol in his hand.

"I'm surprised you remember my name, Avery. Or am I supposed to bow down, kiss some ring, and call you Your Majesty?"

She ignored his insult, her mouth dry and her tongue mysteriously coppery. "What are you doing here?"

"You know what I'm doing here." He stopped a few paces away and gestured at her with his gun, his emerald Rendon eyes as dark as the mountains behind him. "Raise your hands."

The sickening feeling turned into a squeeze, cutting off her breath, but she did what he ordered. Quen relieved her of the small knife in her pocket and laughed as he ran a leathered finger down the blade.

"One knife, Avery? I thought Drex would have taught personal security better than that." He narrowed his eyes. "Maybe deep down he realized you'd eventually betray him, too. Maybe he always knew you weren't worth his allegiance."

There was no way to hide the tears that tried to appear at the mention of Drex. "It's for the *okaucros*." How she wanted to plunge it into his leg and dart up the hill.

Quen grinned again, then pulled a pair of night vision goggles out of his black tactical vest and strapped them on. "Well," he said. "Sounds like your Haederan friends didn't give you enough of a briefing on the local area. Lots of other dangerous things out here." He pointed out into the darkening desert with his pistol. "This way."

"No. I want to talk to you, Quen. I've wanted to talk to you for years." She couldn't help how high pitched her voice had become.

"Oh, we'll talk first. We're just going to do it a little farther out in the desert."

"I'm not going anywhere with you. You can kill me right here." They'd find her body then, at least. And the longer she kept him from taking her somewhere else, the greater the chance that Chase or Merritt would realize something was wrong.

Quen's lips twisted into something more like a sneer than a smile. "You think I'm by myself? You'll come with me now, or my darling nephew dies, too." He shrugged. "Such a tragedy—I think he would've had gray eyes like his daddy."

Avery sucked in a breath. Lucas had to be safe. Merritt was with him. Chase had gone back up there. Kern had to be there now, too. Dozens of Imperial Security officers roamed Windhaven. Maybe more. Kern hadn't told her exactly how secure the place was.

Yes, Lucas had to be safe.

But what if he wasn't?

She raised her hands into the air again, this time in appeal. "Fine."

* * *

The underbrush cut against her bare ankles as Quen pushed her along, quickening their pace every minute. It was becoming harder and harder to keep steady, to keep herself from the downy cactuses that were thickening with every step. Avery steadied herself the best she could—if she fell into one of those, she'd be covered in spines that would take forever to remove. As if she had forever. As if cactus spines were her biggest worry. No, that pistol at her back deserved that honor.

Quen grabbed her arm and pulled her to a stop, then gestured toward a small wooden building that she'd have probably walked right by in the darkness.

"Straight ahead."

"What is it?"

"You're going to use the time you have left on inane questions? You haven't changed a bit. How would I know what these people have out here in the middle of nowhere?" He pushed her inside, against the far wall, then backed up to light a small lantern on the floor before yanking his goggles off.

She blinked in the dim light. The lantern wasn't bright enough to alert anyone over the hills and at the main house of her predicament, even between the missing slats that had once made up the walls of the building. It looked like the shack had been a spring house, back when wells had been needed at Windhaven. The circle in the center of the floor, paved over now, gave it away. She wished there was still a hole, one she could jump into and escape this nightmare.

"So." Quen lowered himself to the floor against the door and propped the pistol on his knee, leveling it at her chest. "It's been a long time."

"It has." She leaned against the wall so he couldn't see her shake. "Where have you been?"

He cocked his head. "Here and there. But where I've been isn't that interesting. I want to talk about what you've been up to first."

You mean like fighting a war, being tortured, and running our home planet because you *couldn't be bothered?* That probably wasn't what Quen meant.

"What I've been up to? Like what?"

"Like how you've suddenly become so very friendly with the Haederans." He shook his head. "The Haederan Empire, Avery. The murderous, imperialist bastards. Why?"

"I get the feeling you aren't going to give me time for the whole story."

He waved the pistol. "Go ahead. Start. I'll let you know if I get bored."

What did he want to hear? The truth? Or his twisted idea of the truth, warped beyond recognition? There was no way to know which version would placate him until Merritt or Chase found her.

"Fine." She took a breath. "Then I'll start with this. I didn't want that war. I didn't want to be queen. I was happy enough with Father—I was happy enough with Uncle Victor as king and you as prince-elect. You know me, Quen. I don't want power. I don't want fame. But things don't always work out the way we want."

"Don't I know it."

She ignored his commentary. "Yes, Mother and Father were murdered. I want those who did it to pay. But there are other things now—"

"Things more important than avenging their deaths?"

"Revenge is not ours to give." Quen knew that. Drex had warned them both as children.

He actually snickered at that. "Don't tell me you've suddenly discovered your long-lost faith."

If he kept this up, she was going to slap the sneer off his face.

But underneath her annoyance was fear—this was Quen, and he knew her. Knew her weaknesses. As if a mother's weakness was a secret.

"So what if I have?" she asked. "What does it matter to you?"

He shrugged. "It doesn't. Just proves how much you've changed."

"Not nearly as much as you." Was that even the truth? She sank to the ground and watched him, unable to stand any longer. "Please. Tell me what's happened to you."

"All right." Quen leaned against the door and steadied the pistol. "It started in Sabino," he said. "A friend told me he'd pay double if I provided him with a few cases of wine for off-world use. It was easy enough to sneak them off the estate and hand them over to him at a shuttleport. The money was nice but knowing I'd slipped right by Drex and his people unnoticed was even better. Eventually he offered me a position on his ship, so I left."

"To smuggle."

He pointed a cheeky finger her way. "To learn how I could best outsmart a society that had given up on me. To find my family."

He might as well have slapped her across the cheek. "No one gave up on you, Quen. Never. Father cried when you disappeared. Did you know that? I caught him one night just after you left, and he made up some excuse about losing a crop. I believed him for a long time, and I hated him for it. And then I found out we hadn't lost anything that year. It'd been our best yet."

"You're lying."

"I'm not. Even after everything, the senate still wanted you as prince-elect, Mother cried over you, and Father and the king . . . they never gave up looking for you. Not until the Haederans came." Too late, she saw the change in his demeanor. Mentioning the Haederans had been a bad idea.

"And the Haederan embassy in Cadena?" he asked.

"It was part of the agreement, Quen. It had to be done, as much as I disliked it. They didn't give me a choice."

"You always had a choice, Your Majesty. You were the one who ended that war."

"People were dying!" She leapt to her feet, forgetting the gun. "I couldn't continue that fight. I couldn't let our people suffer through that any longer, and don't tell me you wouldn't have done the same if you were in my position. You don't know what it was like."

Quen hadn't seen executions up close like she had, after all. He hadn't seen Jon Gavni, practically a child, fall to the floor, dead. He probably hadn't even seen their parents' grave.

"Father would have rather died than make a deal with them. It seems he did." His eyes narrowed, and the pistol stabilized. "So what's going on, Avery? Are you screwing the Haederan emperor? What about that Imperial Security officer who seems so fond of you?"

"Am I what?" He couldn't be serious. Of all the accusations he could have made—

"You heard me."

"I won't even dignify that with an answer. You know me better than that."

"Do I? You're a traitor, Your Majesty. I don't know who you are anymore."

"Takes one to know one, Quen."

"Enough." He waved the pistol. "I'm done here."

"You haven't answered all my questions. You said you'd answer them first!"

"I changed my mind. Turn around."

"Quen." She hated the way her voice shook. "You don't want to do this."

"Do it or I'll kill the rest of them, too."

He wasn't lying, that much was clear from his tone. She spun toward the back wall as slowly as she could. Merritt would come. He knew she hated being alone. He'd notice she was missing, and he'd tell Chase, and Chase would tell him they'd been talking out in the desert and that she hadn't returned, and they would find her. They had to.

"On your knees."

She sank to her knees, the rough stone scraping her skin through a rip in her pants. Quen's footsteps and breathing grew closer, and she trembled.

"Quen—"

No. She wouldn't plead. She wouldn't give him the satisfaction. Ever.

"You want to beg, Avery? It's not going to change my mind, you know, but I've dreamed of hearing you do it for over two years now. Go ahead. Ask me. Ask me to spare you. Ask me to spare Parker. Ask me to spare that Imperial Security officer who harbored you. Ask me to spare—" The pistol pushed against the back of her head, hard, and she flinched. "—Lucas."

"Leave him alone," she whispered.

"I don't think I will." He pushed her head lower with the pistol. "Anything you want to say? Maybe I'll feel like telling my darling nephew what your last words were when I go to see him."

She thought of shaking her head, but she was done with Quen.

Holy One, protect Lucas and Merritt.

Quen took a breath.

Forgive me.

A soft whir behind her. It was such a quiet and strangely slow sound for something so loud and quick in the end. She sucked in a breath.

One last breath.

The pop behind her was deafening, so loud they must have heard it at the estate, and she fell forward, her head slamming against the concrete with her full weight.

Pain.

That was all there was.

CHAPTER SEVENTEEN

PAIN.

Pain and dizziness and an intense white light. Her chest wouldn't expand; her body wouldn't obey her commands any longer.

This was death.

Why was death so painful? It shouldn't be painful. If she wasn't with the Holy One now, she should be in some black void, awaiting His judgment. She managed to draw in another breath, though the movement felt like a mockery of her situation.

Another breath?

It took most of her strength to lift her head and the rest to push the weight off her body. Her forehead ached, yes, but when she brought her hand away, there was only the slightest amount of blood. Like a—could it be a scrape? Quen's pistol had been pushed against her hair, and there was no way he could have missed. She blinked and rolled onto her side, afraid to move further. If she wasn't already dead, then moving could be deadly. He had shot her somewhere, that was certain, and she needed to make sure she wouldn't bleed—

Avery gasped as the dizzying white light faded into lantern-lit dimness. Quen lay next to her where she'd pushed his body, face up. His eyes were open, and a pool of blood was spreading under the back of his head. She sprang away from him, away from the blood, away from his pistol, which lay harmless on the ground.

Had she—*but how?*

A shadow moved outside, just visible through one of the missing slats in the wall of the spring house. Without thinking, she swiped the pistol and bounded to her feet, trying to hold it steady. It was a lost battle. Her eyes shifted painfully between the darkness and Quen's body, then the door swung open.

Chase.

He didn't lower his pistol, but there was relief in his eyes as he skirted around her and placed his fingers on Quen's neck. His shoulders sank, then he shoved his gun into the holster under his shirt and pressed his eyes closed with a hand.

Her head throbbed as she watched him, and before she could make her mouth move, something inside her heart snapped. Chase was *reassured*. He was happy she was alive and Quen was dead, and he wasn't allowed to be relieved over more violence. Quen was lying there dead, her brother who she'd always loved in spite of everything—in spite of his childish practical jokes and his abandonment of his own family and the pain he'd caused her parents and the deaths he was responsible for on Asria and on Iythea and the threats he'd just made toward Lucas.

"You." She glanced back at Quen—what had once been Quen —the overdue tears spilling over. They turned the lantern light into a flickering haze of pain. "He's dead. You killed him. You killed him." Other accusations, threats, and pleas rushed through her mind, but it was all she could say over and over again.

"I kept him from killing you." Chase's voice was calm. Too calm. Like he didn't understand what he'd just done.

"No." Quen's pistol shook as she stepped toward him. So did her legs. Both so heavy. "He wouldn't have. He wouldn't have done it. He was only trying to scare me. He was only trying to get me to change my mind about Haedera, about you, about Owin. He wanted to make sure I was still loyal to Asria. To our people.

He needed to be certain I hadn't changed my loyalties. That was all."

She was only a pace away now. Chase wasn't wearing armor, just the shirt he'd been wearing earlier. He had no chance of survival at this distance. He would pay for what he'd done. She'd thought what he'd done to her had been bad enough, but this was worse. Now he'd taken everything. Everyone. Down to the last person. She could already see blood soaking the gauzy white fabric of his shirt, if she could only move her finger. She could smell the metallic tang in the air. Chase's blood would mix with Quen's, right there on the ground, and it would be no more than he deserved.

"Avery. Put it down. Just drop it right there on the floor." Chase hadn't moved, was simply standing frozen inside the doorway, his hands out from his sides.

"Don't." She inhaled sharply as she closed the distance between them in less than a heartbeat, her finger wavering on the trigger as she pressed the gun against his chest. "Do not call me that. You have destroyed the last bit of my life. I won't let you destroy anything else. I won't let you destroy anyone else."

He looked down at her, almost expressionless, then away, toward the slats that made up what passed for walls.

"Give me the gun and we'll talk about it."

"No." She pressed it harder against his chest, feeling the lack of armor, the vulnerability there. "I don't want to talk to you. You deserve to die."

She tried to wipe the tears away with her other hand, but it wasn't just the pistol that was heavy—it was her entire body. The wetness fell down her cheeks, hot on her raw skin.

"Your Majesty, listen to me. If you wanted to shoot me, you'd have done it by now. Take your finger off the trigger. Can you do that? Move your finger, and then you can scream at me all you want. You don't even have to give me the gun. Just move your finger."

"I can't." She shook her head and pressed harder. She couldn't let him off that easily. He needed to be dead, lying there on the cold ground next to Quen. He had the chance to redeem himself, the chance to be forgiven, the opportunity to make things right with the Holy One, and now he'd robbed her own brother of that chance. How would she ever know if Quen would have changed his mind now?

"Yes, you can. I know you can. Let's just start with that."

"No." It was all she could say, all she could think. "No."

"My lady, you can."

With those words, she hated him more than ever, for what he was doing was obvious. He'd done it often enough in that bright room of her nightmares. Frightening her had worked most of the time, yes, but it also did the opposite when her state of mind simply wouldn't permit her to survive more fear. Chase had known when she'd hit her limit back then, and he'd reassured her, brought her back from the brink. He couldn't get any decent intelligence out of someone who was babbling in terror.

And now? Now his calming tone was doing something to her, bending her to his will, even though she knew and hated him for it. It was a brick wall she needed to push through to get to the place where hate allowed her mind its sovereignty, but try as she might, the wall held firm.

"I know you're stronger than this," he said. "You're the strongest person I know. You've survived so much, and you'll survive this, too."

His assertion broke her more thoroughly than any beating ever could have. Her finger slipped off the trigger, though it took physical effort to unbend her stiff knuckle. Chase reached down, his gaze not leaving hers, and unwound her hand from the grip. The gun disappeared from her sight—to where, she couldn't see through the blinding tears.

"You're all right," he said softly, reaching for her. "You're going to be all right."

"No," she repeated. "No." Her knees buckled, but Chase caught her before she fell and eased her to the ground.

And then she hit him.

She hit him for every lie he'd ever told, starting with the day they'd met. For the terror he'd infused into her very soul every time she'd seen the crossed swords that had meant her death. For every time he'd struck her in response to her defiance, every time he'd threatened and coerced and terrified her. For the things he'd done on Haedera that she'd never, ever know about—and didn't want to.

For what he'd done to Quen.

Her fists, weak from fear, didn't do much damage, but she lashed out at him again and again from her knees—at his head, at his chest, at his face, at his arms, screaming until she was hoarse and her head pounded. The sane part of her brain knew he'd throw her to the ground, but he didn't try to deflect her strikes, didn't speak or look away. Not until she landed a solid blow to his jawbone.

"Shhh. You're going to hurt yourself even more. You've beat up on me enough for right now—hold still and let me look at your head, and maybe you can continue later."

How dare he shush her with that detestable, calm tone? What did he know about hurt? What did he know about pain? He didn't know a damn thing, that's what he knew. Still, she didn't fight him as he grabbed her wrists and pinned them to her sides. He pulled her closer and tried to check the wound on her head, and she didn't fight him, just screamed and sobbed harder into his shirt as an older memory assaulted her.

He'd appeared in her cell one day, without warning and during a particularly ruthless beating. The guards, seizing the opportunity to prove her nothing more than an inept spy, had shouted at her to stand in the presence of a ranking officer—*didn't the Commonwealth teach you to respect a colonel, you useless waste of oxygen?*—but she hadn't been able to move from her knees. Not even to acknowledge he was there above her. Not even to plead for mercy.

She'd vomited on his boots instead.

Expecting another blow as punishment for her weakness, she'd recoiled from him, but he'd only ordered the soldiers back and removed the handcuffs, then wiped her mouth and poured a little water down her throat. It wasn't fair. Even now, the indignity of it all made her sick. No one could withstand that blend of cruelty and compassion, and he'd known it, just like he knew it now and was using it against her.

She'd fought his closeness that day, had spit out the water and loosed some ineffective slaps in his direction, until finally, with a few sharp words to the guards, he'd released her to wait for the medic alone on the cold concrete. She should do the same now, because the pain—oh, *kusir*, she hadn't felt pain like this in so long. It should have been familiar, comfortable, something to hold on to, but she could only cling to him and cry.

But through her tears and his hollow reassurances, new voices appeared in the distance, in between the golden sparkles that danced around her, oblivious to her grief. Some of them she recognized, but most were unfamiliar Haederan ones. Wynne's voice joined them, then Merritt's. The scent of sandalwood and the warmth of his body gave him away, even if the entire well house was going black around her. He was walking her—or maybe carrying her—back up to the guest house. There were harsh lights, shrill voices that hurt her head, silk sheets, Merritt's hand gently combing out the tangles in her hair, and then . . .

And then blessed darkness.

CHAPTER EIGHTEEN

The Imperial Security medic who Kern had sent for put down
his scanner and shrugged at Merritt. He had not been informed of
the no-uniform rule—an intentional oversight by Kern, no doubt.
Avery tried to ignore his attention and the swords on his collar,
but the memory of the Imperial Security medic healing her eye in
that cell in Cadena weighed heavily on her mind. It certainly
didn't help her headache.

"It's a concussion. Not so bad. She'll be fine in another day or
so." The medic glowered at her as she curled up in the leather
chair in the corner of the bedroom, then turned back to Merritt.
"Just keep her quiet. Try to get her back in bed and let her sleep as
much as she wants. Keep that baby away from her, too."

"I'm not deaf, I'm not brain-damaged, and I'm not a prisoner.
You can speak directly to me," Avery snapped. It might have been
rude, but the anger was an improvement from the hours she'd spent
sobbing in bed, at least. "And you won't keep my child from me."

Keeping Lucas away was antithetical to the quiet peace the
medic wanted for her, anyway—he'd been screaming for her ever
since Merritt had carried her back to the guest house the night
before. Avery closed her eyes, wishing they'd have sent the man

away without seeing her, even if he'd come all the way from Rebet just to make sure she wasn't seriously injured.

Go back to making sure your victims don't die on their torturers.

"Of course, my lady." The medic gestured Merritt toward the door with his eyes. "Quiet," he repeated under his breath, like she couldn't hear that either, then disappeared.

Merritt shut the bedroom door behind him and turned back to her, hands raised in appeal.

"You heard what the nice man said. Back to bed."

"I don't want to." Petulant sounding or not, the huge bed in the center of the room was the last place she wanted to be, no matter how comfortable it was. She wasn't broken, and she didn't need to be treated like a child.

He sighed. "Being distraught isn't going to make you feel any better, and it certainly won't change what happened."

"He's dead, Merritt." Her eyes ached when she cried, but she didn't care. "I loved him."

"I know." He squeezed into the chair next to her, and she laid her head on his shoulder. "If you don't want to go to sleep, how does a bath sound?"

"Like heaven," she mumbled into his shirt. "As long as you join me."

His eyes crinkled at her invitation. "Let me just go find a servant to run it, then."

"Mer." She tried to laugh, but even that hurt. "Even on Haedera, even with a concussion, I'm capable of running my own bath."

"I was kidding. Obviously." He ran a finger across her forehead. "I'm glad to see you can still smile a bit, love."

Only because Lucas was safe. It was the one thing that made this nightmare better. What if Quen had gotten to him first? Or worse, had made her watch? It didn't bear thinking about. She followed Merritt into the expansive bathroom, shedding her grimy clothes from the night before as she closed the door behind them. He hadn't bothered to remove them, and just getting rid of the dust and blood was a start.

"Hot?" he asked. She nodded, and he rolled his eyes with a laugh. "Even in the middle of the desert."

Merritt didn't understand—hot water was the only thing that would wash the blood away. Silent, she shook a handful of lavender-scented salts into the large white tub and dipped a toe in. Blistering, just how she'd wanted it. Merritt stepped in behind her, and she leaned against his chest, savoring the feel of his skin on hers. His fingers met her shoulders, massaging the tension away —or at least trying to. It wouldn't do any good, not today, but she wouldn't tell him that.

"Where is Quen?" she asked.

Merritt's hands paused at her question, then started again, though not as firmly.

"The Haederans took him to Rebet. Procedure, they told me." His voice dripped with skepticism. "I think the lord of the manor just wanted him away from Windhaven. But what happens next is your call."

A small bird landed on the cactus outside, drawing her attention away from Merritt's touch.

"He needs to go back to Asria," she said, focusing on the bird's scarlet feathers. "I want this kept quiet. As far as anyone but Grant Baylen needs to know is there was an accident somewhere off-world, and he's come back to Cadena to be buried as a Rendon." The secret wouldn't last, but they could do some damage control before the real story broke.

"I'll make sure that happens." He brushed the damp ends of her hair behind her back. "Hair?"

She handed a small bottle of cleansing oil over her shoulder, and Merritt worked the oil through her limp waves. The scent— oh, if it was possible for a smell to feel good, the vaguely citrus fragrance did.

"He called me a traitor, Mer," she said. "And I—"

Was she? Did other Asrians feel the same about her? She

ignored the rumors and gossip on Asria as a matter of course and had since she was a child. *That young Lady Avery will be a problem one day,* she'd once overheard a neighbor at Sabino say. *It's a good thing the king is marrying next month. I hope children follow shortly.* Minding her own business became easier after hearing such unflattering comments. But what were her own people saying about her now?

"You're not a traitor, love," Merritt said easily.

"I made an agreement with the Haederans. I signed that armistice. I've met privately with the Haederan emperor."

"To end a war. A war that should have never happened and had already gone on too long. It was courage, not treason. And as someone who personally benefited from the end of those hostilities, I'll dare them to say anything to your face or mine."

"But I told Chase things. Things I never should have said."

Hadley had absolved her of those things she'd done and said while imprisoned, and the Commonwealth Navy and Special Operations Forces medals she'd been awarded spoke for themselves, but there had to be people in the Commonwealth holding it against her. Maybe even on Asria. It was surprising she hadn't heard the criticism in person yet.

"No one blames you for that. No one who matters, at least." He began to rinse the oil from her hair. "You kept the most valuable intel from the Haederans, and that's all that matters to the Commonwealth. And the senate. And to me," he said with a kiss on her earlobe. "And do you know how I know you didn't do anything wrong?"

"How?" She furrowed her forehead at his reaction as he wiped off the excess oil.

"Because a certain Imperial Security interrogator is still fascinated by the fact you bested him at his own game. He wouldn't have this inexplicable admiration for you if you'd betrayed the Commonwealth. He knows the score."

But she'd betrayed Asria and the Commonwealth in the end, even if the information she'd given up hadn't mattered. She'd broken, more thoroughly than she'd ever imagined was possible, and Chase had been responsible. How was she supposed to admit that to Merritt?

"I was lucky," she said instead.

"Sometimes luck is enough." Merritt sighed. "What about us? I don't want to rush you, but what happens next is up to you."

"I want to go home." Avery closed her eyes as he rinsed her hair. Just being clean made her feel a thousand times more alive. "The sooner, the better."

"We can make that happen, too." Merritt kissed the back of her neck, then pushed himself out of the tub. "For now, you just relax. I'll be back in a bit."

* * *

After a four-hour nap, clean clothes, and ample hugs from Lucas, she felt halfway human again. Her headache was gone, and even the dehydration that had stalked her for weeks was subsiding. The bed and sleep called to her, true, but so did the sun out in the courtyard. With warmth spilling onto her face, she stared at the man sitting at the small table in the middle of the main house's patio, not trusting her feet to move.

Merritt gave her hand three quick squeezes. "You don't have to have dinner with him, you know. He shouldn't have asked it of you."

"I have to face him eventually, don't I? There's no point in putting this off, as much as I wish I could." It was surprising Chase had given her the breathing room he had. She'd half expected him to be waiting in the great room of the guest house when she'd woken up that morning. Guilt, especially Chase's seemingly all-consuming guilt, was a powerful thing.

"All right. I'll see you in an hour then." He gave her a quick peck on the cheek and walked off, leaving her standing there alone.

No, not alone. Kern appeared in the edge of her vision, though why he was still following her around Windhaven was a mystery. Quen was dead, wasn't he? She was safe.

Safe from him, at least. She certainly wasn't safe from Chase, who stood as she approached, a distrustful look in his eyes and a light bruise on his cheek. What did he expect? For her to attack him again?

"I'm glad you came." He exhaled and gestured to the empty chair across from him. "I didn't think you would."

Small talk wasn't going to happen. Not yet. Avery sat, her eyes darting about at the wine she couldn't drink, the small salad already on her plate, the cactuses that surrounded them, Kern's not-so-inconspicuous presence—at anything but Chase.

"A quiet dinner, then. That's fine. Wouldn't be the first." He blew out another deep breath as he sat. "Your Majesty . . . I'm so sorry."

"You could have stunned him," she said to her glass of water. *Why hadn't he?* For the first time since she'd arrived on Haedera, water wasn't appealing. She looked up at him, eyes questioning.

"I don't carry a stun pistol at home." Chase took what on first glance appeared to be a calm sip of wine. Was it her imagination, or did his hand shake? "Anyone sneaking onto my estate has harmful intentions in mind."

"But—"

But what? How could she refute that? She could argue until she was blue in the face, but she knew—and more importantly, Chase knew—that she wouldn't have survived last night's encounter with Quen if he hadn't intervened. But gratitude? That would have to come later. Much later.

He set the water down. "Look," he began.

"You're lying," she interrupted. Nothing about him gave it away, but that was pure Chase. One simply had to guess about his honesty at random, and he had to be lying now. "You don't wander around Windhaven armed at all. Don't even try to convince me that you do. Why would you need to? You brought that pistol last night knowing you'd kill anyone who crossed you. You did this on purpose!"

"You don't know what you're talking about."

"Then tell me."

He pressed his lips together. "You've never been stunned, have you?"

Avery jerked her head, unwilling to shake it. He knew very well she hadn't. And he knew exactly why not. She'd tried to get stunned—oh, how she'd tried. Getting herself stunned had been the only idea she'd ever come up with to avoid his questioning while she was imprisoned, but Chase had been onto her. Those Haederan Army soldiers had been given orders not to shoot her, never to stun her. Their Imperial Security Command master couldn't interrogate an unconscious prisoner.

They'd beaten her senseless instead.

"When you're stunned, you do not just fall down unconscious and drop the weapon you have pointed at someone's head. There's a delay. You twitch. You spasm. Sometimes the stun pistol malfunctions completely. What if he'd convulsed after I shot him? We wouldn't be having this conversation now, I can tell you that much. Do you understand what that would have done to Asria? To Colonel Rendon? To your child?" He glanced away, then back at her, and his voice cracked. "Do you know what that would have done to me? Desperately seeking your forgiveness and then losing that chance?"

Five seconds earlier, she'd wanted to scream at him, but the words had fled.

Chase cared if she lived or died?

It was hard to believe. Or maybe not so hard, when she thought about it. A bit of her anger melted away—as terrified as she'd been last night, Chase hadn't escaped untouched, either. He'd brought her to Windhaven, to Haedera itself, the one place she feared more than anywhere, to protect her, and that decision had almost resulted in her death. The guilt he must be feeling had to be unbearable.

But that guilt was his fault. It was his fault Quen was dead, too. She'd tell herself that over and over until she believed it.

"Forgiveness?" she repeated. "I can forgive you for the things you did to me, but I can't forgive you for this."

He blinked at her, wordless for once.

"Colonel."

She glanced up at Kern's voice. His face was hard, his jaw tight, but that wasn't anything new, not really. It just wasn't a version of Kern she had seen on Haedera so far. No, this version was the Imperial Security officer she'd known back on Asria, and she much preferred the relaxed man he'd been the past few weeks. But Fiona—it was Fiona, standing next to him, who looked even odder. Her normally tawny complexion was pale, her eyes strangely bright and glassy.

Avery jumped to her feet. "Did something happen to Lucas?"

It should have been Wynne notifying her if something had gone wrong in the guest house, but what if something had happened to Lucas and Wynne was dealing with it there?

"No, my lady. The prince is fine." Just those words seemed to drain Fiona. She squinted at Kern and stiffened.

"This isn't a good time," Chase bit out, looking pointedly at the gate on the other end of the courtyard. "We're in the middle of a private dinner."

"Yes, sir." Kern, bless him, sounded completely unflustered by Chase's irritation. "But I think you need to hear what she has to say. Now."

"Then say it." Chase took another sip of wine.

"My lord," Fiona began. "Last night—" She swallowed, after another stricken glance at Kern. Like she was terrified of him for some reason. It wasn't all that surprising, but she hadn't ever seemed to mind him much before. "I—"

Her mouth moved a few more times, silently, then shut.

Chase leaned back and threw his hands in the air. "If you're just going to stand around and stutter, I'd like to have dinner in peace. We can discuss whatever it is later. Better yet, talk to Lara about it." He turned back toward Avery and picked up his fork.

"I told Quen Rendon where to find her." The words escaped Fiona's mouth in a wheezing rush of air toward Chase's back. She twisted her hands together, her fingers shaking, her knuckles almost white. "I told him how to infiltrate Windhaven. I told him where the queen would be last night."

She—Fiona had done what?

Kern's mouth fell open. "That's not what you told me! Sir—"

Chase ignored him and twisted back toward Fiona. If he was taken aback at her spontaneous confession, it was impossible to tell. He tilted his head sideways like the hawks that flew over Windhaven, stillness personified, eyes on his newest prey. "You did what?" he asked in a voice Avery recognized.

How glad she was that his tone wasn't directed at her. But Fiona—*kusir*, she'd been alone with Lucas, she'd been in her and Merritt's quarters on the courier ship, she'd had unrestricted access to the guest house at Windhaven. Suddenly, she couldn't breathe.

Fiona stared at Chase like she'd realized what she'd just done.

He stood. "Don't make me ask again."

Fiona's lips trembled as she tried to speak. No sound came out, and she covered her face with her hands as a small whimper escaped. Avery's gaze flickered from Fiona to Chase. Had he ever looked at her with that predatory stare?

"Don't want to tell me now?" Chase asked. "Realized the kind of trouble your bravery just got you into? That's fine. I suspect you'll change your mind shortly." He glanced at Kern. "Major?"

Kern blinked, then seemed to recover from his shock once he realized he wasn't in Chase's line of fire. "Let's go." He put a hand on Fiona's arm.

She jerked away, her steps quick. "No," she said to Chase. "My lord, you don't understand—"

"I think we all understand well enough," Chase said. "Get her out of here, Major. Now."

Avery looked away, toward the small cluster of purple cactuses beside the table. It seemed spineless, but she didn't need to see Kern dragging Fiona off to her fate. Her screams and protests and the footsteps of the Imperial Security personnel who'd evidently met him around the corner told most of the story. The tightness in her chest told her the rest. Her body knew what was happening, even if her brain didn't want to admit it.

The shrieks and boots faded off in the distance, and Chase blew out a deep breath and sat down to his salad like nothing had happened.

"That's it?" she asked. "You're just going to let them drag her off like that?"

"Yes, that's it. What else would you like me to say?" He shrugged and picked up his glass of wine. "I'm sorry you had to see that?"

"But what will happen to her?"

Chase took a sip, focusing on the glass. "You know what'll happen to her."

"Colonel, please." Even Fiona, no matter what she'd done— what exactly had she done?—didn't deserve this.

"This is an internal Haederan issue. Stay out of it, my lady. Believe me when I say that you do not want to make it your problem." He downed the rest of his wine in one swallow and nodded at her. "Just enjoy your dinner."

CHAPTER NINETEEN

Food, Haederan, Asrian, or any other kind, was one of the most unpleasant ideas in the world right now. The outdoor café was as comfortable as any place on Haedera could be, but Avery could do nothing but push the chilled tomato salad around with her fork. The automatic movement didn't help her appetite, and she risked another glance at Kern.

Even though his arm couldn't have been fully healed, gone were the casual pants and loose shirt that allowed her to be in the same room with him without shaking. Gone was the pistol hidden under that shirt, replaced by one he wasn't bothering to conceal. It was his green Imperial Security uniform that was responsible for their ability to eat lunch in broad daylight in the capital city of Rebet without being harassed, but even so, if she'd had any appetite before leaving Windhaven, which she hadn't, it was gone now at the sight of him.

The only saving grace was that Chase had disappeared after their awkward dinner a few nights before. Whether he was back to work harassing Haederan subjects or simply hiding away somewhere at Windhaven, Avery didn't know and didn't care. Besides Kern in uniform, Chase was the last person she wanted to see—and, it appeared, he knew it.

Merritt squeezed her free hand under the table as she laid her fork down once more.

"Not hungry?" he asked.

She shook her head and looked at Kern. "I just want to get this over with."

Kern tossed his napkin on the table and pushed his chair back, standing with something that was almost sympathy on his face.

"It's a short walk—just around the corner. And if I'm not mistaken, you could use the distraction of a walk."

She nodded, numb. Even Merritt's arm around her waist as they walked down the street—it felt unreal. The whole thing did. How long had it been since this had been her greatest fear? The end of her life? It seemed just days ago. And now her feet were carrying her, however unwillingly, to . . . to what?

You can still back out.

But she wanted to know. Needed to know. Fiona might be the only one who'd had any idea what had gone on in Quen's mind at the end. She might have been the last one to speak with him. She was certainly the only one who could explain her part in this mess.

And it was Fiona being held there. Not her.

Never her.

She repeated the phrase in time with her footsteps. She'd repeat it as often as necessary until they were out of the terrible place they hadn't even reached yet.

Not me.

Not me.

Not me.

"We're here," Kern said quietly.

She'd walked the entire way with her gaze on the sidewalk without even realizing it, and it took effort to look up, more than she had thought she could summon. A tall building stood in front of them, its windows black glass. Impenetrable. Hostile. Fearsome. Not the vague, indistinct building from her nightmares, true, but bad enough. Two uniformed Imperial Security

Command men stood in front of the large glass doors, but it had to be a formality. More threats, more fear. No doubt there were others stationed on the roof and around the block. Or maybe regular Haederans avoided this area of town just like she would have preferred. The thought forced a shiver up her arms.

"Avery?" When she didn't reply, her gaze firmly on those two officers in green, Merritt placed a hand on each side of her face, cutting through the detachment. "Remember, you can leave," he said. "Whenever you want. Just say the word—hell, just give me the right look, and we'll leave. Understand?" Given no response, he gave her a little shake and brushed a loose piece of hair from her cheek.

"And hey." Kern gave her a crooked smile as she peeled Merritt's hands away. "Remember, too, you're going in through the front door."

She laughed at the idea of going in any other way, an ugly, breathless noise.

"Then let's get this over with."

With Merritt's arm wound protectively around her, they ascended the stairs.

* * *

It wasn't what she'd expected. Not that she'd given much thought to her expectations beyond what appeared in her dreams. The screams of doomed prisoners, perhaps. Instead, Kern led her and Merritt down a series of corridors, then into an open area surrounded by glass-walled offices, each furnished with a table and several chairs. The brightness was unexpected, nothing at all like her nightmares. That was something, at least.

"Offices for initial questioning. Sometimes prisoners react better if they think there's some hope for them," Kern said, catching her interest. He shrugged. "It doesn't usually work."

She opened her mouth to tell him to stop—his explanation was too close to Chase's technique, one she'd been subjected to so long ago. Kern was right. It hadn't worked, not on her.

Kern made a frustrated, or perhaps guilty, noise at her silence.

"Sorry. But again, you're going in the front door. Prisoners take the elevator up from the ground floor on the other end, already inside the secure area."

As if that was supposed to make her feel better. They kept walking, following Kern's quick steps down another hallway. And at the end—there at the end was the worst thing she could think of.

Chase stood in front of a solid door with a keypad. She should have known. He wouldn't leave her alone with Kern for this. In his mind, it was probably better for him to be there. But she couldn't. She just couldn't be around him. Not here. Not now. She clutched Merritt's hand tighter and turned toward Kern.

"You never said he'd be here." She couldn't look at Chase. Couldn't speak of him, to him. "Why didn't you tell me, Major? No warning, no mention of it?"

"Sorry we're early, sir." Kern ignored her and stepped to the side, leaving nothing more between her and Chase than a few paces.

"And I'm sorry too," Chase said, rubbing a palm across his eyes.

Sorry for what he'd done to her, what he'd done to Quen, what she was about to experience, or just sorry he was going to be the one prying her off the floor after she passed out? There was that breathless laugh again. Even Kern stared at her that time, like he didn't want to be the one to help Chase drag her limp body back downstairs.

"Colonel Rendon," Chase went on, dragging his gaze from her and looking at Merritt with a little more courage, "I'm afraid you'll have to wait outside."

Merritt gaped at him and edged the tiniest bit closer to her, just enough to be inappropriate in public.

"I'm not leaving her." He glanced from Chase to Kern. "Especially with you two."

Especially with you, Colonel Chase was what he should have said. How could Merritt betray her like this? How could he not let his anger at Chase show? Through the fog, she realized what a silly hope it was—Merritt at least had good enough sense to act like nothing Chase did bothered him. But that didn't matter. In that moment, she hated him and his good sense.

Chase sighed. "I tried. Even I couldn't get you in. It took Owin's clout and a whole lot of begging for Lient to even allow it of Her Majesty. You're lucky to be allowed in the building."

Her Majesty. Not *Avery.* Not *my lady* with a friendly, mocking undertone.

The numb feeling returned. She'd made her feelings clear by avoiding him after Fiona's arrest, and he'd accepted them with minimal protest. Without any protest, really. A stranger stood in front of her now.

No—not quite a stranger. A stranger would be preferable to who he truly was. Again he was the man who'd tortured her, the one who'd ruined her life. And now she had to go into this row of holding cells alone with him, the man who'd killed the only family she had, or she didn't go at all. And she had to know what Fiona knew about Quen. She just had to know.

Merritt shifted. "Do you think it's appropriate for you to handle the questioning of one of your own servants?"

"Major Kern is handling the questioning. I'm only a witness."

"Oh, please." At her outburst, three heads shifted toward her. "He's not even pretending!" Chase didn't flinch, and she took a deep breath. There was no way she'd win. "Fine. Whatever. Pretend whatever you want. Let's just get this over with."

Merritt shot her a questioning look.

"I'll be fine," she said to him. "Just fine. But I'll need you when we're done in here, right?"

He bobbed his head in understanding—though his last glance at Chase was anything but pleased—and let Kern lead him to one of the empty offices. His absence was physically painful, a chill at her side.

She risked a glimpse at Chase while they waited in silence. Clean-shaven, hair trimmed, and immaculately dressed in a freshly pressed Imperial Security uniform, he looked as uncomfortable as she felt. That tense muscle in his jaw always gave him away. Was it her? It had to be. It certainly wasn't his surroundings. This was the life he'd never truly left.

"Ready?" he asked once Kern came back.

She nodded, even though her chest was tightening by the second. She yawned behind her hand, but it didn't make a difference.

Chase pressed his fingers to the pad and keyed in a code. Lights flashed, and he slid the door open. Luminosity behind her —it was silly to imagine she could feel it—and darkness in front of her. When her eyes adjusted, she was in another world, one she had thought she'd left forever.

Cells, each with a heavy metal door, lined each side of the hallway. It wasn't as dark in the corridor as she'd imagined—the sunlight blasting through the windows on the nonsecure side had fooled her eyes into thinking it was darker than it was—but there was a certain despair about it, one not quite as tangible as the lack of sunlight. The environmental system sent an icy chill through her, and suddenly Kern's suggestion to wear heavier clothes that morning made more sense.

Chase stepped inside with a questioning glance at her, and she followed, though it was more to show him a modicum of nonexistent bravery than a real desire to face what was on the inside. Kern slid the door shut behind them. There must have been a separate environmental system for the holding area, for the door didn't just cut off the outside, it cut them off from the rest of the planet. What had Fiona felt when they'd first brought her here? Terror? Or just relief that the pretense was over?

They walked, Chase in front of her, Kern behind, twenty paces to an open door. *An open door. Don't forget it's an open door.* They'd take her out, back to Merritt, whenever she asked. Even now. Avery opened her mouth to plead for just that, then shut it again.

Chase stopped outside the doorway and pointed. "They'll bring her here. I'm not making you stand in a cell to have this discussion."

She stared at the two chairs that sat in the corner of the otherwise empty room, unable to force her legs to move. This wasn't real. This wasn't happening.

"Hey." Chase reached a tentative hand to her arm and shook her. "You there?"

Avery blinked at him and took a deep breath, then doubled over. Something heavy sat on her chest, choking off her air. It was humiliating to show her fear, but it was the only way she could inhale, even a little.

"I can't—I can't breathe," she gasped.

Kern swore under his breath. "I told you so, sir."

Chase's shadow shifted in what had to be a silent rebuke of Kern for that comment, then he bent down in front of her. "Close your eyes."

"Don't—don't play—" She looked up at him and tried to take a shallow breath. "Don't play your mind games with me."

Without another word, he straightened and shrugged at Kern. "Take her back out, Brennin."

Kern's hand wrapped around her wrist. Avery uncurled herself and prepared to fight, even though the move made her chest even tighter.

"No!" Then, a little more quietly. "No."

"Then do as I say."

That tone. She knew it, though she hadn't heard it in so long she almost didn't recognize it at first. It was the tone that forbade defiance—or else. She couldn't fight that. Her broken mind wouldn't let her fight it, especially not here. Her eyelids fluttered closed, then jerked open again as Chase's palms landed gently but firmly on her shoulders.

"Keep them closed. Try to relax."

Try to relax? Who was he kidding? Against her will, she shut them again.

"Now breathe. Slowly. Think of something beautiful. The Gallis Mountains, maybe?"

Through the terror, the sheer absurdity of Chase's suggestion—the spot in the wilds outside Cadena—hit her. One slow breath. She and Merritt were sitting in the meadow, surrounded by wild cylva. Two. The breeze blew her curls about, and Merritt tucked them behind her ear. Another breath. And another. The shadows stopped spinning around her; her chest loosened. How long had it taken? There was no way to know, but that didn't matter. She opened her eyes and pulled her lips into a smile. Anything to convince Chase she wasn't as broken as he knew she was.

"There you go. Better?" he asked, loosing her from his grip.

She nodded, afraid to say a word.

He motioned inside, toward the chair. "Sit down, Your Majesty." It was an order this time, but not an unkind one. She sat. Chase leaned out the door and rapped on the wall with a bang the entire building must have heard, then stepped inside. "It shouldn't be too much longer. They were notified you were on your way up."

Avery couldn't look at him. She took a deep breath and blinked, then examined her shoes. And when she looked up again, there was Fiona.

She had an Imperial Security guard on each side of her, gripping an arm. Shackles surrounded her ankles, and her wrists were cuffed in front of her. The clothing she'd been wearing when Kern had escorted her from Windhaven had been replaced by a shapeless jumpsuit that might have once been red, or maybe orange. As faded as the fabric was, it was hard to tell. Her shoes were gone, and the jumpsuit was a little dirty now, yes, but what exposed skin there was looked untouched. It seemed they hadn't physically abused her. But the haunted look in her eyes—that was something Avery understood.

Fiona's gaze flickered from her to Chase. If it was possible, she became even paler at the sight of him.

"My lord—"

"No," Chase said quietly, though the softness cut like a knife. "You no longer have the privilege of calling me that." Fiona focused on the ground, tears spilling on her feet, and he looked at the guards. "Ten minutes."

They nodded and released her, closing the door behind them as they went. It made a whooshing noise as it sealed shut, and she wasn't certain if she or Fiona flinched harder. Kern simply crossed his arms and relaxed against the wall with the air of someone awaiting a performance. If he knew Chase as well as Avery suspected he did, perhaps he was.

For a minute, the room was quiet. Quiet except for Kern's fingernail scratching aimlessly behind him on the wall. Except for her own heartbeat. Except for Fiona's ragged breathing.

Except for Chase's sudden footsteps.

"You betrayed me." He edged next to Fiona, looking her up and down. She stiffened at the proximity. "You lied to me and you betrayed my trust. In my own household." His voice was so quiet Avery had to strain to hear it, though she was certain Fiona didn't have to struggle at all. "You betrayed your emperor. Your empire."

Fiona whimpered. Avery held her breath.

"Why?"

Such a simple question, the answer so fraught with peril.

"He—" She looked up at Chase. He intentionally looked away at the wall, breaking eye contact, and she looked back down at her feet. "He told me he loved me."

A soft chuckle. "You did this because a man told you he loved you?"

How did he make such a significant thing sound so silly, so inane? Avery glanced at Kern. He raised a shoulder in silent approval.

Ass.

Fiona stared frantically from her to Chase to Kern. "And because he was right."

"About?"

"About her." Fiona met Avery's eyes, some of the fear turning to hate.

Chase turned around without a word and settled into the other chair.

"Why don't you start from the beginning?" he asked. "Where you met him, how he convinced you to do this, how you kept in contact with him, how you got him into Windhaven. Everything."

Everything would take much longer than ten minutes—but Chase had to know that. He knew Fiona would be so determined to fit her defense in before the guards returned that she'd tell him every detail, no matter how irrelevant. How obvious his tactics were from this side of the questioning.

Fiona's face hardened as she turned toward them. "There was a café in Cadena that I used to visit. They served Haederan food. There was Haederan—company." Her eyes grew blank, like she was looking into the past.

"And you were lonely," Chase prompted.

"I was proud to serve Lady Sophie. And you, my—" Fiona swallowed down the unwelcome title. "I'd have died before I asked to be sent home. But Asria wasn't Haedera. It wasn't Windhaven. And yes, I was lonely. For the atmosphere more than the company, I think. But then he started coming around. He didn't look Asrian, didn't sound Asrian. Said he'd spent some time there as a child but that he'd been off exploring the quadrant since he turned fifteen."

It was Avery's turn to swallow, though her throat was dry. Why hadn't Quen come to *her*?

"We just talked at first. Talked and listened to the music and drank coffee and ate. And then one night, he invited me back to his flat."

Oh, Quen.

Chase was silent.

"It was another month before he told me who he was. He told me his sister had seized the throne from him, that she was a Haederan sympathizer, that she'd allowed the Imperial Haederan Army to operate on Asria, and that she planned to hand their own planet back over to us when the time was right. He said she deserved to pay for the things she'd done and the things she planned to do."

"Quen Rendon was Asrian. An Asrian who hated Haedera and all we stand for." Chase shrugged. "He hated us. He hated you, underneath it all. Why did you help him?"

How could you have fallen for his manipulation?

"He was loyal." Her chin went up, and she brushed away a single tear that had trickled down her cheek. "He was loyal to me, loyal to his people. That meant everything to me." Something must have clicked in Fiona's mind, because fear overcame her sorrow. "He said the person bankrolling him would kill me otherwise. I only wanted her dead! That's all he wanted! I didn't—I'd never have influenced our plans for Asria!"

"I know you wouldn't have." Chase waved his hand. Was that the truth or an attempt to calm her so she would keep talking? Whatever his intent, it seemed to work—Fiona breathed again. "Who was bankrolling him?"

"I don't know. One of his pirate friends, it must have been. There's more money out in deep space than I could ever imagine." She fumbled a bit with her hands. "So when we left Asria, I sent him a message and told him we were headed to Haedera. That you would be sheltering her at Windhaven. Lady Sophie was in one of her moods and wanted to pack herself, so I ran out and met him that evening. I promised I'd help him. I didn't see him again until we arrived, here in Rebet."

"The trip to visit your mother last week."

If there was underlying anger in Chase's statement—and how could there not be?—he didn't show it.

Fiona nodded. "He'd found some run-down flat in Cristead, on the north side. I don't know where he got the money for it. He seemed to have credit on a dozen planets. He'd dyed his hair, bought new clothes, worked on his accent. It was enough to pass for Haederan. I—I told him it would be enough." She brought her hands up to cover her face, but her voice broke. "And then I gave him maps. Schedules of the security teams. Her favorite places on the estate, and when she seemed to be away from Lucas and the prince."

No matter what Quen had threatened, Fiona hadn't wanted Lucas harmed. That was something, at least. A bit of her hatred, a bit of the fear, melted away. She could handle Fiona's hatred toward her. It was a necessary hazard of her position, something she had to deal with even on Asria. Even those who loved her— did they mean it? It was so hard to tell anymore. Hate was honest, at least.

"And the night it happened?" Chase asked.

"I didn't know when he was going to show up. I didn't think he'd be able to get through the security anyway. I didn't know anything had happened until the prince carried her back to the guest house."

"What about Lucas?" Judging by the way Kern stiffened, Avery wasn't the only one surprised by her own voice.

"He told me that once you were dead, I was to kill him." She inhaled. "But I would have never—"

"Why did you admit to it?" Chase interrupted. "You should know by now that you surprised everyone. It's quite possible that you might have gotten away with it. No one would have been the wiser."

"I don't know." Fiona pressed her fingers harder against her cheekbones, leaving small pink marks. "Lady Isobel would have been so disappointed in me. I knew you would be, too."

"You knew what the outcome would be," Chase said, gesturing around. "You weren't afraid of this?"

Fiona nodded, slowly. "I suppose I didn't care at that moment." She looked at Kern, who'd absorbed himself in an apparent hangnail.

"Do you care now?"

What was Chase doing? Where was this going? Nowhere good, that was for sure. Avery dug her toes into the floor, primed for an escape. But the door was locked. No one was coming to help her. She shot Chase a panicked glance.

"Yes. I care now." Fiona's voice cracked. "It's worse than I ever imagined."

"You committed treason. You may as well have plotted to kill Lady Avery yourself. What do you think should happen to you?"

"I know I will die for this." Her voice quivered. "I only pray it happens quickly."

Avery jumped at Chase's deep sigh. He looked at her, the question left unasked.

And you, Your Majesty? What kind of vengeance do you want?

She stared at him, and the purpose of the entire ghastly visit fell on top of her. He was making Fiona her problem. Didn't he realize how much grace she'd already extended to Haedera over the past few years? How could he ask this of her?

Because she wanted vengeance. She wanted Fiona to pay—for what, she didn't know. Lucas was safe, Merritt was safe, she was safe. Fiona's actions might constitute treason on Haedera, but that wasn't her problem. She wouldn't let it become her problem. Her head jerked on its own in a movement that resembled something like denial.

Chase gave her a look she couldn't read in response, then stood to face Fiona.

"You understand I can't promise anything. I cannot promise that your life or the life of your mother will be spared, and I certainly cannot promise your release."

Nor, Avery suspected, did he want to.

Fiona stood frozen, her lips just barely parted, eyes glazed and unblinking. Like she'd finally found a way to retreat from his hell into her own mind.

"Your audience with His Imperial Majesty is in four hours. We'll discuss the matter further with him. They have clothes for you." Chase looked her up and down. "I suggest you find a way to clean yourself up as well."

"What?" No longer lifeless, Fiona trembled for the first time. "No. Please, no! Keep me here forever, kill me right now, but please don't make me do this." Her voice grew quiet, and the tears began. "Anything but this, my lord."

The reaction was strange at first, but then, Fiona knew a different side of Owin than she. Than even Chase did. A bit of pity danced through Avery's mind, but the door swished open, dashing the pity to shreds before she could examine it—and probably Fiona's hopes along with it. The guards pulled her out, still sobbing and pleading with Chase over her shoulder.

Chase sank back into the chair next to her, and that time the closeness wasn't as welcome. Avery jumped to her feet and backed toward the door, thankful for her unexpectedly steady knees.

"Sir." Kern narrowed his eyes at him. "Are you all right?"

"Why wouldn't I be all right?" Chase snapped at him. "She's nothing but a servant and a traitor." Perhaps ashamed of his noticeable irritation, he took a deep breath and looked at Avery. "And she was certainly easier than you."

CHAPTER TWENTY

IF SHE'D HAD ANY DOUBTS AS TO JUST HOW EGALITARIAN ASRIA WAS, this visit to the imperial palace had just smashed them to pieces.

While Kern hovered next to her, Avery stared at the large columns that broke Owin's study into two distinct halves. Curved glass on the bottom, wood on top, they looked like something that belonged in a—museum? That wasn't right. This was what people thought of when they thought of royalty, not the small palace in Cadena that had been her home for so many years. The highly polished floor reflected her image like a mirror, and the statues? She didn't want to breathe anywhere near them lest they come crashing to the floor.

Kern turned to her and grinned. "Don't break anything."

She laughed, partly to conceal her nervousness of the purpose of their visit, partly because she could only imagine half of how his class-averse mind was whirling. From her position at the bottom of the low stairs, she could barely glimpse Owin's desk in a small alcove. He stood as a guardsman announced them, then stepped around his desk. As fastidiously dressed in a dark suit as the last time she'd seen him, he gave her a brilliant smile as he made his way down the steps.

"Avery." Owin clasped her hands between his. "I suppose it

goes without saying that I'm very glad to see you alive and unharmed. And surprised to see you here, to be honest. Surprised but thrilled." He shrugged. "It turns out my security people"—a quick glance at Kern—"weren't happy about me visiting Esro, and I didn't think I'd get the chance to see you again on Haedera."

So they weren't going to talk about her audacious request in the Linden family garden before they'd been attacked. That was probably just as well. Of course, there were more pressing matters at hand. Owin had probably lost count of the attempts on his life, anyway.

"Yes, well . . . Colonel Chase is persuasive," she said.

It seemed like the correct answer, the expected one, even though she hadn't even seen Chase since she'd dashed out of the Imperial Security headquarters earlier after his offhand comment about breaking her. But Chase would have been persuasive if they had discussed visiting Rebet, wouldn't he have? It wasn't truly a lie.

Owin laughed. "That he is. And perhaps when this is over, we can talk about more pleasant things."

"I look forward to it."

Owin sighed. "But for now—"

He marched up to the middle step and gestured at the guardsmen flanking the heavy wood doors behind them. The doors swung open, admitting Chase, two Imperial Security guards, and Fiona.

She was pale, so pale, and her knees buckled when her eyes landed on Owin. She stumbled, but Chase whispered something in her ear, and she nodded, stiffening. The guards fell into place behind them as he escorted her to the bottom of the stairs.

How glad she was that Fiona's fate was ultimately Owin's decision. As much responsibility as she had on Asria, few judicial things fell to her—the removal of senators for certain crimes, perhaps—and for that, she was grateful. There was responsibility, and then there was responsibility. Even ordering military action, a dreadful thought that had been in the front of her mind since the Haederan invasion, wasn't personal. How did Owin live with this kind of power?

Next to her, Kern flinched as Fiona fell to her knees in front of the emperor, though Owin didn't look happy about the situation, either. He jerked his chin at the officers behind her, and one pulled her back to her feet. She didn't fight, but she didn't look at Owin again, either.

Owin's eyes flicked to Avery, then back to Fiona.

"We're going to skip these formalities. I'm not inclined to change my mind because of a little groveling by a traitor."

Her stomach twisted. This would have been her standing shackled in front of Owin's father if things had gone differently. How many times had Chase threatened her with this very scenario? Light-years from home, beaten, broken, and terrified, pleading for her life in front of a man who had every reason to want her dead and no reason to proclaim mercy.

Fiona's stare hadn't moved from her feet. "No, Your Majesty. I am sorry."

"The time for apologies is over." Owin's hard stare turned to Chase. "Colonel, I've read Major Kern's official report as well as your personal input."

Naturally. That's why Kern had been there that morning. Chase couldn't have been officially involved with the investigation of one of his own servants. Not that ethics had stopped him. Chase wouldn't have given up the opportunity he'd had this morning for anything.

"Anything you would like to add?" Owin asked. "This was, after all, a problem in your own household, Your Grace."

The courtesy was clearly a threat, a warning to make sure there were no further issues in said household, but Chase didn't flinch.

"Nothing. I leave the verdict to you, sire."

Coward. Of course he would let someone else make a decision of this magnitude. Chase had never seemed spineless before, but . . .

No, that wasn't right. The last time Chase had argued with his emperor, his child had died. Not spineless, then. He was protecting someone. Maybe even Fiona herself.

"Yes, and I'm sure you're happy to do so." Owin sighed and motioned toward the door on his left. "My lady, I didn't have as much time to think about this today as I'd have preferred. Let's discuss this in private, if you would."

Away from Fiona he meant.

Chase stepped toward her as she moved to follow Owin. "Sire, out in the afternoon garden? Alone? That's not wise."

"Really, Gareth." Owin sounded like he was losing patience. "You are not on my personal security team. I realize you have a difficult time understanding the concept of a holiday, but I don't think Lady Avery is capable of—"

"It's not your safety I'm worried about. It's hers. I failed her once before, and it's not going to happen again. Not while she's on Haedera."

"The palace is secure. Yes," Owin said with mock patience, adding as Chase opened his mouth again, "even the afternoon garden you hate so much."

"Then leave your own bodyguard here." Chase didn't back away from her as he issued the challenge.

Owin shook his head and narrowed his eyes. "Fine. Outside, then."

Wonderful. A private conversation with Owin was bad enough, but now she had Chase trailing along behind her as some kind of ironic self-appointed protector. Didn't he realize how paranoid he sounded? He'd already killed the one person who wanted her dead. What was the point any longer?

She took one last look at Fiona before cautiously following Owin across the polished floor. The doors he'd motioned to opened to a large garden, almost like the courtyard outside the guest house at

Windhaven but much more expansive. Why did Chase, in Owin's words, hate the garden so much? It was certainly beautiful. Straight cactuses lined each side of a long stone walk that went—where? Somewhere magical, it had to be. Avery wanted nothing more than to reach her hand out and brush them as she and Owin walked through.

"You wanted names, my lady," Owin said as the cactus fence opened into what looked like empty desert. No wonder Chase didn't like this so-called afternoon garden. The place probably gave Owin's guards nightmares.

Avery glanced at the lizard skittering by her foot and the mountains in the distance.

"Yes, but—" *But that's not what this meeting is about.*

"We're still on the palace grounds. Walled in by static fields." He smiled at her, then glared at Chase. "It only looks open, but Imperial Security still hates it. They hate anything beautiful. Thankfully I can overrule them in most aspects of their authority."

Most. The word wasn't lost on her.

"Yes. I assumed it was safe enough. But I was under the impression the names were not going to happen."

Owin crossed his arms. "Just like I thought it was clear when we met in Cadena that I cannot be accused of compassion. You asked me for it anyway. To put it bluntly, giving you those names at this time would not be in my best interest, the best interest of the Haederan Empire, or the best interest of your own system."

Her stomach tightened. Again with the reminder that Asria wasn't as free as she wished. That *she* wasn't as free as she wished. Why hadn't she declined Chase's offer to shadow her? His presence, a feeling she could sense in the prickle on the back of her neck, was the last thing she needed right now.

"And yet," Owin went on. "I think we can make a deal today that will be mutually beneficial. This woman will be an example, a public one. It will show things have not changed on Haedera. She will be proof that I am not someone to be trifled with, and I will tolerate treason as lightly as my father did."

She clenched her hands at her sides, twisting the silk of her dress into small knots.

"You still mean to kill her."

"You speak as though you have no idea how things are done on Haedera. From Gareth, I am certain you know that's not the case." Owin glanced at Chase. "Her execution is scheduled for tomorrow. You give me your approval for this sentence, officially, as queen of Asria with the implicit backing of your senate, and I'll hand over the names I have in my pocket right now. If not . . ."

Heat washed over her. Owin had the names she'd asked for, right here, right now. But he expected her to trade Fiona's life for the names of the ones who'd attacked Merritt. Expected her to choose Asrian justice over a Haederan woman. How could she do something like that? It was an impossible choice. Wasn't it?

Or was it just too easy?

Chase's lip curled. "Sire, with all due respect, you can't ask that of her."

Owin ignored him, just like he'd been ignoring his own guard. "I need your answer in the next thirty seconds, my lady."

She looked back at Chase, wishing he was Merritt, wishing he'd step in and say something, but he only placed his hands on his hips and shrugged at her. And with his surrender to Owin's authority, she knew.

This wasn't about Merritt's attackers or Fiona at all. It was about controlling the queen of Asria, about manipulating her, about making her remember how easily he could change his mind and send thousands of troops back to Asria in defiance of the Commonwealth's military and her own agreements with him.

Haederan.

The word was a curse threatening to burst forth from her lips. Owin had her trapped and he knew it, the bastard. What was she supposed to do? She'd promised Merritt. Not to his face, but in her heart. And not as his wife, exactly, although she'd spoken as that too, but as his queen. Finding those men had meant something. It would have meant that the Haederan Empire no longer controlled Asria, that they could no longer do whatever they wanted to her planet, that they couldn't destroy more of her people's lives.

And now, it seemed, that hope was a lie.

"I need more than thirty seconds to make a decision like that."

Owin lifted his arms to his sides. "Perhaps you're right. Think about it on the way back to Windhaven and let Gareth know what you decide. He'll get word to me. Martyn?" He gestured at his guardsman. "Escort the queen back to Major Kern and to their aeroflyer. Gareth and I have some unfinished business here."

The guardsman gestured her back through the cactus fence toward the study, and she hesitated at first. Chase hadn't wanted her out of his sight, but that was a silly thing to worry about, wasn't it? Naturally she was safe with one of Owin's guardsmen. Reluctantly, she allowed him to lead her back to the study. If nothing else, Kern was there, and without realizing it before now, she'd bestowed him with a grudging trust.

But when they entered Owin's study again, Kern wasn't there. Avery ground her heels into the marble, and the guardsman shrugged at her.

"He's probably at the flyer already, my lady. I'll take you."

"I'd much prefer to wait for Colonel Chase."

"His Grace will be along shortly, my lady. If not, there's no shortage of flyers. He'll catch up at Windhaven."

More manipulation. Owin wanted her away from the palace, back to Windhaven where she could have ample private time to think about his offer.

"No worries of that, Martyn." Chase slipped inside the study, and her heart began to beat a little slower. "If you're ready?"

Avery gave him a grateful smile. "How did you escape?" she asked as he guided her outside into the long corridor.

"Well, I rather think I used up all Owin's good graces for the next five years."

"You mean you left him standing there shouting after you."

The boyish grin she'd seen only a few times—and never since she'd arrived on Haedera—appeared on his face.

"It seems you have me figured out."

"Hardly. What did he want?"

"No idea. He stuttered and stumbled about how long I was planning on staying on Haedera, then threatened me again to get my estate in order. That's when I walked out."

Her eyes widened. "And he didn't come after you?"

"Owin? Chasing is beneath him. Has been since he was a child." He pushed open a door and gestured her into the industrial tunnel that led to the aeroflyer pad. "He'll go back to his desk and send me a dozen irate messages, and then he'll forget about it by nightfall."

The warmth of outside air from the open door at the bottom of the tunnel hit her face. If only Owin would forget about his deal along with everything else. She fell silent as Chase helped her into the flyer. He didn't seem upset at what had transpired inside Owin's study and in the afternoon garden, so why should she allow her anxiety to show?

"Next to you or across?" he asked.

She smiled at his courtesy. "Across is fine."

It wasn't fine in the least. Anyone sitting across from her in a flyer still gave her flashbacks to that awful morning at Alcaris, but she could pretend. And if she kept pretending, it would become reality. And the reality was they were on Haedera, not Asria, and Chase wasn't here to hurt her.

"Hell, sir," Kern called from the pad outside the flyer. "There you are. I've been searching all over for you. He wants you back immediately."

"Too late." Chase knocked on the wall behind their heads. "If you want a ride, better hurry up and get in."

Kern practically leapt into the flyer before the pilot could react to Chase's order. "Uppity bastards told me to take the queen back to Windhaven immediately instead of waiting for you," he vented as he snapped on his harness, uncharacteristically talkative.

"Since when do those guardsmen think they run things, anyway? I swear, Rebet never changes. Bring in a few farm boys and give them guns and they think they own the place." He slammed his mouth shut at Chase's withering glare.

Avery leaned her head against the window as the craft powered into the air. Wynne should be here to stop Kern's one-sided bickering and keep the memories at bay, but Wynne had accompanied Merritt back to the estate hours before. The skyscrapers and slums below turned to sweeping, empty desert as she tried to force the thoughts from her mind, and with a silent prayer, she looked back inside. The memory of Chase and Rhys Linden in the shuttle at Alcaris didn't strike her that time, but the recollection of Chase's words that morning did.

She was certainly easier than you.

It had been his own pain talking, but that didn't make it any better. Would anything? Maybe not, at least until she and Merritt stepped foot on Asria again. Not until she remembered everything, and that would be even further in the future.

You need to change the subject.

"Major Kern," she said, her voice surprising her. "You don't like Rebet. Why?"

Kern snorted. "Rebet is an *alig*'s den of power-hungry subjects jockeying for imperial favor. The capital attracts the worst of the system and always has. It's disgusting," he said with ease. "Present company excluded, of course, sir."

"Of course." Chase's eyebrows were as high as she'd ever seen them, though it was amusement, not shock, that tinged his features. Clearly this kind of outspokenness from Kern was nothing new.

"And your hometown is . . ."

Kern grunted and folded his arms.

"Yes," Chase said. "Tell Her Majesty about Knighton, Major. A hotbed of loyalism, is it not?"

Kern sighed. "Knighton is the site of one of the largest resistance groups in modern history, and consequently, one of the largest massacres. It was an intelligence failure on the part of a dozen agencies. It should have never gotten as vast as it did, and the response was well out of proportion. Ninety percent of the aristocracy and half the populace wiped out, just like that. We never fully recovered, and I have no desire to be a part of the remaining nobility that's inflicting their particular brand of justice on innocents."

Had Kern—had he just spoken ill of Imperial Security?

"I don't understand," she said. "What difference does it make if you're doing the same thing for Imperial Security or under your father's name?"

"Because contrary to what you think"—Kern's tone turned sharp—"I don't believe in indiscriminate killing, which is what His Grace would have me doing. Imperial Security shows more restraint than you'll ever understand."

There was no arguing with that kind of rationalization, as much as she wanted to. Did Kern really not understand what kind of terror his organization brandished over their system?

"There's a reason we have so much power," Chase added. "We don't just frighten everyone into submission—though you're right in thinking that would make things easier. I know the Commonwealth thinks we keep peace by just existing, but nothing's ever that simple. Devan had his share of attempts, though none of them came close, and Owin . . ."

He frowned. "Owin's different, and we don't need to rehash why. But he's known of the risk since he was a child. He knew he might not even make it to adulthood. There are too many others waiting for the chance."

"Even with you watching over him."

"We exist to preserve the Haederan Empire," Kern said. "Preserving the emperor is secondary to that aim."

"You preserve your empire through fear." Avery sighed and looked out the window as the flyer dropped far enough to send her stomach halfway up her throat. The turbulence was worse the farther they flew into the desert. The midday heat always did it. "Never mind. I know I'm wasting my breath."

"Arguing what you believe is never a waste of breath," Chase said. "Especially to me."

"Colonel." A new voice, the pilot, broke in. "We've got a problem. Oil pressure just went—"

A grinding noise shot through the cabin of the flyer, and her hands went automatically to her harness. She yanked on it, hard, so fast she could barely breathe.

It loosened instead. *Kusir.* The latch had completely detached from the mesh fabric.

"—just hang on, sir. It's going to be a rough landing. Going to try to make Laegih."

The pilot didn't sound panicked, so there was no reason for her to be. These things happened. Ships made emergency landings, and pilots trained for them. She had, hadn't she?

"Over here." Chase shifted toward his window, holding out the harness to the seat between him and Kern.

On shaking legs, she changed seats as the grinding became louder and louder. Kern helped her snap herself back in as she took another look outside—they were not, thank the stars, anywhere near the mountains that crisscrossed the desert outside the capital, but the cactuses below were growing larger and larger by the second. They weren't going to climb out of this one. Transmission failure, had to be. The flyer might as well be eating itself alive.

"You ever been in a crashing aeroflyer?" Chase sounded nervous for the first time.

"Brace!"

They weren't going to make Laegih after all.

She exhaled and grabbed the handhold on the seat next to Kern. The cactuses weren't just growing larger now, but the angle was the strangest thing she'd ever seen.

The flyer slammed into the ground nose-first, then rolled. To the left or right, she had no idea, because black spots filled her eyes, and up and down ceased to have any meaning. Dust—or maybe sand—filled the cabin and her lungs. For a moment, the only important thing in the universe was taking one more breath. She couldn't see Chase or Kern, though someone in the distance seemed to be calling her name. She couldn't hear much of anything over the crunching and grinding and earsplitting noises of the flyer being torn apart. They rolled one more time, settling upside down.

Then, finally, there was silence.

CHAPTER TWENTY-ONE

"MY LADY."

The Haederan lilt filled her head, cool and familiar. Avery coughed, then opened her eyes to Chase couched on the floor of the cabin in front of her. They weren't upside down anymore; at least, she didn't think they were. She didn't feel the pressure in her shoulders that would mean she was hanging from the harness, but it was difficult to tell what direction they were facing with the metal and insulation that covered the floor and seats.

"You're not injured. Just sore, I'm sure." He unfastened her harness, and she slid away from his grip. "But we need to get you out of here, and if you can't walk, I'm going to carry you, no matter how much you scream."

"I can walk."

She spit the dust from her mouth and pushed herself up. Sharp metal dug into her palm, but they could clean the wound later. Her feet were another matter. One shoe remained, and the other—who knew where it had flown off to? She grimaced at the floor of the flyer, strewn with debris and twisted metal, then at Chase's heavy boots.

"No, you can't."

She grabbed what appeared to be a solid piece of metal above her, some piece of the flyer that had been exposed in the crash, and used it to steady herself as she tested a clearing on the floor with her bare toes.

"You're not going to carry me. Where's Kern?"

"Outside tending to his busted shoulder. You'd rather him carry you out of here?"

She refrained from rolling her eyes. "I'm concerned."

"You're stalling. Do you smell that?" Irritation speared his question as he pointed at the liquid dripping down the forward bulkhead behind her. "We might not have much time."

Fuel. She smelled it, acrid and burning, and she knew he knew she could.

He held out his hand. "I'm not going to hurt you."

Why should she believe that? He'd done it before, hadn't he? He'd slapped her and pushed her against the wall and done who knew what else. And now he expected her to allow him to lift her out of this flyer? He didn't know what he was asking of her.

She froze, her hand above her. What would be the purpose of that abuse now? In Chase's mind, his cruelty always had a purpose. He wasn't going to throw her to the deck of the flyer for the fun of it. With some reluctance, she nodded, even though the memories fought with the smell of the fuel, threatening to over-take reality.

"Fine," she said, letting go of the handhold. "Just be quick. And don't drop me."

"I wouldn't dare drop you, my lady."

There was a hint—just a shadow—of his familiar mocking grin as he lifted her straight up and strolled through the wreckage toward the hatch. The accident had crushed it, leaving a strangely shaped hole instead of the rectangular exit that had been there before, and she had to duck her head against his shoulder as they moved through the opening. Before she had the chance to stop shaking at his touch, he'd deposited her on the ground outside next to Kern.

"Both of you stay right there," Chase said. "I'm going to check up front."

She waved off Kern's attentions, and after checking the scratch on her hand, surveyed their surroundings. The flyer had crashed in an arid wash, and the soft sand probably accounted for their survival. Able to move without much pain except where the harness had bruised her shoulders—likely Kern's injury as well—she walked a few paces toward the edge of the wash. There was no fuel smell here, which meant the flyer wasn't leaking enough to turn the riparian trees that surrounded it into an inferno. Some good news, at least.

Chase emerged from the hatch as she made her way back around to the side of the flyer, shaking his head.

"How bad?" Kern asked.

"Flyer's done for. Pilot slammed his chest against the controls, best I can figure."

Her heart sank. "But the harnesses."

"His harness was tampered with, too. Microtears along the edge. He would have never noticed during the daily inspection."

A chill wound down her back despite the heat clinging to the desert, and she sank to the ground and put her head in her hands. It was too much. She should be dead and that pilot should be alive, off doing whatever it was that Imperial Security officers did when they weren't tormenting their fellow subjects. Instead, she was stuck in the middle of the wilderness with the last person in the galaxy that she wanted to be with.

"And they must have done something to mine as well," she said.

"Likely." Shifting evening shadows moved around the corners of her vision as Chase sat down beside her. "Are you hurt?" he asked.

"I'm fine. Just a little shaken."

"You had a concussion not that many days ago. I'm concerned about that, Your Majesty."

She wound her fingers through her hair, matted with dust and sand, to avoid answering. Was this what being queen was like? Everyone, even Chase, constantly concerned for her safety and well-being? It was suffocating, especially after the things he'd said that morning.

"Again, I'm fine. I know the symptoms, and I'll let you know if I'm not." Not that there was anything anyone could do for her out here if she had a skull fracture. "But I don't understand. Who had access to the flyer? Is the Imperial Security Command involved in this?"

Kern snorted. "Of course not."

He sounded uncomfortable, though, like the thought had occurred to him as well. But that was nonsense. The idea of Imperial Security assassinating her was just her imagination running wild. The simplest explanation was that radical traditionalist Haederans didn't want Owin ruling, didn't want the Haederan Empire's tenuous relationship with the Commonwealth, and didn't want the queen of Asria on their planet except in chains. Anything else was silly conjecture, the product of a fearful and inventive mind.

Wasn't it?

"We'll talk about this later," Chase said. "I'm going to find the emergency kit. It's going to get cold soon, and we could use the blankets. And water."

"I'll help you." Anything to dispel her pounding headache. Not a concussion—she would never admit that to Chase—but dehydration and fear? She needed to do something to avoid focusing on those.

"Not barefoot. You'll sit right there and rest within eyeshot of Major Kern." His tone sharpened. "Please, my lady."

Avery ignored him, pushed herself up, and marched to the back of the destroyed flyer. Fuel was leaking from the stub wing now, yes, but it was easy enough to avoid, and if it hadn't caught fire by now, it wasn't going to. Chase disappeared inside the mangled hatch, then tossed a light out to her without any further argument. A stack of emergency blankets from under the rear seats followed.

"I suppose I did need one of you," he said, his reluctance obvious. "Much easier than holding the light myself. And believe it or not, you argue less than Brennin."

Silent, she kept the light on him as he grabbed the portable shelter and water generator. They'd need it soon. Chase sat back on his knees, so she blew out a breath and headed around the front of the flyer toward the small cockpit with one of the blankets he'd thrown to her. A few days out here with him was an excruciating thought, and she needed a break.

He ducked his head outside the hatch when her light disappeared. "Where are you going? I need that light."

She stopped and clutched the packaged blankets to her chest. "To cover up the pilot."

Chase jumped out the opening and stepped in front of her. "We'll need those tonight."

"I doubt that. We have a shelter, and there are four blankets in this package. I'm using one to cover him up."

He sighed and held out his hand. "I'll do it."

"No. Me. It's the least I can do."

He cocked his head sideways, as if in acquiescence, and moved aside.

It was a tight fit through the crushed doorway to the small flight deck. Bile rose in her throat at the sight of the pilot. He was leaning back in his seat, eyes closed. Yes, Chase had been thorough in his examination. She held her breath as she ripped open the package with her teeth and spread the silver blanket over his battered body. It didn't seem like enough.

Holy One, protect his—she managed to avoid adding *Haederan* —*soul.*

Silent, she passed Chase and hopped out of the flyer, only for her legs to buckle. He watched, arms crossed, as her knees hit the ground. *Kusir,* how she wanted to remain on the ground and sleep, even in front of him, but she spit sand from her mouth and brushed it from her skirt as she stood again.

"Sure," he said. "You might not have a concussion, but you're too shaken up to be doing any of this." He grabbed her by the arm and half dragged her out of the wash to an empty patch of sand where Kern was inventorying their supplies. "Sit down."

The familiar itching in her brain began again, the start of a flashback. She jerked her arm away, but there was no point in fighting it if it was going to happen. And Chase was—oh, she didn't want to even think it. Chase was right. She took the blanket he offered and flopped onto it.

"Now stay there." He dropped the rest of the supplies in front of her and glanced around the desert. "Brennin and I have got to get a fire started. It might be hot now, but it'll cool off rapidly once the sun goes down."

"I can help."

"Sit," he said, with a gesture toward Kern. They didn't stop to make sure she obeyed, just walked off a short distance into the desert, only to return with armloads of dried cactus spines. "They burn well, at least," he said with a tired smile.

Avery busied herself with the water generator as he and Kern stacked the spines. Six clean cups came out of the packaging first. More small mercies. Even more miraculous was the small flashing light on the side of the box and the drops of precious water that began to flow out. That immediate predicament dealt with, she glanced up at Chase, then back down.

She'd let him touch her. Chase, the one who'd terrified and threatened and struck her. She'd always sworn if she somehow escaped that prison in Cadena that she'd make him pay, but instead, she was depending on him in one of the most desolate areas of his own planet. What a sick, cosmic joke. Was the Holy One laughing at her right now? Or was this another attempt to force forgiveness?

"How long until they come for us?" she asked.

"The emergency transmitter was disabled," Kern said. "A few days, if we're lucky."

"Cut harnesses and a disabled emergency transmitter. And you're going to say it wasn't intentional?"

"I said we'd talk about it later." Chase fussed with the last few spines, then collapsed on the ground next to Kern.

"It's later. What do you know, Colonel?"

"I know as much as you."

"Who had access to your flyer?"

"The pilot and palace security. That's it."

"Then how do you know Imperial Security isn't behind this?"

"Why would we want you dead?" Kern leaned backward on his elbows.

She waved her hand out toward the mountains.

"I'm Asrian. Don't tell me the armistice hasn't made me unpopular here as well."

"Perhaps," he replied, "but the palace staff wouldn't dare. You saw how seriously His Majesty took this latest incident. More importantly, they saw it."

Kern's reassurance didn't make her feel any better. What if this had been the desired outcome? What if she hadn't been meant to die in the crash but out here alone in the wilderness? Kern and Chase were armed, and no one would ever know . . . would she even see it coming?

She tensed, and judging by how Chase shifted away from her, he'd noticed.

"Imperial Security is not behind this. Do you understand?" he asked.

"Then convince me otherwise. I'm sure you've got some idea of what those other options could be."

Kern ticked them off on his fingers. "Traditionalist Haederans unhappy with the armistice. A colleague of your brother's who didn't like that the job wasn't finished. Someone who mistook your transport for the emperor's. You can guess how many of those are hanging around Rebet."

"But none of them would have had access to an Imperial Security aeroflyer parked on a palace pad surrounded by your guardsmen."

"No," Chase admitted. "They wouldn't."

"So we're right back to where we began. You."

"No." He scratched at his forehead and looked at Kern. "I swear to you, this was not Imperial Security. It's not possible. Lient . . . I know this will make you uncomfortable, my lady, but it should make you feel safe. He has an odd respect for you. Any order to take you out would have to come from someone high in command, and he'd hear about it. He hears everything to begin with. Believe me, he'd never allow your assassination unless he personally desired it."

"Well, that's comforting," she said sarcastically. The idea of Lient tacitly ordering her murder didn't bear thinking about. "So that leaves who?"

"Only one person, I would think." Chase drew a few idle marks in the sand, then looked up. "His Majesty."

CHAPTER TWENTY-TWO

Avery burst out laughing.

Haederans and their paranoia. Owin was trying to kill her? Of all the nonsensical things Chase had ever said, this topped them all. She looked toward Kern, desperately needing to share her humor, but he wasn't amused, and the hot sand underneath her suddenly seemed like ice.

"You're serious," she said.

"You challenged him," Chase said. "I know you know better, but I also know that's never stopped you before. Owin, however, took it personally."

"How—"

"He told me what you'd asked of him on a call that same night. A rather long call where he vented about your rebelliousness and disrespect and told me he wouldn't put up with it, no matter what he'd agreed to."

"You never warned me," she said.

"Would it have changed anything if I had?" Chase gave her a small smile. "I didn't see the need to let you know. What was done was done, and I didn't think you'd see him again for a long time, perhaps not for the remainder of your stay here. I'd hoped his anger would have died down by then, and I certainly didn't think he'd throw the decision regarding Fiona at you earlier today."

"You think he changed his mind so suddenly to get me back on that aeroflyer."

Chase shrugged. "It would explain why he held me back and sent Brennin to escort you back to Windhaven without me."

"Some of us are more expendable than others," Kern added.

At the bitterness in his voice, Avery whipped her head toward him. Had Owin forgotten Kern was likely one of the officers who'd helped put him in power? He'd either made a grave mistake in threatening one of his most ardent supporters or had been attempting to tie up loose ends. Neither looked good for Kern, but that meant she'd earned herself another ally.

"And now?" she asked. "Is he going to come after us out here?"

"No." Chase sounded convinced. "An aeroflyer crash can be explained away. An aeroflyer crash followed by an attack by bandits or the like? That would raise too many questions. But listen . . ." His certainty faded away. "I don't want to say this either, but this means Fiona was wrong about Quen's patron. I'm sure of it now."

He didn't say anything else, and she knew.

"It was Owin," she breathed. The color drained from her face. "All because I challenged him. And Quen would have made the perfect assassin. Already angry, motivated by money and his hate for me." Her voice broke. "But I would do it again. And I'm going to keep doing it until we're free."

"Listen to me. I'm not going to risk your life. Ever. If he wants to hurt you, he'll have to come through me first. You know that, don't you?"

"I think so."

"Good. I'd rather you believe me, but I'll take unsure." Chase leaned back and sighed. "It was Owin's idea to go for a walk in the Linden garden, you know."

"But that was before I even mentioned withdrawing your

troops. You're saying he set up that attack? And maybe even the one in Cadena?"

"His Majesty isn't stupid," Kern broke in. "And you, my lady, are"—a slight smile crossed his face—"rather insistent when you set your mind to something. And predictable, if we're being honest. He knew what was coming. You argued against the surveillance base in open committee, after all—did you think that wouldn't reach his ears?"

Chase nodded. He met her eyes, solemn, then turned to Kern.

"Brennin—I think it's time for that shelter, if you would."

Kern didn't blink. "Seems like it, sir. Back in a while." He disappeared into the rapidly setting sun, and silence fell upon the little camp. A breeze picked up, but it didn't mitigate the heat as much as she wanted.

"I need you to trust me. Instead you're afraid of me." Chase flicked the starter at the pile of dried cactus spines. Flames burst into existence, licking the sweltering air. "Still."

It didn't matter how much she pretended otherwise, he could read her. Yes, she was angry, but the terror—the terror always ended up overriding the anger, and oh, how she wanted to be furious instead of afraid. She would have to be flippant instead. It'd always been the only way.

"After your performance this morning," she said, strengthening her tone, "I find it impossible to believe that's such a shocking reaction. You have a rather short memory, Colonel."

"I remember everything. More than you do, you know. But I'd rather hoped . . ." He looked at the fire and shrugged. "I was out of line this morning. I'm sorry."

What did apologies mean anymore? Empty words. They were nothing but empty words, especially from Chase.

"I remember enough," she said. "I remember being terrified and cold and hungry and in pain. I remember exactly what that room looked like and what it was like to sit there for hours, knowing whatever resistance I had left wouldn't be enough. Some days—some days are fine. And others? I jump when a sentry comes around the corner because I'm afraid they'll be in a Haederan uniform."

"I can imagine." It sounded like the same false soothing tone he'd used on her that morning, and her anger grew.

"Can you? Have you ever been in my position? I don't think you have, so you can't possibly imagine it from your side, no matter how long of a career you've had."

She tilted the water generator to the cup. It hadn't produced much so far, but it was better than nothing.

"Yes, I have memories, but there are so many things I don't remember. Hadley said I didn't tell you anything important, but I don't remember. I have no idea if that's true or not. Black holes in my memory, remembrances that seem like hazy dreams. Maybe they *are* dreams. I have so many nightmares that I don't know what's reality and myth any longer. Maybe I am a traitor."

What wasn't she remembering? What had she told him?

In the distance, something howled. An *okaucro*? Perhaps it really was time for that shelter, even though the idea of sharing it with Chase and Kern made her stomach flip. The last time she'd fallen asleep in front of Chase, he'd slapped her. She'd shown a moment of weakness, and he'd taken advantage of it. That, she remembered.

The flames reflected in his blank face for a long time.

"My lady," he said abruptly, his voice uneven. "I could tell you what you told me, but I know you'd never believe me, even if you wanted to. I don't blame you for that. Only, I have the interrogation notes and those of the medic. Both are personal copies of the same daily reports I sent to Lient. They are"—he swallowed—"extremely detailed, as one would expect of a high-level prisoner. Of any of my prisoners. And they're accurate. If you're anxious to remember what exactly went on in Cadena, what precisely you spoke of to me and endured there, they are yours."

She set the generator in the sand and covered her eyes against the low sun. Her body had gone numb; her mouth had gone dry.

It was a gift he'd just offered, wasn't it? A horrifying one, but a gift nonetheless.

"Think about it." He stood. "I'm going to help Brennin with that shelter."

* * *

She woke screaming, damp waves of hair clinging to her forehead. Small bits of light danced through the shelter's walls, and she sat up, clutching the blanket across her chest. The shelter was empty, and not nearly hot enough to account for the profuse sweat that covered her. Before her heart settled, Chase stuck his head inside, though he didn't look concerned.

"I'm guessing," he said, handing her a fresh cup of water, "that was one of the frequent nightmares."

The water cooled her throat but not much else. Avery tucked the curls behind her ears and motioned him outside. The shelter had been cool thanks to the integral fans, but the desert was anything but, even so early in the morning. Heat shimmered against the distant mountains, and across the wash, Kern paced on the far side of the flyer, his jacket tossed haphazardly across one of the wings.

"It warmed up quickly," she said to Chase, more to change the subject than out of curiosity about the heat. If he thought she was simply hot, maybe—perhaps—he wouldn't truly believe how terrifying the nightmare had been.

He didn't miss a beat. "A hundred and seventeen already. It's going to be hot."

At least the breeze felt good for now. "How long are we going to wait before we start walking?" The very idea made her body heavy.

"Another day, at least. Those mountains over there"—he pointed toward the west—"are at least sixty kilometers away, and you're not acclimated."

"Neither are you."

He graced her with a sour look as he pointed toward the fire. "I was heating coffee when I heard you screaming. Would you care for some?"

Guilty. He was feeling guilty, and his sniping was a dead give-away. Avery nodded and settled onto the blanket by the fire, trying to squash the anger threatening to boil up. Surely they had a better use for water than coffee. But Chase knew Haedera, didn't he? Maybe the generator had produced enough during the night.

And, it appeared, it had. Chase dumped a package of coffee crystals into a fresh cup, and she breathed in the familiar scent.

"What's going to happen to Fiona?" she asked.

Chase picked up a rock and tossed it toward a shallow hole he'd dug about ten paces away. A pile of them sat in the center; he'd been at his game a while.

"Just what my esteemed brother-in-law said." His voice was steel. "Nothing can prevent our ceaseless march toward our own destruction. Since you're supposed to be dead and therefore unable to protest, her sentence has undoubtedly already been carried out. She's one less loose end for Owin to worry about."

The heat of the desert settled into her gut.

"I'm so sorry," she said. "I wish there was something I could have done."

"There was no way around it. Not while Haedera is Haedera. Not even if you'd agreed to give up those names in exchange for her life." Chase tossed a rock, then another. "You know there was nothing I could do about it, either, only mitigate the damage that had already been done. Her mother is safe, at least—I made sure of that. It was all Fiona asked of me." He fell silent, and the pile of rocks grew.

She could take a hint.

"And me?"

"I told you. I won't do anything to risk your life. You'll go home, and you'll be safe there. As safe as you can be."

His real concern was obvious. Even if Owin backed off, as long as she was queen of Asria, she would never be safe. She would always be angering the wrong people, making the wrong decisions, traveling to places where no sane person would go. The quadrant had changed since her carefree days as a child at Sabino, and the only thing left to do was change with them. Chase understood that more than most.

"I want that surveillance station gone," she said. "I want the Imperial Haederan Army off my planet."

"I know you do."

"I'll fight until it happens. Until Asria is completely free again."

"I know you will." Pride shone in his eyes, tempered by concern. "I wish you wouldn't—but I know you will."

There wasn't anything else to say. She drew a few circles in the sand, but it didn't assuage her fears. Best not to focus on the future. Not right now.

"Didn't you sleep last night?" she finally asked with a nod toward the hole, now almost full.

"Not really. I spent most of the night lying on my back looking at the stars." Chase gave her a tired smile. "My father loved them. I don't, and I've always wondered why."

"If he was anything like me, they meant freedom. Or did at one point." She squinted for any remaining stars against the glare of the high sun. As soon as it'd crested the faraway mountains, their camp had warmed. Haederan court attire—the long skirt and elbow-length sleeves she wore—made things worse. On the other hand, they were light and flowy, and she wouldn't end up sunburned. Better still, the deep rose silk stood out against the sand, and any rescuers would see her long before they saw the crashed aeroflyer. Chase's wool service uniform looked less comfortable, though like Kern, he'd ditched the jacket.

"He thought so, too. I used to stare at pictures of his father and grandfather, but it took a long time before I connected their uniforms to the reality of their frequent absence. When I figured it out, I felt betrayed. What could space offer that I couldn't? Why did he prefer those stars to my younger brother and sister and me?"

Avery shifted uncomfortably. It wasn't a criticism of her decision to leave Asria, but it felt close. She'd left Merritt behind to fly for the Commonwealth, after all. If Victor hadn't abdicated, if she'd never been forced from the academy, Lucas would have never existed.

"I'm sure he didn't prefer them." How odd it felt to comfort Chase. "I'm sure he loved you."

"I know that now. And yet . . ." Chase sighed. "I always wonder what would've happened if I'd chosen his path. Who would I be today?"

My life would have gone much differently.

Or would it have? If it hadn't been Chase, it would have been someone else. Maybe she wouldn't have survived. Maybe she'd have escaped with her life but ended up physically maimed as well as emotionally traumatized. Or maybe even . . .

She pinched the skin between her thumb and finger to stop the runaway imagination. The potential futures, twisted and string-like with infinite possibilities, weren't worth the agony.

Chase must have read her mind with that particular talent he had, because he looked away, over the mountains in the distance. Leaving her with her thoughts, he craned his neck and checked his chronometer, then pointed west.

"Aeroflyer. Looks about five minutes out. They were faster than I gave them credit for."

Only five more minutes alone with him. The knot that had turned to iron in her stomach slowly began to unravel as the unmistakable promise of rescue filled her ears. She'd experienced one of the longest afternoons, nights, and mornings of her life, and she'd survived. She blinked at the aeroflyer, just to make certain it truly existed, then glanced back at Chase. He was still staring off into the distance, and as she watched his profile, the most outrageous thought flew into her mind. Fate had always been an indefinable, nebulous thing. The sovereignty of the Holy One had been just a story she'd been taught, but maybe . . .

She smiled at his back. Maybe, just maybe, they'd been fated to meet. Put on their particular string of life by something greater.

"Colonel?" she asked as the aeroflyer touched down on the other side of the wash.

He turned, eyebrows raised, just like in her nightmare. Tears filled her eyes, only this time, they were tears of relief. Just relief. Not fear, because she would never let herself be afraid of him again.

"When we get back to Windhaven, I'd like to see those notes."

CHAPTER TWENTY-THREE

AVERY REACHED OUT HER FINGERS AGAIN, THEN PULLED THEM BACK. The disk sat on her palm with a look of perfect innocence, almost as if it were watching her. All she had to do was stick it in the tablet that sat next to her. All she had to do was read words. Just strings of letters, retyped a dozen times, not even written in Chase's hand. Letters and words couldn't hurt her, could they? Not like a beating could.

Chase cleared his throat from the chair across from her. "You don't need to rush this."

"If I don't, I'll never do it."

"You can do it in five minutes," Merritt said. "Or five days, for that matter. There truly is no rush."

"We're leaving in two," she pointed out. Their belongings were already packed and sitting in a corner of the guest house. The only thing left were final preparations and provisions for *Mayfair*. Neave would want his ship back just like he'd loaned it, and neither she nor Merritt wanted to stop for supplies.

"Yes. Yes, of course." That frustrated tone was in Merritt's voice, the one he could never hide when she was overly literal in his presence. "You know what I mean."

"I know." She stuck the disk inside the tablet before she could change her mind once more. "The order is self-explanatory?"

Chase nodded. "Chronological, starting the day you were transferred to Imperial Security custody."

She nodded. Her mouth was dry, but she couldn't move even a finger toward the glass of water next to her. Merritt slid his hand over hers, and she began to read.

Time: 1528. Date: 78 Cael.

Interrogator escorted prisoner to personal office in temporary IHA prison. Prisoner reacts appropriately to standard rapport-building techniques and spontaneously confessed to holding a Commonwealth Navy commission in direct contradiction to information given IHA military governor. Interrogator attempted to confirm extent of prisoner's misinformation, suggesting leniency might be an option given enough cooperation; prisoner stated she would rather die than accept interrogator's assistance. Handler and further network to be determined in future sessions.

The memories didn't exactly take over as she skimmed over the first entry, but a few flickered into the front of her mind. She was sitting in that chair in Chase's office on a warm autumn day, watching the golden trees outside flaunt their freedom. Uninjured but terrified, she'd known the brief reprieve wouldn't last. Even if she talked that very second, she would never tell him everything he wanted. And when she stopped? That's when it would truly begin. Chase had watched her from only a few paces away, calm and collected, as she shook from that realization. Too calm. He'd known, even then, that he'd win.

"I need a break." She glanced up at their concerned faces. "Just a few minutes. I just—I just need some time to gather myself."

Need some time to forget how he looked at me back then.

Merritt squeezed her hand. "Of course. We'll check back in."

He gestured to Chase, and they disappeared with no argument. Avery set the disk to the side and paced the library. The sun streaming through the windows should have warmed her, but it didn't seem that anything would ever settle the chill in her soul. What was she about to learn? Would it solve everything, or would it ruin the scant peace she'd lived with since the war?

"My lady?" a quiet voice broke in.

Avery jumped as she twisted away from the windows. Sophie stood just a few paces away, immaculately dressed and styled as always. Only this afternoon her feet were bare, and dark circles ringed her eyes. She'd been crying, and for a long time by the looks of things.

"Sophie?" She glanced around the library for the source of the emotion. There was no one, not even Wynne. That meant Kern had people close by, and she shivered at their unseen presence.

"I'm sorry for interrupting." Her voice was soft, lilting, tentative. "I was wondering if I could talk to you. Please."

"Of course." Avery motioned her to the sofa by the window. "What's wrong?"

Sophie followed, wringing her hands. "Please don't tell my father I came here to see you."

Practice for ten years from now. "I can't promise that. But I can promise I'll listen. And then if you need to talk to him about it, I'll help you figure out what to say."

Sophie sat next to her and stared at her bare feet for a full five minutes. Finally, she looked up, one tear on her cheek.

"It's my fault he's dead."

"Who? Marc?"

She nodded without blinking. "We had a fight that day because he'd been in my rooms again. Moving my stuff around, reading my journal, that kind of thing. He was always messing around in there, and I was so angry with him for it, especially when we fought over it and he did nothing but laugh. So when they showed up for him . . ."

The one tear became a flood.

"When Father's people came, he didn't want to go. He loved visiting Grandpapa, but he had my journal hidden in his room and he was going to spend the day reading it. He'd been taunting me about it for a week, so I told him he needed to go to the palace and Grandpapa would be angry if he said no." She grabbed a leaf off the large plant next to the sofa and crushed it between her fingers. "I convinced him to go with them so I could sneak in and get it back without him knowing."

Avery reached out and pulled Sophie against her, mostly to hide her own tears. How was she supposed to explain betrayal and death to an eleven-year-old when she didn't understand it herself?

"What happened to Marc was not your fault," she said. "You didn't cause it, and you're not responsible for it."

Sophie looked up with a bit of hope. "If that's so, why does he resent me so much?"

"Your father?"

Sophie only pressed harder against her side.

"Oh, Sophie, no. I promise you that he does not resent you, and he does not blame you for this." Defending Chase was harder than it should have been. "He's hurt, yes, and grieving, and he doesn't know how to deal with that. But he does not resent you for living. He knows you had nothing to do with this. He loves you."

"Really?"

"I'm certain of it."

"But he lied. If he loved me, he wouldn't lie to me."

"What did he lie about?"

What hasn't he lied about? was probably more accurate.

"He said he was going to retire. No more Imperial Security Command. That it would be just me and him here at Windhaven. No more trips off-world. No more secrets. But there've been so many of them around that I know he hasn't been telling the truth." Sophie bit her lip and looked at her hands.

Avery sighed. "Well, Major Kern is only here to watch me. To make sure I'm safe."

To make my life miserable.

"Yes, my lady. And his men. I see them all over the estate, even though they think I don't. They think I'm a baby, and that they don't need to hide from me. I don't like them, but they don't frighten me."

Avery stifled a laugh. Trust a child to see through Imperial Security.

"But the rest of them," Sophie went on, her eyes wide, "the ones who aren't here for you, they've been visiting so very frequently since he returned. Sometimes even General Lient."

The laugh faded away like she'd imagined it, and her stomach dropped.

Your service ends with your death, in case you've forgotten. Not when you decide it's no longer worth your while.

Chase would never leave Imperial Security.

Because Imperial Security would never let him go.

She wanted to hug Sophie, to tell her everything would be fine, that Chase would retire and live out his days at Windhaven —but that wasn't the truth. The real truth, the one no one in the Commonwealth wanted to accept, was that Haedera would never change, armistice or not. Perhaps Owin wasn't as bad as his father, but he wasn't a leader the Commonwealth would ever allow to remain in power on one of their own planets. And Chase? It didn't matter what he wanted. He was trapped as surely as she.

"Sophie, I—" Avery jumped as the library door swung open, and Chase stepped inside with a strange glance at both of them.

"Can we talk?" he asked. "Somewhere else."

"Now's not a good time." She reached for Sophie's hand. How could he not notice how upset the child was? She wouldn't force a conversation between them, not yet, but Chase should know enough to ask what was wrong with his own daughter. "Sophie and I are talking."

He didn't break eye contact with her. "It's urgent that you and I speak. Alone. Now."

Avery blew out a deep breath and nodded at Sophie as she stood.

"Why not here?" she asked Chase as she swiped the disk off the table and followed him into the corridor. It'd been his idea to view the notes in the library to begin with. *Fewer prying servants,* he'd said. *They know not to interrupt me in here.* "I'm ready now. If someone can find Merritt, we can get started. Does this really need to be done now?"

"Yes," he said. "It does."

His soberness touched her heart, but the familiar panic began to war with her anxiety.

"I'm not comfortable with this," she replied. "Perhaps someone can find Wynne first."

"Please, Your Majesty."

The serious look on his face was nothing new, but this time something was wrong.

"Yes," she said. "All right. But you're concerning me now."

He smiled. "It's nothing to worry about. Trust me. Let's just go for a little walk."

* * *

As they approached the hillside chapel, the gradual unease she'd felt in the library turned to the blaring alarm bells she'd heard mentally ringing in Chase's presence only once before. It was so loud it overcame the squawks of the birds that watched her from the building, and just like the last time, she couldn't force her legs to run away.

"Here?" she asked, standing awkwardly inside the doorway.

Chase picked up Marc's picture and dusted it off with his hand. "It's peaceful here. A good place for a talk. Don't you think?"

"I suppose." She lifted her shoulders in partial disagreement.

Peaceful wasn't the word she'd have chosen, not with the stark reminder of Marc's death staring her in the face. Heartbreaking. Poignant, maybe. But not peaceful.

"I don't know why you bother trying to lie to me. You've never been accomplished at it." He kissed the photo before replacing it. "I leave for Ventana IV tomorrow," he said abruptly.

Avery blinked at him. "Ventana?"

"To turn myself in."

"But—" Her heart closed in on itself.

Chase rolled up the sleeve of his loose shirt and angled his body for her to see.

"Even Owin's influence has limits when it comes to the Commonwealth," he said, softer than she'd expected. "They don't trust him, and they certainly don't trust me."

She stared at the small implant that barely protruded from the skin of his upper arm. Her fingers reached out of their own accord, but she yanked them back before they could brush against him, her face red.

"You said everything was fine. That you'd been cleared and released. You lied." Her breath caught, and she did everything she could to fight through it. "You lied to me and you lied to Kern and you lied to Owin and you lied to Imperial Security."

Chase shrugged, avoiding her eyes.

"So what is this? Some kind of parole?"

He nodded but didn't seem inclined to say anything else.

"How much time did they give you?"

"As long as I needed to make sure things were taken care of here. They know I have a child." He pulled his sleeve back down and smoothed out the wrinkles. "Though I suspect they'd be happy if I simply never showed my face on a Commonwealth planet again."

"You're telling me you couldn't have cut that thing out of yourself? You're out of the Commonwealth's reach here. They won't come after you, especially with Owin being who he is." None of this made any sense. Chase was a lot of things, but reckless and impulsive wasn't one of them. He'd changed his mind in the span of ten minutes? "As long as you stay here," she went on, "they won't care. That's all they want, anyway, for you and the rest of Imperial Security to stay on Haedera and leave us alone. They won't bother you if you stay here and away from any Commonwealth world."

Especially Asria.

"I could have had it cut out," he replied. "I chose not to. What I did to you was wrong, and I'm going to answer for it."

"Is this about the notes? If they're bothering you that much, then burn the disk. I'll survive. You don't need to play the martyr here, Colonel. I'm standing right here, the person you wronged, telling you that you do not need to do this."

"I don't think you know the definition. It's about atonement, not martyrdom."

How was she supposed to argue with someone who'd made up his mind? It was like bashing her head against that brick wall again, only this time it was his will she couldn't bend, not her own.

She looked back at Marc's picture. Had Chase forgotten Marc wasn't his only child?

"But what about Sophie?" she asked. Did he even remember she was waiting in the library?

That muscle in his jaw, the one that was the only betrayal of his emotions, tightened.

"I'll tell her tomorrow morning. Sophie has family on Haedera, and she's my sole heir. It's not as though she'll be left destitute. Besides, she barely knows me as it is. Never has, and that's the way it needs to stay. She deserves better."

He had no idea. Had Chase let Sophie cry on his shoulder? Had he let her mourn her brother and mother?

"But she loves you. She needs you. Not her uncle the emperor who's too busy for anything but running his empire, not the million distant imperial cousins you have hidden around Haedera, and not the servants at Windhaven who are afraid of her because she's your daughter. You. The man standing right here in front of me, daring to claim she deserves better. You would take her father away from her after she's already lost her mother and brother?"

And grandfather. Don't forget that one.

"She's been traumatized, not that that's any surprise to anyone who's met her, and she needs you. She needs your love and your time and your forgiveness for something she didn't even do."

Chase's eyes turned cold. "I've made my decision. I'm telling you as a courtesy because I think you deserve to know, not so you can stand here and argue with me."

"And there's nothing that will change your mind? Nothing I can do? Nothing I can say? Colonel, please. I'm begging you. Don't do this. This is all in your control. You don't have to do this, especially out of some misguided penance."

"Are you really trying to change my mind?" Chase stepped toward her until she was pushed up against the cool stone wall. "Are you really standing here telling me what I should and shouldn't do?"

"You asked for my forgiveness." Avery tried to shrug him off, but his hand gripped her shoulder, and he dug in his fingers before she could slip out the door. *Kusir*, more tears. She had to stop them. Tears were weakness. Tears showed him he had control over her, and he couldn't know how badly she was still affected.

"That was a mistake," he replied. "Do you think you're allowed a say in whether I've atoned enough or not?"

His voice was low, dangerous. This, she remembered. *Felt.* This was the Chase of that bright room, with eyes like ice. She pressed herself against the wall, putting as much distance between them as she could, but he closed the remaining space between them until she could scarcely breathe against his chest. Speaking— fighting—both were out of the question.

"You betrayed the Commonwealth because I forced you to," he said into her ear. "You became a traitor. I could make you do it again in five minutes if I wanted, right here, right now. You're so broken that you'd do anything I asked. And that's just today. Another week and I'd have you landing on Ventana IV and killing the supreme commander of the Commonwealth herself if I wanted you to."

Her heartbeat pounded in her ears; the chapel went gray. The scorching chapel disappeared in her mind; the walls turned to the cold concrete of that interrogation room.

No.

But somehow, buried in the terror, she found her voice.

"Let me go. Colonel, please."

"You don't hear yourself, do you? Well, I do. You sound just like you did back then, begging and pleading for mercy even as they struck you, knowing it didn't matter—that I'd do whatever I wanted to you, make you say whatever I wanted you to say, and you'd lose. Get out of here."

He released her shoulder and shoved her toward the door, then turned toward what was left of Marc to light another candle.

Her chest hurt. Her head hurt. Her soul hurt. And when she darted back to the guest house, not caring that Kern had come up behind and was calling for her over and over, not caring that Merritt was going to question her about the tears . . .

Chase didn't follow.

CHAPTER TWENTY-FOUR

Mayfair was too quiet. Avery hadn't realized just how much noise and chatter had filled the spacecraft on the way to Haedera until they were two weeks out from Windhaven, captained by a Haederan crew who was stiff and formal toward her while being chummy toward Merritt in the same breath. Ignored again, not that it was a surprise. And the children? Sophie had always been quiet, but now the girl's absence was tangible. But now, even Lucas's screeches that rang out as he toddled around the ship, even Merritt muttering under his breath at his tablet, even the low Haederan music that echoed through the washroom—none of them could break the strange silence.

She would never admit it was Chase who was missing.

Never.

Because she'd given him too much credit. Had fallen for his kindness, his lies, and this many weeks later, her own mistakes filled her mind. He'd saved her from Quen, yes, had probably saved her from Owin's assassination attempts at the Linden house and in the middle of the desert, but for what purpose? To simply turn around and traumatize her again only a few days later?

With a sigh, she waved off the lights in the washroom. If his quiet conversation with himself was any indication, Merritt was busy with work as usual. That was something else that would change when they reached Cadena, because settling into his minor duties as prince consort would take priority for the next year. He'd promised. It had taken long pleas and negotiations to have that official leave approved, but the Defense Forces had at last relented, and Merritt had received word just a week ago. They'd really had no choice.

And after his year of royal obligations? The waving and events and looking good by her side? The Defense Forces medical board was so very close to clearing him, and if they did, he'd go to a part-time flying billet like he'd always dreamed. Things would be perfect. Finally.

She pulled the curls off her neck and settled into bed next to him. "What are you working on?"

Merritt smiled at her. Or more precisely, she suspected, what she wasn't wearing. "Just some things. Nothing important."

She leaned over his shoulder. It was hard to tell what he was working on through the crack in the glass that ran from one corner of the tablet diagonally toward the center. *Strange.* She'd spent half her time at Windhaven curled up against him like this while he worked, and she'd never noticed a crack.

"Did you drop this?" she asked, running a light finger across it. "I'm sure we can find you a loaner if you'd like. This looks like an annoyance to work on."

"Hmm?" He stuck his arm under her back and pulled her closer, sounding distracted. "Drop what?"

"Your tablet. It looks like it's about to break in two."

Two.

Heat rushed over her. How had she never noticed? She hadn't seen Merritt working ever since their desert walk just before Chase had suddenly returned to Windhaven. She hadn't seen him working on this cracked tablet, not on any tablet. Not since . . .

Nausea joined the heat.

Not since he'd left it sitting on the foyer table in the guest house at Windhaven.

And he thought she would never notice. That she'd never put everything together. That she'd never figure it out. How could she have been so trusting? How could she have been so distracted?

His friendship with Kern.

Chase's rescue of him.

His defense of Chase.

The way he'd suddenly changed his mind and gone to Haedera with her after claiming that he couldn't possibly leave Asria.

"You bastard." She sprang out of bed, the heat settling in her cheeks. The silk lingerie that left nothing to his imagination seemed a mockery now. She wanted nothing more than to cover herself up. To put light-years and layers upon layers of fabric between them. "You're working for them."

Merritt set the tablet aside and furrowed his brow. "Excuse me?"

"How long?" Her voice shook.

Sudden realization touched the creases around his eyes. He jumped across the bed and up in front of her, his hands in front of him.

"Avery, listen. We can't talk about this here."

"Don't touch me. How could you do this?"

She glanced frantically around for a weapon. Or a robe. Or a pillow to hold in front of her. Or even Wynne, but Wynne knew not to interrupt. Wynne had been told not to interrupt tonight. If she screamed, would Wynne hear? What would Merritt do to her now that he knew she knew the truth?

And why had he done it in the first place? Had they brainwashed him? Tortured him? Of course they'd *tortured* him, but had they changed him? Made him believe things? Chase had joked about indoctrinating her so long ago, before she'd even known he was Imperial Security, so maybe the idea wasn't so far-fetched. And there was always Elex Feye. They'd done it before.

Or had the whole thing been a lie? Had Merritt willingly cast his lot in with the Haederan Empire? With Imperial Security?

Her hand hit her mouth. How naïve she'd been to trust him. No—not naïve. How long had she known Merritt? Practically half her life. This wasn't her fault. It was his. That, at least, was the one certainty, the one bright side in this nightmare. She'd done nothing wrong.

"I didn't have a choice," Merritt said. "Teruel needed someone."

"Teruel?" The name of the Royal Asrian Defense Forces leader —Merritt's commander—sounded foreign on her lips. "What does he have to do with this?"

Teruel. Her heart sank. He'd pushed through Merritt's leave, had always supported her in her role as queen. How was she supposed to tell him his senior aide was a traitor?

Merritt shook his head.

"Well, I do work for him. Regretfully sometimes, I think. What's gotten into you? I knew you'd be angry over this, but I never thought you'd be this upset." His eyes narrowed, then widened in shock as she pressed herself against the wall, shaking. "Stars, Avery. You think I'm working for the *Haederans*? Have you lost your mind?"

Avery blinked at him. At his cheeks, red with fury. What had he said? Had he denied it? She sagged against the wall, tears spilling over. *Yes, Mer, I've finally lost my mind.* Taln Perrin had always taunted her about how damaged Merritt was, but she was the broken one, the person who couldn't trust the one man who'd always been there for her.

Merritt dropped one of his hands to his side and reached for her with the other. "I'm sorry. I shouldn't have said that. Come here."

"I can't. Mer—you're right. I'm too broken, and I don't know how to fix it."

"Shh." Coming from anyone else, the hushing would sound dismissive, but as she found herself engulfed in his arms, it sounded anything but. "You're not broken. Not beyond repair, anyway. And if little pieces of you are chipped off, we'll fix them, right? With gold, even."

"But I don't understand what's going on."

"We can't talk right here, love. And not until you calm down." Ever so gently, he pushed her head onto his shoulder and stroked her hair. "I love you, and I love Asria, and I'm sorry I made you doubt either. Yes?"

Her breathing became regular again. Slowly. Because something was still off. Even if Merritt wasn't handing over information to the Haederans, he was up to something, and he couldn't be up to something. Last time, he'd almost gotten himself killed, even after she'd begged him to not get involved. He knew better than that now.

"I'm sorry, Mer. I just—"

The compassion, and the remainder of his anger, fell from his face. "Let's go in the washroom."

It was difficult to believe the Haederan ambassador's ship was bugged—or maybe not so hard. The Imperial Security Command had their hand in everything, and Neave especially wasn't immune. Perhaps Merritt had seen something suspicious in his search of their quarters, but she couldn't ask, not now. Hand in his, she followed him inside the small chamber.

Merritt flipped on the faucet. It was a risk since water was limited aboard a starship, after all, but the only real choice. Drinking water was a separate system, and they'd survive if they ran out of bathing water.

"It was nothing," he said under his breath. "I don't want you to worry that I'm caught up in something messy and dangerous. Just a bit of misinformation. We're not doing well."

She knew that from the incessant senate meetings, the closed-door, limited-attendee kind. Rebuilding a shattered military, even one meant for defense only, took time. Their fleet was all but destroyed, and the personnel? Too many were dead. Too many more were broken.

"Bad enough for a disinformation campaign?" she asked.

Merritt didn't need to say anything. His hesitant nod was enough.

And the Haederans couldn't know. It was obvious now what he'd left on that tablet back at Windhaven—fake troop buildup numbers, an incorrect and overstated status of the Defense Forces fleet, maybe even plans to turn their defensive force into an offensive one in the wake of the war. Anything to make the Haederans think their former protectorate was a threat. Not a planet to be trifled with.

And the Imperial Security Command, where the information doubtless was right now, wouldn't think twice about Teruel's aide having access to that kind of intelligence. As volatile as things had been with the Rendon family lately, they wouldn't think twice of Merritt accidentally leaving it around, either.

"I couldn't tell you," Merritt went on, as visions of destroyed Nightflares danced through her head. "I'm sorry."

"Why couldn't you tell me?" she asked. "Or at least warn me?"

"Because . . ." He stiffened and took a step away from her, still close to the water but out of striking range. "Because it was a Defense Forces operation, Avery. Even Grec doesn't know the details. And Teruel wasn't sure—"

"Teruel wasn't sure what?"

His lip curled up a bit. "That you wouldn't feel obligated to tell Chase."

"How dare you."

The words spilled out as her cheeks flushed. Or had the blood drained from her head? By the sudden dizziness, maybe it had. She'd been transported off *Mayfair* to some kind of strange place where everyone lied and thought the worst of her.

"I never said I agreed with him!"

"Well? Do you?"

"Avery—"

She put a hand on the wall to steady herself and keep from

dashing out the door and hiding with Wynne for the rest of the voyage like a child.

"Don't *Avery* me. Do you agree with him? Do you think I'm a traitor, that I'd go running to Chase with something like this? Do you think he's gotten into my mind that badly? Were you lying when you said Quen was wrong about me? What, Merritt? What exactly do you think about me?"

Merritt blinked a few times. "I think I love you, that you're more loyal to Asria than anyone else in the system, and that Teruel should have kept his mouth shut."

"You're trying too hard," she said, fighting to keep a grin from her face. Angry. She had to act angry. But Merritt always knew the right words to say.

A smiled appeared, the one that never failed to warm her body. "Is it working?"

How could she be angry with him now? Half of her felt manipulated, but the other half—this was Merritt. He wouldn't lie. He'd make her happy if it was the last thing he did. He'd push through her anger if it were the right thing to do.

"Keep working at it," she said, "and I'll let you know."

"I can do that." His lips were against her ear before she could lodge any ineffectual protest, though she made a dutiful attempt to push him away. "Does this help?"

"A bit." Her breath quickened as she dropped her hands from his chest. He'd already done his job; the temptation of his body against hers was too much to bear for much longer. "But you know this isn't fair."

"Fair?" His tone was light as he nipped at her earlobe. "Who said anything about fair? You did order it of me, my lady, and far be it from me to ignore your commands. You may want to be careful what you ask for."

"Mer—" She didn't have enough breath left in her lungs to finish his name.

"Shh." He put a finger against her lips. "No more talking."

Her eyes fell closed; his lips touched hers. She should be angry. She should pull away, disentangle herself somehow, and stalk out of the washroom to put on a robe. He was clearly distracting her from Teruel's comments and the disinformation campaign, but none of that mattered now that his hands were—

Merritt pulled away, sending a rush of ice through her.

"What's this?"

"What's what?" It was impossible to keep the annoyance from her voice that time. Were they to be continually interrupted tonight by some manufactured drama?

His gaze burned into her eyes, then landed lower. "What happened to your arm? It's all bruised."

"Nothing happened to my arm." She glanced down to see a light green line of fingerprints marching down her bicep.

"Those are finger marks, Avery." His jaw was tight, the desire of thirty seconds ago gone. "Who did this?"

"No one. I—"

She pulled the strap of her lingerie back over her shoulder and ran her palm over the marks. They didn't hurt, and she'd stopped looking in the mirror after they'd boarded. No one needed to see what they looked like after a week in space. Merritt had been so busy he'd never noticed.

"Don't lie to me. Who did it?"

She closed her eyes.

"He did, didn't he? What the hell happened?" A long curse, and not even under his breath for the benefit of the surveillance equipment that time. "I'll kill him. I don't care if he's locked up behind a hundred doors on Ventana, protected by a thousand security people." Merritt's fist hit the glossy wood panel next to the door; his cheeks went as red as she'd ever seen them. "I told him I'd kill him, and I'll make good on that promise if it's the last thing I do."

"No. Merritt, you don't understand."

Why was she defending Chase again? How was she supposed to explain this? He'd hurt her, he'd terrified her, and there was no excuse for what he'd done, no justification, no way she could rationalize any of this.

The familiar nausea welled up again.

"Mer, listen to me." She swallowed down her shock. "Please. He did it because he knew if he hurt me, if he made me think he was that same person back in Cadena . . ." Her chest tightened, and the tears fell freely. "He knew I wouldn't help him. He knew he had to give me a good reason to leave him alone, a good reason not to fight for his freedom. Hurting me, making me remember, it was the only way he could stop me from—"

"Stop you from what?"

Merritt looked incredulous that she was defending Chase once more, covered in bruises from his hand, no less. She couldn't blame him. Would he ever believe what had happened?

Oh, Chase.

She pressed her eyes closed.

"It was the only way he could stop me from heading to Ventana and pleading for his release."

CHAPTER TWENTY-FIVE

SHE'D ALWAYS WORRIED IT WOULD COME TO THIS. GUEST QUARTERS AT the Commonwealth Navy's headquarters for high-ranking visitors were better than average, true, but it was still military lodging. There was a huge spray of fresh flowers on the table by the window, though, and the purple blossoms went a long way to transform the four-room flat into a place she could stand for more than five minutes.

Avery pinched one of the blooms. It didn't smell, and she tossed it into the incinerator chute, much to Lucas's dismay.

"You're not going to eat the flowers, little man. Not now, not ever. Sorry. And I'm fine, Mer," she said to him as he paced uneasily by the windows.

She'd been insisting the same thing for the past two hours, ever since security officials had shuffled them in here. She eyed the bouquet again, then stepped away from it and scooped up Lucas. It wasn't worth destroying the beauty with her anxiety or his toddler curiosity.

"You don't look fine." Merritt sighed and sat down in front of her. "Come here."

Reluctantly, she sat and leaned into him, letting his hands wrap around her. Lucas's wails turned to soft snores as she rocked from side to side.

"I don't know why I'm here," she said. "I don't know if there's anything I can do, and I'm furious at him for doing this. I'm furious with him for even putting me into this situation."

"To be fair, he didn't know you would decide to take a side trip to Ventana. Did the best he could to talk you out of it, in fact, if I'm recalling correctly."

Avery pulled away. "You didn't just say that. You're going to change your mind about him that quickly?" It'd been only a few short weeks since Merritt had threatened to kill him. "Don't even think of siding with him. Don't even think of defending him."

"I'm not defending anything. I'm still angry at him for what he did to you, but that only means I'm even prouder of you for doing this."

The buzz of the door interrupted him. Wynne jumped up from her chair to admit their visitor, too quickly for someone who hadn't been listening to their entire conversation.

The man who entered was almost unrecognizable, dressed in the Special Operations Forces uniform she was technically authorized to wear but had only glimpsed a few times in real life. His hair was shorter than she'd ever seen, which shouldn't have been a surprise here at headquarters.

But the grin? The grin left no doubt.

"Hadley." Despite the long trip and circumstances of their visit, she couldn't hide her own smile. "You don't know how happy I am to see you. And your other guest?"

"Arrived safely yesterday. He's writing up some reports and getting ready in his quarters upstairs. I'll send for him in a bit."

She handed a sleeping Lucas over to Merritt and put her face in her hands. Overwhelming relief. It was all she could feel. The first step in their plan—one of the most important, if not the most fragile—had gone well. Stev Kanmar was on Ventana.

"You will never learn not to be surprised, Your Majesty." Hadley laughed at her reaction as she forced herself to her feet and crossed the room to greet him properly. "It doesn't matter how many times I surprise you. You asked for him, and I delivered. Did you honestly expect anything less?"

"With that kind of attitude, Major, I can't believe I've missed you this much."

"The women here keep telling me I have that effect on them." Hadley planted a kiss on each of her cheeks. "I'm happy to see you, too. And Colonel Rendon—under better circumstances this time, sir. No, don't get up. As much as I'd love to steal him from you for a while, Lucas looks too comfortable."

"Much better circumstances," Merritt agreed, holding out his hand. "Being trapped under a sleeping baby is an improvement over being trapped in a clinic bed."

"No doubt. And the leg?"

"Holding up. I can run again, though I haven't yet decided if that's a good or bad thing."

"A bad thing," Hadley replied. "Always a bad thing."

"So the flowers? They have Zenos Hadley written all over them," Avery said.

Hadley chuckled. "I seem to remember promising you some in your quarters at some point. You got a husband instead, so I had to make it up to you." He gave them an approving glance and a small wave. "Rachel picked them out. Some sort of Ventanan violet, she said. Very nice. Me . . ." He shrugged his ignorance of floral design. "Let's just say you're lucky I wasn't in charge."

"Rachel? Has the confirmed bachelor been holding out on me? Being stationed on Ventana IV for the next two years isn't as bad as you'd expected, is it?"

His eyes crinkled. "She's nice. We'll see."

Even Merritt chuckled at that.

"I hope it works out," Avery said. "You deserve it." She leaned back onto the sofa. "I'm too tired to play the social game right now, Hadley, and much too worried. How is he?"

Hadley ran his hands over his face and fell into a chair by the window. "He's physically fine. Don't even worry about that. But you know how isolation messes with you, even after only a week."

If she knew anything, it was that. *Move on, Hadley.* "Yes. And a trial?"

"Already over." Hadley shrugged. "It was fast. I was allowed to observe as someone who has 'direct secondhand knowledge of the information,' whatever that means. They begrudged every moment I was in those chambers, but nothing they did could make me leave. It was awful, Avery. He confessed to all sorts of things right in front of them, things that are in direct conflict with your reports from Asria. And they're trusting his outlandish stories over you and Colonel Kanmar. But you know how he is, persuasive as all get-out. He's taken everything you told Major Malvern and me about your detention and twisted it around to make himself look evil. It doesn't make any sense. It's almost as if . . ." He looked up at the ceiling and sighed.

"Almost as if what?"

"Almost as if he doesn't care that they want to make an example of him."

That sounded like Chase—at least the Chase she'd said goodbye to on Haedera. He'd walked away from Sophie, after all.

"I don't think he does care. He wants to serve his time here to punish himself. It didn't matter how much I argued with him that it wasn't necessary."

"That's going to be a problem." Hadley's face twisted into a pained expression. "He didn't receive the sentence he so desperately seemed to want."

"What do you mean? If they're just going to send him back to Haedera, he wouldn't be in isolation right now. He's been here for at least a week already, and if that's enough time for all these hearings, surely that's enough time to make transportation arrangements for him. He can take *Mayfair* if it comes down to it. I'm sure the ambassador won't mind when he hears the entire story. Hadley, what—"

Oh.

Bile. She could taste it rising up in her throat. The Commonwealth couldn't.

They *wouldn't.*

Would they?

Merritt's hand reached for hers, but she jerked it away and pressed it against her mouth. She couldn't be sick right here in front of Hadley and Merritt and Wynne, but . . .

Hadley closed his eyes as he spoke.

"They're going to execute him, Avery."

CHAPTER TWENTY-SIX

Her mouth was so dry. In the haze, she thought Merritt had left her side and was digging through ice and drinks at the bar, but she couldn't be certain.

"They can't. Hadley, they can't." Her hands curled into fists, and she pressed them into her forehead. How many people would hear if she screamed in fury? No, not fury. It was physical pain.

"They're angry. I told you they want to make an example. He's going to be the first of whatever Haederan 'criminals' they can lay their hands on, I think." Hadley exhaled. "You know how it goes. War changes things, and principles be damned."

But that was the whole point. The Commonwealth was supposed to be better than the Haederan Empire. They weren't supposed to stoop this low. Even the less progressive Commonwealth planets didn't sway in ethical breezes like this, not after joining, at least. And Asria? The death penalty had been banned after the civil war. But then, maybe that was why the Commonwealth was taking matters into their own hands. Maybe they didn't trust her planet to mete out justice. Didn't trust *her*.

"I signed an armistice." Her voice was breathless as Merritt set a glass of ice water in her hands. "It was a war. They aren't criminals. Not all of them. He's not a criminal."

Hadley scoffed. "Good luck convincing them of that. When I argued his innocence, they called me naïve."

Naïve was the last word she'd ever use to describe Hadley. "Then what can I do? Hadley, I have to do something. I can't let this happen."

"I'd like you to visit General Torin with me. Right now, if possible. He's the only one who has any sway with this board, though he can't threaten their impartiality by setting aside the verdict completely. We'll bring Kanmar with us and try to convince Torin to let both of you testify. They might be star-bent on revenge, and they might be running this tribunal in secret, but they still need to do everything by the book. It's a long shot, but with both of you on-world, they have no reason to rely on reports." Hadley scratched his head. "These officers aren't bad people. Perhaps just a little overzealous right now. Gavan Davidson in particular despises Haederans—his son was some sort of technical officer who was killed in a skirmish on Naraka when they first invaded."

Avery nodded and took a small sip of water. It only made her stomach worse.

"Yes. Yes, I can do that."

Hadley squinted at her. "Are you certain? If you need some more time, we can wait a bit. You've only just arrived, after all."

"No. No more time. Not while they've got him locked up."

He stood. "Then let's go."

* * *

Torin's office was across the base from the visitor quarters. It was spring in Efa, the city of the Commonwealth's headquarters, and the flowers were like nothing Avery had seen on any other planet. But she couldn't focus on them today. Just like the blue autumn sky had done during her first interview with Chase, the brilliant jewel tones of the plants mocked her. Nothing could be allowed to be so beautiful while this was happening. Hadley ushered her into a windowless conference room on the third floor of the Special Operations Forces headquarters building, and it was almost as if she could feel the electronic interference that buzzed through the structure, preventing any listening devices from functioning.

But that was all in her head, wasn't it?

She tried to ignore the smell of the coffee brewing in the corner as Hadley tapped his fingers on the table. They shouldn't be drinking anything so normal, just like the flowers shouldn't be showing off. The door cracked open as she stared at her empty cup without touching it, and she looked up, expecting Torin.

But it was Kanmar, in a fresh Defense Forces uniform and with dark circles under his eyes, come all this way from Asria after nothing more than a guarded message from Hadley. Even after Chase had been powerless to protect his children from Perrin's wrath. Didn't the Commonwealth understand what it meant for Kanmar to be here? How much he respected Chase even now? Would they understand? Could she make them?

Even though he had to have known his queen was waiting, Kanmar's eyes widened as Hadley ushered him inside. He bowed, heedless of the fact they weren't on Asria and she wasn't on Ventana as anything but a lowly Commonwealth captain.

"Colonel." Avery hid a smile. "Thank you for coming."

She hurried around the table and extended her hand instead of laughing. Overly formal and proper Kanmar hadn't changed a bit since she'd first met him in Jeph so long ago. Such a long trip, and for him to make the journey, leaving who knew what official business undone on Asria to defend a Haederan . . .

Kanmar looked from her to Hadley as he shook her hand, uncomfortable as the casual gesture had to make him. "For this, it may as well have been just across the city, Your Majesty."

"You don't need to call me that," she said. "Not here. Not now. Please. We're just a few people trying to save his life, yes?"

Her appeal had probably fallen on deaf ears, but Kanmar

nodded. Avery stood between him and Hadley and stared at her fingernails until the door slid open again.

Torin this time.

The general scanned the room as he entered. "Quite the group you've assembled, Major Hadley," he said in greeting as he gestured for them to sit. "But as I know you're aware, the tribunal is finished. They've made their decision."

Hadley held out her chair, then headed for the coffee machine. "They can always decide to hear more information, sir, especially in a capital case."

"I don't know why they would," Torin said. A frown.

Avery folded her hands on the table. "General, I'm quite concerned about the stories Colonel Chase has told the tribunal. I don't think—I *know* they aren't the truth. There must be something I can do. Appear on his behalf. Tell the truth. Anything. They can't make such a decision with inaccurate information."

"Inaccurate?" Torin reached for the cup of coffee Hadley set in front of him. "The tribunal has reviewed copies of your debriefings with Major Hadley and Major Malvern. I heard your story myself on *Triphane,* and they've read that report as well. Zenos has been filling in the rest of the details for them."

"Those are just debriefings, General," Avery said. "They're nothing more than unemotional, impassive written words. They're mostly about the verium, as well, not my imprisonment, which is what this is truly about. And with all due respect to Major Hadley, he wasn't there the entire time. He only knows the few things that I told him shortly after my rescue. He doesn't know the details. I barely remembered my own name when he initially debriefed me, and not much more when you did. I remember quite a bit more now."

A lie.

"And Colonel Chase is lying. I couldn't tell you why he's doing so"—another partial lie—"but I am certain he is."

Torin spun around in his chair and stared at the wall for a long time, long enough to finish his coffee in several long sips. The room was deadly silent as he thought. Hadley rolled his eyes toward her in an *I told you so* motion, and Avery shook her head in reply. Torin had to change his mind. He had to.

"You are aware that they will ask you very pointed questions," Torin finally said, turning back to her.

Will.

Her heart flipped in optimism.

"I am."

"Questions that you—having taken an oath to the Commonwealth, I might remind you—will be required to answer truthfully. There cannot be any indication that you're lying to protect him, or the outcome would be more disastrous than it already is."

Like that was possible. "I understand."

"And you're further aware that the questioning will make our discussion on *Triphane* feel like two old friends chatting over tea."

"I am aware of that as well, General."

Her breath became short. Was Torin trying to protect her? From the tribunal? From the memories? What? It didn't matter. She'd answer whatever they asked. She'd do anything to save Chase.

"Major Hadley has informed me"—Torin ran a finger around the edge of his empty cup and Hadley jumped with more coffee— "that you've suffered continual flashbacks since the events on Asria. I'm concerned that your testimony might be ineffectual and harmful."

Avery hid a sigh of frustration. Hadley had probably thought he was helping. Protecting her. It wasn't his fault that he'd made things worse.

"Continual is a bit of an exaggeration," she said, but Torin didn't blink. "Fine. Yes. It's been difficult. But as everyone here knows, I've been through worse than some questioning by my own side. I don't have anything to hide. I'm especially not going to hide my respect for a man who, yes, hurt me both physically and mentally, but who has been trying to make up for it ever since."

And I won't go away until you allow this, General.

Torin exhaled. "That's all very impassioned, and you've persuaded me to an extent. I'll make sure Colonel Kanmar has his say in front of the board. Whether his story will make a bit of difference to them or not, I'm not able to predict. I wish I had more control, but you know that's not possible." He leaned back in his chair and spread his hands. "But I'm afraid I can't allow you to speak in front of the tribunal."

Her heart sank. "Why not?"

Torin looked her up and down and raised his eyebrows. A slow smile, almost like Hadley's, spread across his face.

"Because you're out of uniform, Captain."

Her stomach might as well have been spinning in circles, but she couldn't conceal her grin.

He was giving her a chance.

"I'll remedy that immediately, sir," she said.

* * *

"I'm not thrilled at the idea of not being able to hear your testimony." Merritt glared at her from the bed like his exclusion from the proceedings had been her idea.

"I'm not, either." Avery avoided his eye, tugging at the stack of clothing in front of her. "But you heard General Torin."

And Torin, to no one's surprise really, had told them in no uncertain terms that Kanmar would only be allowed inside the tribunal room to give his own testimony. He wouldn't be allowed to listen to hers, and Merritt wouldn't be allowed in at all. She shook off the injustice. The general must have his own reasons, even if they were some silly, irrelevant Commonwealth regulations. At this point, she needed to convince herself to be grateful for any opportunity.

"Oh, yes. I heard him." Merritt tossed her belt to her and gave her another doubtful look. "But I don't have to like it. Are you sure about this?"

"I feel like I'm going to be sick," she said as she fastened the last button on the blue jacket of the uniform Hadley had delivered earlier. He'd done her a favor and fastened the accouterments for her. "I can't look at a glass of water without wanting to be sick. But yes. I owe him this much, even if he's intent on destroying himself. And I don't have to say a word to them until later, only listen to Kanmar for now. That'll let me ease into it."

Ease into it, yes, but most of her wanted to scream in impatience about the delay. The tribunal needed to hear everything, and they needed to hear it now. They couldn't leave everyone hanging like this. But it was a problem of her own making, wasn't it? She was the one who'd put the shred of hope in her own head.

"I'm still concerned."

"I know. But I'm going to be just fine, Mer. I can do this. I have to do this." She threaded the belt around her waist and turned toward him, trying not to stare at her reflection in the opposite mirror. If she looked at herself, she wouldn't want to be anyone else, especially Her Majesty the Queen of Asria. "How do I look?"

Merritt tilted his head and examined her. "Like a decorated Commonwealth Special Operations Forces officer determined to do the right thing no matter how terrifying it is."

Her heart sank. The tribunal couldn't see her fear.

"It's that obvious?" she asked.

He jumped off the bed to face her. His eyes skimmed the gray diamond rank on her collar, the bronzed wings from her academy days, the medals for which Torin had pushed through the authorization—including several with classified citations—and the dark curls she'd so carefully pulled into a knot on her neck.

"Obvious to anyone who knows you, love, and probably most who don't." His lips brushed hers. "But you're doing this anyway . . . and that's what makes me love you even more."

CHAPTER TWENTY-SEVEN

The small conference room turned tribunal chamber was nothing like she'd expected. Instead of a formal planetary courtroom with spacious windows like the ones on the seventh floor of the senate building, this was a small, sparse space with no wall décor or windows. And it was cold, enough to make Avery wish she'd chosen long sleeves under her wool service jacket. The same underlying electronic noise she'd felt while meeting with General Torin buzzed in her brain, and the air conditioning blew a stray curl around her forehead. She tried to tuck it back into place, but it proved to be an unsuccessful struggle.

Hadley motioned her to a hard chair against the side wall, perpendicular to the long table in the front. Five Special Operations Forces officers in blue uniforms like hers and one woman in a fleet captain's uniform were behind it already, tablets in front of them, their faces like stone. They nodded at her and Hadley.

"Captain Rendon."

The officer in the middle—the one with three diamonds on his collar—nodded again. General Gavan Davidson, Hadley had called him, though she'd never heard of him before today. General Torin's direct lieutenant and heir apparent to the Special Operations Forces throne, he was tall and lean, his shaved head showing off a recent scar across his temple. Avery tried not to stare, tried not to wonder about the cause.

"I assume Major Hadley has filled you in on our previous decision?" he asked.

She swallowed, falling into long-unused Commonwealth Navy protocol. "Yes, sir."

"Then you're aware of the exception we are making in allowing you and this Royal Asrian Defense Forces officer to add your narratives to the record."

"Yes, sir, I am." She hadn't considered throwing her position about inside the tribunal room itself, but his tone left no doubt—he'd never allow it. This didn't sound good. This didn't sound good at all. "And I speak for both Colonel Kanmar and myself when I say we appreciate the tribunal's willingness to permit it."

She glanced at the others. Colonel Eliza Barton. Colonel Miklos Takach. Colonel Aron Vastel. Colonel Aubert Ryall. Captain Matilde Ingrams. All Special Operations Forces except Ingrams, the cruiser commander. All looked back at her with the same blank expression. And all knew her story now.

Most of it.

"Good. Just so we have that understanding. Sit down." He nodded at the security officer by the back door. "Send Lieutenant Colonel Kanmar in, please."

Her knees gave out as the door opened and Kanmar's footsteps echoed through the small space. Hadley gave her a questioning look as he sat next to her, and she nodded in reassurance. *Fine.* She was just fine. She only had to sit and listen to Kanmar's testimony for now, and she'd already heard most of his story from Chase. It was horrifying, yes, but she could sit and listen without breaking down.

But what if they don't listen to him? What if they didn't listen to either of them? Davidson seemed like he'd already made his decision, and he had to be infuriated that Torin had stepped in and ordered them to consider more information—all because the monarch of a Commonwealth planet had requested it of him. It was all she could do not to cry in front of them all. She stiffened her spine instead and focused on Kanmar's words.

". . . was part of an explosives team captured while attempting to retake the Royal Asrian Defense Forces headquarters at Alcaris. I witnessed the executions of twenty-seven Defense Forces personnel before being held in an Imperial Haederan Army prison at Alcaris for four months. During that time"—he took a breath—"I was subject to daily torture and isolation for the entirety of my detention."

"Excuse me." Colonel Barton, the intelligence division chief, raised her finger from the end of the table. "For the record, could you please detail the nature of the torture in question?"

Kanmar's left hand balled into a fist.

"Six broken ribs as well as both my arms, several severe burns, and a mild traumatic brain injury. All since healed," he added stiffly.

"That's the outcome," Barton replied. "I'm specifically asking about the nature."

There was a long pause. "Sleep deprivation. I was allowed two hours a day when I wasn't hanging naked from the ceiling by my wrists. Sometimes they hosed me down when they did that just so they could laugh while I shivered. They burned the soles of my feet with a lighter from the temple in my hometown." Kanmar's eyebrows flickered up in feigned politeness. "Shall I continue, ma'am?"

"What was the reason for this kind of treatment?" Barton raised her shoulders.

"Reason?" His Cadena accent, already out of place on a man from Tarragona, suddenly sounded even stranger on Ventana as his politeness turned to anger. "You think they had a good reason for this kind of thing? That it was my fault?"

"Your own report detailed your suspicion for your torture," Davidson interrupted coolly. "I think it's a reasonable question."

Avery gnawed on the inside of her cheek as Kanmar took a dozen deep, slowing breaths.

"I spit on the Haederan military governor shortly after the invasion of Asria." His tone was clipped. "He was . . . offended."

And I have absolutely no problem doing the same or worse to you was left unsaid.

"Continue," Davidson said with a sigh.

"One day, Colonel Chase arrived. I'm not sure what he told the guards, but the next thing I knew, they were loading me on a transport. The army didn't look disappointed to be losing their punching bag, and now I realize they thought I was in for far worse treatment. But instead of transferring me to Imperial Security custody, I was sent to the Imperial Haederan Navy prison camp on Emot. After I'd recovered from my injuries there, Colonel Chase appeared again. Told me he needed my help. That the queen needed my help."

He shot Avery a look she couldn't interpret.

"So he based his decision to release you on your agreement to do what he wanted?" Takach asked.

Kanmar made an unenthusiastic sound of dissent. "No, sir. This happened months after I was transferred from detention at Alcaris. I was safe on Emot. I could have bided my time trying to escape from that camp for years. I didn't need him. And my answer was never in question. As soon as he mentioned Her Majesty's name, I knew what I had to do."

"You must have distrusted Colonel Chase when he proposed this," Vastel said. "Why agree to his demands? Were you that desperate for your freedom?"

Kanmar flushed—in anger, Avery was certain.

"He didn't demand anything from me, sir." He cocked his head, eyes narrowed. "If you think I did this to save my own skin, to escape that camp, you're wrong. I would never betray Asria like that. I was home with my family for less than a day before I swore into the Imperial Haederan Navy, just so I could hand Her Majesty back over to Colonel Chase. And even that visit with them was a sham, a way to throw off the Haederan troops in

Tarragona and make them think I was a collaborator. It wasn't a holiday."

Another quick look and deferential nod at Avery.

"Yes, I was that desperate to help Asria. To help the queen. For her, I would have agreed to help the Haederan emperor himself if he'd asked. I suppose Colonel Chase knew that, but in my opinion, he didn't coerce me. He simply knew the right person to ask."

Davidson flipped through a tablet. "And your family . . . ?"

It wasn't a question. No, it was common knowledge, especially in that part of Asria. Heat washed over her, the same feeling as the day it'd happened. She'd screamed and sobbed at Chase that evening the entire way from Tarragona back to Cadena on the shuttle, had spent the next evening throwing up in her locked room at the palace—and that hadn't compared to what Kanmar must have experienced when he'd learned.

"My children are dead, sir." Kanmar was a little quieter now. "In the Tarragona mine collapse."

The collapse that Perrin had engineered. Six hundred Asrians, dead in an instant, in a false flag operation intended to both discredit the fledgling Asrian resistance movement and test explosives to destroy Villiers. Six hundred people . . .

. . . including Kanmar's three sons.

"Because Colonel Chase gave the names of your sons to the Haederan military governor just so they could be subjected to his own people's wrath," Davidson said, his voice growing louder. "He lied to you about their safety. I wouldn't call that the action of an upstanding man. Perhaps you didn't act fast enough or with enough gratitude for him?"

Avery couldn't help her sharp inhale. Davidson glanced her way, and she stiffened.

"Captain Rendon."

She stood. "Yes, sir?"

"It sounds like this is news to you." A spark flashed across Davidson's eyes.

He thinks he's caught me in a lie.

"Y—yes, sir. Because it's not how it happened."

"Then enlighten us."

"I was there when it happened," she said. Kanmar turned toward her, but she didn't make eye contact as she spoke. "Colonel Chase was with me in Tarragona at the time of the explosion. He didn't know about Perrin's plans for the mine. He was there—"

Kusir, they'd never believe this, especially Captain Ingrams, who was now staring at Hadley, eyes narrowed. She was wasting her breath. Torin had been right.

"Governor Perrin was the one who ordered me to Tarragona, but Colonel Chase escorted me there." She closed her eyes. "I was placed in Imperial Security custody after I was repatriated to Asria, and he was directly in charge of my detention. His presence, wherever I went, was expected and not unusual, including his accompanying me to Tarragona. But I found out later he had a secondary purpose for going."

She blinked back tears as her eyes landed on Kanmar's. "Occasionally, he'd disappear from the palace at irregular times, and he was visiting Tarragona then, too. Once a week, the entire time Colonel Kanmar was with the Haederan fleet, and later, while he was detained again back on Emot. His wife told me, much later."

"He was bringing her messages from me," Kanmar added. "I was lucky. Most others never heard from anyone the entire time we were deployed. Emot was a little better, but not by much. Once he started coming around, the local garrison soldiers must have thought—anyway, the harassment from the Haederan Army ended when they noticed his visits. Until—"

Until the explosion.

"He took photos of the Haederan soldiers involved in the false flag operation," Avery added, "solely to prove Taln Perrin and the Imperial Haederan Army were behind it. Those photos are safely in the custody of the Asrian Defense Forces now, and if you'd only request them, you'd see."

Her jaw tightened. Why hadn't she thought to ask Hadley for those as well?

"Excuse me, my lady." Kanmar pulled a disk from his chest pocket. "But those photos are here."

Takach raised his eyebrows as Kanmar laid the disk in front of Davidson. "You understand, Captain Rendon, that I'm finding all this hard to believe."

"Yes, sir. I understand."

"The two of you are asking us to believe that per the orders of the Haederan emperor, a man known for torturing his own people arranged the release of an Imperial Haederan Navy prisoner simply to coordinate your apprehension in deep space so you could be placed back on the Asrian throne?"

There's no actual throne in Cadena. Hasn't been for five hundred years.

"Yes, sir. Because that's how it happened."

Davidson rubbed his eyes, then shoved the disk into his tablet. "Captain Rendon. Did Colonel Chase's actions have a direct influence on your ability to take control of Asria?"

"Yes, sir, they did. If Colonel Kanmar hadn't arranged for my ship to Ventana to be intercepted, I can't predict how things might have gone on Asria. I wouldn't have made it home for months, if at all. I wouldn't have been in place to negotiate an armistice with the Haederan Empire. Who knows how much longer the war might have continued then?"

"Very well."

She collapsed next to Hadley.

"Lieutenant Colonel Kanmar," Barton asked. "Did Colonel Chase force you into working for him?"

"No, ma'am."

"Coerce you?"

"No."

"Did he promise you anything in return for your release and subsequent enlistment in the Imperial Haederan Navy?"

"No, ma'am. He did not."

"Not even the safety of your family?"

"He said he would do what he could for them. And after speaking with him, I believe he would have done it regardless of my decision."

Barton looked at Davidson, then back at Kanmar, and nodded. "Very well. Thank you for your testimony. You're dismissed."

Kanmar nodded, turned on his heel, and walked out.

"Captain Rendon." Davidson jerked his head toward the spot Kanmar had vacated. "Your turn."

CHAPTER TWENTY-EIGHT

She would rather fly twenty training sorties in a row than stand in this room with so many eyes on her. Still, Avery forced herself up, forced herself to move in front of them. There was a scuff mark on the institutional plastic floor, like Kanmar had been grinding the heel of his boot into it the entire time he'd been speaking. Probably he had.

Davidson sighed again. At her for standing there, at Torin for ordering him to consider more information, or at Chase for causing the hearing in the first place? Who knew?

"Let's cut right to this, then, shall we?" he asked. "I think we all know where it's going to go."

She squared her shoulders and lifted her chin in invitation.

"When you were arrested, did you tell Colonel Chase that you were a Commonwealth Navy officer?"

"I wasn't arrested by Imperial Security, General. So, no. I did not volunteer that information when the Haederan Army ordered my arrest, which was for my refusal to swear allegiance to the Haederan Empire as the princess-elect of Asria, not because of my other activities. At the time, I thought it important to keep my military status with the Commonwealth a secret."

Had she rambled too much? Perhaps. She certainly hadn't

answered Davidson's question, and judging from the look on his face, he knew she'd intentionally evaded the answer.

How do you think I kept information from Chase for so long?

"That's not what I asked." Davidson rubbed his forehead. "But fair enough. Once the Imperial Security Command discovered the extent of your activities and transferred you to their custody, did you tell Colonel Chase that you were a Commonwealth officer?"

"Yes. I did."

Kusir, that had sounded too defensive already.

"And he did what?"

She closed her eyes and shook her head. She couldn't lie to them. But she couldn't tell the truth, either.

"What was his response, Captain Rendon?"

The climate system blew another curl across her forehead. She let that one go. Did it really matter that her hair was out of regulation now?

"He said my military status didn't matter to him." It was a whisper, someone else's voice. "That it didn't matter to Imperial Security."

It's actually Lieutenant Rendon.

She'd stuttered her rank at Chase to correct him when he'd used her royal title. She'd stuttered a lot those days. He'd never mocked her for it or acted frustrated, only grown more patient.

Is it now? he'd asked, curiosity and triumph written on his face. *Commonwealth or Defense Forces?*

C—Commonwealth.

I thought as much. He'd smiled at her then, confident. *Did they tell you that would protect you? That any kind of military status would make a difference if you were arrested? It doesn't, you know. Not to me. They didn't warn you about Imperial Security, did they?*

"And then what? Did he say he notified the Commonwealth of your detention? Did he let you speak with a Commonwealth or Defense Forces official? Or even the Haederan Army?"

"He—he moved on with his questioning."

"So it would be fair to say that the charge of failure to acknowledge your military status is accurate, yes?"

"Yes, but—"

"This isn't a trial," Barton interjected, "and you won't be disciplined for anything said here. Say what you want to say. I, at least"—she looked at Davidson—"would like to hear the full story."

"In his mind, I was engaged in illegal espionage on a Haederan protectorate. To him, it wasn't a military matter, and there was no need to follow that protocol. My status as an Asrian citizen and Commonwealth officer was irrelevant to the crimes he believed I had committed. I don't believe what he did was unethical at all. Misguided, perhaps, but nothing more."

"That's an interesting defense." It was Captain Ingrams, the sole fleet officer on the tribunal.

"On Haedera this wouldn't have been an issue, and that's what he was used to. He wouldn't have intentionally done something malicious. He . . ." What else to say about Chase? "He has honor."

They all stared at her.

"Did he rape you?" Vastel asked.

Finally, an easy question to answer. It was hard not to laugh at such an absurd one.

"No," she said. "He did not."

Chairs creaked, like they'd all shifted uncomfortably at the same time.

So sorry to destroy your delusions.

Barton flicked a finger across her tablet. "It is Major Hadley's assertion and this tribunal's opinion that you have some rather large gaps in your memory caused by your traumatic experiences. How can you say for certain what did and didn't happen?"

Kusir. She should have taken up Merritt on his offer to read the notes beforehand.

She steeled her voice. "I remember. And my medical records,

which General Torin has already provided the tribunal, will bear that out."

"Are you saying Major Hadley is incorrect? Or maybe you suddenly happened to remember?"

"I—"

She should have known they'd walk her right into this. And they couldn't get their hands on the disk. Not even Hadley could know of its existence.

"Captain Rendon . . ." Barton glanced at her tablet and frowned. "I'm going to read something, so there's absolutely no doubt of what we're speaking of here. Colonel Chase's statement from two days ago says, 'Lieutenant Rendon was subjected to multiple, sometimes daily, sexual assaults throughout her incarceration. A typical interrogation session would begin with blindfolding the prisoner, stripping her, and marching her from her cell to the interrogation room. There, I or one of the Imperial Haederan Army guards would proceed to assault her. After that, the interrogation proper would commence.'"

Avery flinched as Barton dropped the tablet on the table, apparently unflustered by the image she'd just given the entire room.

"Is that not the truth?" she asked.

Her face had gone red, there was no question about it. Avery chanced a glance at Hadley, but his mouth was hanging open in horror like this was the first time he'd heard these details. Well, General Torin had told her that the tribunal would be blunt, hadn't he? That they'd ask pointed questions that would be uncomfortable to answer? And Chase was . . . well, she had to give him credit for his imagination. It was no wonder the tribunal had ruled the way they had.

She shook her head, though whether it was denial or just annoyance at the situation Chase had put her in, she didn't know.

"Colonel Barton, it's a creative piece of fiction. He's lying."

Barton looked suspicious. Davidson's gaze wandered, though

he seemed to focus on Hadley more than once. Vastel looked like he'd swallowed something distasteful.

Her shoulders sagged. "I won't say I wasn't terrified of just that happening the whole time I was there," she said. "Every single time the cell door opened, every time they put their hands on me to search me or hit me. But he's lying," she repeated, staring straight into Barton's eyes. "No soldiers ever paraded me around naked, and no one ever took my clothes off."

That wasn't quite the truth—the medic had a few times, but that didn't count, did it?

He said no pain relief today, the medic had said at one point as he'd frowned at the wounds on her back. *But this will prevent infection.*

Thank you, she'd almost replied. She'd stopped herself just in time, could still taste the blood from biting her tongue. Her left eye watered at the memory, and the wall of the tribunal room grew blurry. Oh, of all the inopportune times . . .

She shoved the memories into the past where they belonged.

"And no one ever raped me. Not only is he lying about everything he told you, he did the opposite. He protected me from the Haederan Army guards who initially wanted to do exactly what you just read. Threatened them with stars knows what if they so much as looked at me the wrong way in that regard."

"Why would he lie about something like that?" Ryall, who'd been silent throughout Kanmar's testimony, propped his elbow on the table and focused on her.

"I couldn't answer that, sir." The lie slid through her lips too easily.

"Then explain to us how a typical session did go," Davidson said, his attention back on her at last.

Avery swallowed. No, perhaps this was the uncomfortable part Torin had mentioned. Dismissing Chase's outlandish story was easy, but this . . .

She blew out a deep breath and called what little she remembered back to her mind. It had to be enough for them.

"They came for me every few hours," she began, "although I suppose sometimes it may have been every few days. It was impossible to tell. They'd search and blindfold me, then lead me around until I was too disoriented to know where I was." Just like Chase had done the first time he'd removed her from her cell to question her. That she remembered, especially the burning self-hatred for her failure. And those army guards had learned from him, though sometimes not quickly enough. "After I tried to escape before the first session, they—"

"An escape attempt? There's no record of that." Ryall cocked his head. "How did Colonel Chase react? He must have been outraged."

"He didn't react at all. The guards . . ." It was almost impossible to see out of her left eye now. She rubbed it lightly with her fingertips, but the blurriness didn't clear. "They pistol-whipped me."

"Which he allowed to happen," Takach said. It wasn't a question.

"I don't think he did. Not then, at least. He looked surprised at my condition when they brought me to the interrogation room that day. And he brought the medic in to see me. He couldn't do much, only gave me some ice, but at the time, I was grateful for and surprised by any medical care. It had mostly healed by the time Major Hadley found me, and what he and Major Feye couldn't treat with the field kit, the Defense Forces medics took care of when we arrived at Villiers. You have those records as well. It was nothing."

All six stared at her again like they couldn't believe she was defending Chase. Or maybe they couldn't believe she'd mentioned Elex Feye. How many of them had known Feye? How many had worked with him, joked with him, drank with him? How many had wept over his treachery and death?

"Continue."

She blinked away Feye's face.

"Then I would sit in the interrogation room for hours while he stared at me or talked. And I would ignore him for a long time, as long as I could. When that silence became too uncomfortable—because he was so good at that stare that implied all sorts of horrible things were going to happen to me unless I did what he asked—I made up stories, told him all sorts of lies, and then once he seemed to be temporarily satisfied with what I'd told him, I would ignore him some more."

"Your failure to give him any kind of useful intelligence must have infuriated him as well," Ryall said.

"No." Her vision focused, for just a second, on the back wall behind Davidson, then blurred again. "It didn't seem to anger him. Colonel Chase was patient, so patient I couldn't believe it. In fact, I think his resolve was the most terrifying aspect of the entire ordeal."

Her voice broke. "He knew he'd win eventually, no matter how long it took. He was willing to wait me out, was willing to wait until I finally broke out of nothing more than terror and fatigue and shame. And when he finally decided he was tired of trying to crack my resistance, or maybe when his superiors threatened him to hurry up, he still didn't touch me."

It sounded so silly now. What would they think of her? Well, they had to know she'd stand up here and try to defend Chase, didn't they? They knew she'd betrayed Hadley and Feye to him already.

"He did nothing more than threaten to send me to Haedera. He'd already implied I'd be tortured and executed there. He'd told me not two days before that I'd been sentenced to death in absentia for treason and espionage by the Imperial High Court, but that if I cooperated with him, he had the authority to request the emperor overrule their verdict and commute my sentence to life instead. And I was finally so broken that his threat was all it took."

She shrugged, trying to signal the end of her story. "Now I understand why Imperial Security—why the Haederan Empire itself—gave him such leeway in his work. I understand it was nothing more than a psychological ploy."

And beyond that, I think he enjoyed the challenge.

"But the Haederan Army guards beat you. You were certainly bruised enough in the photos Major Hadley took after your rescue." Davidson flipped his tablet toward her and scrolled through a few.

Avery couldn't help wincing. Those damn pictures. She should have known they would come back to haunt her one day. In the first, she was in Hadley's safe house on the wrong side of Cadena, her eye swollen shut and a light bruise from Hadley's own hand across her opposite cheek. The second showed the green and yellow healing injury on her ribs. Had she looked that bad? It was so hard to remember how painful breathing with broken ribs had been. The third—she couldn't remember the guards grabbing her by the throat, leaving a ring of finger marks on the delicate skin, but apparently they had.

The familiar rage brewed again. How dare Chase make her stand here and relive all his abuse to save him?

"They did hurt me," she said, as evenly as she could. Visualizing their deaths was all too tempting, but she needed to hide the anger in order to save Chase—and to not transfer it back to him. They could fight more about what he'd done later. Merritt would be welcome to slug him in the face if that's what it took. But not if he was dead.

Slow, steady, deep breaths. Just breathe.

"They hurt me more than I ever imagined was possible," she went on. "And I have no doubt that Colonel Chase ordered it more than he allowed it. I'm aware of his interrogation methods now. I wish I had known before."

"It sounds like you're downplaying the severity."

"I climbed a mountain, didn't I?" She spoke before she could stop herself.

"Adrenaline and the will to live will allow for a great many feats," Davidson said. "And you did say the medic repeatedly healed the worst of your injuries."

At that, she could only shrug. Her mind had gone blank; the pictures and effort the story had taken had forced it over the edge. Now, instead of water, she wanted nothing except coffee. Torin had said this would be uncomfortable, but he hadn't mentioned how absolutely draining it would be to stand here and answer these questions.

"Did Colonel Chase ever hit you himself?" Ingrams asked.

Avery looked at her feet.

Or tea. Even tea would suffice.

"Yes," she answered, trying to force the reluctance from her voice. They were already questioning her loyalty, her sanity. She could see it in their faces—they thought she was a Haederan torture apologist. "He did."

"How many times?"

"I can't remember. Once, I think. Maybe twice. But it was mind games with him most of the time. Not often physical."

"I think you'd remember if it was only once or twice." Barton's tone indicated what she thought of that claim. "Did he ever drug you?"

"Drug me?"

"Drug you," Davidson repeated, emphasizing each word, like she couldn't be trusted to listen, either. "It's come to our attention that prior to his arrival on Asria, Colonel Chase was in charge of an Imperial Security research program—a program testing the effects of a new truth serum. He admitted to it in front of this tribunal."

He had? Nothing Chase said surprised her anymore. But truth serums didn't exist, and even if they did, he'd never mentioned anything to her. Though naturally, if it was highly classified, he wouldn't have, no matter how amicable their relationship had become. Haederans were Haederans, no matter what.

And it wasn't as though Chase hadn't even given her *anything*. He'd given her some sort of sleeping cocktail when she'd been on the verge of a breakdown on *Imperieuse*, and Kern had injected her with who knew what when he'd staged her arrest back in Cadena to save her from Victor. Imperial Security liked their drugs. But a truth serum? No, of course not. It was a ridiculous claim. No matter how much she couldn't remember, she would have known about that.

Answer. You have to answer them.

"He never gave me any kind of drug while I was imprisoned, no."

That wasn't a lie, at least. They didn't need to know about the rest. Chase had thought he was helping her on *Imperieuse*, even though she'd been furious at the time.

"Captain Rendon . . ." Davidson narrowed his eyes at her. "I don't believe you. In fact, I don't believe a word you've said here."

Her heart began to race. "It's the truth, sir."

"I don't believe you remember the truth. I don't believe you remember half of what you've told us here. Major Hadley."

"Yes, sir." Hadley stood with an apologetic glance in her direction.

"As Colonel Barton mentioned earlier, it was your opinion after Captain Rendon's initial debriefing that she was leaving out large parts of her incarceration. Was that opinion erroneous?"

"Sir . . ."

"Well? It's a simple question, requiring nothing more than a yes or no. Was it erroneous?"

"I believe my report was accurate at the time."

Davidson's glance swiveled between Hadley and her. "Then you can see our concern here, Major."

"Yes," Hadley replied. "I do."

"And?"

"What happened was several years ago, and I don't believe there's anything untoward going on here. People remember new things over the course of time, and her initial debrief took place not two hours after her rescue. Normally I'd have preferred to give her a little more time to recover, but the urgency of the situation and the risk that Haederan troops would find the safe house precluded that. She was lucid, honest, and forthcoming about both her experiences and the limited information she'd given Imperial Security."

"It sounds like she gave limited information to you as well, Major Hadley." Davidson turned his attention back to Avery. "You're lying, Captain. The only question is why."

"General Davidson, with all due respect—" Hadley broke in.

"No one's planning on locking up the queen of Asria for lying, so you can sit right back down and let her defend her statement. Because if she's going to show up here and demand the right to give new information, she damn well better be clear on where this information came from. Right now, you haven't changed anyone's mind, and I can't honestly believe"—Davidson's voice grew thick —"the two of you are expecting this board to grant any kind of leniency toward someone who sexually assaulted and conducted medical experiments on one of my officers for weeks!"

"Sir—"

"Shut up and sit *down*, Major Hadley."

The buzzing grew louder, like it was coming from inside her brain instead of the jammer in the ceiling. Davidson hadn't listened after all, and why should he have? It hadn't occurred to her before that he'd taken her treatment personally, but he had, and she couldn't fault him for that.

Her mouth opened, and before she could stop herself from making the biggest mistake of all, the confession flew out.

"His notes," she said, breathless. "I have his notes."

CHAPTER TWENTY-NINE

DAVIDSON AND HADLEY BOTH SWIVELED TOWARD HER, SHOCK ON their faces.

"Excuse me?" Davidson asked.

"His what?" Hadley caught himself mid-sit.

Avery sucked in a gasp of stale air, tinged with ozone. How she was still standing was a mystery.

"I have copies of his interrogation notes. All the logs, all the transcriptions, and all his personal notations as well as the medic's records. They're the same ones he sent to Imperial Security headquarters in Rebet. I have weeks' worth of documentation, as candid and reliable as anything you're going to get. They'll prove he never raped me and that he never experimented on me." *I hope.* "If that's what you're so concerned about, if that's what it takes for some sort of mercy, then I can prove neither happened."

Silence. The buzz of the jammer echoed through the room, but at least it'd vacated her mind for the time being. Hadley cleared his throat twice; Ryall pushed a pen in circles around the table, avoiding her gaze. Davidson simply stared at her.

"How did you obtain these notes?" Barton asked.

"He gave them to me, ma'am."

Davidson clenched his fists—to prevent himself from throwing his hands in the air, Avery suspected.

"You can't honestly believe they're the truth," he said.

"I believe they are," she said, closing her eyes. Chase would have had no reason to lie to Lient about her treatment. "I haven't read everything, not even most of it, but I've read enough to know that they do not exonerate him of all the charges. If they were falsified, I believe they would clear him of everything. He never expected me to come to Ventana and use them for his defense. He never expected me to defend him at all. It was a favor. To help me in my own recovery. Not to provide to the Commonwealth in any manner."

Barton, at least, relaxed at the flimsy argument. So too had Vastel. But the others, especially Davidson? It was impossible to know what they were thinking.

"Why didn't you provide these immediately?"

"I believe you'll understand once you read them, General."

Davidson's expression softened somewhat. "You have them now?"

Avery nodded.

"Hand them over."

Curse her shaking hands. The entire board could see her struggle to unzip her pocket and pull out the disk. Hadley, bless him, took it from her and set it on the table in front of Davidson without a word. The only thing she could do was grasp her hands together behind her back. At least the stance hid the shaking from everyone but Hadley.

Davidson stuck the chip in his tablet, then pushed it toward Ryall, next to him. For a full five minutes, the two read, nodded, whispered under their breath, and then read some more. It was obvious what they were thinking.

She's been lying to us this entire time.

Davidson stood at last, flicking his finger up and down the tablet as he made his way across the room toward her. With raised eyebrows, he handed it over. "I'd like you to read several excerpts of this. Out loud, if you would, please."

Her focus fell from the scar on his temple to the tablet. Chase's notes stared back, a mess of distorted text and light. Davidson couldn't possibly expect this of her. Even if she'd wanted to relive it in front of strangers, she could scarcely make out the words.

"I can't do this," she said. A quick glance at Hadley. His jaw was set.

Davidson ignored her and headed back to his seat. "We're waiting, Captain."

What would happen if she dropped the tablet on the floor and ran out? Would Hadley stop her?

Coward. You're here because you want to be.

She rubbed her eyes and took a deep breath instead of running.

"Time 1232. Date 82 Cael." She stumbled over the unfamiliar Haederan word. Scarcely being able to see it didn't help. "Prisoner arrived in interview room five minutes later than ordered for first official interrogation session. IHA guards claimed escape attempt, accuracy and nature to be verified. Prisoner was offered and declined medical care despite deep gash under her eye and became evasive when interrogator questioned cause of injury."

There. That was enough. Just words. Just the past. She'd survived.

"This was the escape attempt you mentioned," Davidson said.

"Yes. But as I said, the medic eventually—"

"You still have vision problems, do you not?" Ryall didn't wait for an answer. "Keep reading."

Bastard.

She rubbed her eye again. It didn't help.

"Time 0297. Date 97 Cael. Prisoner arrived crying in interview room for the second time in six hours. Removed blindfold and checked for injuries. Chafing on right ankle becoming severe. Removed shackles and requested ISC medic for infection check. Prisoner refused water and juice. Informed prisoner IV fluids would be required if refusal continued. Prisoner drank two pouches of juice while waiting on medic. Medic applied antibiotic cream and bandage and cleared prisoner for further questioning."

"Do you remember this?" Ingrams asked.

Avery shook her head. It could have been any day—or every day, for that matter. Did they expect this spectacle to jog her memory? They had to be smarter than that.

"Next excerpt," Davidson said.

She clenched her jaw instead. Hadn't she read enough?

"Keep reading, Captain."

In the span of a heartbeat, she skimmed the next entry Davidson had highlighted. His and Ryall's previous choices made more sense now—they'd been warming her up. The air conditioning still blew across her face, but heat crept through her, minimizing its effects.

"General—"

"Read it."

Her heart began to pound. She clutched the tablet, the only thing anchoring her to the present, but it didn't help. A wave of fear rushed over her, and she looked back at Hadley, at his short, regulation hair, at his major rank, at the lines around his eyes that hadn't been there a few years ago.

It's all in the past. You're safe. You're safe now.

Hadley nodded reassuringly at her, and with another deep breath, she turned back to the board and looked at the tablet.

"Time 1902. Date 128 Cael. Informed prisoner signed death warrant had arrived from Haedera. Prisoner was blindfolded and moved to interrogation room where she was notified that the sentence was to be carried out without delay. Lieutenant N. asked for any last remarks, prisoner was silent until—"

Tears threatened to fall as she stumbled over Chase's words.

"Until interrogator began last rites, at which time prisoner began to beg. Lieutenant N. and two security personnel stood prisoner face-first against the wall and independently confirmed interrogator's projectile sidearm as unloaded."

Memories trickled back, but that was all they were—memories. The soldiers had handcuffed her hands behind her back, then positioned her against the concrete and given her a stern warning that running wouldn't accomplish anything.

Run, and you'll be standing right back here against this wall on two broken legs. You ought to be grateful he's making it quick, Asrian trash.

She'd believed them. The chill had bitten her skin as she leaned forward, trying to hide her terror while Chase's voice droned in the background, murmuring a Haederan prayer she didn't recognize and couldn't understand. She'd begged the Holy One for mercy as he pressed the pistol against the back of her neck. Waiting for his finger to move had taken forever and an instant.

The tablet became heavy, and she couldn't stop the tears any longer, not even in front of Davidson and the rest of them. It was no wonder she'd attacked Chase in that wellhouse at Windhaven. It was no wonder she'd complied with every single one of Quen's orders. Her soul had remembered that evening deep under Cadena even if her brain hadn't.

Davidson's stare hardened, and she looked down at the notes once more, desperate to forget Quen.

"Interrogator fired once. Prisoner collapsed to the floor and was secured in chair once again for medical examination. ISC medic verified cause of collapse was psychological. Fluids given, vitals stabilized, and prisoner returned to her cell for three hours of sleep. Post-session medical documentation follows."

Davidson leaned forward as she dropped the tablet to her side, his expression as blank as the void of space.

"Even an untrained Commonwealth officer like yourself should be able to acknowledge how wrong a mock execution is," he said.

"Yes." She could scarcely hear her answer. Davidson probably hadn't heard her at all.

"And you're still defending this man."

It wasn't a question. She couldn't even nod.

"Then I suppose," Davidson said, with a certain air of finality, "there's nothing left to discuss. You and Major Hadley are dismissed. We'll review this new information and call you back once we make a decision."

* * *

Hours later, she filed back into the tribunal room next to Hadley, her feet like lead. The six officers were already there, their faces stony. Hadley gave her one last glance before sitting, and Avery all but fell into the chair next to him. How she wanted to sit on her hands to keep them from shaking. Or to cover her face to hide the nausea that was growing worse each second.

The side door opened, and she glanced at her boots as the guards escorted Chase inside and stopped him in front of the center of the tribunal table. It'd been weeks since she'd seen him, and he looked smaller than usual. Or was it the fatigue in his movements that was obvious even from here? One thing was certain, his face was unreadable as always—until he noticed her.

Was it anger then? Fear? Or simply shock at her presence on Ventana IV and her current attire? It was impossible to tell, but his facade had slipped. She stiffened as he processed her appearance, the very picture of the officer he'd tried to destroy, and set her face in that expression that should have been so familiar to him: the uplifted chin, the slight head tilt, the vaguely disinterested look.

This is the person you wanted to see again one day, Colonel. Right here, where you least expected her.

Chase looked away, silent.

Davidson stood.

"Colonel Chase . . ." His lips thinned. "I have four last questions, and I'd advise you to answer them honestly this time."

Chase's shoulders lifted just slightly.

"Did you force or coerce Lieutenant Colonel Kanmar to enlist in the Imperial Haederan Navy?" Davidson asked.

After the briefest of glances at her and Hadley—as if he'd just figured out exactly what had transpired earlier that day, exactly why he'd been brought in again, just how futile another lie to the tribunal would be—he shook his head.

"No," he said.

"Did you, at any point during her detention, rape Captain Rendon?"

"No." His answer was soft, even more immediate—and he kept his eyes focused on Davidson that time.

"Did you conduct medical experiments on her with Imperial Security's truth serum or other drugs?"

"No," Chase said flatly. "I did not."

Barton shifted. Of course—she'd seemed especially interested in that part.

"Did your interrogation of Captain Rendon otherwise include methods that a reasonable person would consider torture?" Davidson asked.

Silence, unexpected silence.

Oh, it was heavy. Like the humidity in Cadena before the autumn rains. But the weight was only her own anxiety, wasn't it? Naturally Chase would deny it. The Commonwealth was seconds from letting him walk away, and of course he wouldn't—

No, she mouthed toward him. *Say no.*

Chase stiffened. He glanced toward her and Hadley again, expressionless, catching the last of her words, then back to Davidson.

"Yes," he said, his Haederan accent more pronounced than she'd ever heard. "It did."

The giddy feeling disappeared in an instant, water smashing against rocks in the high mountains, only this time, it crushed boulders against her heart. It was hotter than that cool mountain stream, too, hot enough to send her stomach into turmoil.

What had he just done?

Davidson exhaled like he was just as shocked at the answer.

"Before we pronounce our decision, this tribunal thanks Lieutenant Colonel Kanmar and Captain Rendon for their testimony and willingness to detail your actions on Asria during the Haederan Empire's occupation. From their explanations, it is clear that the charges brought before this tribunal were, for the most part, inaccurate, a product of hearsay and exaggeration, perpetuated by your dishonesty. Rest assured a full investigation into the initial nature of these erroneous charges will be conducted."

Avery's heart slowed. It was Quen who was responsible for tipping off the Commonwealth. After the things he'd said about Chase, there was no question about that now. She couldn't look at Hadley, couldn't look at Chase. Only at her hands, folded in her lap, knuckles white.

"Therefore, this tribunal has chosen to set aside the previous verdict and find you innocent of the charges of impressment, rape, and illegal medical experimentation."

Her eyes flickered upward. Chase hadn't moved a muscle. Would Davidson not get on with it? Was this simply more torture for all of them? Was she the only one who cared? Chase still didn't seem to.

"With those charges invalidated, it seems death is a steep price to pay for a single accusation of torture—one which we will not impose at this time."

Her hand went to her mouth.

"However."

No.

Not *however*. Not the worst word anyone could hear in a situation like this. She sucked in a breath that the entire room could surely hear. Beside her, Hadley's chair creaked like he'd been caught just as much off guard.

Davidson laid his tablet beside him. "We cannot ignore the magnitude of your extensive crimes against the Haederan people and Captain Rendon herself, nor the fact you violated your parole and remained on Haedera well past the week this tribunal permitted. To do so would be a breach of trust of anyone who has wanted peace, both in the Haederan Empire and across the quadrant, and a travesty of justice—one which we cannot allow."

Holy One, no. Stop them. Please.

She was imagining things. She was dreaming. The nightmares, as vivid as her waking moments, were back, only this time she wasn't the victim. Because this had to be a dream, didn't it? She'd told them everything. She'd argued and articulated every detail of her imprisonment and Chase's abuse, the things he'd done and the things he hadn't. Surely her honesty must have mitigated their anger.

But it hadn't.

Because they were right.

Chase had done horrible things on Haedera. She didn't know what, exactly, and didn't want to, but she knew. He'd done horrible things to her. The photos, her story, the disk—it was all proof. She couldn't excuse the things he'd done. He couldn't escape the Commonwealth's desire for blood. Just this morning, they'd wanted to execute him as an example, and justice didn't swing back toward mercy that quickly or easily. Her blood pounded in her ears as Davidson continued.

"Therefore, this tribunal sentences you to confinement in the Commonwealth Navy detention facility on Ventana for a period of sixty-six years, three years for each year of your Imperial Security Command service—to commence immediately."

CHAPTER THIRTY

Chase didn't move at the tribunal's pronouncement, but Avery's eyes welled up before she could do anything about it. One tear fell on those dreadful indigo pants. The ones she'd once been so desperate to wear, the uniform she was ashamed of now.

Sixty-six years. It was a death sentence for a middle-aged man. The tribunal members had listened to her and Kanmar to an extent, had ruled against executing him immediately, but had handed down what might as well have been a death sentence anyway. Chase would never see Haedera again, not the sunsets at Windhaven, not the dunes outside Rebet that blew and sang in the wind. Not even Sophie. Nothing she'd said had done a bit of good, not even the nightmares she'd relived in front of these emotionless strangers. Her legs tensed of their own accord, and Hadley's hand darted across to her shoulder, pinning her down before she could stand and scream about the injustice.

"Do you have anything to say about the verdict, Colonel?"

Silence.

Davidson stood and nodded at Hadley. "Then everyone is dismissed."

The guards moved toward Chase as she fought the urge to attack them. The chains around his ankles clinked as the small group moved past her, back out the door. She stared at his back, horrified, desperate for one last look, but he never turned around.

"Now you can stand up," Hadley hissed at her. "Calmly, if you would."

She did as he ordered, numb.

"Now walk out," he said under his breath.

Someone else was making her move, because she wasn't in the room anymore. She'd floated away, somewhere where things made sense, somewhere where Chase was safe, somewhere people listened to her and understood that people could change. Even people like Imperial Security officers.

Hadley grabbed her by the shoulders as she stepped into the corridor. She was too numb to say anything about the impropriety, too dazed to scream at him about the futility of his comfort. Voices streamed about them as the tribunal officers departed, but she couldn't comprehend any of the words, only the sickening heat that threatened to eat her alive.

"Listen to me," he said. "This isn't over. Are you hearing me? Don't give up." He shook her gently, then a little harder, his mouth moving silently in more meaningless promises and trite platitudes as he did.

Avery let him, even as she felt Davidson's disapproving stare as he pushed by. When the last of the board trickled out, she stood in that sterile hallway and sobbed.

* * *

No sooner had the tears dried than she forced Hadley to escort her to the holding cells in the west wing of the building. He didn't look happy about it, and the guards looked even less thrilled when she strode through that heavy steel door. But Hadley was as persuasive as always, and in less than five minutes, they'd contacted Davidson. Even with the general's authorization, there was no royal consideration at headquarters like there had been on *Terigon*. Avery gritted her teeth as they patted her down, all too meticulously, then let the warrant officer in charge lead her and Hadley to Chase.

He was still wearing his uniform. Still clean-shaven, still wrinkle-free and as tearless as always. It was almost impossible for her brain to reconcile the sight of this polished Imperial Security colonel sitting in a Commonwealth Navy cell, though the shackles that remained around his ankles helped with that. He vented a dramatic sigh when he noticed her outside the static field, then flopped to his back on the hard bench and closed his eyes.

"I shouldn't let you in there, uh . . . Captain." The warrant officer glanced from her to Hadley, at their comet badges and her eyes—all too uncommon on Ventana. "He's dangerous. And they'll be here to transfer him within the next hour."

Dangerous? She managed, just barely, to not roll her eyes.

"Then I have time. Isn't that right, Mister Rablin?"

"Yes, I suppose you do." His gaze fell to the ground. "And I suppose he's not my problem in another hour, so you can be my guest."

"Good." She jerked her chin at the keypad. "Now, please?"

Rablin sighed and keyed in the code. Avery took one step inside and pressed herself against the wall as the static field appeared again and footsteps echoed outside. She couldn't say anything until Hadley walked the man away for a few long cups of coffee.

"Colonel."

Chase stared at the ceiling, silent.

"Please talk to me. Do you know what I just did for you? Do you know what it took out of me? I stood up and told them all sorts of things that I'd rather have forgotten, and you couldn't be bothered to do the same in your own defense. You could have lied. You could have said you didn't know what you did was against Commonwealth law. You could have said something, anything, to mitigate what you've done. And you didn't need to come back here, especially for me!"

What else was there to say? She had to say something, because he was still acting like she wasn't there.

"How long have we known each other?" she asked. "I know you too well now. I know you're not the person they think you are." She tried to steady her voice, but it was hopeless. "That's why you treated me like you did back then. You could have ignored their gossip and let those army guards do whatever they wanted to me. You didn't need to let the medic treat me, but you did. It's why you were kind to me when we first met and why you prayed for me and why you sometimes talked to me like a human being. It may have been an interrogation technique, but it wasn't only a technique, and don't even bother to argue otherwise."

His boot-clad foot—laceless now—twitched.

"Am I right?" Of course she was right, and with that twitch, he wanted her to know.

Chase tilted his head toward her. "Sure. If it means you'll leave me alone, then you're right. Now go back to Asria, Your Majesty." His eyes narrowed. "And take those medals with you."

Her face grew hot. It didn't matter what had happened in the past, how he'd threatened her, how many times she'd cried in front of him, and the mess he was in now, Chase still had that same particular talent for sending her into a rage with the slightest provocation.

"Do you think these things matter to me?" The low fury in her voice vibrated against the walls. "Do you think I wanted them? I would give up every single one if you would stop this insanity and defend yourself."

Her fingers grazed the award the Commonwealth had given her for turning the fighter over to them. Before she could think better of it, she'd yanked it from her jacket. It was heavy in her palm, and cold.

"Like this one? The one I earned for doing something that ultimately saved thousands of lives but was responsible for the death of the child of someone I care about? Do you think I didn't mourn

Marc—that I didn't *sob* over him—when they handed this to me? I don't want it!"

She flung the cool silver at his head as hard as she could. Her hand was shaking, her aim was poor, and the medal skimmed Chase's scalp and clanged as it hit the opposite wall.

He sat up, his eyes wide. "What the—"

"Or this one?" she interrupted. She ripped off one more. "The one they gave me because I was unlucky enough to end up a prisoner? That was a random chance I certainly didn't handle well. If they only had any idea—which I suppose they do now. It's another one I don't deserve." With her last word, she flung that one at him, too. It clattered to the floor next to his shackled ankles. "I don't want them. I don't want any of them. I don't want the recognition and I don't want the honor. Not if they meant I had to stand there in that tribunal room and watch you destroy yourself."

Something clicked behind her as she reached for a third medal, and she spun around as the static field opened again. Senior Warrant Officer Rablin stepped inside, *kusir*, with Hadley next to him, no less. Had she been screaming at Chase so loudly the entire building had heard her? Or had they been listening to her conversation the whole time?

"Let's go," Hadley said. "Now."

She shrugged off his gentle touch on her arm. "I'm not done with him."

"Oh yes you are. Are you trying to get yourself killed?"

Rablin reached down for the two medals and held them out. Avery waved him off, and he shoved them in his pocket after a hesitant look at Hadley. Chase flopped on his back and ignored the entire scene.

"He's not going to kill me, Hadley."

"That's right," he agreed. "Because you're leaving. This second."

She chanced another look at Chase, but he'd closed his eyes again. Fine, then. It was over. She'd failed. They'd failed. Kanmar had come all this way, Hadley had arranged everything with Torin, and they'd failed. Chase would die here, alone on Ventana IV, and there was nothing she or anyone else could do about it. She nodded at Hadley, took one step toward the door with his hand on her arm, then stopped.

"I saw you, you know." She took a deep breath and brushed off Hadley's grip. "In the Pelancos. You were overseeing a checkpoint on the main road, and you were looking for me. Elex Feye—I was up there on a cliff with him and Hadley, and he was going to shoot you."

She closed her eyes. The wind blew through her hair, and the mountain sun was hot on her cheeks, pale from too many weeks in a prison cell. The healthy scent of pine trees, the cleanest thing she'd smelled in as long as she could remember, floated all around her and Hadley and Feye. The bruises Hadley had photographed still covered her body, making every step across the mountain trail an exercise in suffering.

"He had that rifle on his shoulder," she said, opening her eyes, "and his finger on the trigger, and I—I told him to stop."

Chase's eyes flickered open, though he didn't move otherwise.

Had she finally reached him? She turned to Hadley, still hovering right next to her.

"Hadley, we're all right. One more chance. Please."

He clasped his hand on her shoulder like he had so many times before when she'd been nothing more than a princess-elect and naïve lieutenant, then motioned Rablin out.

"I forgave you then," she said after they'd disappeared. "I just didn't realize it at the time. And then I forgave you again when I found out what you'd done for Merritt. And when you showed me where my parents were buried. And when you told me about Marc."

She wiped her eyes.

"And when you offered to bring me to Haedera to protect me, and when you prayed with me in front of Rhys Linden's grave, and when you told me you'd never allow Owin to lay a hand on me, and yes, even when you saved me from Quen."

How could he just lie there and stare at the ceiling?

"You think you need to earn my forgiveness by sabotaging your own life, but you don't. You can't earn it, no matter how much you try. I've offered it to you freely, and you're pushing it right back into my hands like you don't care about it at all. And I know you care. I know this is what this is about."

He didn't reply to that, either, and she sank to the floor. It was cold, just like that bright room had been, but this time the memories didn't assault her. She sat there in silence, long enough to shiver from the chill that was working its way upward.

"How many people have you killed?" she asked softly.

Chase's eyes shifted toward her.

"How many?" She raised her shoulders in question. "I think I deserve to know."

There was another long silence, broken only by the soft hiss of the air conditioning. She was moments away from standing, seconds away from leaving in disappointment, when he spoke.

"Four."

The single word, spoken to the ceiling in that lilt she'd once hated and feared, cut through the quiet of the cell.

"Four?" Did he mean four hundred? Or four thousand?

Chase ran his hands over his face. "Four," he repeated, lowering himself to the floor in front of her.

She blinked at him.

"When I joined Imperial Security from the army," he said, "I went straight into the clandestine service. It wasn't the usual route, but I had skills. I recruited and ran agents from around Haedera, and then, once I married and became too visible on-world, outside the system. Death wasn't something we dealt in. There's no place for murder when you're a case officer trying to set up a network. A dead man can't give you information. And then it turned out I had another skill. One much more useful and harder to find."

Despite the shackles that forced his legs into an awkward position and the chill in the air, a small flicker of that familiar amusement crossed his face.

"People just couldn't stop talking to me. Except certain Commonwealth spies, perhaps."

She couldn't stop one side of her mouth from lifting into a small smile, as tearstained as it was.

He held up a hand. "Oh, I'm under no delusions about what eventually happened to those who were less than willing to work for us or confessed to treason or whatever else. I never did the dirty work myself, if that's what you're asking, but that's no excuse. And self-defense? Four. Martyn Clough, Darren Baines, Glyn Burrier, and Quen Rendon. Plus a few more at the Linden house in Esro now, I suppose. When I was twenty-seven, Clough put a bullet in my leg. He'd have put several more in my head if I hadn't shot him first. Six years later, Baines tried to escape from Imperial Security headquarters when it became apparent that we weren't going to release him for a very, very long time. He had a hostage and a knife, and there was only one way it could end. Burrier, you know. And Quen Rendon . . . Quen Rendon was a half second away from killing someone who I am very fond of and respect very much."

He looked at his hands.

"I think about them often—yes, even your brother—and wonder if I could have done something different. But it wouldn't have mattered in the end. Except for him, they'd have been executed had they been arrested without incident. And then I think about the people I sent off to certain death, the ones you once accused me of being responsible for. I never ordered any executions directly, but those four may as well have been four thousand, and I wake up every morning knowing that I was a part of that and can never take it back or change the past."

"But sixty-six years." One tear ran down her cheek, and others threatened to follow. "You've done so much to atone, and now you won't walk out of here, no matter how many appeals Owin makes, if he's even still speaking to you after this. I know you didn't expect to die on Ventana. And you just let them do it to you. You didn't speak at all on your behalf."

No, that wasn't correct. Chase hadn't just refused to defend himself. He'd done much worse than that.

"You lied instead," she went on. "You made up some of the most senseless and horrifying and implausible things I've ever heard—things I know you're not capable of."

"You were never meant to hear them."

"That's not remotely the point." She clutched her hands in her lap. Why did he still make her want to pull her hair out?

"It is the point. But now they know the truth, don't they?"

It was the same questioning tone she remembered, but there wasn't any menace behind it this time. Just simple curiosity.

"I gave them your notes. They know everything now." Chase didn't react, and the apology spilled out. "I'm sorry I let them read everything, but you didn't leave me any choice. I didn't know what else to do. I couldn't let them execute you. They weren't believing anything Hadley or I said, and they needed to know the person I do."

"You don't know me." The words were defensive, but the sorrow in his voice was not.

"I know you better than you think I do. From the very first day, you've had your secrets, but you were open with me, too." She frowned as Barton's accusations flitted back into her mind. "Except for one thing. What's this truth serum thing all about?"

"I never used it on you."

Now he sounded defensive. *Kusir*, maybe Davidson was right. Maybe Chase's notes were mere fabrication.

"Did you use it on anyone?"

He sighed.

"The truth serum . . . it's a small program, and still in the research phase. Sometimes people just get picked to run these things, and I was in the wrong place at the wrong time. Lient needed someone he could trust. It was a secondary job, though, and I was constantly being called off on other missions, so it didn't proceed as quickly as anyone would have preferred. Then the invasion happened, and everything was put on hold until after I returned from Asria. I thought that would be the end of it. Lient had promised my involvement in the program was only temporary, and that as soon as I returned to Haedera, he'd find a replacement and let me escape to the counterintelligence position I'd been so desperate to earn for years. I wanted to stay on Haedera with Isobel. I wanted a desk job. Anyway, to make a long story short, that program isn't going to become official any time soon."

"Why not?"

"You always were good at asking questions you didn't want to know the answers to."

Avery tightened her jaw and pressed her palms to the floor, ready to bolt. He was going to hedge after all this? She should leave him here.

"My lady, stop. I didn't use it on you for two reasons. First, because there would have been absolutely no challenge in it." The statement should have been followed by a grin, but Chase looked as serious as ever. "I am—was—proud of my skills. I don't need to drug anyone."

"You know I can't remember everything," she said. "But I do remember the guards injecting me with something more than once. I was so exhausted that I finally gave up and let them do it. What was it?"

Chase sighed. "Saline. Do you think I would have let anyone but one of my own medics near you with anything else? Any symptoms it caused were from your own anxiety."

Her chest loosened. He'd only been manipulating her. Not experimenting on her.

"The second reason . . . it's positively lethal in its present form. We used it on Major Feye, and if Rhys hadn't shot him first, that single injection would've killed him if he didn't return to us. Within months."

She still wanted to run, but her body wouldn't move.

"How?" she asked, her mouth suddenly dry.

"Cardiac arrest. It weakens the muscles enough that stress or physical activity puts too much strain on the heart, and eventually, usually without warning, it gives out."

Heat rose in her cheeks. So it wasn't enough that they'd captured Elex Feye, tortured him, turned him, used him, and eventually killed him. The Haederan Empire had made sure he had no chance from the beginning. And they were doing the same to their own people. She'd given Chase so much credit. Had trusted him. Had believed there was still a bit of good in him, only to find out he was responsible for this kind of atrocity.

She should have known.

"You are despicable." That time she stood. Easily. "I should—I should tell General Davidson—"

"Oh, take your indignant self-righteousness somewhere else. Charming as it is." He leaned against the bench and wrapped his arms around his knees. "Sit down, my lady."

She should turn back toward the door. Scream for Hadley. Run into Merritt's arms. Chase wasn't in her mind. He couldn't tell her what to do any longer. But just like her body hadn't let her disobey when he'd ordered her to stand with her nose against the wall for hours until her calves cramped and her bare feet were numb, it wouldn't let her remain standing now. Though this time —perhaps this time it was a desperate need to believe in him rather than fear.

"No. You have no right to order me to do anything." Her voice shook, even as she sat back down a few paces from him and curled her legs under herself.

"Please. There's more to tell, and you need to hear it."

"You have two minutes," she said, lifting her chin. *And sixty-six years.* "Best speak fast."

He didn't hesitate. "The first subjects began dying after Major Feye received his initial dose, and I'll never forgive myself for not making the connection immediately. But there weren't as many

deaths as you think. After we figured it out, the remaining Imperial Security prisoners had implants placed to prevent that outcome. I wish I'd known earlier. I wish we could have saved Major Feye. I'm telling you, we didn't know how lethal it was at first, and once we learned, we did what we could to mitigate what damage we had done."

The air whooshed from her lungs at the unexpected mercy.

"Somehow I doubt Imperial Security cares what happens to them. You'll continue using it on your own people and justify it by giving them pacemakers to keep them alive until their executions."

Harsh. Too harsh. But true, wasn't it?

"That's so very Asrian of you, my lady." The words were mocking, but the underlying sadness was not.

She was missing something, but with the headache that was building, she was never going to figure it out. Because this wasn't Chase. Not the mocking, confident, arrogant Imperial Security officer she'd known for so long. He hadn't looked this devastated when the tribunal had pronounced his sentence, so what—

Oh.

She scooted a bit closer to him as the last of the hatred floated away and understanding took its place.

"That's why you stayed on Asria, isn't it?" she asked softly. "You suspected they were going to rescind your counterintelligence job offer, and you knew what their plan for you was then, didn't you? But you also knew it would be a death knell for that program if you weren't running it, so you begged Owin and Lient for a break from everything."

Chase's secrets fell into place, and she spoke even faster after a short glance outside the static field.

"A long holiday, I'm guessing you told them you needed, a change of pace. Lient fell for it, so you stayed in Cadena. No one would be the wiser if you were working for the ambassador himself. You sabotaged that research by leaving your Imperial Security duties and committed some kind of passive Haederan treason. That's why Lient and the others were visiting you at Windhaven—they were trying to convince you to come back. Lient even threatened you over it. Merritt and I heard him that night in your library."

And Sophie had understood. She'd known her father was trying to make it right but that Imperial Security hadn't released their claws—and never would.

"And to think I once believed you naïve."

The sadness in his eyes didn't abate, though a bit of pride and relief now tempered it. That, she recognized. Was it happiness that she'd figured it out or relief that he hadn't broken her completely? Maybe it didn't matter.

"Why didn't you tell me any of this before now?" she asked. "Why didn't you tell General Davidson? It might have mitigated your actions as far as the tribunal was concerned."

"It wouldn't have changed their minds, nor should it. I deserve to be here. I can handle their ruling, and I accept the Holy One's judgment. I made my peace with that a long time ago. And anyway, this is the sentence I wanted. It'll save so many, more than you know." He was silent for a long time, and when he looked up, his eyes were glassy. "I won't pretend it's going to be pleasant, and there's so much I'll long for, but . . . stars, I think I'm going to miss your foolish tenacity as much as anything else, Your Majesty."

"Captain Rendon."

It was an automatic reaction, just like that day long ago at Alcaris, though this time it was more to keep herself from crying than to correct him, for hurting him now was the last thing she wanted to do. The words felt foolish on her lips as they echoed in the silence of the cell, the request ever more so, and as the weight of Chase's emotions settled onto her shoulders, she knew.

"And Colonel . . . you haven't yet seen the limits of my foolish tenacity."

CHAPTER THIRTY-ONE

Her heart threatened to pound out of her chest as she approached Davidson's office. Words and questions and pleas spun in her mind, and she forced them into the quietest recesses. This couldn't be planned. If she planned her argument, she would back down out of cowardice. Davidson was second only to General Torin in the Special Operations Forces, after all. She, a mere captain, was about to challenge one of the most important officers in the Commonwealth's military.

Only she wasn't just Captain Rendon anymore.

Davidson's secretary jumped from her desk as Avery flung open the door. "Captain, General Davidson is busy."

After running a two-week tribunal and tormenting her? Hardly. More likely he was taking a nap, to be followed by several large cups of strong Ventanan coffee or a rendezvous with his wife, if there were such a person. Davidson's secretary stood and called after her, but Avery skipped around the flailing woman and pushed the inner door open. With any luck, the presumed wife wasn't actually in his office.

Davidson, alone, thank the stars, stood as she entered. The room was more luxurious than she'd expected for a building where electronic noise vibrated her very bones. His desk floated at waist height above the floor, suspended by the kind of expensive fielding generators even the Rendons scorned. On one side sat a cup of coffee, on the other a stack of papers and data disks, and in the center a tablet lay, its screen overlaid with a black-and-white chart. Davidson slammed his hand over it and the screen went dark, but there was no shock on his face. Perhaps Hadley had been more open than she'd wished about her problems following orders.

"Captain Rendon, the tribunal is finished," he said. "You and Colonel Chase have both had your say, and it's not my problem if he refused to take the chance when it was offered. Major Hadley's informed me you've said your goodbyes—goodbyes you owe me a personal thank-you for authorizing, I might add—and they're on their way over from the detention facility to pick him up as we speak. There's nothing left to talk about here."

She took a deep, silent breath. "I'm sorry, sir, but there is."

Davidson's tablet stylus clattered to his desk. "Then what is it now?"

"I'm concerned for his safety."

"Captain Rendon, really. I realize your perception of the situation is a bit skewed due to your experience, but Commonwealth prisoners are perfectly safe, and Colonel Chase will be held in isolation for the entirety of his sentence. He'll be fed, clothed, and will receive appropriate medical care. His remains will be repatriated in due course, if his family wishes. There's no threat. No torture. This is Ventana IV, not Haedera."

"General—"

"If you have further information, I suggest you tell me now. My patience regarding this matter is at an end."

No going back now. She flashed him her brightest smile, the fake royal one Merritt hated.

"Then you leave me no choice, General. You're aware that the civilian law of a sovereign planet—which Asria is once more, I remind you—supersedes Commonwealth regulation. As the duly elected queen of Asria, it's my duty to formally notify you that the

Asrian High Senate is requesting Colonel Chase stand trial to answer for his crimes committed against me and any other Asrian subjects during the occupation." She lifted her eyebrows in feigned innocence. "You certainly wouldn't want to challenge our sovereignty so shortly after we threw off an enemy occupation."

Davidson let his forehead fall into his hands and sighed, then fixed her with a glare.

"And I'm also aware that your intent is to take him to Asria and have him released in direct opposition to the wishes and decree of this tribunal."

And that's the last thing you want.

She let her smile disappear. "Then it seems you have two choices: hand Colonel Chase over to the Asrian High Senate for trial or alter his sentence to one that will render my demand unnecessary."

He scoffed. "That's coercion."

"Prove it, sir."

Davidson blew out a deep breath. "How serious are you about this?"

"I think I've made my seriousness clear."

"Why are you doing this for him?" His eyebrows knitted together. "I want an honest answer this time, Your Majesty."

Her mouth grew dry. He was giving her a chance. One last chance. She ran down the same story she'd told Bretel—the parts Kanmar hadn't mentioned in his testimony. Chase's rescue of Merritt. What he'd done to protect Lucas from his great-uncle's wrath. The things he'd done for her. Everything Davidson hadn't wanted her to say before spilled out.

"Major Hadley told me about your son, and I know you want justice for him," she finished. "But Colonel Chase had nothing to do with his death, and he needs mercy—as do Asria and the Commonwealth. If we're to heal from this war, all of us, surely there is room for both."

"Mercy." Davidson scoffed. "You're talking reconciliation over justice. I can't allow that. The situation doesn't allow for that."

"No. I'm asking for both reconciliation and justice. I'm certain you can hand down a sentence that allows for both."

"Mutually exclusive."

"They're not," she said softly. "But I think you already know that. And he does, too. Spare him."

Davidson stared at her for a long time, then paced around the room, stopping only to stare at his desk for so long that she took a step toward the door, despairing.

"I will speak with the tribunal," he said at last, scratching his neck. "With this information and your forthcoming request—I suspect we can come to some other arrangement."

Avery hid a swallow as she nodded. "Thank you, sir." She turned toward the door, the ill feeling in her stomach at odds with the relief in her heart.

"Just one moment, Captain."

She froze, hand on the door panel.

Davidson made his way around his desk. Any hint of a smile that might have existed before flickered away, and he folded his arms as he spoke. "Your service to the Commonwealth has been impeccable, and you have my personal gratitude for it." Davidson's focus drifted toward her medals, two conspicuously missing, still stashed in Rablin's pocket. The man could keep them for all she cared. "But considering the timing and nature of this request, perhaps it's time . . ."

He raised his eyebrows in question.

Avery nodded as the door slid open, relief washing away the rest of the sick feeling. Her dreams were gone now, like Admiral Kohren had smashed them to bits in his office so long ago on the other side of Ventana IV. Like they'd floated away when she'd taken her oath deep underground in Villiers and promised to love Merritt for the rest of her life and when she'd watched Lucas smile for the first time. But dreams changed and shifted, and that didn't make them worse. It didn't mean she was settling. It only meant better things were ahead.

"Yes, sir," she replied. "Perhaps it is."

* * *

Hadley followed her into the tribunal room once more, though when the guards escorted Chase in this time, he had less color in his cheeks than before, like the weight of his situation had settled upon his shoulders at last. Perhaps she should have told him her plan, but there'd be some lasting part of her psyche that hadn't wanted him angry with her for trying or disappointed if she failed. Would he have tried to stop her if he'd known she had planned to coerce Davidson?

Probably. She'd meant what she'd told the tribunal. Chase was nothing if not honorable. More honorable than she had a right to claim now. As Davidson—alone, this time—ordered her and Hadley to sit, an almost giddy feeling threatened to overtake her, tempered only by the fear that something could still go wrong. Maybe this was a trap. A game. Punishment for her rash appeal for Chase's freedom.

"Colonel Chase." Davidson stood stiff, almost at attention. "Even though your actions on Haedera have been disgraceful, we were not aware of the remorse you have already shown. That lack of knowledge has consequently been remedied. Therefore, given your remarkable aid to the Asrian royal family, your assistance in the end of hostilities between the Haederan Empire and Asria, and an unprompted—and, may I say, frankly incredible—plea by Captain Rendon . . ."

He paused, appearing to swallow any remaining misgivings. "This tribunal has chosen to suspend the entire sentence on two conditions. You will not set foot in Commonwealth space nor return to your Imperial Security Command duties for the remainder of these sixty-six years. Do you understand this sentence and conditions, Colonel?"

Chase blinked once.

"Yes," he replied.

Something had surprised him at last. Avery bit the inside of her cheek to keep the smile away. Her hand shot sideways, toward Hadley, and his fingers closed tight over hers. She'd grin at Chase later, away from the watchful eyes of Davidson and the rest.

"And do you agree to this?"

Chase's eyes flickered sideways at her, just for one instant. Probably enough that he could see her eyes dancing. She'd hear from him about that, no doubt, but it didn't matter. He could show his disapproval in whatever way he chose, as long as he was safe.

"Yes." His voice cracked. "I do."

"Good. Do not think that our reach, like that of the Imperial Security Command, cannot extend to Haedera in the event you decide not to comply with the second condition." Davidson's eyes softened. "Go home. Retire. Enjoy life. Get to know your daughter." They hardened again as he turned toward Avery. "Captain Rendon."

Her knees shook as she stood. "Yes, sir."

"General Torin will be expecting your resignation on his desk within the hour."

She nodded. It was surprisingly easy. "Yes, sir."

"Asria will be glad to have you home, Your Majesty, but you are welcome on Ventana any time. Just not in my office." He glanced around at the other officers, then at Hadley and Chase. "I trust there are no other issues to discuss?"

Silence.

"Then this tribunal is closed. All of you get out of here before I change my mind."

CHAPTER THIRTY-TWO

Two guards with rifles stood at the exit to the hangar bay, but they didn't look nearly as serious as they had when they'd escorted Chase into the tribunal room the day before. *Mayfair* sat by the large door, her pilots inside running prelaunch checks, her loading hatch open, and her engines venting small plumes of white exhaust. Merritt skimmed her hand with his, then headed out the door with Hadley, leaving her to wait alone with Chase in the humid Ventana air. They'd said their goodbyes, casual and hasty, and now it was her turn.

Chase had spent the night in visitor quarters next to hers, not the detention center—under heavy guard and without access to communications, to be sure—but almost free. There'd been no way to get a message to Brooks Neave on Asria quickly enough to ask for formal permission, so she and Merritt had made the executive decision to loan him *Mayfair*. Neave would be fine with it. She'd make sure he was fine with it as soon as they could arrange for passage home. The ambassador would get his ship back eventually, even though she'd probably owe him something for her appropriation.

"I'm sorry about your commission," Chase said, facing her as the guards closed the door and slid in front of it once more. "I would have never asked you to do that for me."

How many times was he going to apologize?

"I have an entire system to run. It's no loss," she lied, suppressing a shiver. As long as she kept telling herself that, everything was fine. But it was the truth, wasn't it? Her past was gone. Time marched on. Asria needed her.

"Still, I know how much it meant to you."

She looked at her feet to hide her shame. "I can still fly with the Defense Forces when I wish," she pointed out, rubbing her wrist before she could stop herself. "When I can."

But even Chase had to know it wasn't the same. She met his stare and forced a smile. He'd been right—lying to him was pointless.

"Five minutes until the launch window, sir." The pilot's voice rang out the hatch.

Chase nodded toward the ship. "Sounds like it's about time."

"Sounds like. Give my regards to Owin, if you feel it'll do any good. And Sophie. Let her know she's welcome to visit Cadena whenever she'd like."

She bit her lip. Saying goodbye shouldn't be this difficult. A few years ago, she wouldn't have looked twice as he walked away. Maybe she'd have celebrated. And now? There was so much to say, but she hid behind formality and distance.

"Sophie might want to escape to Asria for a visit sooner than I prefer. But since I'm stuck on Haedera for the time being, she's not leaving Windhaven for a long time if I have anything to say about it. It's time we got to know each other."

A knot loosened inside her. "I'm glad. She does love you, even if she doesn't know it." What she wouldn't give to see the joy on Sophie's face when Chase returned to Windhaven. Would Imperial Security leave him alone now? Likely. If it was a choice between his retirement and imprisonment, even they wouldn't harass a member of the imperial family, however minor. And Chase could handle himself.

"I'll see you and Colonel Rendon sometime next season? Owin's already thinking about something official, I'm sure—and my vow stands. It'll stand forever."

Owin was the last person she ever wanted to see again, but if she avoided Haedera for no good reason, he would know she knew. She would play the game, even at the risk of her life.

"We'll make every attempt to be there." She shifted awkwardly, but it wasn't from the thought of seeing Owin again.

Chase glanced at her feet, then back to her face. "You read the rest of the notes after Davidson made his decision, didn't you?"

How—how had he known what she was thinking?

"No," she said. "More. Not all. It seems counterproductive now, but maybe in the future. Though there was one file that looked irrelevant—Merritt and I were curious, but I didn't want to pry if it was mistakenly included."

"Mmm." Guilt flashed across his face, then was gone. "That's because it wasn't for you." Her brow creased, and he added, "I suspect Colonel Rendon might be interested in the contents of that file."

Her eyes widened.

The names.

He hadn't. He couldn't have. But who else but the Imperial Security Command would step right over the emperor's order like this? Who else would have the access and ability to dig for the information?

"But Owin will be furious with me if I use that information to expel any of those soldiers from Asria," she said, suddenly breathless. "I can't imagine what he'll do next."

"Just toss a few others out at the same time, and he'll never know why you expelled them." Chase's face lit up in a real, boyish grin. "Let me deal with him otherwise. It's not as though I have much else to do anymore except participate in entertaining palace diversions, and that's practically a hobby among the family. He'll find something else to try to control you with, if that's what you're worried about."

"Thank you," she whispered. Owin's grip on Asria would tighten again, there was no question about that, but her worry would wait for another day. Today she'd celebrate Chase's gift. "You don't know what this means to us."

"You're more than welcome." He ducked his head as she tried to hide her eyes, filled with tears she would never let spill over. "What's this? Is Avery Rendon actually crying at my departure? I'll add that to the list of things I never thought I'd live to see."

"You're not funny. And I'm not crying." She wiped the few—the very few!—tears away and laughed. "All right. Maybe I am, a little. But don't let it go to your head."

"I'm afraid it's much too late for that, my lady." He glanced back at the courier. "I've got to go. Safe travels back to Asria. Perhaps you can send some of that remarkable Rendon wine back with Brooks the next time he heads home."

"I'll do that. Cases and cases of it, stamped diplomatic. And you have a safe trip as well—send word when you reach Windhaven."

Chase gave her a curt nod and turned to walk away. She should be happy at the sight of his back. And relieved. Elated, perhaps. She should feel healed. But the sadness, the sense of something unfinished, clung to her.

"Colonel, wait," she called after him.

He spun around as she darted toward him, a question on his face.

"I didn't say goodbye." She wiped damp palms on her pants. "But if I do that, then I really will start crying. Then you'll laugh at me, and I'm not sure I can handle that after everything else, so I'll do this instead."

She had to stand on her tiptoes to brush her lips across his cheek, but it was worth the rush of emotions that wound through her—and Chase's reaction.

He flushed. Yes, actually flushed. His cheeks grew red as they stood in the hangar bay with armed Commonwealth guards

surrounding them. Finally, she'd surprised him, and that felt as good as everything else.

"What was that for?" he asked. "And don't tell me it was in lieu of saying goodbye."

He knew. It was obvious that he knew, but she'd humor him one last time.

"For saving me." She lifted her shoulders, the honesty physically painful. "In every way possible."

After the briefest hesitation, his hand landed on her back, and he drew her against him. A flicker of fear shot through her and then disappeared as she embraced him in return, her tears dampening his shirt.

"Don't be ridiculous." His voice grew coarse, heavy with emotion. "You saved me, and you know it."

"You're wrong." She shook her head as hard as she could against his chest. "But I won't win this one, will I?"

He chuckled. "Never. You may as well give up now, my lady."

"You are impossible." She couldn't help her own laugh. "Each other, then?"

Chase disentangled himself and smiled down at her.

"Each other."

ACKNOWLEDGMENTS

As always, there's a list of people who made this book happen: Meghan, who read this book so many times I lost count, Christy, Hope, and Janie, my loyal beta readers, Christi and Grace, editors extraordinaire, and last but not least, Andy, who answered all my questions about the military, even the ones he'd answered a million times before and the ones he thought were ridiculous. You guys are awesome.

ABOUT THE AUTHOR

Anne Wheeler grew up with her nose in a book but earned two degrees in aviation before it occurred to her she was allowed to write her own. When not working, moving, or writing her next novel, she can be found planning her next escape to the desert—camera gear included. She currently lives in Georgia with her husband, son, and herd of cats.

For more information:
www.anne-wheeler.com